Reach
to
Eternity

THIS LAND, THIS TIME

I   Into the Battle

II   A Time of Death

III   Reach to Eternity

IV   South to Destiny

Dobrica Ćosić

Reach
to
Eternity

translated by
Muriel Heppell

A Harvest/HBJ Book
Harcourt Brace Jovanovich, Publishers
San Diego   New York   London

Library of Congress Cataloging in Publication Data

Ćosić, Dobrica, 1921–
Reach to eternity.

Translation of Vreme smrti III.
1. European War, 1914–1918–Fiction.
I. Title.
PZ4.C835Re   [PG1418.C63]   891.8'2'35   79-2234
ISBN 0-15-175961-8
ISBN 0-15-676012-6 (pbk.)

Printed in the United States of America
First Harvest/HBJ edition 1983

A B C D E F G H I J

Reach
to
Eternity

KRAGUJEVAC

DECEMBER 17, 1914

DIRECTIVE FROM THE HIGH COMMAND TO THE SERBIAN ARMY:

HEROES!

DURING TWELVE DAYS OF FEARFUL EFFORT, DIFFICULT MARCHES, AND FIERCE BATTLES, YOU HAVE PERFORMED PRODIGIES OF HEROISM AND GIVEN A SHINING EXAMPLE OF SUBLIME SACRIFICE FOR THE FATHERLAND AND FREEDOM.

HISTORY WILL INSCRIBE YOUR GLORIOUS DEEDS IN LETTERS OF GOLD, AND FUTURE GENERATIONS WILL TELL THE STORY OF YOUR HEROISM. OUR DESCENDANTS WILL BE PROUD OF WHAT YOU HAVE DONE.

THE GLINT OF YOUR WEAPONS WILL SHINE THROUGHOUT CENTURIES TO COME. EUROPE STANDS AMAZED, AND OUR ALLIES ARE FULL OF ENTHUSIASM FOR THE BRILLIANT DEEDS OF THE SERBIAN ARMY.

WITH YOUR POWERFUL ATTACKS YOU HAVE SHATTERED MORE THAN FIVE ENEMY CORPS AND GAINED MANY VALUABLE SPOILS OF WAR.

YOU HAVE TAKEN PRISONER 274 OFFICERS AND MORE THAN 40,000 NON-COMMISSIONED OFFICERS AND SOLDIERS.

YOU HAVE CAPTURED THREE FLAGS, MORE THAN 130 CANNON, 70 MACHINE GUNS, AND A LARGE AMOUNT OF WAR MATÉRIEL.

THIS IS THE THIRD TIME YOU HAVE DEFEATED THE ENEMY.

YOU ARE AND SHALL REMAIN INVINCIBLE.

I AM PROUD TO ANNOUNCE THAT THE ENEMY IS NO LONGER ON SERBIAN SOIL. WE HAVE DRIVEN THEM OUT WITH MUCH BLOODSHED.

PRINCE ALEXANDER

COMMANDER IN CHIEF

OFFICIAL COMMUNIQUÉ OF THE GENERAL STAFF OF THE AUSTRO-HUNGARIAN ARMY:

AS A RESULT OF THE OPERATIONAL SITUATION CREATED BY THE NEED TO WITHDRAW OUR RIGHT WING, IT BECAME NECESSARY TO ABANDON BELGRADE. THE CITY HAS BEEN EVACUATED WITHOUT A STRUGGLE. OUR TROOPS HAVE SUFFERED CONSIDERABLY FROM FATIGUE AND BATTLE, BUT THEIR MORALE IS GOOD.

PETROGRAD, TSARSKOE SELO

TO PRINCE ALEXANDER, COMMANDER IN CHIEF OF THE SERBIAN ARMY:

I HAVE JUST RECEIVED THE GOOD NEWS OF THE VICTORY WON BY THE BRAVE SERBIAN ARMY OVER OUR COMMON ENEMY. I CONGRATULATE YOUR HIGHNESS ON THIS SUCCESS WITH A JOYFUL HEART.

NICHOLAS II
CZAR OF RUSSIA

PARIS

TO HIS ROYAL HIGHNESS, PRINCE ALEXANDER:

IT IS WITH GREAT PLEASURE THAT I CONGRATULATE YOUR ROYAL HIGHNESS ON THE BRILLIANT VICTORY WON BY THE SERBIAN ARMY, AND ALSO ON THE WONDERFUL EXAMPLE OF PATRIOTISM GIVEN BY YOUR NATION.

RAYMOND POINCARÉ
PRESIDENT OF THE REPUBLIC OF FRANCE

LONDON

TO VOJVODA PUTNIK:

IN THE NAME OF THE BRITISH ARMY I WISH TO CONVEY TO YOUR EXCELLENCY MOST CORDIAL CONGRATULATIONS OF THE BRILLIANT SUCCESS OF THE BRAVE SERBIAN ARMY AGAINST OUR COMMON ENEMY.

WE HAVE WATCHED WITH HEARTFELT SYMPATHY THE HEROIC DEEDS NOT ONLY OF YOUR TROOPS BUT ALSO OF YOUR EXCELLENCY, PERFORMED UNDER THE MOST DIFFICULT CONDITIONS.

LORD KITCHENER
BRITISH MINISTER OF WAR

Withdrawing toward the Drina and shooting over the heads of its own supply train, the Austro-Hungarian cavalry dislodged from the road a column of its own division hospital, which during the last three days had been pursued and sometimes overtaken by short episodes of fighting.

Major Gavrilo Stanković propped himself up on his elbows to look at the mindless flight of the Austrian cavalry through the mist. Three days in a cart that continually jolted and got stuck in the mud had caused dreadful pain in his wounded leg; but even more tormenting was the fear that the Serbian army would not catch up with them before they reached the Drina.

"So you feel triumphant, Major?" said Captain Hans Koegner in German. Koegner, who had been wounded in the shoulder, lay beside him, keeping up the Austro-Serbian squabble which had begun the minute Gavrilo Stanković had been dumped in his cart. At first Koegner had been delighted to find that Major Stanković both understood and spoke German quite well. "Bravo, Major!" he had exclaimed. "At last, a Serb with whom one can talk! I found all that killing with not a word exchanged and no communication of spirit quite disgusting."

"My knowledge of German won't afford you that pleasure," said Stanković, trying to silence him.

"Really, Major, didn't you find it degrading, those brutal charges of people in different uniforms? Men shrieking and rushing about like animals? Just think how different the war would be if the opposing sides first talked to each other, if they quarreled and argued instead, if their minds clashed before their weapons. Imagine what victory would mean then!"

"Victory would mean nothing then," replied Stanković, and relapsed into silence.

Gavrilo Stanković was thinking how he and Bogdan Dragović could escape just before dawn, with the help of his orderly, Radojko Veselinović—unless of course the Serbian troops rescued them before then. Bogdan was suffering from pneumonia as well as his wound. The night before, in response to his plea, Gavrilo had given his solemn promise that he wouldn't leave him, that they would stay together until the end of the war; but their decision to flee before they crossed the Drina had been seriously threatened by their separation that morning. He couldn't make the attempt without Bogdan, whom he had come to love like a younger brother after they had both been captured on Suvobor. In Bogdan, Gavrilo loved the young man he himself had once been, and he felt sad, during the nights made sleepless by his wound, that he had no son like him. He might indeed have had such a son.

Mud-spattered horses and soldiers swam up from the mist like specters, then disappeared into the gathering darkness. The thumping of the horses' hooves and the creaking of the munitions carts now prevented them from hearing the explosions of gunfire that had followed them since midday, fanning the flame of their hopes. If the fleeing soldiers were the rearguard of a larger force—a logical assumption—then the Serbian vanguard should catch up with them in an hour or two. How many hours would it take to reach the Drina from where they were now? Radojko Veselinović would know, he came from these parts; but he was with the column of walking wounded who were in front of the ambulance carts, and he had not appeared since midday, when he had brought Gavrilo a handful of prunes. If it hadn't been for Radojko's kindness and resourcefulness for the past two days, he would have had no food at all. Hans Koegner had received no rations that day either, but he had brusquely refused the prunes offered by the Serbian soldier, uttering a lengthy diatribe on the fatal absence of social hierarchy among the Slavs. Without it, Koegner said, they would never become a people of culture. Raising himself on his good arm, he had leaned over Major Stanković. "Can your pride actually endure this kindness from a subordinate? I can't understand what the Serbian army is all about, if the officers take food from the hands of their soldiers!"

Gavrilo had replied slowly and deliberately: "If I couldn't take food from the hands of my soldiers, Herr Kapitän, I couldn't order my battalion to charge against your bayonets or to stand firm against your attack."

Hans Koegner paused, then said firmly, "It would indeed be a misfortune for Europe if by some chance you Orthodox Slavs became her masters!"

"I think you're right; but it would be an even greater misfortune for the Slavs."

"I don't understand, Major."

A galloping horse, spurred furiously, took a fall with its rider; others running full tilt behind collapsed on top of them, so that men and horses piled up high on the road. The cavalry column halted.

Hans Koegner had begun to relate an imaginary triumph: "You'll hear the bells ringing loud and long from all the bell towers of Germany and the Austrian Empire, and the sound, healthy rejoicing of the victorious armies. What a scene! Instead of the salvos of cannon, our Germanic laughter. Are you listening, Major?"

"Yes, but I feel a great need for silence—both now and in time of victory," replied Stanković, who sank back on his mattress.

The clattering of hooves suddenly died down, the fog settled and thickened over the hedges and underbrush, and a dank, chilly silence spread along the highway through the dusk: a silence charged with uncertainty and menace.

If Gavrilo Stanković had known which division was approaching, he would have known whether its commanding officer would halt the advance of his troops that evening. If he, Gavrilo, had not parted company with the conspirators, if he had not resigned his commission and gone to Russia to mix with revolutionaries and fall in love with Masha, he would not now be a prisoner, lying in a cart with his leg smashed, in the company of Hans Koegner. He would be in command of a division, like his friend Kajafa, or he would be divisional Chief of Staff, chasing Potiorek's troops across the Drina and the Sava.

Bogdan Dragović thought that the wounds in his chest had started bleeding again, because of his fall. His breathing and the pulsing of his blood carried the dull pains throughout his body; the Austrian on his right jabbed him in the ribs, as he did whenever the cart got stuck in the mud. He touched the Austrian lightly.

"Why are you hitting me?" he asked. Why indeed should this soldier hit him, a man who probably would not survive his own wounds? Why should this Austrian hate him, a Serb? Was he seeking vengeance for his injuries, or was he simply malicious? Bogdan felt like crying, and not just because of the pain and his increasingly labored breathing.

"Why are you hitting me, you bastard?" he shouted as loud as he could, amid the hospital column's creaking and the darkness.

His neighbor struck at him again, right below the wound. Bogdan cursed and groaned, then grabbed the Austrian by the throat with both hands. The Austrian continued hitting him near his wound. They were suffocating each other.

Radojko Veselinović, Major Stanković's orderly, was in the column of Austrian and Serbian walking wounded; after Gavrilo Stanković and Bogdan Dragović had been shot on Suvobor, he had stabbed himself in the left arm, partly because he had lost faith, and partly to avoid being separated from his commander. He was walking behind an Austrian called Pepi, who had been wounded in the leg. He was sticking close to Pepi, but Pepi kept disappearing in the darkness, determined to slip away from him that night.

"Pepi! Where are you?" Radojko would shout.

"Ja-a!" Pepi would reply from the dismal darkness, but not at once, and each time his voice was fainter.

Radojko listened for Pepi's crutch, then followed the sound of its tapping: he was determined not to let Pepi get away from him before they reached the Drina. As if guessing Radojko's intention, when dusk began to fall Pepi tried to get out of his sight. While helping an Austrian officer get off his horse, which had collapsed from exhaustion during the flight of the cavalry in the fading light, Radojko had stolen some hardtack from the officer's saddlebags. But how was he to get it to the major, and at the same time prevent Pepi from disappearing to escape punishment for his victory in the wrestling match on Suvobor—a match fought in a distillery shed crammed with wounded, and in the presence of Major Gavrilo Stanković? Where was the Serbian vanguard now? Surely they could catch up with the hospital and take them prisoner. He could no longer hear Pepi's crutch; he must have given him the slip again.

"Pepi! Pepi!" he shouted.

"Ja-a!"

Pepi was some distance away; Radojko pushed his way through the wounded toward him. Not a light anywhere, not a single dog barking, no sound of gunfire. This too filled him with fear.

The ambulance cart stopped outside a building from which came a gleam of lamplight, the sound of crockery, and shouting and quarreling in the several languages spoken in the Austro-Hungarian army. All around were darkness and silence. This must be an inn, concluded Gavrilo Stanković. If they didn't spend the night here, they must mean to get across the Drina before daybreak. He called to Doctor Vojtekh, a Czech in Austro-Hungarian uniform, a Slavophile and a friend of the Serbs.

"We've been defeated, badly defeated, Major!" said Doctor Vojtekh in Russian, clearly disturbed.

"Are we going to spend the night here, Doctor?"

"I think so. Captain Schulz has ordered the division's rearguard to vacate this inn for us before dawn. Can you hear them? The whole battalion is drunk. They're staggering around and sprawling in the inn like pigs."

Gavrilo resolved to take a decisive, almost final step. "Listen, Doctor. You must help Bogdan and me to stay on this side of the Drina!" He felt along the side of the cart for the doctor's hand.

Doctor Vojtekh was silent for a long time, and Gavrilo thought his hand was trembling; he pressed it. "I'm no coward—have no fear about that," the doctor whispered, and disappeared into the darkness.

Gavrilo dropped down onto his mattress, somewhat reassured; while he waited for Radojko he listened to the drunken Austrians in the inn, and to Hans Koegner, who was saying that it was no mere chance that there was not a single philosopher among 150 million Slavs.

"Do you think, Captain, that the language we hear from the inn is the language of philosophers?"

"Don't be cynical. They're just a poor bunch of idiots."

"I'd appreciate it if you wouldn't talk any more until daylight."

Radojko stood behind Pepi, holding on to his empty knapsack; the major was calling him, and he didn't know what to do: when the major shouted like that, it meant he needed him badly; but if he left Pepi in this darkness, he'd never find him again before daybreak, and by then they'd have reached the Drina.

The inn was vacated with a lot of shouting and yelling, and a few revolver shots. There was commotion among the wounded. Pepi moved forward, with Radojko hanging on to his knapsack.

Gavrilo was carried into the empty inn on a stretcher. He was assailed by the smell of filth—the filth of an army and a tavern combined—and of brandy; but in his heart he felt as if he were being carried into a Belgrade hospital. Doctor Vojtekh wanted to place him beside Hans Koegner and the other wounded Austrian officers lying on tables pushed against the walls; but this suggestion was firmly opposed by Doctor Schulz, the officer in charge, who insisted that only officers of the Austro-Hungarian army should be put on the tables: "Let the Serbs lie in their own filth—on the floor of this pigsty!"

"You're right, Doctor, absolutely right," whispered Gavrilo. His stretcher lay against the legs of Koegner's table.

Koegner leaned over toward him. "I much regret I'm not on the floor with you, Major."

Gavrilo didn't reply. They also brought in Bogdan Dragović, who didn't care where they put him.

Doctor Vojtekh ordered that Corporal Dragović be placed next to Major Stanković. Bogdan didn't open his eyes; his breathing was labored and short.

"Is he any better, Doctor?" asked Gavrilo anxiously.

Doctor Vojtekh shook his head.

Bogdan heard Gavrilo's voice, opened his eyes, and saw him in a blur; he reached for Gavrilo's hand and squeezed it hard. He didn't know where he was, but he felt safe at last. There was nothing he wished for; everything around him was swaying in a darkness in which a light was dissolving, then blinking on and off. He clutched Gavrilo's hand, his father's hand, to keep from toppling over and to stop that Austrian from hitting him in the chest.

"We won't be taken to a prison camp, Bogdan," said Gavrilo, removing his hand from Bogdan's limp grasp to wipe his hot, sweaty forehead.

By what law or justice should he survive this young man who had sacrificed himself for a pipe—for Gavrilo's souvenir pipe from St. Petersburg, which Corporal Frank had yanked from Gavrilo's mouth as he lay a prisoner in the hospital on Suvobor, at which he gazed and grumbled in German: "Where would a Serb get such an expensive pipe? He must have stolen it somewhere in Europe, the bastard!"

Frank had then carefully wiped the stem of the pipe with his handkerchief and started to smoke. Gavrilo had been so overcome that he had no voice left to protest and couldn't even raise his hand: his pipe, which Zharkov, his closest friend and companion, had given him as a keepsake in front of the lime kiln on the Karpov banks during the St. Petersburg uprising of 1905, right under the Cossack sabers—that treasured pipe had been snatched from him, and now that Austrian, Corporal Frank, was smoking it: the victor!

Then Bogdan Dragović had gotten up, staggered toward Corporal Frank, and like a flash of lightning snatched the pipe from his lips. Gavrilo had been dumbfounded that a man with a bad chest wound could move like that, and had been more amazed at his strength even than at his courage; only then had he been startled out of his frozen numbness and humiliation. Corporal Frank had stood there in disbelief until his compatriots, offended by the bold action of the Serb, began to protest; then with two leaps on his one sound leg he had caught up with Bogdan, who was tottering back to his mattress, and started to beat him violently on the back. Bogdan had lost consciousness before Radojko jumped up to defend him. Doctor Schulz had bellowed from the door of the shed, whereupon the corporal stopped beating Bogdan and told Schulz that a skinny swine of a Serb had snatched his pipe from his mouth. Gavrilo had protested that this was a lie, but Doctor Schulz summoned his orderlies and told them to carry the rebellious young man outside into the snow. It was dusk when Doctor Vojtekh finally brought him back in, half-frozen and delirious, and put him next to Gavrilo; he gave him two injections and threatened Corporal Frank with demotion if he harmed a wounded enemy in any way.

When he regained consciousness the next day, Bogdan, flushed and smiling, brought the pipe out from under the bandages on his chest and pushed it into the major's hand. To thank him would be far too little; to reproach him in a fatherly way for his rashness would be harsh and insincere. In any case he had realized from his encounters with Apis and the other conspirators that people like Bogdan were blind to the experience of others; it was useless to try to teach them about life. So he put the pipe in the inside pocket of his jacket. When Bogdan recovered, he would tell him all about it.

Now he called Doctor Vojtekh and begged him to do something for Bogdan. The doctor gave him an injection, forced a tablet between his lips, and felt his pulse. "A young man's heart. He'll pull through. Don't lose hope."

A crowd of walking wounded came into the inn and filled up the space between the serving-hatch and the tables on which the Austrian officers were lying. Gavrilo called out to Radojko.

"I'm here, sir, don't worry—I'll be with you in a minute," answered Radojko from the doorway, holding on to Pepi's crutch. If Pepi tried to escape now he would take his crutch; without it, Pepi couldn't get away.

Suddenly there was shooting outside. The bullets hit the windows and smashed the glass; someone turned the lamps off, and the wounded crowded together on the floor, groaning in pain. Radojko grabbed Pepi's crutch and crouched in the doorway at the other end. The shooting continued; bullets pecked at the walls and shattered the brickwork. Radojko wanted to shout for joy, so that their liberators could hear him, but didn't dare. He pressed Pepi's crutch between his knees like a rifle and trembled.

With a searing pain in his leg and pelvic bones, Gavrilo raised himself and held on to the poles of his stretcher, trying to follow the course of the battle, the outcome of which he did not doubt. Meanwhile Hans Koegner was talking above him: "I can't understand you, Major. Can't a sensible and educated man like you see how pointless this war is? You say you're fighting for the unification of your people, but what is there to unite but your poverty?"

Koegner seized him by the shoulders. Gavrilo jerked his arm away, expecting Serbian soldiers to appear any minute now. The gunfire had become less frequent, and the shooting was concentrated in the immediate vicinity of the inn.

"Long live the Serbian army! Long live our liberators!" shouted the Serbian wounded inside the inn; there was commotion and pain in the darkness. The shooting outside suddenly stopped. Radojko got up, opened the door slightly, jumped over the doorstep with the help of Pepi's crutch, and crouched down on the steps, trying to figure out what was happening. In front of the inn and on the road the Austrians were making a terrific noise; cries for help from the wounded pierced the darkness. Our boys have given up, concluded Radojko, disappointed; he ducked back inside, where no sound could be heard but labored breathing.

"Pepi!" he called in a low voice, and when he spotted him he placed the crutch next to him.

Several Austrians came in carrying lamps and calling for the doctors; the lamps were lit and hung on the walls. They brought in more wounded, kicking the Serbs on the floor out of the way to make room for the newcomers.

Disappointed at the battle's outcome, Gavrilo didn't know what to say to Hans Koegner. The newcomers groaned on the floor.

"Why are you silent, Major?"

Gavrilo propped himself up to see Koegner's face. Koegner looked at him for some time, then said, as if in confidence: "We simply must annihilate your people, Major. It's the law of history."

"Isn't victory enough for you, Captain?"

"Defeat does not teach wisdom, Major."

"So that's why you impale our children on bayonets, hang our women, and burn our houses and stables?"

"We destroy you by the methods you understand best."

"Aren't you afraid, Captain?"

"Afraid of God, you mean?"

Gavrilo raised his voice. "Yes, that's what I mean!" Then he sank back slowly on his stretcher.

Doctor Vojtekh came up to him, smiling. "Those drunken swine are hitting each other," he said in Russian. "They're frightened. It was a terrible defeat, I can tell you. You're saved, Major!"

Gavrilo dropped back onto his stretcher. The dull pain from his wound permeated his whole body, meeting no resistance. He no longer heard Koegner, who was talking about the virtues instilled in him by his mother and grandmother. Gavrilo turned to Bogdan and caressed his sweaty forehead. If he survives, he thought, will he need my experience? Will the truths I hold have any meaning for him?

Bogdan opened his eyes and for a long time tried to recognize the shadows around him. "Is that you, Major?"

"Yes, Bogdan. We won't be separated any more. Our men will be here before daybreak."

Bogdan tried to smile, then fell back into the darkness.

Radojko came up and gave him the stolen hardtack, apologizing for not having come to see him since noon.

"That Pepi wouldn't let me out of his sight," he said, and felt crestfallen that the major made no comment.

"Go get some straw or hay, anything you can find, to put under Bogdan. He's lying on the bare brick floor, and he's got a high temperature again."

Radojko gave a hurried salute, then went outside to look for straw, but the Austrian guard wouldn't let him pass.

Later, when all the lamps had gone out, Radojko sneaked up and removed a blanket from a wounded Austrian overcome by weariness. With the major's help he placed it under Bogdan, then returned to the doorway to keep an eye on Pepi and listen to a wounded Serb tell how, the night before last in just such darkness, the Hungarians had dragged some wounded Serbs out of the stable one by one and killed them with their rifle butts on the manure heap.

"Whish! Bang! Most went without a squeak. No time. One moaned.

Then again—Whish! Bang! I had crawled under the manger in the nick of time, but I expected them to yank me out by my feet."

"Listen to this, Major." Koegner leaned over Gavrilo and, from a postcard with a picture of Franz Josef in the uniform of a marine, he read:

> "Oh Heavenly Father, Lord of all the suns,
> Be Thou my witness in my despair
> That I did naught to start this conflict;
> My hand sowed no seed of bloodshed.
> But now, encircled by an invidious foe,
> I have called my people to their defense.
> May Thy spirit watch over our weapons,
> Give us the victory—to Thee be the glory!

That's how our emperor prays, Major!"

"I don't like the truth in verse, and still less the lies of an emperor in the form of prayer. Now I want to go to sleep."

"Oh, be a gentleman, Major. This is our last night together. You'll be sleeping tomorrow, and as for me, I'll be . . . oh, well!"

Koegner fell silent. There was a commotion in the inn as Austrian orderlies began to carry out cases of medical supplies.

As Austrian officers hurried in and out, their wounded called out in fear: "You aren't leaving us to the Serbs, are you? Some medical service, you sons of bitches!"

Gavrilo caught sight of Doctor Vojtekh near the serving-hatch; he was holding a lamp which lighted his square, smiling face for the wounded of both armies to see. They were calling to him from outside in German: "Hurry up, Vojtekh! We're leaving!"

Doctor Vojtekh grinned, then lifted the lamp above his head and flung it to the floor, as one might in a drunken brawl. The room was engulfed in darkness.

"You poor wretched Serbs, they've left behind typhus patients who'll infect you," said Vojtekh in Czech. His words startled Bogdan out of his delirium; feeling for Gavrilo's hand, he grasped it firmly.

The inn was quiet. Outside, horses were stamping and carts were being loaded. A wave of dank, cold air, sobering in its effect, came through the open door. The men outside again called to Vojtekh, but he didn't answer. Then there were sounds of departure, soldiers marching close-packed on the highway. The silence was broken by hoarse laughter from the serving-hatch. The Serbian wounded were whispering; Koegner was weeping quietly, and Gavrilo trembled when he heard him.

Radojko Veselinović called out, "Pepi, where are you?"

"Ja-a, Radojko!"

Radojko smiled in the darkness: Pepi had spoken his name—for the first time!—and they had been together for a whole month.

In fact, they had not been separated since their wrestling match in the distillery shed on Suvobor, when they had been taken prisoner; it had been the worst blizzard in living memory and the Austrian officers had fired shots to celebrate Potiorek's capture of Belgrade. "Belgrade has fallen!" The words were whispered or shouted in the languages of both the warring armies. Some of the Serbian wounded sobbed aloud; Gavrilo Stanković, then commanding officer, had wept quietly. It was the first and last time Radojko had seen the major in tears, and the sight blinded him: if he, Major Gavrilo Stanković, was weeping, then Serbia was done for! At that moment Pepi had gotten to his feet —the same man who filled them all with awe because every morning he stripped to the waist and rubbed himself with snow in the frosty air. Then Mirko, a Croat from Vukovar, said that Pepi was the best wrestler in Vienna, and just when Major Stanković burst into tears, Pepi walked to the middle of the shed, tossed his crutch aside, took off his jacket, and stood there in his blue vest and wide belt with four German letters in silver on it. Speaking sternly, he said something to Mirko in German, and Mirko explained that Pepi was challenging the strongest of the Serbs to a wrestling match, to celebrate the capture of "that Serbian henroost, the place where your Uncle Peter lives." Those were his very words, something Radojko would never forget. The wind whined outside, the forest groaned. Snow poured in through cracks in the doors and the Austrians were firing their revolvers, singing, and shouting, "Belgrade has fallen!" Pepi spread out his arms, shook his shoulders, and flexed his muscles. The Serbs buried their faces in the straw; Major Stanković did not attempt to hide his tears; and Radojko was overwhelmed by a hot, burning sensation, as though he would burst. He got up from his mattress, and holding his wounded left arm with his right hand, he walked up to Pepi. He had looked hard at the major, waiting for some word of command; but the major said nothing, so he went up to Pepi and said: "Mirko, tell him in German: 'Fritzie, I'll wrestle with you, but if you touch my wounded arm, I'll kick you with my boot in your wounded leg.' Got that?"

When Mirko explained what he had said, Pepi roared with laughter: his whole body, from his blond head and his big nose down to his bull-like torso, doubled up. Then he straightened himself, looked sternly at Radojko with his feline eyes, and said something to Mirko; Mirko didn't want to say what it was, but he advised Radojko not to wrestle with the Viennese champion, because he'd break his backbone. This infuriated Radojko further, and he cut Mirko short: "Tell him to watch out! There's not a man the length and breadth of the Adriatic coast who could knock me down! Just tell him all I've told you, Mirko!"

Pepi grinned, while Corporal Dragović called out: "Radojko, he'll smash you to bits! You don't know what tricks he has up his sleeve!"

"To hell with his tricks!" he retorted.

The wrestlers grasped each other by their belts. Pepi held Radojko's belt with only one hand, which put Radojko on his mettle and made him equally scrupulous, so he bent his left leg and raised it up to his knee, and hopped around on one leg like Pepi. Evenly matched now, they pushed each other around, drawing close and then moving away, breathing heavily and stumbling over the wounded men, who cheered them on and swore, the Serbs and Mirko from Vukovar supporting Radojko, and the Austrians Pepi, while Corporal Bogdan covered his eyes. Radojko cast a quick glance at the major, whose eyes were closed; it cut him to the quick. The Viennese champion seized his opportunity: he flung Radojko's emaciated body across his knees and hurled him down among the knapsacks and top boots.

"Well done, Pepi! Bravo!"

Outside, the wind howled over Suvobor, and revolver shots echoed. Pepi stood still a minute, smiling, then clapped his outstretched hands, while Radojko collapsed onto his mattress next to the major, whose eyes were closed.

The Austrians must have run away, and our men will be here before daybreak, Radojko concluded—then we'll see what's what! He crept outside and listened for sounds on the road.

Gavrilo listened to Bogdan's heavy breathing and the tearful moans of his delirium. His temperature was still high. The major wiped his face, rubbed his temples, and covered him with his overcoat. Sleep overcame him while his hand was still on Bogdan's forehead.

At daybreak Bogdan was awakened from a deep sleep by the sound of the major's voice: "Tell me what you can see, Radojko."

"It's misty, sir. The sun can't break through. I have a strong feeling we're at a crossroads."

"Where do the roads go?"

"I don't know. They're blotted out by the mist. Maybe we're in a valley with cornfields and clover. Or maybe on a path between the hills."

"Can you hear anything, Radojko?"

"There's a horse galloping, sir—two horses."

Chairs scraped against the floor, straw rustled, voices muttered in two languages. With a great effort Bogdan opened his eyes.

Radojko stuck his head outside, into an icy mist which cast its blue shadow over the wounded as they leaned toward the door. The sound of horses' hooves came closer and closer.

"Our men!" exclaimed Radojko, and rushed out into the fog.

To Bogdan it seemed that the entire inn was dancing around Radojko with mute, motionless shadows. He shivered violently, seized by a nameless fear. He wanted to take Gavrilo's hand, but couldn't bring himself to do it; Gavrilo's face had the same expression as on Previje, when the two of them had gone to the observation post in the beech tree while shells exploded in front of them.

"Our boys have reached the Drina! Do you hear that, Pepi? They're at the Drina!"

That was Radojko, and beside him stood a Serbian sergeant and a soldier with his gun cocked, ready to fire.

"Are there any Fritzies fit to fight here? Anybody got anything to fight with? Long live our liberators! Long live King Peter! Are you sure they've crossed the Drina? What's your regiment?"

A huge head appeared from the serving-hatch, smiling and giggling feebly.

"Free at last! Freedom!"

It was the Czech, Doctor Vojtekh. There he was, kissing and embracing Gavrilo Stanković.

"Please forgive me, Major. I'm drunk!"

"I forgive you, Doctor. And you, Bogdan, now you've got something to be happy about," whispered Gavrilo, stroking his head.

"Yes, I'm happy," muttered Bogdan. He remembered Natalia. Perhaps she would come see him after all.

Gavrilo took his pipe out of his pocket and tried to fill it, but he spilled the tobacco; his fingers refused to obey and he had great difficulty lighting it. He inhaled the first puffs and looked at Bogdan. He could find nothing to say to him, or to the sergeant who was standing at attention and reporting. Or, for that matter, to Hans Koegner, who said as he got off the table: "Allow me, Major! The tables belong to you now. But remember: we will come back and punish you for the humiliation you've inflicted on us. We'll be back and don't you forget it!" He bowed, and sat down on the floor against the wall, covering his head with his blanket.

Radojko stepped on Pepi's crutch and looked down at him; Pepi in turn looked imploringly at Major Stanković and even more so at Radojko. But Radojko wouldn't settle accounts with him here. No, he'd grab him by the collar, take him out onto the road and through the fog to the pigsty where the Fritzies had killed the innkeeper's wife the previous night because she tried to stop them from killing a pregnant sow. He'd finish off that squealing Fritzie, champion wrestler of all Vienna, in the pig shit. He'd put one, two, three bullets in him, the first right through the forehead!

"So now your teeth are chattering, you dirty German dog. Get up, Pepi!"

Pepi lay stretched out on the floor, covering his head with his hands for protection. Radojko looked around the inn: could the major see him? Could the Serbian wounded see what the best wrestler in the Austrian Empire looked like now? But Major Stanković was talking with the sergeant, and the wounded were rapturously greeting and embracing the Serbian soldiers.

Radojko burst out: "Now you're in for it, Pepi! Mirko, tell him I challenge him to a wrestling match." Then he added quietly, "Now, you champion of all Vienna, you and I are going to fight with the Serbian soldiers on the Drina! Get up, Pepi!" He handed him his crutch and took him outside.

Bogdan Dragović wanted to shout at Radojko, but he dared not; perhaps these were specters created by his illness; perhaps Major Stanković was not really smoking his pipe, and the Serbian sergeant was not telling him which regiments had liberated Šabac and gotten through to the Drina. Perhaps it was not really true that Radojko and Pepi were wrestling in the fog. He couldn't make them out clearly. First their heads and then their feet were snatched away by the fog, then it swallowed them up completely. Black, inky shapes were tumbling about; the twitching spasms of movement were wisps of fog. The fog was panting and moaning, the dawn was tottering. A long-drawn-out, hoarse groaning filled the inn.

"Pepi's knocked him out again!" someone said.

"Come here, Radojko!" ordered Gavrilo Stanković.

"Why did you want to call him out when you're weak?" someone scolded Radojko.

"Bend down, Radojko," commanded the major.

A thick, heavy slap on the face echoed through the inn.

"I understand, sir."

Radojko Veselinović walked dejectedly out into the fog and sank back on his stretcher. No, none of this was real, thought Bogdan, it couldn't be.

Vukašin Katić arrived suddenly in front of the first houses of Valjevo. Just below the plum orchard—crisscrossed with trenches and covered with shell holes, shattered fruit trees, and the bodies of men and horses—was the beginning of the town: the scene of victory in the war and also of everyday life behind the front line, where Vukašin Katić must go on with his life as a politician, a leader of the Opposition and editor of Opposition newspapers. Could he go on with it? Could he face meeting people, talking about the war and politics, the government and the Allies? Writing articles about the corrupt and inefficient government, the war profiteers, the shirkers, the rising prices? Could he go back to the old preoccupation with political combinations, and lunches and dinners with foreign diplomats and journalists, convincing them of the inevitability and justice of liberating and uniting all the Serbs and South Slavs? How could he? First he must stand in front of Olga and say, I believe Ivan has been taken prisoner. As proof he would take the cap from his pocket: Look, here's his cap. I remember it by this border and that spot. Ivan and I wear the same size hat and it fits me exactly. He would put the cap on his head and look at her frightened face, then fall silent, his silence joining with her silence, which had never happened before; he would lie beside her sleepless form, unable to sleep himself. Where could he find strength to do all this? He must meet Milena that very day—it was less than fifteen minutes' walk to the hospital—and listen to her weeping, look into her frightened eyes, and convince her that there were grounds for hope. He must go just as he was, wet and muddy, with his broken cane.

For two days he had walked over the slopes of Maljen and through the villages where Ivan's regiment had fought their last battles, looking for him, asking everyone he met whether they'd seen a tall, thin corporal with glasses; but to himself he put other questions: Why hadn't he welcomed his son with a smile when he came home from school? Why hadn't he kissed him as he used to kiss Milena when he left the house? Why hadn't he hugged him as he hugged her during thunderstorms, when he sensed that the boy was afraid?

As he waded across the streams and walked through the woods, lingering in the field where the Austrians had driven the village people in front of them as they launched their counterattack, he prayed to the earth and the trees that he might not find him. All the while he was troubled by a feeling of uneasiness, because he hadn't found time to play with his son, hadn't taken him sledding or swimming in the river or for walks in the woods, as other people had taken their children. He had received the news of his successes at school with tight-lipped coldness, maintaining an attitude of indifference to the praise and admiration that Ivan won wherever he went, because he, his father, had been his sternest judge, thinking that in this way he would make him stronger and stimulate him to further achievement; for he expected much of him.

Whenever he spotted some soldiers' bodies he would take off his hat and remain motionless for a while, staring at the tracks in the mud or snow to see if he could recognize Ivan's footprints. Ivan's footprints were long and narrow, but this one was short and wide; here was one made by a peasant's sandal, but Ivan was wearing boots; here were some long footprints like his, and made by boots, too—by someone who was in a great hurry or running away. Why hadn't he done more to share his son's youthful worries?

Then he caught sight of a new cap caught on a thorn in the underbrush, a cap exactly like the one Ivan had worn in Kragujevac, but he couldn't bring himself to touch it and pick it up. In his letters from

Paris and Skoplje there had been no affectionate words for him, his father. How formal they had been when they said good-by at the Niš station the day Ivan left to join the Student Battalion as a volunteer, behaving as if it were nothing unusual at all. Only when he had made sure that there was not a drop of blood on the snow, the grass, or the footprints was he able to take the cap and put it on his head, then continue in the slush through fields where Ivan also had walked, stopping at every house to ask about a tall, thin corporal with glasses. He went on until finally a peasant woman told him, and he asked her to repeat it to him several times, that the Austrians had brought one of our boys—a tall, thin young man, blond—into a house where their staff was; they had asked him a lot of questions, then taken him away while our men were shooting from the hillside.

With this proof that Ivan was a prisoner, and the cap he had taken from the thornbush in his pocket, he must now continue to live as he had done until the arrival of the telegram from Colonel Miloš Vasić, the commander of the division in which Ivan served: "Your son, Ivan Katić, is reported missing after the engagement on Maljen. Please do not give up hope. With kind regards to Mrs. Katić and yourself. . . ." Suddenly he encountered the enormous gray eyes of a dead horse and, unable to walk past its sightless gaze, he fell headfirst into the mud. Then he got up, jumped over a ditch, and entered the plum orchard, so recently a battlefield. Leaning against a shattered tree trunk, he lit his last cigarette, which he had kept since midnight. As he smoked he stared at the dead Austrians, the rifles and mess kits scattered over the ground, and the fragments of overcoats and pieces of human bodies hanging from the disfigured and bloodstained tops of trees. So this was victory—the victory people talked about behind the lines in the Parliament and coffeehouses, and wrote about in the newspapers, drank toasts to! With what passion and earnestness he himself had written and spoken that word: *victory*. The victory he had talked about, the victory of people behind the lines, his war and their war, the war of ideas and nationalistic propaganda, the blood which flowed in newspapers and poems—all this bore no resemblance whatever to the real war on Maljen, the reality of victory in this plum orchard. Well, he had known that; but no, he hadn't really known. Could he go on talking and writing about the war and victory as he had done up till now in the *Echo*? Would these plum trees ever blossom again, and wait for the harvesters to come and pick their fruit? Would this battlefield strewn with corpses and weapons once more become an orchard, with ripe fruit and yellowing leaves scattered over the grass?

At the bottom of the orchard an old peasant woman was going from one dead body to another, looking them over carefully.

He went out onto the road and hurried past some prisoners who were collecting the bodies of soldiers and horses. He turned his head away from a group of small boys who were clearing away the debris of victory from the street. As he approached the gates of the barracks, then the hospital where Milena worked, his pace slackened. He stopped in front of the gates where groups of walking wounded were standing, surrounded by women and old men bent under the weight of large bags; the wounded were munching bread and chicken, draining bottles of wine and brandy, and talking about something that clearly filled their listeners with anxiety.

He looked down at his feet: how could he meet Milena all covered with mud as he was, and with this cane? He was now in front of the long, low building where he had left Milena three days ago. He stood in the melting snow against an old acacia tree. A few large snowflakes swirled over the dark brown earth. His hands were cold and numb. He couldn't put them in his coat pockets; what would he do with his broken cane?

As she came down the hospital steps, Milena saw her father leaning against the tree trunk. She was finished and could go home with him immediately. What was the news of Ivan? His hat was pulled down over his forehead, so she couldn't see his eyes—not a good sign. She hurried toward him, but stopped dead at the sight of his broken cane: ever since she could remember she had heard its tapping, along paths and up and down steps—the tapping of that elegant black cane, inseparable from her father when he was on the street, and now just a broken handle in his hand.

"Ivan has been taken prisoner, Milena," he said, then saw her eyes on his broken cane. Quickly he dropped it beside the acacia tree, went up to her, and took her in his arms.

"Is it really true, Father?"

He unbuttoned his coat to bring her face closer to his chest, to shelter her right under his heart. He kissed her head and shoulders.

"Yes, it's true," he said. His arms fell limply down, but she did not lift her head from his chest; she simply dared not tear herself away from his embrace, from the familiar and well-loved smell of tobacco and some other indefinable smell associated with her father, which brought back memories of him and her childhood, of her mother and Ivan. Will the war ever be over, Father? she wanted to ask him, but she was afraid to see his eyes and face, while his heart was still thumping as he spoke.

"We have reason to believe he's a prisoner, and that is what we must believe," he said, speaking into the nurse's veil on her head; but from the way she continued to press her head against his chest, he felt that she didn't believe him. "Listen, my dear," he begged, "we mustn't invite trouble by our doubts and suspicions. Tomorrow I'll write to the Red Cross in Geneva and ask them where he is. His life is safer as a prisoner than at the front."

For a long time neither of them spoke.

"I believe you," she said, and removed her head from his chest, quickly drying her tears. There was a smile on his face, and his eyes were dry; so perhaps it was true that Ivan was a prisoner. She didn't hear what her father was saying; he had taken hold of her hand and was taking her off somewhere. That was all for the best; Dušanka could have all her things. Perhaps she should have said good-by to her and to Doctor Sergeev, but what could she say to them? How could she say to them, I can't stand it here any longer—I'm going home! She would write them a letter and tell them why she had to go. She didn't care if they despised her for it.

Flakes of snow melted on the road and were extinguished in the gathering dusk. She recalled the wounds, which had made her faint. The naked, disfigured bodies of the men, the stench and filth, the curses and insults of the soldiers, the piteous cries of the wounded, the trembling jaws and the glazed eyes of the dying, from which there was no escape, anywhere.

Vukašin tried to wrap his coat around her; she was walking quickly, as if running away. What had she lived through? Who had hurt her so deeply that she didn't even want to take her things, or say good-by to the doctors and nurses? She pressed herself close to him, as though someone were pursuing her, and gripped his hand convulsively. He took her head between his hands and looked hard into her eyes. What did he see there? Was it fear, reproach, or entreaty?

"Has something terrible happened, my dear?"

Her lips and chin trembled, but she couldn't tell him.

"What about Vladimir?"

She gazed into her father's eyes; she certainly didn't want him to think that she was unhappy only because of Vladimir.

"Would you like me to make inquiries through the staff of the First Army?"

She removed her head from his hands and started to walk down the street. He caught up with her, took her by the hand, and didn't let go until they reached a place where they could spend the night. They entered a cold room with two unmade beds. Milena stopped in the doorway, halted by the smell of tobacco and boots, the familiar stench of war from which she was trying to escape. She didn't want to spend the night here; she wanted to stay outside in the fresh air all night, with nothing to remind her of the hospital. Her father was tired, though; he was opening the window and had lit the stove. This calmed him down a bit, and he knew he was doing something for her. How could he have gone through life denying himself the pleasure of spending time with his children, thinking up little treats for them? How had he not been aware of the joy of doing things for and with his loved ones? To live only for the common good, for ideas and lofty aims, to make the nation's worries one's own, to consider party politics and writing for the newspapers more important than one's home, where he most frequently arrived tired and depressed and had nothing to say—what sort of a life was that?

The fresh air in the room and the fire in the stove, with its flames leaping up into the fading light, had a calming effect on Milena, too; she remained leaning against the doorpost, looking at the flames. Was it true that she would never go back to the hospital? Never! she said to herself.

"Milena, take off your nurse's apron and cap," said Vukašin, sitting down at the table. He was excited at the thought that they would have supper together, that after such a long time he would once more kiss and caress her before she went to sleep. Like the old days when he used to come home late, go on tiptoe into the nursery, and peep at Ivan; and if he wasn't asleep he would gently stroke his hair, hardly touching it, and then stand over Milena, bending down so that he could hear her breathing more clearly. When there was a moon he would pull the curtains slightly and open the shutters so that he could look at her sleeping face, the shadows cast by her eyelashes, and the slight, restless movement of her lips as she slept.

She took off her cap and apron hesitantly, as if ashamed, and threw them on the bed. Standing in the firelight of the darkening room in her blue dress, she seemed even thinner, her body like a child's. Her arms had grown longer and skinnier and her eyes looked older; her bun made her seem older, too. Her mother would soon put her to rights again.

"Vladimir is dead, Father," she said, a little too loudly, standing beside the bed and looking at the floor.

He went over to her, took her hand, then hugged her to him and comforted her a little.

Milena suddenly pulled away and learned back against the wall. She saw no grief or pity in her father's face; he had not liked Vladimir, and had once said to her mother (she had overheard him from the entrance hall), "That saber-rattler is not the right man for Milena." Her assertion that the young lieutenant was not a "saber-rattler," but a man "as modest and gentle as a girl," had failed to calm him. From then on he had looked at her with a despondent expression, had been grave and gentle with her, as if she were suffering from an incurable illness; but she had brusquely rejected his concern, and never sat in his lap again.

Vukašin returned to the chair beside the stove. He reproached himself because even now he could not grieve for Lieutenant Tadić as Milena would have liked him to; he had seen him with Milena in the street two or three times, and all he knew about him was that he had fought with distinction in Macedonia, but did not seem worthy of Milena. From one of her letters to Olga he knew that Vladimir had been seriously wounded, and that this was one of the reasons she had not left the hospital in Valjevo before the Austrians entered the town. Now it would be easier for her to do so, but he must take her away as soon as possible. General Mišić was an early riser; first thing in the morning he would ask him for a car to take them to Mladenovac or Čačak.

The landlady brought in a lighted lamp, a plate of cheese, and a loaf of warm bread. They sat down to supper. He said he was very hungry, told the landlady how good the bread was, and asked her for some wine. He pressed Milena to take some food and ate quickly himself, talking about the magnitude and importance of the Serbian victory. Milena took a bite of bread that stayed in her mouth; she couldn't swallow it. He stopped dead in the middle of a sentence and stared before him.

"Tell me about Mother."

He gave a start, then told her all about Olga, and how worried she had been about Milena during the Austrian occupation. Suddenly she cut him short: "Father, I read somewhere that love can make you vicious."

He stopped eating; with his hands still on the table, he said in an embarrassed tone: "I don't know what that means, Milena. How could love make one do anything wrong, except in novels? I'm rather dubious about what novelists present as the truth."

"That such people cannot atone for the evil they have done. Is that true?"

He looked into her eyes, but she was looking down at the bread.

"To tell the truth, I've never believed that any evil deed can be atoned for by repentance."

She hid her hands in her lap.

"That's terrible," she whispered after a while. "I've done something wrong."

"How could you do something wrong? What are you talking about? Look what you've done for all those wounded men!"

She heard Vladimir's cry and saw in her mind's eye the white pile of bandages slowly darkening with blood. She closed her eyes.

"Put out the lamp, Father. Please!"

He put out the lamp and remained standing, frightened by the tone of her voice and her dry, protracted sigh.

"Tell me all about it."

"I can't."

"You don't think there's anything that concerns you that I wouldn't understand?"

All over Valjevo dogs were barking.

"I must go to bed, Father. I was on duty all last night."

With hesitant, frightened movements he began to get the bed ready. What could be tormenting her so much that it even blotted out her anxiety about Ivan? Something that she couldn't tell him, in spite of her almost arrogant sincerity and her obstinate self-confidence.

"Don't bother to prepare the bed; I can't undress and lie down in a strange bed. Just remove the cover, then take off your shoes and lie down, and I'll lie next to you."

He did as she said and lay on top of the eiderdown, against the wall; she took off her shoes and snuggled up against her father, like a child nestling her trembling body deep into his warm embrace. He covered her and hugged her even closer; soon her trembling was stilled in sleep. Now she was a child again. He listened to her breathing as she slept, often broken by sobs and sighs. What could she be dreaming? Was he going to lose her, too?

A column of oxcarts passed down the street; when it paused under the window, he could hear the groans of the wounded and their cries of protest. Just as the slow-moving carts had creaked and jolted over the cobbles of Valjevo that night when the Supreme Command had discussed the possible capitulation of Serbia, and the need to give all her children to the war. He had said nothing, though he did not agree, fearing to oppose the sacrifice of the students lest he appear a traitor, lest he offend his political supporters or incur the scorn of his friends. He could see them all in the courtroom bending over the war map of Serbia; he could hear Putnik's asthmatic coughing, the scraping of Prince Alexander's chair, the tapping of Pašić's cane; could see Mišić with his thumb poised over the colored patch on the map indicating the combat area, then making circles around it. It had all made his eyes swim, so that he scarcely heard Mišić demanding that the government send all the students to the front without delay. If he's a prisoner, where is he now? The creaking of the slow-moving carts, with their burden of sick and wounded men, ground through his backbone. His shoulders grew stiff, and his weary feet were numb in his damp socks; but he kept still, so as not to wake up Milena.

"Is that you, Father? Where am I?"

"It's still early; go back to sleep."

"It's getting light," she whispered, shivering. The wounded men will be waking up now, she thought. My God, how could I think of leaving them? She tore herself away from her father's arms, jumped out of bed, and started to look for her shoes in the gray, chilly room.

"Where are you going, Milena?" He felt unable to move. Was she going to run away?

"I must get back to the hospital, Father. I go on duty at six." She put on her shoes without tying the laces.

"I thought we had decided to go to Niš. Your mother is expecting you. We must be together until we get news of Ivan, and you're so thin. Things are different now. The hospital can manage without you."

"No, Father, it's impossible. Please try to convince Mother that I'm well and happy, and that she needn't worry."

"But, Milena, I can't go home without you. I can't leave you here. There's typhus," he muttered, still lying down.

She sat beside him on the edge of the bed, wearing her nurse's apron and tying on her cap. "Father, do you remember what you said once to Ivan and me?" Her tense, strained voice broke, and her eyes filled with tears.

"Yes, I know, but, my dear, we've paid our debts to humanity."

"I simply couldn't sleep in Niš knowing that Dušanka was on duty all night, alone with two hundred sick and wounded men. While my colleagues are still in the hospital, it's my duty to be there, too." She took his hand between hers. "Don't be unhappy, Father. After all, I'm your daughter." Her head sank down on his chest.

He embraced her and said in a whisper, "Yes, my child, you must go."

"Let me know as soon as you have any news of Ivan. Good-by, Father."

Milena left without shutting the door behind her. Vukašin remained on the bed, motionless.

When the front door creaked shut behind Vukašin, Olga leaned against the window and parted the curtains; he was walking slowly away between the frozen chrysanthemums; then he paused, as if to pluck off a dead flower, or perhaps to come back to the house to tell her something, or explain in military terms the meaning of the telegram from Colonel Vasić: Missing in the last engagement on the slopes of Maljen.

Since receiving the telegram, which they had each read several times, they had decided after a brief discussion that he should at once go to Valjevo to see General Mišić; then they had said nothing more before he left. It was only after Vukašin had walked out into the street, stopped beside a lime tree, and leaned against its dark trunk that she suddenly began to weep with her whole being for her son and for his father.

Her neighbors, refugees from the combat area, knocked on the door to express their sympathy and comfort her. "He's only reported missing!" she would say, and lock herself in. However, she had to receive her cousin, Najdan Tošić, her nearest relative on her father's side.

"Let me in, Olga! I have good news," he said, scolding her, then he kissed her on the forehead as he always did, though this time she found it repugnant. "I asked Apis to go personally to Colonel Vasić and make inquiries. Ten minutes ago he telephoned that all the facts clearly indicate that young Katić is a prisoner. They think that he probably broke his glasses and got lost near the enemy position."

"What if he wandered in among the Austrians?"

"They would take him prisoner. He's a corporal. A retreating army has to look after its prisoners, especially the corporals."

"Yes, provided there aren't some wicked people out for vengeance in that army."

"They're beaten to their knees, Olga; Mišić gave them such a battering on Suvobor that their one thought is to get out of Bosnia and Srem as soon as possible. I'll send a telegram to Geneva, to a Hungarian baron who's a good friend of mine, and ask him to find out where Ivan is through their General Staff."

She listened intently and perhaps would have felt some spark of hope if Najdan hadn't said all these things with undisguised anxiety and lack of conviction. She could hardly wait for him to go, so that she could lie down on the bed, cover her eyes with a scarf, and once more direct her thoughts inward.

She strained every nerve to remember the first time Ivan cried, how he grew up, went to school, left for Paris, then came back home—everything connected with him until that fateful day, the eleventh of December, when he disappeared into the fog and darkness: the branch of a tree had hit his face and broken his glasses, she was sure; or the glasses had dropped into the water while he was jumping a stream; or else he had stumbled over a fallen log in the forest and broken them. She read all the letters he had written from Paris, and in one of them she sensed for the first time that he was in love. That letter was written only to her, and as she read it through many times it caused her no pain that the feelings of love and sadness that he expressed to her, his mother, were really intended for a girl whom he didn't even mention. It certainly couldn't be that Kosara from Skoplje whom he had talked about when they said good-by; just as the train was moving off, he had said that she was a marvelous girl—beautiful, intelligent, noble, with a wonderful soul. Olga's memories mingled and intertwined, from the time she saw him in the midwife's arms to the railway station in Niš when he waved from the train taking him away; at that moment he was for her a baby once more: his face clean and rosy as it had been in his cradle, the hands protruding from his overcoat transformed into little clenched fists waving from his swaddling clothes. The scenes mingled, faded into the confusion of her memories: the baby ill with diphtheria was succeeded by the soldier wearing a cap too big for him, hurrying toward her from the barracks at Skoplje through the dusty courtyard the first time she saw him there; then the boy coming home from school, crying because he had broken his glasses while playing; then the stern and serious young man, confidently discussing with friends the latest books, and the annexation of Bosnia and Hercegovina, arguing impatiently with his father every day at lunch, putting forward the claims of Knut Hamsun and Nietzsche in opposition to Vukašin's authorities, Montaigne and Anatole France. Then she saw the small boy with large, rather protruding greenish eyes, smiling gently when she came into the room to wake him in time for school; she had done this, whatever time she went to bed, so that his day might begin with some tender words from her. She remembered every word he said to her the morning he left to study in Paris, how he wouldn't be troubled or changed by contact with Europe as so many of our people are—all this aimed at Vukašin; and how she had looked at him when he unexpectedly came back from an excursion; and how, though she felt tense and frightened, she hadn't even embraced him, realizing that he had just dropped in for a short time, in the course of a journey he had decided upon in Paris.

Her thoughts returned most often to that evening in their vineyard on Topčider Hill, when he had looked up from her arms at the August sky, crowded with stars, and asked, "Why is the sky so black, Mummy?"

"How can you say it's black, darling, when it's covered with stars? You couldn't count them in a hundred years."

"What are stars, Mummy?"

"Surely you know what stars are?"

"I know about them from fairy stories, but I've never seen them."

"Can't you see them now?"

"No, I can't."

She thought she would drop him. "You can't see the stars in the sky? Little fires burning a long way away like lamps, like colored flowers?"

"No, I can't. The sky is black, Mummy. The Old Witch lives there."

"No, the stars are there. The Old Witch lives in a cave in the forest. The stars are shining up there," she murmured as she carried him to bed. In tears, she waited for Vukašin to come home, to tell him that Ivan couldn't see well.

She was deeply troubled that her child could not see well, and felt guilty about it; and when they bought him some glasses just before he went to school, she could hardly wait for the night to come. She held him in her lap on the terrace as they waited for the night to fall, just the two of them, telling him stories of fiery dragons flying through the sky with flaming tails, fighting each other for princesses. Above Srem and the Sava the stars had already come out in their countless numbers; she was waiting for him to say that he could see them, but he said nothing. She made up a story about the dragons flying from star to star; still he didn't say anything, but he looked at the sky from time to time. She could restrain herself no longer: "What can you see in the sky, Ivan?"

"I can see the stars."

"How many can you see?"

As he began to count them she clasped him to her breast, and didn't carry him to bed until he had fallen asleep in her arms.

She just couldn't imagine him taking part in these battles, charging and fleeing from bayonets, shooting at the Austrians and hiding from them; there was no image of him in the fighting on Suvobor. Except for his glasses falling off, she could picture nothing of the fighting in which he was reported "missing."

She had no idea how long she slept or what she ate after Vukašin's departure to bring Milena home. Voices inside the house were muted; from time to time she would hear the clatter of dishes, the shuffling of mules and padding of slippers, the creaking of doors. Neighbors came in without knocking, bringing her tea, coffee, and cakes. Their whispered talk was of the typhus spreading through Serbia; but she did not respond to this, she had no room for other anxieties. Najdan often dropped in, to tell her that he was expecting a telegram from Geneva any day now. She begged him not to come until the telegram arrived, but he came just the same, worried now about Milena, telling her that there was a typhus epidemic in all the areas that had been occupied by the Austrians. People were so frightened, he said, that they no longer talked about the victory over Potiorek; they were terrified, just as they had been after the fall of Belgrade.

"That husband of yours still goes on ranting against the government!"

"Najdan, you know I can't stand your opinion of Vukašin!"

"He said that all the merchants in Serbia and all army contractors are thieves. He said they should be court-martialed. My name was the third on the list. Who should I steal for anyway? Who's going to inherit from me? His own children!"

"Have pity on me, Najdan. After all, you're my cousin. You and Vukašin must do things in your own way. Please go; I'd rather be alone!"

Once more she pressed her head against the window, resting it on one of the iron bars until it grew warmer. She scarcely moved as she stared out at the gate, recollecting how Vukašin used to come home with his chest thrown out, walking with long strides, waving to her with his hat or cane from the terrace, or calling her name and announcing unexpected guests for lunch. She was always cross because they were never alone together with the children, but it was no use. As he became a more important public figure and his reputation grew, they were even less alone and belonged less and less to each other. When she tried to make him share her anxiety about the reality of their life together, she soon realized that he was not aware of anything lacking, or afraid because they were so seldom alone. She tried in vain to resist the discovery that at bottom Vukašin was not so very different from most men, with their inherited conviction that a woman had all she could possibly want if she had money and her husband was important. She suffered because the world and life were taking Vukašin away from her, and because every time he left the house he would belong a little less to her when he came back. She tried to believe it was not his fault. Meanwhile she found comfort only in the children—in Milena because she took up her time, and in Ivan because he filled the house with his affairs. She winced with pain as she banged her forehead on one of the iron bars on the window.

She looked up, unable to believe her eyes: there he was, tearing himself away from the trunk of a lime tree, looming up from the cobbled street between the clusters of wet, dead chrysanthemums, bent, haggard, and without his cane. To steady herself, she gripped the window bars until her hands hurt.

Vukašin slowly opened the door and stopped on the threshold: now the moment had come that he had dreaded since his departure from Valjevo. He struggled to pronounce the first words he must speak to Olga, standing there amid a pile of trunks and boxes. Suddenly he felt deprived of the hope with which he had tried to convince himself, so that he could also convince her.

She walked toward him, took both his hands in hers to still their trembling, and looked straight into his eyes. "What's the news?"

"I'm sure he's a prisoner."

"Is that what you think, or have you proof?"

"At the army headquarters they say there's not a single fact to indicate that he was killed."

"Is that all, Vukašin?"

"I myself went to the battle site. He's not there; but in the next village a peasant woman described a corporal who had been taken prisoner who looked just like Ivan. Only he wasn't wearing glasses—but that would explain why he was taken prisoner."

"What else did you find out?"

"Mišić is convinced that he's a prisoner."

She let go of his hands and sat down on the bed. "What about Milena? Where is she?"

"Milena's fine, only she's upset about Vladimir. He's either been killed or died of wounds, I couldn't find out which."

"Why haven't you brought her home? There's an outbreak of typhus there."

"She didn't want to leave her job. I tried to convince her that she had every right to come home, at least on leave, but I couldn't."

She pulled herself away from his suddenly hoarse, broken voice, silent in the face of his grief, twisting herself up in this silence, feeling that she would straighten herself only when she had acquired the strength to comfort him, to ease his burden a little. He sat down noiselessly on the bed, without taking off his hat and coat, and slowly, quietly lit a cigarette. He wanted to lay his hand on her head, to perform some wordless action, but he didn't know what. So they remained silent and motionless, until darkness slowly filled the room. She moved up to him, put her hand on his shoulder, and spoke in a quiet but intense voice: "I'd feel ashamed of myself now, ashamed of both of us, if you'd listened to me that night. If you'd used your influence with people to keep Ivan from being sent to the front. I'm no heroine, you know that; but at least our son has chosen his own destiny."

"Ours, too."

"That's right. Now take your coat off and wash your hands, and I'll get supper ready."

Vukašin embraced her with tears in his eyes; he wanted to speak words he hadn't uttered for years, to speak about the long silence between them and his own sternness toward Ivan; but his pain filled him with shame. She sensed it and felt even sorrier for him, so she lingered a long time in his arms, open to his trembling.

At supper they talked about Milena in strained, broken whispers. Vukašin was grateful to Olga for making everything about that supper seem as if he had just returned from the Parliament or the newspaper office. Again he reproached himself for his infidelities, and even more for his lack of understanding, his sense of security that had gradually become indifference.

He remembered two or three occasions when she had tried to warn him, always with the same words: "We're together, and yet we're alone. Aren't you afraid, Vukašin?"

"Surely you and I don't have to convince each other of our love?"

"Yes, Vukašin, we must, as long as we're alive."

"Then for goodness' sake, what is it I should be afraid of?"

"Of loneliness, loneliness that you can never escape."

"Well, Olga, that's a misfortune that you and I will suffer. I'm sure of that."

"But that's what I'm afraid of, and your courage in the face of loneliness. Yes, that's what I fear." She had begun to nod, her eyes wide open with fear, but he had firmly put an end to their conversation, aware that he was leaving her feeling sad. Now he was sorry.

As soon as they had gone to bed and were lying in the darkness, once again he surrendered to thoughts about himself: he would have to change his life; but how? Supposing there was no war—should he abandon politics and become a judge, a lawyer, a civil servant? Or should he retire to their vineyard in Topčider and live on Olga's inheritance? Did his plans have any significance in a country which Ivan would perhaps never see again? Everything that he had considered his nature and his gifts—his knowledge, wisdom, and conscience;

all that he had wanted to share with his friends and his nation—all this, now that he had no one to inherit it, seemed pointless. It made no difference that Ivan had set out along a different road, that some Vladimir would decide Milena's fate. He felt deeply that his political struggles for the advancement of Serbia, everything he had done and wished to do for the common good, all his newspaper articles and speeches in the Parliament, all those ceaseless conflicts with environment and tradition, the many times when he had refused to acknowledge defeat, his hard-won reputation—all this had in fact been intended for his son. In the same way his own father had acquired land and power for his sons, and his father-in-law Todor had done the same for his daughter. Does it really take a great misfortune to bring us back to our true selves? Was it only through Ivan's fate that he was learning what sort of man he really was? No, he hadn't deceived himself, and he wasn't deceiving himself tonight either. In every real misfortune there was something truly great, something of great importance for the mind and soul. Here alone there resided some vital truth that he wouldn't want to be deprived of, ever; but he would have given his life if by some miracle Ivan, wherever he now might be, could know his thoughts and feel his shuddering. If Ivan could feel what he was feeling, he would die a happy man, but that was quite impossible. Those who believed in God were fortunate. Yet belief—a pure firm conviction—was possible: at this moment it really was possible to believe in God as this power, this hope, struggled toward birth.

Olga knew that he was still awake and gently stroked his hand and hair, so gently that he didn't feel her touch; for a moment she could hardly restrain her tears, desperately unhappy that he didn't take her in his arms, that this night he didn't embrace her as his wife. Couldn't he feel how strongly her pain yearned for love? How her love was the measure of her pain? Perhaps he couldn't emerge from his own loneliness, or understand pain because of his strength. Maybe he didn't love her. My God, she thought, it's terrible to be alone tonight. He lay there beside her; she could hear no other sound but his breathing. His heart beat beneath her outstretched hand, burning and wide open, waiting for his touch.

When he woke up in the morning and saw her with a scarf across her face, he raised himself in the bed and timidly put his hand on her breast.

"What are we going to do, Olga?" he whispered.

"We must get on with our lives. We must live for our children," she said at once, as though expecting just such a question.

"Do you think we can? Can I go on with my usual duties?"

"We must. You must go on opposing the government, you must go to the newspaper office and the Parliament."

"What will you do today?"

"I . . . I'll make sure that people don't see only my unhappiness."

"Is that really so important to you?"

"Well, I'm sure it's important for Ivan. I'll go to the Red Cross today, and as soon as we have news of Ivan, I'll go to Valjevo to fetch Milena."

Although the drum had not yet sounded through Prerovo to announce the arrival of letters from the soldiers and the list of killed, wounded, and missing from the district command, ever since daybreak old men, women, and children had been trudging and floundering through the slush and along the muddy lanes toward the district office. If they greeted each other, they did so quietly. Not everybody greeted Aćim Katić, and he for his part did not respond to the greetings of the young men. He was walking slowly behind his son George when suddenly George motioned him to stop. Aćim stopped and looked at his son, who was hunched under his fur hat, and so shrunken that from behind he was recognizable only by his clothes and cane. Aćim was tipsy. Since his return from Valjevo, he hadn't left the still and had talked only to the animals. For fifty days there had been no letter from Adam, and during the past week no word from the district command about the soldiers at the front. Aćim Katić's throat swelled as he peered despondently before him at the clammy dark brown fence bending toward him, with dogs poking their noses between the stakes, and footprints of men and animals decomposing in the mud. Had God willed it that Adam would never again come thundering down this lane in the moonlight at full gallop, disturbing Aćim's first sleep with mingled anxiety and joy that he was a hellraiser and a night owl? Surely his nest among the ash groves was not to become empty, and the Katić family continue only in Belgrade, with Vukašin and his family and that strange grandson Ivan? His cane slipped from his hand; George disappeared behind a bend in the road as he followed slowly.

If no letter has arrived overnight, thought George, at noon I'll go to Valjevo and Šabac to look for Adam. He had had a dream about him the previous night, a dream that he saw him looking very thin, all skin and bones, barefoot and in rags like a beggar, riding past a fence, not theirs, dozing. O Lord, tell me what I must do to have Adam back alive and get a letter. Should I give everything I own to a monastery, or become a monk myself and stay buried alive? I'll do anything! Whisper in my ear, Lord, what I must pay to have Adam back. I'll do what no man has ever been able to do.

In front of the district office he walked past a crowd of women clustered around Tola Dačić, who since his return was telling his usual lies about General Mišić and what they had said to each other. He leaned against a hollow elm and rolled a cigarette, as he looked at the open door of the district office: the head man was there, so the mail must have come.

Meanwhile Tola Dačić, holding his grandson by the hand, continued to talk. Of his three sons, whose name was on that black-edged list? Even in peace God did not take the bad folks, as was right and proper—but aways the best, damn it! Those who would suffer longest, and most deeply. If the power of a great empire was to be halted, broken, and thrown back across the Drina and the Sava, the toll in human lives and endurance would be well-nigh impossible to bear.

The head man came out of the office with the list and stopped on the steps, then looked around the assembled crowd as if seeking out someone. He looked at his list, then once more at the women, children, and old men thronging in front of him.

Natalia Dumović ran toward the office. If there was no letter from Bogdan today, she would go with George Katić to Valjevo to see Bogdan's mother; she would know whether he was still alive; but how dare she think he was not?

Prerovo seemed engulfed in a dense silence—or had fear robbed her of her hearing? Or had those people standing beside the elm tree and in front of the district office been struck dumb? Natalia stopped a few paces behind her father and Aćim Katić: she was carried away by the silence, and Bogdan's old letters lay like a weight against her heart. Why was the man looking at the list and not speaking? Couldn't he read? No, it wasn't that; he could read all right. What was her father up to, slowly climbing up the steps of the office in this silence? Suddenly all the people looked fearfully at the schoolmaster.

"Listen, folks, our army is victorious, Serbia is saved! Prerovo will be full of people again. Men will be cursing and shouting again, and there'll be weddings and feasts beside the Morava." Natalia trembled as her father stammered out those words; the women shrieked and moaned as if from a slap in the face. "Give us our letters!" shouted Aćim Katić; he would have waved his cane, but he couldn't extricate it from the mud. "That's right!" said Tola Dačić. "Let's have the letters first."

The head man went into the office and quickly returned with a small bundle of letters and postcards. Kosta Dumović, the schoolmaster, descended one step and leaned against the wall. George Katić did not raise his eyes from a footprint which seemed to grow wider and deeper. Natalia came up to him and whispered: "Uncle George, I want to go with you to Valjevo." He didn't understand why she wanted to go to Valjevo, but he couldn't ask her because he was listening to the head man calling out the names, and to the cries of the women: He's alive! Give me that letter, it's from my son! My boy's all right too, thank God! Natalia, come read this for me! I need help too, Natalia! I want you too, dear—have a look at this last word and tell me what it says!

Natalia trembled as she waited to hear her own name. "He's alive! They're all alive!" cried Tola Dačić every time the head man called out a name. Then he looked at Natalia running up to get a letter: "You're a lucky girl, Natty, but you've had a long wait." He heard his own name, and threw his fur hat in the air. "Bring it to me," he shouted to Natalia. "What? Only one? Open it and tell me who it's from."

"George and Aćim Katić, two letters!" Aćim dropped his stick and walked toward the head man; a voice he didn't recognize broke in: "The cavalry are always all right, everybody knows that; it's the infantry that gets killed." He took both the letters; one of the two wasn't in Adam's handwriting, and yet it looked familiar. Impossible —it couldn't be from him, today of all days! The world must be coming to an end if it really was a letter from Vukašin!

"Now, folks, we have to face it. You'll have to hear which of our boys won't come back to Prerovo. That's fate. Professor, you're better at reading than I am. You read the names of the dead—our old pupils. Will you women please be quiet!"

George Katić raised his eyes; in front of him, in the hands of someone he didn't know, was a large blue envelope with the letters of his name swarming like bees in Adam's handwriting. He crossed himself, then took Adam's words, Adam's envelope, but couldn't open it. The schoolmaster, Kosta, took off his hat, and so did the head man. Snow-flakes swirled past, as big as the palm of his hand.

Tola Dačić read only the end of his letter: "Your unhappy son, Miloje," then pushed forward, trying to make himself heard above the shrieking of the children: "Is my Aleksa's name on that list, Profes-sor?"

"You must wait; I'm going to read them all out." Kosta Dumović continued to read, slowly, almost inaudibly, the names of the dead from Prerovo.

"Speak up, Professor! It's only right that the names of those who stay out there should be heard properly," said Tola, holding his grandson's hand as he pushed his way through the crowd of women up to Kosta Dumović, who at that moment raised his eyes from the list and said, "May God have mercy on their souls."

"A soldier has no need of God's mercy, Professor!" cried Tola. "He's repented enough for himself and for his grandchildren. Go on reading!"

"Now, the wounded . . ."

"Well, wounds will heal," said Tola to himself and his grandchild, Blagoje's son, and listened to the names of the wounded with his head turned the other way. There were a lot of them. His grandson began to shiver. "Better wounded than a prisoner," he whispered to him.

"Now, folks, listen to the names of our boys who are missing—taken prisoner by the Austrians." Kosta Dumović finished reading and re-turned the list to the head man.

"Run home and tell them our boys are alive, and that we have a letter from Miloje," said Tola, sending his grandson on his way. Then he opened the letter:

It's good to know that all you folks are safe at home. Greetings to Mom and Dad though it would be better if we weren't here and greetings from me to the rest too if they ask twice how I am though a lot the neighbors and the rest of the family care I'm all right. Well the war news—some folks managed to get across the Drina and the Sava but when we bashed the Fritzies you couldn't move for dead bodies or see the water for blood. I was just looking forward to a leave doing something for myself for a change in-stead of for the government, then when I was on sentry duty beside the Drina, everything quiet, one of those damn Fritzies got me—broke my arm above the elbow. He was aiming at my heart but I moved a bit to the left, but the dumdum caught me and smashed the bone. Serves me right for not taking cover behind the trees but I got that interested looking at the fish jumping from the Drina at dawn then I was lying in Pecka until they took me to a freezing filthy inn at the back of beyond. So look out for a grave for me thats what I deserve no more news your unhappy son Miloje.

"Looking at the fish, you idiot!" muttered Tola. "Now if it had been some women rinsing hemp or washing! There he was staring at the fish, damn him! Fish, indeed!" Then he asked the schoolmaster where was this place Pecka? The schoolmaster didn't reply; he was on his way to the school, bareheaded, stooped. "Natty, do you know where Pecka is? You poor girl, where did your man get killed?"

Leaning against the hollow elm tree, Natalia was unable to take her eyes off her letter:

Natalia,

Any time now the First Army staff will send us students to the trenches. I have a feeling that I'll be killed in the first battle, and I can't let that happen and not tell you how much I loved you, and that my love for you was the greatest thing in my life.

In the train from Skoplje to Kragujevac, among us thirteen hundred students going to the battlefield, I was the only one who was happy. That was because you were waiting for me in Kragujevac. I felt there was nothing I couldn't do, nothing I couldn't dare to do. But you didn't come. That was my first defeat in the war. Can you imagine how painful it was? Try!

From the time we left Kragujevac until we got to a village below Rajac, I doubted everything about myself. I didn't even have the strength to walk right. I was completely alone, facing those men who were going to kill me. It was as if I had never lived, as if I had never been born.

If you still exist anywhere in the world, I no longer exist for you. I have gone out of your life forever, and can never come back.

Bogdan

"Have you lost somebody?" asked the women sympathetically, as they gathered around her with their letters. She didn't reply, but read them their letters. She had no idea whose letters she was reading, or to whom she was reading them; she hurried so as to be alone as soon as possible, alone with her own letter. I have gone out of your life forever. If you exist anywhere in the world. If I exist for him? She hurried on with the reading.

"Mother, was it my fault I was late meeting that train? Tell me the truth—don't spare my feelings!" she said, seizing her mother's hand. Then she rushed into the room she shared with her sister. "Milica, don't you remember how I didn't sleep a wink that night. How I got everything ready, and how I was weeping for joy and talking about him all night?"

She left the house and ran to her father at the school; he was arranging lighted candles on the pupils' benches. "Father, was it really my fault that I was late for that train?"

"No, it wasn't your fault, but you should have arrived there in time, my girl. You just mustn't be late when you're meeting a soldier on his way to the front."

Natalia looked at her father in amazement. She would have cried out in protest, but it seemed so unfair she couldn't even open her mouth. To hear such words from her father, too! Trailing her hand along the wall, she went out of the schoolroom, just as she used to when her father scolded her because she had not done her homework properly. Outside, in the slushy, frozen snow, she listened to church bells and women sobbing.

Meanwhile George Katić went into the big kitchen of his house, carrying Adam's letter in his hand. "His horse has been killed, but only his horse, thank God," he said to Zorka, his second wife, and Milunka, Adam's grandmother, who had stayed in the house to look after him when Simka, his own mother, died. Both of them begged him to read Adam's letter. "Where am I going to find him a decent horse?" he continued in worried tones, as he held the damp envelope over the stove. "Now you two listen to my orders, which have to be obeyed until Adam comes back. No one is to leave our house without receiving what he asks for! Neighbors, beggars, gypsies—give everybody what he wants; never mind whether they're thieves or paupers, friends or enemies. No one is to go away from our house with hate or evil thoughts in his heart. You, Grandma, are to go to the monastery tomorrow and give them five ducats, and tell them they're to say prayers for Adam every feast day. As for you," he said, turning to his wife, "I don't want any tears in this house!" He dried off the envelope, then put the letter in his wallet. It had never been so full and heavy. There were four letters from Adam there, and Aćim had two others; but why wasn't he home yet?

The women wiped their tears with their aprons and begged him to read the letter. He had already read it three times, but he sat down and read it to them again, word by word, slowing down every time they sighed, pondering on the meaning of what Adam had presumably not written:

Dear Dad and Grandpa,

I expect you've heard how we dealt with the Austrians, and how the Serbs won a great victory. Now the whole world knows which army is really heroic and unconquerable. They know that we Serbs are a race of men, strong and tough when God is squeezing the life out of us and the devil is scratching our eyes. Until we got to Suvobor and Rudnik, the Austrians couldn't kill us fast enough. How we got out of that mess only the good Lord knows. But what is all that to me, when I no longer have Dragan? I'm afraid he's gone, poor creature. There was a fog, far worse than when Grandpa and I went out shooting wild geese and the Morava was frozen. I was at my last gasp rushing to the Drina when I saw a great mass of dead and living horses, but no sign of Dragan. If the poor beast isn't rotting on Suvobor, then some German sausage of a general is now riding him to Vienna. It makes me feel miserable. So, Dad, please go up and down the Morava, as if you were out buying pigs, and have Grandpa drop in on the people round about, as when there's an election, and both of you do your best to find me a horse fit to ride. It must be young, and the best-looking one you can find, and see that it has a big flower on its forehead, and white forelegs, so that it looks like Dragan. And Grandpa, please see that it's a black horse; and don't you buy me a sleepy old cart horse, Dad. I don't want to ride a cow. Try to bring the horse as soon as possible, because they say the Germans will be invading Serbia any time now to punish us for beating the Austrians and Hungarians and the rest. Go to Valjevo, and ask there for the cavalry squadron of the Morava Division, second draft. I'm getting all mixed up and forgot to ask whether any refugees have come to our house, people I met and traveled with for a time—an old woman with her grandson and her granddaughter Kosanka. The old woman is a nuisance, but Kosanka's a marvelous girl. Don't bother about the old woman, but do look after Kosanka, and don't let them go back home until I come on leave. When the war's over I won't mind all I've gone through.

"He doesn't mention us!" cried Milunka, disappointed.

"You're not at the front, that's why," said George. "Now, Grandma, please cross yourself and be quiet, and don't either of you forget what I told you." Then he fell silent as he listened to the tolling bells and sobbing from the village.

Aćim came in and sat down on the couch, exhausted. "Ivan's reported missing," he said, running his fingers through his beard.

"You mean Vukašin's son?" asked Milunka.

"Light the stove in Vukašin's room," said Aćim to Zorka, after a pause. "George, give me Adam's letter." He put on his glasses, took the letter, and began to read it, whispering to himself. "He's still on about Dragan . . . still crazy about his Black Beauty. . . . Even the war can't teach sense to some people. 'Please go up and down the Morava . . .' Where are we to find him the finest horse in the world these days? . . . As if that weren't enough, you expect me to look after some old woman or other. Your head's still full of petticoats . . .'"

He finished the letter and handed it to George. "Don't worry about him any more. Vukašin will put in a word to get him transferred to the telephone service."

"How do you know that?"

"The other letter's from Vukašin."

"When will he do it?"

"He'll do it, that's what he says in the letter. His son's missing, and his daughter's working as a nurse—you've seen the place where she is."

He felt he must read Vukašin's letter once more, so he went into the old house where Vukašin's room was, next door to his own. He waited for Zorka to light the stove in Vukašin's room, so that they could sit and talk there. Perhaps Vukašin might even come himself, now that his heart was broken and he had written a letter. Yes, now that his heart was heavy, he would have to come back to his own people.

"Listen, Zorka. Please change the bedding on Vukašin's bed, dust the cupboards and the windows, and get everything nice and clean. Put some good apples and quinces on the cupboards and the windowsill, and from now on light the stove in his room every day."

My dear Father,

My son Ivan is reported missing—at dusk on December 11, that's what they say, since he hasn't been found on the battlefield. I've been looking for him myself on the slopes of Maljen for three days.

Yes, my boy, you love your son as I love you, but it hurts even more!

Your grandson was nearsighted, but he volunteered anyway. He's worn glasses ever since he started school.

Well, he didn't get his poor eyesight from the Katići. It's from his grandfather on his mother's side. All those liberal eggheads wore glasses.

He was quiet and thoughtful, always poring over books or looking inward at his own thoughts.

And what use is a man like that to the world?

He wanted something quite different out of life from what you and I had.

Yes, what you and I want are two different things; but why didn't your son Ivan want to follow in his father's footsteps?

He didn't have time to learn that there's no escaping our fate, and that our life is not our own.

No, it certainly isn't. It was just chance that a decent man found your grandfather Luke under a willow tree beside the Morava, when he was camping for the night while on the run from the Turks. He took him home like a young rabbit, gave him some milk, and covered him with a blanket. So he grew up somehow or other, like a hawthorn in a stone quarry, but if the Turks hadn't killed the squad teacher Vasili, and if your grandmother Kata hadn't been widowed, and if the Morava hadn't carried that shepherd and miller Luke off one dark night, he would have been buried at the end of the cemetery where they bury beggars and bastards. Only the good Lord knows why I'm still alive. I can't count how many times I've been shot at from ambush, how many kings and princes have wanted to put a noose around my neck. Do you remember once when I was bringing you home from high school for Christmas, two shots were fired at us from behind in the darkness? It's a wonder you're still alive, too, with all the enemies you've made. Have you at least told Ivan what a tightrope we have to walk, how we must grab at every straw?

I feel I owe him a great debt, Father.

You needn't burden your soul with guilt. He was never barefoot or hungry or without clothes. He never knew want or fear. Everything was easier and better for him than for you. You've nothing to feel guilty about, and there's no greater unhappiness than remorse.

He's pigheaded, just like you, and takes after you in some other ways, too.

Is that all?

He often asked me about you, and wanted to come see you.

How could you deprive me of my grandchild? You left home and went your own way, did what you wanted; but Ivan's my grandchild. When God or man takes away your son, there's still your grandchild —his father's first joy, his grandfather's last. So that while life may be a den of wolves, we're not always with the wolves, and so we're less afraid of the end of life. Didn't all your book-learning teach you at least that much?

If he comes back, I'll bring him to Prerovo right away. I'll bring your grand-daughter Milena, too; she's a volunteer nurse in Valjevo.

Vukašin

Well, see that you *do* bring them, my boy!

P.S. Tell George that I'll recommend Adam for a post as telephone operator.

He got up and opened the door of Vukašin's room, determined to keep it open as long as he lived; then he went in and stood in front of the photograph of Vukašin taken before he left for Paris. He rested his fingers on the frame and the glass and stared at the youthful face, with its high, frowning forehead and large, stern eyes: So you've lost your son, too? He must have grown up quickly, to vanish so quickly; and I never even set eyes on him. The frame shook from the trembling of his hand, and flakes of plaster fell from the wall. "But I forgive you, my son," he muttered, and burst into tears.

Najdan Tošić, merchant and supplier to the army, stood at his dining-room window looking out at the bare lime trees in the twilight; his heart was heavy as he listened to the rain and thought about the infectious disease that was spreading through Serbia, bringing totally unexpected misfortune as well as plenty of business. For him especially, business was booming. Drugs, soap, sugar—what else would be in demand? Next morning his first visit would be to Doctor Levi. Or should he go see Kostić? He must ask them what medical supplies to order from France. What supplies were most urgently needed from Greece? They would come through within five days, and in a business of this kind time was crucial. Immediately he must buy up from all the pharmacies in Serbia the medicines needed to treat the recent infection, and deposit them with his friends in Kragujevac, Ćuprija, and Leskovac. Such goods would have to be sold under the counter—a risky business. Now that every eye was watching him, thanks to that blockhead Vukašin, wouldn't it be safer to work through the Greeks and the Jews? He would concentrate entirely on getting medical supplies—time, money, personal contacts. It would save the lives of his people and at the same time be profitable to himself. That was right, for life is beyond price and every price carries a taint of sin. Yes, that was a fine idea, but what a job! No one must see where it started. Pharmacists, the army medical service, and all the petty shopkeepers in the country would be fleeced. In this horrible squalid wartime existence, only business on a big scale can still excite. Money can move mountains these days! That stupid nephew of mine, Ivan . . . In the summer I could have got Apis to help send him to England to buy blankets for the hospitals and cloth for officers' uniforms; but that pigheaded idiot's son had to volunteer for the Student Battalion! Blind as a bat when it comes to fighting, deaf as a post to the voice of common sense. Hopeless. Poor Olga.

"Shall I set the table?" asked his Aunt Selena; she was his foster mother, his father's sister, who had remained unmarried in order to look after Najdan when he was left motherless at the age of six months, and had accompanied him when he went to study in Berlin and Zurich.

"Yes, Auntie, go ahead," he replied, feeling sad that he could not rejoice at this moment: he had arranged a dinner party for his friends, some diplomats and foreign newspaper correspondents, in honor of the Serbian victory. He loved entertaining, and few things gave him greater pleasure than preparing the house to welcome guests, especially when the whole house from attic to cellar was filled with the excitement of work done with devotion and an atmosphere of festivity, and when he waited impatiently for guests to appear on whom so much effort had been lavished, so that they could all have a good time. It was always his wish that in his house the cordiality of the welcome should exceed his wealth. Here, however, he was in an uncomfortable rented house—all he could get as a refugee, with provincial furniture and kilims from Pirot. There was Aunt Selena strenuously resisting the very idea of a celebration while they still didn't know for certain whether Ivan was a prisoner; he was her favorite nephew and she was full of anxiety about him. In such circumstances, how could he welcome his illustrious guests—foreigners at that—in a manner worthy of himself and the occasion?

"How many places should I set?" asked Aunt Selena pointedly.

"Twelve. Thirteen with me," he replied, without turning around.

"Where did you find twelve people?"

"Five of them are ladies, actually."

"Ladies?"

"Yes, widows. Officers' wives, really distinguished ladies."

"I know your widows and your officers' wives! They're women who sing in cafés, prostitutes! You should be ashamed of yourself, Najdan! The whole town is talking about how those women come to this house, while your wife is in Athens."

"Now, Auntie, where would I find five beautiful but decent women in Niš today? Gay and witty, too. All the nice girls and ladies from the best families are busy with patriotic activities now, working as volunteer nurses."

"Well, what's wrong with that?"

"They're sad, or pretend to be. They dress in rags; it's a sort of wartime refugee chic."

"So our neighbors will be raising their eyebrows tomorrow?"

"They can raise their eyebrows all they want! It's not my fault that only a certain kind of woman is pleasant company in Serbia these days. They're the only ones who can still laugh, sing, and dance."

"Will they sing and dance in our house this evening?"

"What's wrong with that? I want my guests to have a good time," he said quietly. His aunt caught her breath. He felt sorry, but what could he do? The poor creature would have fainted if he had told her that it was those very "prostitutes" who represented the last remnant of psychological health among our women; only they could banish fear and the boredom of wartime existence, remind people of peace, and awaken some hope for the future.

"Look at me, Najdan!"

"What is it, Auntie?"

"I refuse to have your 'widows' in my house tonight, sitting at this table and eating a meal I've prepared! Get us out of this as best you can!"

"Good heavens, Aunt Selena, the guests will be here in a couple of hours—several ambassadors, and journalists from Russia, England, and France. I haven't invited them just for the pleasure of it. You know I have commitments to the High Command and to Apis."

"Well, you know what I think; and if you don't do as I say, you'll regret it," she said, trembling as she put the plates on the table. Then she hurried out of the dining room, but turned around at the door. "Just think how Olga and Vukašin must be feeling tonight. Remember what's happened to Ivan!" she said crossly as she went out.

He was hurt by her reproaches. Next to Olga, he loved Ivan more than anyone in the world, in spite of his impudence and his contempt for "filthy commerce." It was as if he were responsible for the fate of that pigheaded son of Vukašin's, that cynic, the genius of the family! He had cried in front of this awkward young man, pleaded with him: "Please don't be the cause of your mother's death, Ivan! There are a thousand ways in which a man can do his duty to his country."

"Such as what, Uncle?"

"The country doesn't need only our blood, you idiot! It needs money, good sense, and well-educated people. A nation does not live on heroes and heroism alone. I don't believe any division commander is more useful to Serbia than I am."

"Don't make me laugh, Uncle!"

"Don't you make me weep because of your crazy idea about what's sensible."

"Stop wasting time, Uncle. You're losing money, and I could be reading something interesting."

"Listen, Ivan, when the war's over I'll build the biggest library in the Balkans in your name. I'll build a students' hostel and a refectory. I'll give all the money I make in the war to good causes and charitable foundations."

"Forgive me, Uncle, but you're talking nonsense."

"This is the last thing I'll say to you, Ivan. You'll inherit my money—you and Milena. Would you like me to send you a copy of my will?"

Ivan smiled scornfully, just like his father, and simply said: "Give Mother my love. Good-by, Uncle!" Then he walked off into the barracks, hardly able to drag the weight of his boots.

So now, while he's a prisoner of war, I shouldn't entertain in my house! He was about to go to the kitchen, but paused on hearing a noise from the hall, the sound of umbrellas being shaken. He recognized the voices of Dimitrije Lepenac and Melamed Albahari, both merchants. How could he get rid of them?

The maid showed them in and he greeted them, but didn't ask them to sit down.

"I'm expecting guests, gentlemen, and right now I can't worry about anything else. We can talk business tomorrow."

"At these times, Najdan, only death can be put off until tomorrow. Typhus is spreading, as you know. It's swept through Mačva and Posavina, and now it's come to Niš."

"Yes, I know, Dimitrije," he broke in, staring at Dimitrije's clothes: a soldier's cap, breeches, leggings.

"This is the season for wax—sickness, funerals, memorial services—and there's no wax in Serbia. Why don't the two of us import some from Rumania?" continued Dimitrije, who irritated Najdan with his uniform, his banal patriotic decorations, his petty dishonesty.

"I'm not interested in funeral stuff. Not in the least. To hell with your wax!"

"What about soap, perfume, and face cream from Greece? After all, we're the victors. The soldiers are going on leave, they'll buy these things for their wives. Why don't we fill up the canteens in the military zones and the shops near the railway station?"

"You know I don't like this kind of petty shopkeeping."

"All right, Najdan. Would you like me to double the orders for black cotton and silk?"

"I don't want anything to do with funerals, Melamed," he said. Then he noticed the field glasses on his chest and the black ribbon on his sleeve. He inclined his head disdainfully as he listened.

"People in the High Command tell me that in a few days we'll have at least twenty-five thousand prisoners of war in Niš. Twenty-five thousand! That certainly means two or three thousand officers—gentlemen, educated Europeans—and nothing in our shops in Niš to sell to them! Obviously luxury goods, top-quality haberdashery, and high-class groceries will be in demand."

"Who are you in mourning for, Melamed?"

"For my brother. Anyway, the epidemic has started."

"I didn't know you had a brother. Where was he killed?"

"Surely I have the right to grieve for someone!"

"Yes, you have the right, Melamed, but not until someone close to you has been killed. Just as you have the right to have an officer's field glasses around your neck, but at Mačkov Kamen or on Suvobor."

"You don't have to be so sarcastic! This is no time for spiteful remarks. Terrible times are ahead of us. I tell you, it'll be like Milan in the seventeenth century, when the plague carried off people and rats."

"Mind your own business, Najdan," said Dimitrije, "that's how it is now. Uniforms are everything. We've got to adapt ourselves, wrap things up. There's no alternative. Have you got anything to drink here?"

"Why do you have this stupid feeling of guilt because you're buying and selling? Because you're doing a job without which the people couldn't live or the army fight? Good God, the only jobs you needn't be ashamed of in this country are being a village constable or a politician. Well, all right then; I'll see you tomorrow at eight in front of the Hotel Europa. Sorry, gentlemen, but I can't spare another minute."

He didn't see them out; he found their subterfuges, their meanness, their petty, dishonest greed too odious. He lit the lamps and helped the servant finish laying the table. As for those people with the high-flown ideas, all spirit and high ideals, they too were scoundrels who would set the whole world on fire for their shitty ideas and principles! People who despised all beautiful things, to whom this lovely white Rosenthal porcelain or those delicate Czech wine glasses on the white linen tablecloth meant nothing. At least he had all these good things from his house and would not feel ashamed of his table that evening. Those Baroque silver candlesticks which he had bought in Dresden, that splendor of form and light which made the most banal remarks seem gay and convivial, lent beauty even to ugly women as they sat around the table. In this anxious atmosphere, and on such a wet night, he wanted his guests to feel festive the minute they entered the house. In such a splendid light, words would be carefully chosen and prostitutes reduced to silence.

He heard Aunt Selena's voice: "Tell him I'll throw the food on the floor! That's what I'll do."

What on earth could he do? The carriages were already pulling up in front of the house; he must greet his guests with a smile. The first to arrive was the Bulgarian ambassador, Chaprasnikov; he would keep him as long as possible, or until he learned from him what people in Sofia thought about the Serbian victory. Chaprasnikov was wearing a new lilac-colored vest and a jacket cut in the English style

—but fifty years out of date, of course. He was holding a bunch of laurel branches, and asked for Aunt Selena.

"Unfortunately she has a terrible headache," Najdan said; then he greeted Saltikov, the Russian ambassador, who was grumbling about the rain. "In Russia, in Petrograd, there's snow up to your waist," he said tenderly. "Blizzards, troikas, skating . . . Good evening, gentlemen!"

Najdan held the coat of the Rumanian ambassador; he had to squeeze out of him every bit of information about the postponement of Rumania's decision to enter the war on the side of the Allies. He showed the ambassadors and other guests into the dining room and begged them to make themselves completely at home, then excused himself, saying that he must wait for the ladies, who were all coming together on foot and would be wet.

When they arrived, he was pleased with their appearance: all dressed in black, with black veils over their faces. He whispered to them that they must look sad, and talk only about the suffering caused by the war and the heroic deeds of their late husbands, until "the gentlemen were mellowed by wine and began peering at their bosoms." He went into the dining room after the "widows," who were disconcerted by the bright lights and didn't know what to do with themselves. Najdan introduced them to the gentlemen according to the rank of their "late husbands" as the wives of majors, captains, lieutenants. He was glad that none of them knew more than a few words of French or German. The diplomats were exchanging impressions of the reception given by Prince Alexander and Pašić that they had attended that day.

"Why is the regent always so restless? There must be something on his mind. Those burning eyes seem to devour you."

"He has a very pleasant voice, Monsieur Barbi, and he smiles like a young girl."

"What do you gentlemen think of Prime Minister Pašić?" asked Najdan in French; he was pleased with the appearance of the table and the polished manner in which the servant was offering Italian vermouth and port. The sight of the "widows" also gave him pleasure, and the fact that Perkins, the British military attaché, wanted to drink only Serbian plum brandy. He took a glass of port and proposed a toast of welcome.

"If I may speak with Slav frankness," said Saltikov, "I cannot say that I am much impressed by the personal qualities of Monsieur Pašić. He doesn't drink or smoke, and has never gone after women. He loves only power and political victories—a dreadful man. I'm told that no one has ever seen him in a café. Is that true, Monsieur Tošić?"

"Unfortunately it is, Monsieur Saltikov."

"Then why do you Serbs adore him so?"

"Because he's not like us. You see, we Serbs don't respect ourselves, and Pašić is a complete contrast to our national type."

"You Serbs are like us Frenchmen! You swear, talk scandal, and mock even the things you value most."

"That's true, more or less. In addition, Pašić certainly has qualities particularly pleasing to the masses: he doesn't talk much and has a magnificent beard. Honest men think he's an apostle, and the dishonest think that there's nothing he doesn't know."

"Ah, yes, today he seemed so wise and dignified, as he sat there saying nothing. Didn't you feel that everything you said in his presence seemed superficial?"

"That's the privilege of all old men, Monsieur Papakostos," said Najdan, looking hard at Ruža, the "lieutenant's widow"; her cheeks were burning, and her eyes had a strange, feverish look. Could she be ill and infect them all this evening?

"Of all great statesmen, Monsieur Tošić, Pašić really is quite a genius, the way he talks German to us Frenchmen, Bulgarian to the Russians, and French to the Bulgarians. No one really understands him."

"The fact is, he's an old man," said Najdan. Ruža's appearance worried him; she seemed to be shaking with fever and not listening to the Rumanian ambassador, who was talking to her quietly in a mixture of French and Serbian.

"Why don't you go into politics, Najdan Tošić? You're an educated man. In Serbia even old women are interested in politics."

"That's because the Serbs think politics the easiest and dirtiest business there is, Monsieur Saltikov!"

"Bravo! Bravo!" exclaimed Colonel Perkins.

"The Serbs," Najdan continued, "think that such a repulsive and immoral job should be done by those who can't do anything useful, and who are even more corrupt than the people they govern."

"Ah, so you're a Nihilist? Why aren't you a member of the Opposition?"

"My dear fellow, I'm a businessman," he said to Stepan Trofimović. "From what you say, your place is in the Opposition. I wouldn't be surprised if you didn't turn out to be a Serbian Kropotkin—just like that!"

"Well, you might say that the government needs businessmen to get things done, and an Opposition to enhance its reputation." Then he fell silent, feeling he had already said too much. He again directed the conversation to the current political situation and Serbia's victory over Austria-Hungary. From the kitchen came the sound of banging plates and Aunt Selena's sharp voice: "This evening will be the death of me!"

The guests suddenly stopped talking, turned their heads toward the kitchen door, and looked inquiringly at Najdan. He raised his voice: "Gentlemen, have you read the German newspapers and seen what they make of Potiorek's defeat?" Then he looked at Ruža, who was rolling her eyes and shivering. Yes, she must be ill. What a pity!

Colonel Perkins criticized the Serbian High Command, who had not known how to take advantage of the enemy's rout and continue their advance across the Sava and the Drina.

Then Najdan went over to Ruža, and apologizing to the Rumanian for depriving him of her company, took her firmly under the arm and led her into the hall. "Are you ill, my girl?"

"I feel cold and shivery."

"Then why did you come? Do you want to spread the infection through my house?"

"Well, you know I've had my eye on that Rumanian for a long time."

"Here's some medicine for you to take. Go home and straight to bed!"

"Are you sending me away, Najdan?"

"For your own good. Here's some money to buy sugar and tea. I'll come see you," he said, pushing her out into the rain.

He was filled with foreboding as he stood there on the steps under the porch, watching Ruža disappear into the pouring rain. The darkness smelled of something unfamiliar and repellent. He sighed with relief as he realized what it was: the smell of his dead father as he lay on the couch in their drawing room, surrounded by lighted candles and bunches of boxwood branches. Where was the smell coming from? He grasped the wet, clammy handrail of the steps. Was it his own fear of sickness and infection? The night was full of the smell of his dead father; he would never forget that sweetish, clinging odor, redolent of grief, emanating from his father's couch. He stepped back into the hall, but didn't close the door. No, it was a smell of carbolic, or perhaps camphor—that was it, camphor! A small knot of people came trudging down the street along the fence. He hurriedly closed the door and looked around him; some misfortune was going to happen to him, some great misfortune. He could hear his guests arguing about the strategy and tactics of the Serbian High Command. He could not go back to them in such a fearful state. He wiped his forehead and the top of his head, which was spattered with rain, then forced himself to smile, to assume the manner of a kindly Slav host toward his guests.

Colonel Perkins was arguing heatedly, in bad French mixed with German: "General Mišić should be in Zagreb today. And Stepanović could easily have reached Pečuj. After such a crushing defeat for Potiorek, no great commander would stop at the Drina and the Sava!"

"Does Colonel Perkins really think we Serbs are just making hay?" interrupted Anka, the "captain's widow," for whom Chaprasnikov was translating the Englishman's remarks. "Mišić and Stepa have whacked the Austrians as if they were cattle in a cabbage field. Mišić is the Napoleon of this war!"

Najdan returned to the table, smiled at Anka, and remarked, "My dear ladies, I would prefer it if you were a little less aggressively Serbian this evening!"

"The Austro-Hungarians couldn't dig a single trench this side of Ljubljana and Budapest!" continued Colonel Perkins. "General Mišić is a brave man, but a poor strategist, and Putnik is a soldier of very limited range. The Serbs have let slip a unique opportunity. What a pity! Do you agree, Monsieur Chaprasnikov?"

"No, I'm afraid I don't, Colonel. The Serbs have really scored in this last battle. We Slavs are proud of our Serbian brothers."

"Forgive me, Monsieur Perkins," exclaimed Barbi, "but the Serbs are magnanimous as well as heroic. Did you notice the dignified silence with which the people of Niš greeted the column of war prisoners two days ago?"

Najdan could hear Aunt Selena weeping in the kitchen. What should he do? It was time to bring in the hors d'oeuvres; all the guests had now arrived except Scitti, the Italian ambassador, who must have stayed away because of the epidemic.

"All honor and glory to the Serbian army and its leaders!" said Barbi. "But if the Serbs did not have such women . . . ! You know, Monsieur Tošić, your women are enchanting; they're so witty and imaginative! Just look at them!"

Barbi must have noticed my uneasiness, Najdan thought. He must say something—anything. "I'll tell you what it is, Monsieur Barbi. It's our kings' scandalous love affairs that have stimulated such likely imagination in our women. There's no country in Europe that can boast such a dynasty over the last few decades. Our Serbian women have been able to talk against kings and princes to their hearts' content; and when you combine a wagging tongue with a beautiful face . . ."

"Let him serve the food himself! Yes, let him get on with it!" came a voice from the kitchen. All the guests but the Frenchman turned their heads toward the kitchen door.

"Marvelous!" cried Barbi. "Absolutely marvelous!"

Najdan poured out more drinks, proposed a toast, then got up to tell the servant to bring in the hors d'oeuvres. Meanwhile Chaprasnikov continued: "One thing I'm sure of, gentlemen: the peace that will follow this worldwide cataclysm will be the triumph of parvenus. When this slaughter is over, it will be their turn to be on top, don't you think, Monsieur Trailescu?"

Najdan stood in front of the kitchen door, pretending to listen to Chaprasnikov, but feeling quite desperate: how on earth could he calm Aunt Selena and avert a scandal which would be all over Niš tomorrow?

"I don't really think that would be a bad thing. After all, 'parvenu' means 'youth,' Monsieur Chaprasnikov."

"I believe, gentlemen, that the peace will reflect the defeated; they give the peace both its countenance and its spirit. The war belongs to the victors."

"Typical Russian philosophizing, Monsieur Saltikov . . ."

Najdan went to the kitchen door and quietly told the servant to bring in the supper. She brought in two large plates of goose livers and put them on the table.

The kitchen door opened with a clatter; Najdan jumped up and saw Aunt Selena in the doorway, looking furious.

"What is it, Auntie? Excuse me, ladies and gentlemen, you know my Aunt Selena—my foster mother."

The guests looked at her, embarrassed; some nodded by way of greeting. Her shawl fell from her shoulders as she spoke in a hoarse, sibilant voice: "Gentlemen, there's a great epidemic coming here—a great epidemic!" Then she slowly returned to the kitchen, leaving her shawl on the floor.

"It's the war, gentlemen," stammered Najdan. "She's getting old, suffers from migraine. And then the rain . . . The rain is enough to drive the wolves crazy, let alone people of delicate sensibilities. Take up your glasses, ladies and gentlemen! With all my heart I want this wartime night to remind you of peace. We all deserve to rejoice a little. Your health, ladies and gentlemen!"

Barbi asked that the glasses be filled up, then began to speak, smiling and taking obvious pleasure in his words: "The nation to which I belong is not adorned by the virtue known as modesty. This evening, gentlemen, I ask you to allow me to behave as a typical Frenchman, and to be the first to propose the health of our host. It gives me great pleasure to do so in the words of Victor Hugo, from whom I first learned of the existence of Serbia. In Victor Hugo's *Rappel*, written in the 1880s, one of the characters exclaims: 'Are they killing off a whole nation? Where? In Europe . . . But the future is God, whose chariot is borne by tigers. And the future is on the side of Serbia.' Long live Serbia!"

All those who understood French applauded, and Chaprasnikov, the Bulgarian ambassador, asked permission to translate Hugo's words for the ladies. They too applauded, but without noticeable enthusiasm; now it was their restrained patriotism that displeased Najdan. Fortunately the spirits of the company had suddenly lifted, and he felt that the mood was as spontaneous as if Aunt Selena had not behaved outrageously. How could he forget her voice, hoarse with emotion, uttering the words, "Gentlemen, there's a great epidemic coming!" But now he must control the mood at the dinner table, stimulate it continually with drink and witty conversation, ply his guests with food, maintain the tempo. He was making an effort to remember something from Victor Hugo, of whose works he had not read much, when he was struck by a sudden silence: all the guests were staring at the open door, speechless with astonishment. There stood Ruža, the "lieutenant's widow," wearing red Turkish trousers, holding a tambourine above her head. He was stunned. He met her threatening eyes between the candlesticks and had no idea what to do. Was he seeing a vision? Perhaps he himself was ill. Or was this prostitute having her revenge on him as she banged the tambourine above her head, then twisted and swayed her hips in time with the tambourine, and performed a belly dance. The silence was even more intense than when Aunt Selena had spoken her menacing words. Najdan could restrain himself no longer; quickly he rose from his seat and blew out the candles.

If I knew a trade, I would now summon all my strength to make something: a chair, a shoe, a flute, a toy—anything. But I can't even sew on a button. My skills include the ability to read very fast and write legibly, and I have also learned how to aim a gun accurately. My knowledge of History is not needed by the Sick and Wounded. In any case, I'm not sure what I think about the teacher's job, notwithstanding the glory heaped upon it by those wily Greeks.

As I said, I feel an irresistible desire that something of mine should live on after me, that I should leave some sign or trace of myself behind me. In this century, the beginning of which saw some wonderful and some monstrous things, I want one tiny moment to be mine, I want the whisper of some word of mine to be heard in the distant thunder; I want to leave some trace of my existence, apart from the school records and my signature on the pupils' certificates, and I don't want to say anything about myself when I was healthy, except what has significance for Sickness.

Before the war I was a History teacher and disseminated knowledge about the past; but I never told my pupils that History could teach us about life, for I myself had no such faith. Still, with what knowledge I had I did plant some seeds of error. I taught the young to use their memories and to ask questions, although I knew from experience that people find it difficult to remember. And in any case they find it easiest to remember lies and evil deeds. Nevertheless, at that stage of my life I had no alternative but to strive to do something which was in the last resort pointless.

Now I am Wounded. Sick, too. Sickness has for the time being postponed my participation in war, and probably put an end to it, and has taken the place of Death. I will find out about Death, but not now. Still I am dedicating myself to Death, because my Sickness is tormenting me, killing me by inches. So I have time to reflect on Death, to take from her something of the future, which belongs to her, and to give to her something of the present, the only time I have. If in my present state I am incapable of performing the bold deeds which bring recognition and glory, which set one man apart, perhaps I will be allowed to see some particular error, without any consequences. The healthy will not derive any benefit from this, or even hear what I have to say. The truths which I discover will only serve to enhance my own dignity in the face of Death, who, I now believe, is not indifferent to everything human.

Everything in this world, everything inside a man, is a concentrated whirl around Pain—for Pain and against Pain. To alleviate Pain, or to cheat it, is an aim which only the Sick can understand. That aim may be worth the torment and the risk of words. For those words are subject to no punishment, nor do they merit any praise and glory. They suffer the fate of Pain; when it is finished they too wither away. Indeed how could they survive? Are there any words inside me which could outlive Pain?

Ever since I was brought from the front to the Valjevo hospital, whenever my temperature falls and I can reflect on life, I begin to see that something outside us and above us, something invisible to us, must be concealed in the cause and purpose of this war, of so much Sickness, of such great suffering, and of so many deaths. It bothers me—this thing which is above and beyond visible and known facts—and I believe in that which is unknown to us.

So my short and barren report from the Serbian Epidemic of the winter of 1914–15 must from the start be disappointing to some earnest seekers after truth: I shall make no effort to convince those who are well—the more so in that many truths, many facts which are of the highest significance for the healthy, are rooted in vanity and have as their aim the pursuit of personal advantage. I lack hope to make the effort to discover these truths.

Those who are well have invented the lie that great suffering gives birth to great hope. I now think that we can talk about great suffering only when it is total, when nothing else exists, when it contains no trace of hope, when even its very extremities show no glow of faith; yet even when nothing exists but Pain—torment and filth, freezing cold and drenching rain, and stench and alienation and darkness such as I now experience in this hospital in Valjevo—I want to go on living.

Yes, in this state, in such a world, I want to go on living. No need to confess what I'm prepared for, only that I might exist.

Maybe a man exists as long as he exists in the minds of others. The people around me do not groan simply because they can't help it, but because they want others to hear them. The cripples and the dying, those rotting away with gangrene or raving from the fever of typhus—they all want to exist in the minds of others—through their groans or their silence, their kindness or cruelty toward the orderlies, through their jokes, songs, or curses. Everybody has some means of existing for others. Those who cannot or do not want to comfort others or offer them something, or even just change their position, can scratch themselves, offend those around them, and stink. People do both good and evil because they believe that in this way they can best prolong their existence. The Sick, however much they may suffer from their Sickness, suffer even more from the indifference of the healthy, for their injustice in failing to remember and acknowledge the part the Sick have to play in human life and History.

For Sickness is the very basis of human existence. I suppose the Paradise from which we were expelled was a state of health and an absence of pain. Eve plucked the apple from the tree of Sickness, and its fruits were knowledge and freedom. If we do not acknowledge that they have their origin in Sickness, we can easily see that they find many outlets in it. The history of the world is nothing but the untold history of Sickness. The past of mankind has seen many more plagues than wars, and more people sick than healthy. Sickness is the creative force in History: History is fear of Sickness, knowledge of Sickness, the consequences of Sickness. Man first began to construct buildings in order to protect his body from Pain, lessen the torment of fear, and defend himself from danger. Soothsayers, diviners, and medicine men—these were the first crafts practiced by man, and they began because of Sickness. The Sick have created nearly all the great wonders of the world. It was they who in their Pain and sleeplessness invented God. They also, because of the sickness inside their heads, set in motion all the greatest wars and military campaigns. Their manic fear has built up and then destroyed cities, magnificent temples, pyramids, monuments—all great works of architecture that can never be repeated. And the Sick have saved themselves by creating works of art; this is the fact about them which people most easily recognize. In their moments of despair they have thought up ideas which have tormented mankind for centuries; and in their hatred of the healthy they have inspired those evil deeds which rational people cannot explain.

However, the Sick have also been the creators and instigators of nearly all rare and noble virtues. A world without Sickness would be the most stupid and brutish place imaginable: a world without the pain, helplessness, and fear which most effectively restrain human savagery, temper the innate stupidity of every man with caution, give courage a more rational purpose, and sound the warning note of anxiety necessary to our arrogance. Sickness gives birth to that life-saving fear which keeps the world in a state of equilibrium between joy and sorrow, giving meaning to joy and alleviating both. I am now convinced that a world without Sickness and Sick people would be a world without real and effective consciousness of Death, which is what has removed us farthest from animals.

As we have long known, man's knowledge of himself is for the most part knowledge of the world around us; but it is Sickness which compels us to know ourselves. Perhaps the worst thing about the coming Epidemic is not that we shall suffer and die, but that we are doing nothing to get to know ourselves, nothing to make ourselves wise. Getting well is neither the most difficult nor the most important thing for the future. We must learn to know ourselves. Yes, we shall die, but therein lies our real opportunity.

In the late morning when my mind is clearest a great fear springs up inside me, the fear that this present war, like all previous wars, will poison the peace with all the old stupidities and follies, the same prejudices about victory and defeat. Once more the survivors will lose the peace; if they listen to those who are healthy and those who have recovered, and read newspaper accounts of our Serbian victory on Suvobor and Rudnik and on the Kolubara, the victors will enter the peace with delusions of more lasting significance than that of their wartime victories. But a mistaken notion prevails about great delusions, as about great misfortunes.

Even as I say this I regret my self-confidence. For surely the very words I say will only nourish yet unborn prejudices.

It seems that our human soul is a breath of some other being, some inhalation which we breathed in and choked on the very moment our umbilical cord was severed, taking away our Mother and giving us this world—a breath from some other being which we breathe in to nourish us for our existence in this world, and breathe out when our heart stops beating; then our breath is spread out through the air, to be breathed in once again by those whose umbilical cord is severed, who do not know how immensely dependent they are on all who have existed before them, and those who will exist after them.

I understand other things as well whenever Sickness allows me to think in words, and the lice become sated and drowsy. But they have come right at me, covering my body and sucking my blood, ceaselessly crawling over me. I can't sleep because of their scratchy feet walking over my skin. I loathe the idea of killing them and dirtying my fingers. Anyway, is there anything more senseless than struggling against lice? You can fight against emperors, tyrants, and popes, against lions and bears, pythons and crocodiles, but not against the sucking louse and the eggs it leaves behind. It's no use killing them; anyway, it's ridiculous and pointless, because they must endure until death, ours or theirs. They must endure stench and Pain too, all the more so as Pain is the most reliable measure of truth; for although small, short-lived pains easily grasp at lies, a lie can find no resting place in real Pain.

FROM THE *Pall Mall Gazette:*

ALL ARMIES SHOULD RISE TO THEIR FEET AND SHOUT: LONG LIVE THE SERBIAN ARMY!

FROM *The Observer:*

THERE HAS BEEN NOTHING MORE MOVING IN THIS EUROPEAN WAR THAN THE EXCEPTIONAL VICTORY WON BY SERBIA JUST WHEN SHE SEEMED EXHAUSTED AND DONE FOR. ALL FRIENDS OF FREEDOM NOW HOPE FOR THE TRIUMPH WHICH WILL ENABLE SERBIA TO COMPLETE THE UNIFICATION OF HER PEOPLE. THE SERBS HAVE SHOWN CLEARLY THAT THEY ARE WORTHY OF A GREATER FUTURE, WHICH NOW SEEMS TO BE ASSURED BEYOND DOUBT.

BUCHAREST

FROM *Indépendence Roumaine:*

AT FIRST ONE IS TEMPTED TO REGARD THE BRILLIANT SUCCESS OF THE SERBIAN ARMY AS QUITE INCREDIBLE. SUCH NEWS CAN HARDLY BE GRASPED. BUT, JUDGING BY THE EMBARRASSED TONE OF THE AUSTRO-HUNGARIAN PRESS, BY THEIR SIGNIFICANT ADMISSIONS AND THE OMISSIONS IN THE LAST BULLETIN FROM VIENNA, ONE IS FORCED TO BELIEVE THAT THIS MIRACLE HAS INDEED OCCURRED.

FROM *Word:*

ONE HUNDRED AND SEVENTEEN YEARS AGO THE AUSTRIAN GENERAL AL-VICHI, HAVING PUSHED BACK THE FRENCH, IMMEDIATELY INFORMED VIENNA OF HIS BRILLIANT SUCCESS. MEANWHILE NAPOLEON LAUNCHED A LIGHTNING COUNTERATTACK, AND FIRST SMASHED THE AUSTRIAN CENTER AND THEN THE COLUMNS ON THE WINGS. THE SERBS HAVE DONE THE SAME THING WITH POTIOREK, WHO, RELYING NOT ON HIS KNOWLEDGE BUT ON HIS GREAT NUMERICAL SUPERIORITY, AFTER HIS FIRST SUCCESSES SENT A TELEGRAM TO KAISER WILHELM ANNOUNCING THE CAPTURE OF BELGRADE. LIKE NAPOLEON AT RIVOLI, THE SERBS FIRST SMASHED THE AUSTRIAN CENTER AND THEN PROCEEDED TO SMASH FIRST THE LEFT WING AND THEN THE RIGHT.

THE SERBIAN ARMY HAS COVERED ITSELF WITH UNPRECEDENTED GLORY. EVEN THE MOST BRILLIANT VICTORIES ON THE EASTERN AND WESTERN FRONTS GROW PALE IN THE FACE OF ITS HEROISM.

GENERAL SHERFIZ, WRITING IN *Echo de Paris:*

THE SERBIAN OFFENSIVE HAS LED OUR ALLIES TO VICTORY EVEN MORE DECISIVE THAN OURS ON THE MARNE. IT WAS A MAGNIFICENT BATTLE OF MOVEMENT, MANEUVERING, AND ATTACK, A BATTLE IN THE REAL SENSE OF THE WORD, NOT THE TRENCH WARFARE THAT WE ARE ENGAGED IN WITH GERMANY.

FROM *Figaro:*

THE SERBS HAVE A GOOD REASON TO BE PROUD; BY THEIR OWN UNAIDED EFFORTS THEY HAVE MADE A DECISIVE CONTRIBUTION TO THE FUTURE DIRECTION OF EUROPEAN AFFAIRS. FROM THE MILITARY POINT OF VIEW, THEIR SUPERIORITY OVER THE AUSTRIAN ARMY WILL HAVE INCALCULABLE CONSEQUENCES. ONCE AGAIN SERBIA HAS SHOWN HERSELF WORTHY OF THE GREAT ROLE THAT FATE HAS ASSIGNED TO HER.

FROM *The New York Times:*

SERBIA'S OBITUARY HAD ALREADY BEEN WRITTEN. EVERYTHING WAS FINISHED. THE SMALL SERBIAN NATION INDEED DESERVES OUR WONDER AND ADMIRATION, FOR IT HAS NOT ONLY REPULSED BUT REDUCED TO DUST AND

ASHES THE ARMY OF A MIGHTY EMPIRE, AND THIS AT A TIME WHEN THE SERBIAN PEOPLE HAVE NOT FULLY RECOVERED FROM TWO WARS FOUGHT LAST YEAR.

VIENNA

ALL NEWSPAPERS WRITE AS FOLLOWS:

IN RESPONSE TO A REQUEST SUBMITTED ON HEALTH GROUNDS, GENERAL POTIOREK HAS BEEN PLACED ON THE RETIRED LIST. LIEUTENANT GENERAL ŠARKOTIĆ HAS BEEN APPOINTED SUPREME COMMANDER AND HEAD OF THE REGIONAL GOVERNMENT OF BOSNIA AND HERCEGOVINA.

KRAGUJEVAC

FROM *Wartime Diary:*

HIS HIGHNESS PRINCE ALEXANDER, HEIR TO THE THRONE AND COMMANDER IN CHIEF OF THE ARMED FORCES, HAS SENT A TELEGRAM TO GENERAL ŽIVOJIN MIŠIĆ, INFORMING HIM THAT HE HAS BEEN PROMOTED TO THE RANK OF VOJVODA.

"Here's Valjevo at last—and the hospital!" the drivers shouted in the darkness. They hoped that after several days of exhausting effort along a road choked with abandoned enemy supply trains, they were now at the end of their ordeal with their wet, silent burden of men with festering wounds and burning fever.

Major Gavrilo Stanković removed a wet tent flap from his face. "This is your birthplace, isn't it, Dragović? Well, we'll be all right now. We'll sleep in a bed, have something hot to drink, then supper," he said joyfully as he lay in the cart beside Bogdan Dragović. Bogdan was suffering so much from the dull pains in his chest that it didn't matter where he was. A little later he cautiously removed the tent flap from his head: in the dim light cast by two small lamps he caught sight of the artillery barracks, which he had always hated. It was a long, long time—decades ago—when he had set off for this barracks during mobilization.

Just before they parted his mother had pushed a candle into his knapsack. Does she want me to have my father's candle with me when I die? he thought. He had looked straight into her eyes: yes, she was thinking death. From her eyes the fear of his own death spread through him for the first time in his life. Until that August dawn he had never thought that he could die; but that candle and the expression in his mother's eyes suddenly made death appear to him as it really was: the end of everything, nothingness. I'll be killed, he had said to himself, and looked at the ground. In front of him something had dropped with a dull thud. He had shivered, then felt embarrassed. "It's a ripe pear," said his mother, Petrana, and bent down to pick it up. Suddenly he had walked on ahead—to avoid seeing her again, to avoid taking that pear.

"What did your father do, Bogdan?"

"He was a candle maker. His name was Vasa," muttered Bogdan. The candle he had brought with him to the war was one of the few left that had been made by his father.

"An old, clean craft. A fragrant craft. I like the smell of wax, Bogdan. My father was a priest and his hands used to smell of wax when he came home after the church services."

From the darkness and the snow Bogdan breathed the scent of wax, a scent he could never forget, the scent that had been absorbed into his very pores, and which even after several years had not disappeared from his father's workshop, now Bogdan's room. Pierced by bullets and inflamed by pneumonia, his lungs would now be healed by the old fragrance of his father's wax.

He was not listening to the major's angry reproaches against the doctors and the orderlies for not carrying them out of the cart. He didn't care when they took him out that night. He was in Valjevo. And tomorrow his mother and sister would take him home. There, in his own room, he would again see the deer preserve full of flowering lime trees bathed in sunlight, and hear the drowsy, drawn-out hum of the bees, and Natalia, as on those summer nights. No, that could never be. It was all over between him and Natalia. Still, with the scent of his father's wax, he would be well again within a week. The sound of dogs barking echoed through the darkness: the loud, mournful fear that filled the nights of Valjevo, and the streets near the Kolubara and Gradac, bringing back the weariness of those erotic yearnings he had felt as a schoolboy; the sleepless nights before he went away to Belgrade to study, the conflict between his ambition and his pity for his mother, who with his sister toiled day and night to pay for his education. Eagerly he listened to the dogs: perhaps they were from his own street, his own neighborhood. He knew their eyes and nostrils, and the way each one wagged its tail. He thought about their masters: some away fighting, some shirkers, some already dead.

What about the women and girls? The war would be a test of their faithfulness. He wouldn't love anybody until the war was over; he was quite sure about that—nothing would make him change his mind. Was his mother asleep now? He had never actually seen her sleeping. All night long she would be sitting at her loom, her eyes following the dark brown and black threads of the wool of an unfinished kilim for one of the ladies of Valjevo. His mother at her loom, the scent of his father's wax, these dogs—that was home to him. Victory and freedom. This barracks, too, now a hospital, which he used to skip past as a schoolboy with a book under his arm, going barefoot through the summer holidays, and feeling sorry for the village boys drilled by sergeants from morning till night.

"How do you feel, Bogdan?"

"Sad, sir," he replied, and immediately regretted his outburst, the first since the major had slapped Radojko's face for having lost the wrestling match with the Austrian. Since that incident, the image of Major Stanković had somehow become tarnished in his soul: he was no longer that exceptional major with his black beard, his wonderful pipe, his gentle, tired schoolmaster's voice; no longer the good, kindly, fearless commanding officer who loved the students like his own sons or younger brothers; an officer who identified his country with justice, and both with freedom. He no longer felt the same intimate affection for him; or did it just seem so now because his head was full of burning darkness?

"If only I could see my mother tomorrow," said Major Stanković, speaking loudly as he tried to move his wounded leg, that poor rotting limb with its dull throbbings, now so swollen that it felt as if it could fill the whole cart.

His orderly, Radojko, was hovering over him. "What can I do for you now, sir?"

"Ask the doctor on duty why we aren't being carried into the hospital. Wait, Radojko! Move my leg a bit to the left." Radojko moved his leg with utmost gentleness, then saluted and disappeared into the darkness.

How could he have Radojko with him in the hospital? Radojko's wound had healed; he would have to return to the ranks. How could he repay his devotion? Never in his life had he been indebted to anybody—except, of course, to his mother, now paralyzed, unable to leave her house near the cathedral in Belgrade, waiting for death from a shell. The pain in his leg increased, and the leg seemed to be growing. Taking it in both hands, he tried to put it back in its former position.

"Sir, the doctor on duty says that the hospital is full to overflowing. There's no room for us anywhere till morning."

"What do you mean, there's no room?"

Bogdan raised himself up on his elbow; the sound of a guitar came from a house next to the hospital, like the sound he used to hear when he went on school picnics by the Kolubara.

"I couldn't see his rank because of his white coat, sir, but I said to him, 'How would you like it, Doctor, if you were badly wounded, and you'd spent three days in an oxcart with nothing to eat but a few dried prunes?' He just said, 'That's not my fault.' "

"Bring that doctor to me, Radojko. Tell him Major Stanković wants to speak to him."

The wounded were shouting and cursing.

"Can you hear the guitar, sir?" asked Bogdan.

"I can hear dogs barking and men swearing."

"No, it's someone playing a guitar, and singing. A party. They must be celebrating something."

"Lie down, my boy," said the major, feeling Bogdan's forehead. It was burning; he was delirious again.

"The doctor won't come, sir. He says he's not under your authority. He says we'll be put up somewhere in the morning."

"Get up, Milena. You must get up!"

"I just fell asleep!"

"Vida got sick last night. In Wards Seven and Eight there's no one on duty except Mane."

"Let me sleep while you undress."

"I *am* undressed. My God, they've brought in hundreds of wounded. We can't possibly cope. They must have brought in at least fifty cartloads last night. We'll all die."

"We'll see. Get into bed and I'll warm you."

Half undressed, Dušanka crept under the blanket and pressed against Milena's warm body. She whispered into her ear: "I saw Kaća slipping into the director's office. She'd left her post, the bitch. Men are pigs, Milena! Last night he had Ruška there, and that French girl the night before. Four different girls in five days, and him a married man! We idiots work ourselves to death looking after these faithless rats! You're nice and warm, Milena. My feet are like ice. I didn't sit down all night."

"Is it snowing? Don't talk so much."

"A bit of snow, just a thin cover. That blond corporal, the one who looked so sad, died about midnight. He never complained, never groaned. He was the most romantic patient in Ward Six. All the handsome young men are dying. What on earth will it be like after the war?"

"Do be quiet for just one more minute!"

"But I haven't told you—last night just before midnight they brought in such a handsome man, a dream! He was wounded in the stomach; they put him in Ward Three. I was so disappointed; but I'll fill in for Kaća when she's looking after the director. You must help me answer those last three letters. I haven't written to anyone for a whole week."

"Yes, I will. Now be quiet. When this damned war is over I'm just going to sleep and sleep."

"Me, too. I didn't dare stand still last night, or I'd have collapsed. Just before daybreak I felt like killing myself, honestly I did. If it wasn't for those handsome young men, so romantic . . ."

"How can you notice them in this hell?"

"No problem!"

"*Please* be quiet!"

"I was just thinking last night: there's no one to compare with Vojin. He's more romantic than Saša. Nobody has eyes like his— nobody. Why are you so cross? Well, when *are* we going to talk if not now? Ugh, even my heart is cold! Come on, Milena, get up. Sergeev has been waiting for you in the operating room for ages."

"Just a few more minutes. Count to fifty," Milena whispered. She's lucky, Milena thought, the way she can fall in love so easily. Why aren't I like that?

"Vladimir is a selfish, hateful man—a swine! You can take that from me!"

Milena jumped up. "How can you say such a thing?"

"Sorry, Milena, but there was no other way to wake you up. Don't be angry!"

Milena could hardly keep back her tears. She was overcome by nausea. The chill air was steeped in the smell of naphthalene and gas. She got out of bed and began to dress, but her hands would not obey her. If only one could have some peace and quiet in the morning! In the other three beds they were changing over from the day shift to the night shift; the gray light of the room was full of soft, twisting movements, the rustle of underskirts, the placing of hairpins, and talk.

Milena left the room. Outside it was snowing, the first time it had snowed since Vladimir's flight and death. Yes, the first snow since the night when she had walked back and forth in front of the hospital, remembering their walk in a Belgrade park last winter. She could hear their rhythmic footsteps over the thin cover of soft snow, and his description of the snowdrifts on Kozjak when he was campaigning in Macedonia. She could see them both pressed against a lime tree with their fingers intertwined. Then she had decided to go see Vladimir again and tell him that he was not dead for her, as he had written on the envelope of her letter immediately after his arrival in the hospital; she would tell him that she would go on loving him no matter what. Yet she had felt hurt to the point of despair: how could he think that she might not love him just because a piece of Austrian shrapnel had torn open and disfigured his face? Even before she reached his bed, Vladimir had sensed her presence. He heard her footsteps and her heartbeat and began shaking his fists wildly. "It's snowing, Vladimir!" she had said to him. The white mass of bandages that was his head darkened as the blood oozed through; she moved away and stumbled. Doctor Sergeev took her by the arm and led her out of the corridor into the snow outside. "Just keep walking, Milena. People are their own worst enemies. You've got to remember that." She pressed herself against him, her one source of protection in enemy-occupied Valjevo. But it seemed to her that the dark stain on Vladimir's bandages was spreading over the snow under the lamp at the entrance to the hospital and gradually merging with the darkness filled with gunfire.

Later, in Sergeev's room, she began to speak: "Why do people act against themselves?"

"My dear, only a fool would try to answer that question! God Himself steadfastly refuses to say anything."

"Do you think I must try to understand all that's happening now?"

"If I were you, I would make no effort to understand anything in this life; it's something bleeding and rotten, the sepsis of our planet."

Suddenly two powerful explosions shook Valjevo. Sergeev put the light out, pushed the bed against the door, put her on it, and covered her with a blanket. In the morning he woke her up and told her that Vladimir had fled the hospital. She went out and stood on the steps, afraid to set foot in the snow.

By now the pale light of dawn was rising above the dark hospital building. The yard was crammed with oxcarts, among which a few fires were burning. From the carts came the sound of typhus patients who in their delirium were coaxing cattle, charging against the Austrians, cursing, and singing.

Perhaps there was someone among them from Ivan's regiment, she thought. "Is there anyone here from the First Battalion of the Eighth Regiment?" she asked as she went from cart to cart, but she met only silence or the ravings of delirium. Then she went from one fire to another, where the orderlies were warming themselves. "Do any of you know a cadet corporal by the name of Ivan Katić?"

"Why don't you ask about somebody in the ranks, lady? For two freezing days and nights we've been dragging them along, while you nurses and doctors keep warm and snug. When are you going to take these poor bastards away? You're all dolled up in a white cap, you've got nice shoes, you're warm and dry, so all you need now is your sweetheart, right?"

Milena hurried into the hospital. Why did those people insult her so—people for whom she was doing so much, working to the point of exhaustion: people who might well give her typhus. It was because of them that she had not gone home with her father, home to her mother. Why did they get angry and curse as soon as they saw something white and clean, as soon as they set eyes on a woman? She paused on the steps. I'll run away, she thought, I'll leave by the next train. Never mind if she was a coward, a spoiled child; her friends could think what they liked. Behind her she heard the short, quick steps of one of the nurses; as she entered the corridor she was stopped in her tracks by a warm stench that almost made her faint. If she put her nurse's veil over her lips, she would again offend these men lying in the corridors or sitting against the wall, groaning and moaning under the pale light of an electric bulb at daybreak.

"Good morning, Miss Katić! Why are you so downhearted so early in the morning?" said Mane the orderly. Mane was a Serb from Lika who had worked in a circus in Vienna as a clown and surrendered to the Serbian army at Mačva; after that he had been slightly wounded and had become a hospital orderly. She didn't like the circus tricks he performed for the wounded, or his clown's nose, or what he said. She frowned, not knowing how to respond.

"If we don't laugh, dear lady, we'll all get ill. We'll die if we don't laugh, believe you me! After lunch I'll do some of my numbers in Wards Four and Five. I've never been seen before in the Balkans. Come and see them; they'll make you laugh."

"Thanks, I'd love to," she said, to get away from him. Then she pressed forward through the stench, past the raving typhus victims, taking care not to step on them.

"Milena, you look as if you've had another sleepless night," said Doctor Sergeev hoarsely in Russian, as she entered the operating room; he was leaning against the operating table, cracking his knuckles.

His concern and kindness during the past few days had again made her feel afraid. For a long time she had sensed that his feelings were more than brotherly. She could not forget that night, just before the liberation of Valjevo, when he had been drunk and talked quite wildly: "Love is the most sacred thing in this world, but rare, like genius. It is an offense against God to despise the love of another person—an offense which will not be forgiven. Remember that, Milena," he had whispered, snapping his fingers. She had felt frightened and left the room. At daybreak, Doctor Sergeev had found her leaning against an acacia tree.

"Please forgive me, Milena. I'll never talk to you again as I did last night. You needn't be afraid of me."

"I'm not afraid of you, Doctor. You're like a father to me." She had taken his hand and felt like kissing it.

His beard quivered as he said in Russian: "Thank you. Thank you very much."

Since then she had again gone to see him in his room, and listened while he talked about the steppes around Kuban, and about the dead who would one day rise and call the living to account for failing to remember them.

Since yesterday, however, she had again been afraid that he might say or do something that would make him feel ashamed in her presence, that would make her feel ashamed to look at him and work with him and receive kindness from him. More than anyone else here, he would be disappointed in her if she left the hospital. She simply couldn't go away without his approval. How could she say to him, I can't stand it any more!

"Are you tired, Milena?"

"No, Doctor. I slept well. Shall we do the dressings in the wards first?"

"We'll have to amputate a gangrenous leg and arm right away. Of all amputations, I find an arm the most painful. An arm working against an arm—horrendous. All the things it could do—that poor, wretched arm! Milena, can you remember the first time you ever felt anxious?"

She gave a start and looked at him in embarrassment. "I can't remember exactly. Perhaps it was when the sun began to melt the snowman that my father made for my brother and me. It was a big one, a beauty! First of all the sun bit off its arms . . ."

"Wonderful! That's really marvelous! Not just a matter of chance, either!" Sergeev clapped his hands.

The orderlies brought in a wounded man on a stretcher; behind them, walking uncertainly, came a middle-aged peasant with some colored bags over his shoulders, and two peasant women, one of them young.

"What relation are you to him?" Sergeev asked them in Serbian.

"His parents; and this is his wife," replied the father despondently.

"Milena, please translate every word I say for them. Your son's life is in danger. We can save him only if we amputate his leg immediately, but we must have his consent."

Milena began to translate into Serbian, but when she got to "amputate his leg," she paused.

"Tell them we must amputate his leg. Tell them!"

"Doctor Sergeev says that his leg must be removed to save his life," muttered Milena, staring at the wounded man's deathly pale face.

The man looked at his father.

"I won't let you cut off his leg," said the father firmly.

"I won't either," said his wife.

The soldier looked at his mother.

"What do *you* say?" asked Milena. She walked up to the old woman, who was looking silently and intently at her son.

"Cut it off. He's good enough for me even without his leg," she said loudly, never taking her eyes off her son.

"Then cut it off, Doctor," said the son, shutting his eyes.

Silence filled the operating theater. I'll run away from the hospital, Milena thought, so that I don't have to watch Sergeev cutting off arms and legs any more, so that I don't have to help him . . .

Her father had once talked to her about duty, taking pleasure in his words, as if he were bringing her some happy news: she had been sitting on his lap, resting her head against his chest, listening to his words booming away, enjoying them without bothering to understand what they meant; it was only after her arrival in the hospital at Valjevo that she had fully grasped their meaning. Her father himself had had no idea of the weight and value of his own words—not until she had refused to let him take her home last Sunday. Her father had done *his* duty by instructing them in the virtues. Was this intended to help her and Ivan find happiness? He had believed so at the time. After Vladimir's death and her experience in the hospital under Austrian occupation, however, she no longer regarded her duty as a heroic deed performed for her country, nor did she consider it an act of mercy or something noble, as she had been taught at home and in school. Everything she did in the hospital had become for her a higher imperative, increasingly difficult to fulfill, and outside the virtues which adorned one's character. Something that brought with it bitter suffering, and for which any recognition and reward were at once too little and too much. Something from which it was increasingly hard to escape. Something from which even her father could not save her, so that he had been forced to say, "You must go, my dear."

Just now she wanted to press her forehead against the wall, against a block of ice, to stop the burning sensation in her head; but even this was impossible. No, I can't do even that, she said to herself as she moved to the operating table with the surgical instruments, the syringe, and the gas.

What am I without my right arm? What will I be to the folks in Prerovo, that greedy, ill-tempered bunch? Such were the questions that Miloje Dačić, son of Tola, asked himself all night long, and even more insistently as dawn approached, as he lay against the wall on a thick layer of straw which he had stolen the night before last from underneath two moaning comrades. It was the first time in his life that he had stolen anything for himself, not counting a few walnuts or cherries, and occasionally a particularly fine button in a game of tiddlywinks.

All night long he stared at the window, waiting for the first murky light to appear, pondering what the doctor had said to him the evening before when he finally condescended to look at his wounded arm, which was only after Miloje had promised a whole dinar to Paja, the orderly, the biggest ass on two legs (or four, come to think of it), to get the doctor to come at all. The doctor came along with his legs wrapped in rubberized cotton, to keep the lice out of his pants, and stood over Miloje as over a heap of dirt, pushing away Sibin, his neighbor on the right, and kicking the straw as far as he could from his boots. Then he asked Miloje, as if from the ceiling: "What's the problem, soldier?"

"Doctor, my arm hurts so much that I feel like biting it off."

"Undo the bandage and let me have a look."

With some difficulty he began to unwind the bandage from his right arm. Paja, the orderly, bent down to help, but Miloje just nodded, thinking, When the war's over, all you'll get from me is a flea in your ear and not a dinar. The sight of his own arm terrified him and he couldn't bear to look at it, so he shut his eyes tight.

"Soldier, it's your arm or your life. You've got until tomorrow morning to choose."

"What choice do I have, Doctor?" he asked, closing his eyes again so that this villain couldn't read his thoughts.

"That's your business."

Then Miloje opened his eyes to look at the doctor and explain everything point by point, but the doctor was already hurrying out of the room on tiptoe, jumping over the sick and wounded.

"Look here, Paja, why didn't that damned doctor give me something to ease the pain? Something to make it easier for me to choose between my arm and my life."

"There's no medicine left, Miloje. If it's got to come off, what's the point of giving you an injection? Just stick it out for one more night," said Paja, rewinding the bandage around his arm.

"Well, Paja, you're not going to get a cent from me, not even if they cut my head off," he said. He had no further need to curry favor with Paja.

"That's your business, Miloje; but it's my duty to help you if I can.

When you begin to feel sparks flying out of your eyes, call me and I'll bring you a powder," said Paja unctuously, his eyes darting about as he ran off to help friends in distress.

Miloje was staring at the darkening window, thinking about what the doctor meant by "That's your business." Well, his arm certainly was his business and what needn't be removed when his arm was cut off was his business, too—but not his life. Except that sometimes he would use it to think how he could deceive and evade those who did make the decisions about his life, and how to protect himself from thieves and gluttons. The decisions about his life were made by the State; he first realized this as a recruit in the barracks. In war it was always like that. That oath you took in front of the priest—having taken it, how would you ever dare run away from the Austrians? As for the State and the Fatherland, why all this business about taking an oath? The State—well, in Prerovo it meant the head man. In the marketplace it was the tax collector and the granary, which must never be empty. The Fatherland was first of all the corporal, then the platoon leader and the battalion commander, right up to the top man in the regiment, and that's where all the decisions concerning his life were made; that's where they decided whether his head would stay on his shoulders. As for his right arm, there was nothing for him to decide there either. Even the biggest fool in the world wouldn't hesitate between his arm and his life! If a real decision had been necessary—for example, his life or both arms, and both legs and his head, too—there still wasn't any choice to be made: he, Miloje T. Dačić, would choose to live. Yet what was the point of it? What was left for him—a servant, a hired man, a soldier in the ranks—when the doctors, hateful and heartless creatures, decided what to do about his arm and his life? Just because the State and the Fatherland decided about his life, now he had to submit to those bastards in white coats and stretch out his arms and legs for them to cut off like a reed or a piece of rotten wood.

First of all he was going to lose an arm—his right arm, too—and what could be worse? He wouldn't be able to mow or plow, to dig or gather the harvest—the jobs that provided him with food and clothing and made him mean something to other people. A man with one arm couldn't harness horses and oxen to a cart. A one-armed man had only one hand with which to stroke a woman, and it would have to be a quiet and kindly one—if there were any such in the Morava region

—because no woman likes to have only one leg and one breast stroked. A one-armed man couldn't dance the *kolo* with two or three girls. A rich man with only one arm could lead the dance, but a poor man would look like an ass. Yes, that's what he, Miloje, would now be forever! Children would call him "Uncle," women would smile at him in a patronizing way, and bullies would kick him when they felt like it. If he continued to think about it he might lose his head tonight.

Come on, Miloje, look at it another way! You'll be alive, and when you're alive you can scratch, bite, and spit at any bastard. You can have a sheepskin jacket with two sleeves; one may be blowing loose in the wind, but you can carry a knife in the other. You can practice using your left hand, and the strength from the right will flow into it; no one can hit as hard as a one-armed man with his left hand. Aćim Katić would have to arrange for him to be a field worker, or better still a constable taking news of danger or a summons around the village, in return for a glass of brandy and a bit more besides. Why, half the folks in Prerovo were afraid of the constable and on the lookout to do him some service! As for marriage, it was a big war, thank God, and the epidemic would carry off a lot of people, so there'd be plenty of widows. He'd find an old and ugly one, and they'd help each other out. A man didn't need much to keep in good health. He'd catch fish in the Morava, look after cattle, beget children—let them work for him. He'd be alive! He could whistle, earn a bit by singing a song now and then, swear at the dogs and the stars, even laugh at someone weaker and sillier than himself. He'd be able to fool those who were easily fooled and tell lies to blockheads—things Tola had taught him from his cradle, since he too had been raised on the bread of Prerovo and by the streams of the Morava. Now just get this into your stupid head: you'll be alive, and there's a lot of folks in the platoon and in Prerovo—neighbors and relatives of yours, and more than you can count—who'd be happy to see you dead! So you've got to live to spite other people and be a nuisance to them—that's the best sort of life, the very best! First because of the doctors, these hateful bastards in white coats who are scared to touch a sick man, as if he were a skunk, and who cover their mouths and noses with bandages so that they don't breathe the same air as those scoundrels who lie rotting and gasping on the bare floor with no straw under them, which even cattle have. One must go on living to spite the orderlies, too: he didn't care if a whole firebrand flew out of his eyes, let alone sparks; he wasn't going to ask Paja to bring him a powder to take the pain away. To hell with him! If it has to rot, let it rot right away. I want to live, he thought, like a frog, a dog, or a cat. I don't care if I'm a flea, as long as I'm alive!

His arm was hurting, burning; it felt as if it was being slashed with knives, hit with hammers.

As he listened to the roosters crowing and the dogs barking, it occurred to him that they sounded much the same in Prerovo. He preferred the Prerovo ones and felt pleasure as he remembered them, but those damned doctors who sawed off people's limbs! Still, his biggest worry was that knapsack he had taken from an Austrian. What would happen to it while he was in the operating room having his arm chopped off? Those greedy bastards next to him would steal his bag, grab his blanket, and take his straw. When he came back without his right arm, he'd have to lie on the bare bricks like a lizard.

The doctors were quite right to do their butchery, cut off arms and legs, because people are all rats and thieves. They're no different— worse, in fact—when wounded, maimed, and crippled. Everybody in this damp, icy room, whether groaning from wounds or gasping with typhus, would swipe all the blankets and tent flaps if they could, all the rags from the entire hospital, and shove them under their own behinds, and wouldn't give a fuck if others shivered all night long. During the past few nights, when he couldn't sleep because of his arm, he had seen those who could get about stealing straw from under the delirious patients, ransacking their bags, grabbing anything they could. Those greedy bastards would sit up as soon as it was day-break, pretending that lying on the brick floor gave them sores; there they were, sitting up, goddamn thieves that they were, ready to pounce like wild beasts and plunder anybody who had croaked in the night, before the orderlies came to do the same themselves, then carry the poor bastard off to his hole in the ground. When they had scooped up everything the dead man had left—everything he'd managed to get hold of or steal—they lit a candle in the place where he'd been lying and told lies about his heroism, and what a buddy he was. As for that thief Tisa, who could read and write—the one who wrote letters for the poor fools who couldn't, in return for tobacco or money—he wasn't going to get anything out of Miloje Dačić, not if they cut off both his arms! He wouldn't give him as much as a cigarette; he didn't care whether his parents, Tola and Andja, knew when his arm was cut off, or when the orderlies threw what was left of Miloje into some hole. Why should Prerovo know about Tola's son Miloje, the servant and hired man of George Katić, the greediest pig in the district? His parents could take it the same way all those folks did who made sons just for the war or an epidemic to carry off. He'd been a fool to send that letter telling them he was wounded. Let the folks at home, the neighbors, and the whole village think he was alive and well! Let them hope he'd come on leave—and to hell with that other business! There'd be a report from headquarters: Miloje T. Dačić died of wounds in the hospital at Valjevo on such and such a date. No, those politicians, the bastards, would add a lot of crap about the Fatherland. He'd been an idiot to tell Tola and Andja that he had gotten wounded because he was watching fish jumping in the Drina. He should have said he was wounded during the liberation of Šabac. He should have his head examined!

The dim morning light appeared in the window; he could just barely open his eyes. Paja, the orderly, was about to appear, to take him to that place where he had no choice between his arm and his life. But his arm had calmed down; it didn't hurt any more—he couldn't feel it at all! It had grown numb with fear, knowing what was in store for it. Too late. You've got to stick it out. Why didn't you play this trick yesterday, instead of all but wrenching my shoulder off and making me promise Paja a whole dinar? You don't even want to move a finger. Too late. Your fate's sealed.

He didn't want to listen to any of the mutterings and whisperings in the room, to the groaning and moaning, the raving and gasping, but he couldn't help overhearing that good-for-nothing Stanoje and that liar Perica quarreling over the knapsack and blanket of Corporal Žika, who the previous night had said, "Listen, friends, I leave all my things to the pal who'll light a candle for me."

That was why Miloje didn't trust anyone, and least of all his neighbors and relatives, and all who said they were his friends. That was why he had retreated into a damp, icy corner where at least he had no one beside him on his left, even if there was someone pressing against him on his right, and his feet were cramped. The minute the man lying next to the wall died, he had rushed to grab his place, then took out his knife (nobody in the whole division had a better one) and said slowly and quietly, so as to make it clear that he wasn't making empty threats: "This corner belongs to me. If anyone tries to take it from me, I'll split his gut wide open, even if I do have to do it with my left hand." Now again, however, he had a neighbor on his right, Sibin, actually, a liar and a cheat who offered everybody all he had; the old fox had never cursed or used bad language ever since they had brought him in with a shrapnel wound in his back, so that he had to lie on his stomach. He must keep his solemn word to Sibin to leave him his blanket and the knapsack he had swiped from the enemy with some nice things in it, including coffee and some pictures of Vienna. The bag of buttons he'd collected as the most skillful player at tiddlywinks in Prerovo and around the watermill—a bag full of all sorts of buttons—that he'd take with him, and also his knife.

Why isn't my arm hurting now, damn it? Why did it shut up at last?

What if the orderlies swiped his bag of buttons and his knife while the doctor was cutting off his arm? That's right, while he was knocked out they'd steal from him. Should he leave his belongings with Sibin, on condition of a solemn promise and oath? What could a man swear by when he had no children? He turned his head: Sibin was lying on his stomach looking at Miloje. They smiled at each other.

"You're pleased those bastards are going to cut off my arm, aren't you?" he said at last.

"Why should I be pleased about that, Miloje? All night long I've listened to you moaning. I'm worried about you. What kind of life can a peasant have without his right arm?"

"I guess you'd rather I kicked the bucket; then you could spread yourself out and settle in my corner under my blanket."

"That's not the way a friend should talk," said Sibin, turning his head away.

They were the worst of the lot, Sibin and the likes of him, full of fine words. But what could he do? It was growing light, and any moment now Paja, the orderly, might call out, "Get up, Miloje!" What could he do with his knapsack? Nothing, except leave it with Sibin under a solemn promise.

"Listen, Sibin. Here we are, neighbors, the doctors are getting a noose ready for me and we don't know what we care for most in this country or in this world. Tell me, now, what would you give your life for?"

Sibin looked at Miloje dejectedly; he was thinking up some lie, the cunning old fox.

"Sibin, what would you die for, without blinking an eyelash?"

"Well, if I had to, I'd die for my mother. For a good friend, too."

"For your mother, or for a friend? I come from Prerovo, you know, and I don't know of any man from either side of the Morava—from all three rivers, for that matter—who'd give his life for his mother or a friend. You'll have to think of something better, Sibin; that idea's lousy, as far as I'm concerned."

Sibin frowned and again turned his head away. He knows, the old sinner, that I'm in real trouble. He won't get anything of mine, the bastard.

What happened to my arm? Why isn't it hurting, damn it?

"Miloje Dačić, to the operating room at once!" cried Paja from the corridor.

"Don't you bastards lay a finger on my things!" said Miloje, speaking loud enough for half the room to hear. Then he got up, took the knapsack in his left hand, and bent down. "You'll answer me with your life for this blanket, Sibin."

His arm began to hurt as if someone was hitting it with an ax; it knew what was in store for it! Then everything went black, and someone he didn't know led him away. There he saw that son of a bitch in the white coat with his little beard, hovering like a vampire.

"If we're to save your life, you'll have to lose your arm. Do you agree to this?"

"What if I don't?"

"Where do you come from?"

"From my mother's belly!"

"I'm asking you a serious question."

"Well, my arm grew in Prerovo, and the rest of me, too."

"You're from Prerovo?" cried Milena Katić. "My father comes from Prerovo; his name is Vukašin Katić. I have a grandfather and an uncle there, and a cousin at the front. What's your name?"

"I don't know that family."

"Don't be afraid, it won't hurt. As soon as you're well enough, we'll send you home. You're young, and you'll soon—"

"I know all too well what sort of a life I'll have there without my right arm. You might just as well stop cackling about that and cut my arm off, since that's what you've decided; but if you cut off the good one instead, I'll finish you off with my teeth!"

Milena stepped back.

"And don't let there be anything missing from my bag while I'm here!" added Miloje, looking with tearful eyes at Doctor Sergeev, who was walking toward him with his syringe.

Gavrilo Stanković was jolted hard in his stretcher by the orderlies, as they caught it in the doorframe of the operating room. He did not care where they were taking him, he felt so humiliated at having to lie outside all night in the oxcart in the slush, and then for another two hours squeezed on this same stretcher in the damp, foul-smelling hospital corridor in front of the operating room. He caught sight of the white coats and instantly shut his eyes in anger. The orderlies put him down, removed the tent flap, unbuttoned his jacket, and opened the bandages just as the constricted swelling was about to burst. He felt better, and caught a whiff of some sweetish smell. Fingers began pressing around his wound and pierced his emaciated thigh with something blunt. All he wanted was for these repulsive orderlies to remove him from the touch of that hand. He could hear them whispering: "My God, what a wound!"

He started on hearing a woman's voice, opened his eyes, and saw a beautiful, frightened face. Not for a long time since had he seen such a beautiful woman's face and such warm eyes. Why was she frightened? He wanted to smile at her.

"Are you a senior officer?" a man asked in bad Serbian; he had a small goatee and was wearing a white coat.

"Yes, unfortunately; but how does that matter in this pigsty of yours?" His eyes were still on the girl's face; her eyes now looked dark and stern.

"You aren't from the Eighth Regiment, by any chance?" she asked in embarrassed tones.

"I'm Major Gavrilo Stanković, commanding officer of the First Battalion of the Eighth Regiment. Where do you come from, Nurse?" He raised his head to get closer to her eyes, which were now dilated with fear and hope.

"I'm from Belgrade. My brother, Ivan Katić, was a cadet corporal in the First Battalion of the Eighth Regiment. Do you know him, Major?" she asked, seizing his hand.

His hand was dirty and he wanted to wrench it away from hers, but he left it where it was: it was a long time since he had felt the touch of a hand like that. He kept silent until the wave of sorrow had spent itself.

"Yes, I know him. I suppose you're the daughter of Vukašin Katić?"

"Yes," she said, letting go of his hand.

"I have great respect for your father. I'm happy you are sharing in our suffering."

"What do you know about my brother, Major Stanković?"

"A brave young man and of powerful intellect, like his father, but too sensitive, unfortunately—and then his poor eyesight. I left him fighting in the battle in which I was wounded."

"How did that battle end?"

He didn't reply at once: tears were welling up in her eyes. How long was it since he had seen anything like this?

"I don't know. I lost consciousness, and was taken prisoner the next day. I suspect the battalion withdrew, since ours was the rear-guard regiment. I'm sorry I can't be more helpful; but his comrade, Bogdan Dragović, was brought here with me. They were very good friends."

"Where is he?"

"In the corridor near the main entrance."

"Doctor Sergeev, may I go out for a moment?"

"Not before we've bandaged the major."

"Let her, Doctor. Are you Russian?"

"Yes, my name is Nikolay Maksimovich Sergeev."

"I spent nearly six years in St. Petersburg—the most important years of my life. Such wonderful friends . . . Almost everything that matters to me in the world was left behind in St. Petersburg," he said quietly in Russian, excited at speaking it for the first time after so many years. "At least I shall be able to speak Russian with you in this pigsty. If you don't mind, that is."

"Silence is the hardest thing to bear in times of misfortune; but your leg is bad, very bad indeed."

"Are you a Slavophile, Nikolay Maksimovich?"

"I'm on the side of those who suffer for their beliefs. When were you last bandaged?"

"A week ago. Where were you in 1905?"

"Your wound is bad, very bad indeed."

"I understand. There's nothing quite like the feeling a man has when he's away from his own country and his family, fighting for an idea—when he feels a special kind of loneliness in the premonition of sacrifice. That great sense of purpose in St. Petersburg on the ninth of January, when we set out toward the Winter Palace . . ."

Sergeev moved away from the wound, put aside his tweezers, and crossed his arms on his chest; his face was stern and gloomy as he listened to Major Stanković.

Milena Katić knelt down beside Bogdan Dragović, took his hand, and gazed at his unshaven face with its luxuriant moustache, his flushed cheeks, and dull, bloodshot eyes.

"I've heard a lot about you. I feel I know you, Bogdan."

It hurt him to breathe, and Ivan's sister, whom he had imagined somewhat differently, seemed to be swaying in a mist. She was even prettier than Natalia.

"Ivan is a real man," he whispered.

"Tell me about him."

He turned his face away from her; her gaze remained riveted on him as she waited for him to speak.

"Where was he taken prisoner?"

"Under Maljen. In our regiment's last battle. I was unhappy when we got separated. Very unhappy."

"Tell me all about him."

"We thought he was a bit of a sissy. Nobody believed he'd turn out such a fine soldier."

"So my brother was a brave man?"

"Yes, he was braver than me. In facing the truth, too."

Milena remembered Ivan's letters, in which he had railed against the army and teased her about the newspaper publicity she received for her work as a nurse. She remembered, too, her own sharp reproaches against Ivan for his faintheartedness.

Turning away from Bogdan, she said softly: "I scolded him and offended him. Did he ever mention this to you?"

"Yes, he read me one of your letters."

"He read it to you?" exclaimed Milena, staring straight into his eyes.

He could feel her breath and the scent of her hair, which reminded him of Natalia. His heart stirred, and he felt a desire for greater intimacy. "Yes, Milena," he said. "We read letters to each other."

She looked slowly away from his large, feverish eyes. "How did he come to be taken prisoner, if he was so brave?"

"Perhaps he broke his glasses."

Her face darkened, and she fell silent.

"Could you go to my house and tell my mother I'm here?"

"First we must make you comfortable. What was Ivan doing when you last saw him?"

"He was in a hut, next to our commanding officer, who had been killed. Luka Bog, his name was. He was standing over my candle. They had lit it for the C.O. When I feel better I'll tell you all about that night on Suvobor."

"What did he say when you parted?"

"The fire was spluttering. I lost consciousness. I had two bullets in my chest. He stayed in the hut by the fire. He was bending over the fire to get warm. I feel terrible. It would be awful if he's been taken prisoner." Bogdan's lips trembled.

An orderly told her to come at once to the operating room. She bent down and gently touched Bogdan's face with her forehead: he was now her brother. She couldn't leave the hospital until he was well.

As he was being carried through a corridor from the operating room Gavrilo Stanković closed his eyes, not only because he felt humiliated by his condition, but also to block out the dirt and disorder of the hospital; he didn't want anything to interfere with his reflections on Doctor Sergeev's ominous diagnosis of his wound. He heard Radojko talking to the orderlies. They were carrying him past Bogdan Dragović; well, that was all right with him; the next night he would talk to Bogdan about how he had risked his life for the pipe, and about slapping Radojko's face, after which Bogdan hadn't spoken to him.

They put him down where it was warmer and the stench even stronger. He felt someone's body beside him, heard moans in his ear, and opened his eyes: he was lying next to a man whose head was bandaged. Summoning all his strength, he moved himself to the edge of the bed and, catching sight of a white coat beside the pillow, shouted: "You, there! I've never shared a bed with anybody since the day I was born! I demand that the State I serve provide me with a place where

I can lie down and draw my last breath alone! I wish to be alone, is that clear?"

"This is a room for officers. Consider yourself lucky that you're only two to a bed."

"So I'm lucky to be here, am I?"

"Yes, you are. This hospital is equipped to take two hundred wounded, and with those of you who were brought in last night there are already more than five hundred."

"Doctor, you're talking to Major Gavrilo Stankovič!"

"Be quiet, Radojko! Call an orderly and get me out of here. Take me into the corridor. And you," he said, turning to the doctor, "get out of my sight!"

He had been prepared for suffering and sacrifice on behalf of freedom and country—that was his duty and mission in life—but he had never imagined that in this same country he could be left all night in front of the hospital gates and have the experiences he had had that day—and after a victory, too. All around him, angry murmurs dissolved in the foul smell of the wounded.

Radojko soon returned with some orderlies, who lifted Gavrilo onto a stretcher, carried him into a cold, damp place, and put him on the floor.

"What's wrong, sir?"

"Oh, is that you, Bogdan?" He looked gratefully at Bogdan and felt better. "This is horrible. Have you been bandaged yet?"

"No, not yet. I've had a talk with Ivan Katič's sister."

"Radojko, fill my pipe and light it. It's a long time since I have seen such a sweet, pretty girl as young Miss Katič."

Radojko handed him his pipe. "Would you allow me, sir, to go into Valjevo and bring you a bed?"

"A bed? Where would you find a bed? Get us something to eat, Radojko. We're not going to get anything today from this pigsty. They didn't provide rations for us. Buy some good beef and a bottle of red wine, and some sheep's cheese, if you can find it. Grill the meat over a charcoal fire and bring it here for our lunch."

Radojko gave him a grateful smile, saluted, then hurried away down the corridor, pushing past the orderlies and walking wounded.

"The Russian doctor tells me that there are more than a hundred cases of typhus in this barracks. See those men sitting against the wall, dozing? They don't know where to put them. Typhus is spreading like wildfire in the town; the prisoners are coming down with it like crazy. I feel worried about Doctor Vojtekh. I must send a message to the Valjevo headquarters, suggesting they send him here to the hospital; but what would he do in this pigsty?" Finding the tobacco distasteful, he put out his pipe.

Bogdan was being carried to the operating room; Gavrilo followed him with anxious eyes. Someone in a white coat called his name from the end of the corridor. He refused to answer. Again the voice called out for Major Gavrilo Stanković, angrily this time, and bawled at the orderlies to find him; the major covered his face with a tent flap. The dank chill from the muddy brick floor seeped into his bones, into the crown of his head, into all parts of his body except his leg, which seemed to be on fire. Dead or crippled—was that his only choice?

"Major Stanković! The director wants to see you."

Above his head he could hear the gentle, kindly voice of Milena Katić. He must control himself in front of this girl. He removed the tent flap: her face was even prettier than he had thought in the operating room, and he wanted to give her a grateful smile and speak some kind word; but beside her stood a giant of a man in white, looking as if he had squeezed himself out of the wall or emerged from the ceiling—an enormous head, a handsome, fresh face with a moustache and beautiful teeth—smiling down at him.

"What do you want?" he asked gloomily, raising himself on his elbows.

"I am Doctor Aleksić, Major, the director of this hospital."

"So you're in charge of this pigsty, this stinking torture chamber?" he asked, then fell silent, disconcerted by the increasingly benign expression on that smiling face.

"My dear Major, I feel worse than you; but what can I do in an artillery barracks which the Austrians turned into a hospital with two hundred beds? I've already crammed in about three hundred seriously wounded, more than a hundred walking wounded, and over a hundred typhus patients. In this pigsty, as you call it—somewhat intemperately, if you'll forgive my saying so—I have only three doctors, one medical student, about ten orderlies, and a few volunteer nurses like Miss Katić." His smile changed into an expression of compassion. "There are at least fifty patients on the point of death, and the less said the better about food and supplies."

"Don't talk to me about any of these things! I'm not interested in facts."

"Colonel Kajafa, commander of the Danube Division, has been making inquiries about you through the staff."

Gavrilo fell silent; he had been under Kajafa's command since the beginning of the war, and this was the first time Kajafa had shown any interest in what had happened to him. It was some years since they had sat down together over a glass of wine; yet they had been friends, and fellow conspirators, too, taking the same risks. He said firmly: "Tell Colonel Kajafa that I suggest he occupy Valjevo immediately and blow up the hospital! Don't laugh, I'm not joking."

"I apologize, Major, but I'm simply not in a position to provide you with a bed to yourself. If the influx of patients continues, we'll have to place five officers to every two beds."

"What is your rank?"

"Captain, second class, in the medical corps. In the reserve, of course."

"Then, Captain, I order you to withdraw at once!"

"Listen to me! Sergeev has told me about your condition. I've ordered your leg amputated immediately."

Gavrilo cut him short: "I'll make the decision about my leg, not you! Is that clear?"

He regretted his outburst: Milena stepped back and Doctor Aleksić said simply, "As you wish, Major. Your life is indeed your own business!" He withdrew from Gavrilo's range of vision.

"Well done, Major! Well spoken! Would that God would give you an arm long enough to reach to Niš and strike down Pašić! He deserves it for this freedom and this victory, which we certainly don't."

These words broke the silence that had suddenly fallen; he could no longer see his fellow sufferers, but he felt ashamed in their presence. Once again he covered his head with the tent flap. The groaning around him grew stronger; the footsteps continued. Nothing he could do about it. As long as another human body was not touching him, as long as no one was breathing down his neck . . . but why did Kajafa remember him? Was it the magnanimity born of victory, or did his conscience burn him? He's the division commander, and I'm a battalion commander. I'm under his command. My God, Gavrilo Stanković, what sort of a country is this? Why does a man deliberately humiliate himself? What is it he is ready to die for with conviction, and to kill for without compunction?

"Major Stanković," whispered Milena. How delighted he was to meet this beautiful girl! Was it his longing for Masha that made her seem so beautiful? She reminded him of Masha. Not in her appearance, though. Was it possible that his pain for Masha would persist even here, the pain that had disturbed his sleep and oppressed his moments of silence over the last six years? If God were kind, a miracle would happen. The tent flap fell away from his face and he sank into those warm eyes, not quite near. He blinked at their light—as one does just before a kiss.

"Shall we put you in the same room with Bogdan Dragović?" she whispered. A slight tremor ran through him, right down to his wound, a tremor of sorrow and disappointment.

"Yes, please. Thank you," he said dejectedly. The orderlies lifted up the stretcher, and she gently supported his head. He trembled at the touch of her hands, the hands of a pure, free child, like Masha's hands. He dropped his head, so that he might sink deeper into Milena's hands and feel the touch of her fingertips more intimately. It was all the same to him where they were carrying him; all he cared about was that his head should rest in her hands as long as possible. Why should he be afraid of death? Why, indeed?

Gavrilo Stanković was startled from his drowsiness by the banging of the door. In the doorway stood Radojko Veselinović, smiling triumphantly, seeking out the major with his eyes.

"Here I am, Radojko," the major called out testily, angry because Radojko was making such a big thing out of a piece of meat among these hungry wretches who lay writhing on thin layers of straw, covered with tent flaps and torn, dirty blankets, their bags and crumpled overcoats serving as headrests.

Radojko stood at attention, saluted with a wide, firm movement of his hand, then cried out, "I've brought it, sir!"

"What have you brought?"

"I've brought you a bed! The very best in Valjevo! May I bring it in?" He stepped into the room.

Behind him in the doorway appeared a large, white-painted iron bedstead, adorned with shining brass knobs, and with birds and roses painted in vivid colors on the headboard and foot. The bed was tilted on its two back legs while the front ones, decorated with brass loops, were upraised, as if ready to leap into the room. Rearing, it towered for some time over the pain of the wounded, filling them with confusion and astonishment, reducing them to silence, its bright surface gleaming, its roses blooming, its colorful birds flying about in the sky.

"For God's sake, Sibin, what is it?" whispered Miloje Dačić, now minus his right arm, from his corner.

"I've never seen one like that before. Shut your eyes and don't move, or your wound will bleed."

"What do you mean, shut my eyes? Why should I shut my eyes? I'm not dead yet!"

"Miloje, those are birds and roses all right."

"Make way for the bed!" said Radojko, preceding it.

"Where did you find it?" asked Gavrilo quietly as he stared at it; it made him want to sleep. Onward the bed came, white and shining, wide and deep, sailing through the room over the heads of the wounded men, who were dumb with astonishment. Where had he seen this bed before? Not in Belgrade; in St. Petersburg, perhaps, or in Budapest when he was about to leave for Russia? No, it was the bed he had seen in a dream where he was locked in a long, unusually sensual embrace with an unknown woman.

"I pick the biggest and finest-looking house in Valjevo. I go in, and there I find an old man and a young, pretty woman—most likely the old man's daughter-in-law, and his son's gone to war. I say to them: 'Major Gavrilo Stanković is badly wounded, and there he is in the hospital, lying on bare bricks. I think, sir, he deserves better from his country than that.' 'What are you looking for, soldier?' the old man asks me. 'I'm looking for a bed. So that he can be ill properly, like a gentleman.' 'You take everything you need for a wounded Serbian officer. Give him that bed, Desanka, and everything that goes with it.' We go into a big room and there it is, shining."

Yes, it was the bed from his dream, and yet it wasn't the same. Perhaps he was dreaming now. The bed seemed to be growing right up to the ceiling, becoming broader and broader until it filled the room with its shining light, rustling with a soft, clean sound, like his mother's sheets. Darkness was slowly, very slowly falling, the sky above the Sava was aflame with the setting sun, and the linen smelled of his mother's hands, as on Sundays when he slept longer, covering his head with the eiderdown to prolong the night, while the bells rang out from the cathedral and passers-by talked about all sorts of things.

"Now stop all this chatter! Get out of the way so that we can put the bed down. You'll have to stay on the stretcher, Major, but only for a moment. Now just a bit farther. Give that man there a shove, it's time he was carried out into the shed anyway. What do you mean, he isn't dead yet? Sorry, Corporal, but you'll have to move. Where to? Well, you could go under the bed. Matter of fact, you'd be better off there. We're only carrying out orders; it's not our fault it's so big. A great bed, fellows, isn't it? Good God, those birds look real. Just you smell that rose, you characters! Well, you won't be bored any more. It's true the bricks are hurting your back, the lice are biting you, and your wounds are rotting, but you've got something fine and big to look at. What more do you want, you bastards? Now then, Major, just you go to sleep."

To lie there, to spend the rest of his life lying in that bed in its soft white bedclothes, to sleep in a clean bed until death came—that was happiness, freedom, the Fatherland. To sleep.

Bogdan Dragović felt a cool hand on his forehead and out of the dull murmuring heard someone call his name. He would have answered, but he had no voice. He could not open his eyes because of that cool, strong hand which moved over the burning surface of his brow.

"No, he's not asleep; he has a high temperature." It was the voice of that girl, Ivan's sister.

"Let me take him home!" Who could that be?

"We can't let him go until his temperature is down. Who can look after him better than I can?" Yes, it was she.

"He must be under medical supervision for at least a few more days. That's the doctor's orders."

"What, here?"

"Don't worry, I'll look after him. Bogdan was my brother's friend."

"What shall I do, then?" Yes, it was she. He forced his eyelids open: there were his mother's fingers, dark red, blue, and black from the dyes of the rugs. He touched her fingers with his eyelashes and saw their wrinkled skin; they were pressing his forehead, his eyebrows, his eyes, rising and falling with his breathing, lifted up by the pain in his chest. What will happen to her if I die?

"Nurse, could you arrange for me to stay beside him while he's here? I'll help you, and I'll keep an eye on everybody in this room."

"Have you brought me some pears?" he whispered.

"I've brought you some quince preserve, my darling."

"Don't take your hand away. Keep pressing my forehead. Where is Milica? She should be working as a nurse."

"Your sister ran away when the Austrians came."

"Where is she?"

"No one has seen her. I'm worried."

"Milena, I'm thirsty. I'm burning."

"I'll bring you some tea right away."

"Where were you hit, my darling?" asked his mother.

"In the chest."

"Was it on Friday evening, the week before last?"

"I don't know."

"I was weaving, when suddenly my hands went numb, as if someone had struck them. The lamp flickered, nearly went out, and the thought flashed through my mind—something has happened to him."

"Give me your cool hand, Mother."

She put her cool hand on his forehead, but without moving the other one, hot and damp from his sweat. He pressed her palms onto his burning forehead and eyes.

"Mother, tell me about all the dreams you've had since I went away to the war."

"Just let me take you home, then I'll tell you all my dreams. One at a time. Like I used to when you came home from Belgrade for the holidays."

"Tell me now."

Petrana Dragović, famous throughout Valjevo as a weaver of rugs, bent over to tell him about a dream she had had twice, almost exactly the same the second time, speaking as if disclosing a family secret: "I was weaving with the green thread, and the shuttle got entangled in the basic color, so I couldn't bring the green across. Just then a sound of barking and meowing came from in front of our house. I looked up and there you were, my darling! You were wearing your officer's overcoat, but you had no moustache, you were quite young, your face was the same as when you went to high school. Our courtyard was full of cats and dogs, standing all around you, so that you couldn't budge. You called out to me, but the thread was wound around my hands, I couldn't get them out. I pulled the thread tight and tore it, but it did no good. . . ."

Bogdan let go of her hand. Milena brought a cup of tea and bent down to give it to him. Bogdan drank, then muttered: "Bring me a pear, Mother."

His mother stood over him, her eyes dry and lifeless, swaying as if about to utter a wailing cry, but with her lips pressed tightly together.

Gavrilo's leg woke him up at dusk. It was a different kind of pain, which he had felt since the previous night: a dull, burning sensation that seeped through his leg and throbbed into the pelvic muscles at the base of his torso in rhythm with his heartbeats. He recalled the ominous diagnosis of Doctor Sergeev and realized that he was lying in that white bed, a clean and elegantly appointed bed in which he had fallen asleep the moment his head touched the large, white, sweet-smelling pillow. Eagerly he breathed in the scent of clean bed linen and felt sad because of the very cleanness and whiteness, which seemed unreal, like peace, indeed like everything in his life that had possessed beauty and meaning—gone beyond recall, like everything he had loved.

The wounded men called to the orderlies to put the light on and asked for supper, or water. The hospital seethed with groans and the clatter of tin cans. The pale yellow light from the feeble bulb, spreading over the ceiling, seemed to quiet the evening clamor of the wounded. What had happened to Bogdan? Gavrilo raised himself on his elbows, but his wounded leg refused to budge and he couldn't drag it onto the floor. He saw a thin, slight woman bent over Bogdan; she was wiping the sweat off his face.

"Are you Bogdan's mother?"

"Yes, sir, I am."

"I'm his commanding officer and his friend."

"I'm grateful to you for that, sir. May God preserve you, as you have preserved my son."

"Take him home as soon as possible," he said, and sank back on his pillow.

"The doctors won't allow it, sir."

"I'll give orders that they're to let him go."

Petrana Dragović thanked him and offered him some quince preserve. He didn't like preserve, but took some to please her. He couldn't taste the quince; this worried him and reminded him of Doctor Sergeev's words.

Radojko arrived, carrying a basket covered with a towel. "Here's everything you wanted, sir!"

Gavrilo was delighted at the sight of the hot meat grilled on charcoal embers, the large chunks of cheese, the white bread, and the red wine. Radojko was overjoyed by his pleasure, and as he spread the towel over the eiderdown, he related how he had found a kilogram of meat and a woman to make the bread in a town crammed with sick and wounded men and prisoners of war. The major listened to him and looked at the food.

He had always lunched and dined in company, taking a special pleasure in courteous service, fine china, and elegant settings. He was known for his gastronomic inventiveness and his culinary vocabulary; he had his own terms of praise for every dish and every occasion. Good hostesses delighted to have him at their tables and boasted when "Major Gavrilo" dined in their cafés. He had no patience with people who were indifferent to food and drink, who took no pleasure in this noblest of vices. He hated Serbian inns because they were dirty and smelled of onions and brandy; whenever he had the money, he patronized only the best cafés and first-class restaurants. Now here he was among a crowd of sick and wounded men, surrounded by the hospital smell, sitting on his bed with Radojko's crumpled peasant towel in front of him, with meat in a saucepan, cheese on a tin plate, and a coarse, cracked cup for his wine. Radojko was urging him to eat, saying that the meat would get cold, that the bread was particularly good.

However, he could taste neither the beef nor the bread nor the cheese. He felt depressed. He took a few more mouthfuls, then stopped.

"Finish the rest for your supper, Radojko."

"Isn't the meat to your taste? You're always angry if it's overdone. Perhaps there isn't enough salt?"

"It's all fine, but I've no heart for it, Radojko. Take the food away."

"But, sir . . ."

"Take all this food out of my sight at once! I'll keep the wine."

He opened the bottle and took a good swig; he felt no sensation but bitterness and the taste of iodine; still, he felt he would like to get drunk.

"What did you see in the town, Radojko?"

"A lot of sick people, sir, sitting against the walls and fences, dozing in the snow. Some of them get up, stagger about like sleepwalkers, then topple over. All the courtyards and sheds—even the pigsties—are full of sick prisoners of war. People in town say it's an epidemic. Nobody talks of the victory."

"Are you afraid, Radojko?"

"Not while I'm with you, sir."

Gavrilo stared at his dirty hands on the clean, pale blue eiderdown, jerked them away in order not to dirty it, then dropped them down again, staring once more at his emaciated fingers. "Do your best to find me some soap by tomorrow morning," he said sternly.

"I will, sir. I'll turn the whole town upside down."

Is it possible that even dirty hands bother me now? he asked himself as he looked at the dirt under his nails.

"Major, would you sell me some of your bread? I'd like to taste a bit before I die," said a wounded man.

Gavrilo moved over and stared from his bed at the men lying on the floor in the dim, quivering light. They were pressed close together, covered with rags. Many had raised their heads and looked hungrily in his direction.

"Radojko, distribute this food among the soldiers!"

Quivering with fury, Radojko made no move to obey the order.

"Take some yourself if you haven't had any supper."

Making no attempt to conceal his anger, Radojko divided the major's supper among the wounded, then left the room without his usual salute.

Gavrilo again took some wine, but after he had swallowed a few mouthfuls the bitter taste made him shudder, and he slammed the bottle down on the floor. He stared at the ceiling and the long zigzag crack across its surface. In the corridor the wounded were quarreling about a blanket and the orderlies were shouting. Someone let out a loud wail, as though pierced by a bayonet.

I'd clout that man if I could get my hands on him, he thought. Nothing infuriated him so much in wartime as stealing on the battlefield and soldiers wailing. To endure suffering with dignity and to die nobly—that was something a man owed to himself. No one could love life who didn't also love death. Why didn't Sergeev come to take a look at his leg?

Milena Katić came up and stood by his bed. She looked at Bogdan, then at him, but the look was different this morning. Was she reproaching him on account of the bed, perhaps? Why did he find this girl so disturbing? Why did she remind him of Masha Rayevska, so that his whole life seemed to be nothing but his wound and a feeling of helplessness? This was not really true, nor did he want it to be. He had not been unhappy over those forty-odd years, nor were they going to end in defeat.

"Milena, would you move my wounded leg toward the wall?"

She rolled back the eiderdown and shifted his leg with deft movements. Was she frowning because of the smell of his wound? He would have liked to ask her why Sergeev didn't come to look at his leg, but she suddenly turned around and bent toward Bogdan, as if to escape from him, as if she were leaving him forever. Just like Masha Rayevska. So once again this evening, as always, he had to go back to the beginning, to the moment when she had turned away from him with sudden scorn in front of the whirligig at the fair in the Imperial Meadow the week before Lent . . .

. . . It was their fourth visit to the fair, her favorite outing, an event to which she had looked forward since Christmas. The poor people of St. Petersburg went wild in their enjoyment of food and drink, singing and dancing: it was their revenge on incurable poverty and the boredom of winter. At that time the despair born of poverty emptied out into orgies, and everyone vied with everyone else in outrageous behavior—there was nothing they dared not try. He found this uninteresting and alien to him, but Masha loved to see it all, to try to experience everything. She was always in the highest spirits, as if it were her last carnival. He had to take her around the fair, making great efforts to conceal his "Serbian sulkiness," as she called all his moods opposed to her own; so he pretended that for him too the fair was "wonderful," and agreed with her that "only the Russian people know how to enjoy themselves to the full, because they dare to be sincere." In any case, during the last year of their love he often indulged her increasingly strange ideas. It was easy for him to do this, since he was superior to her in knowledge and experience, being sixteen years her senior; but he was not pretending or lying when he agreed with her that nothing brings people together so much as great fear. "Fear that makes a nation," she had said the first time they met, confidently and firmly repeating an idea not her own. For his part, he didn't wonder how this young girl had come to such an idea about the world; it was her fear that had drawn him to her and aroused his excitement when he had first caught sight of her during the Blessing of the Waters at Epiphany, standing in the crowd on the banks of the Neva, leaning forward over the frozen river. She had been completely carried away by the hymn: "The voice of the Lord cries out above the waters . . . come all of you and receive the spirit of wisdom, the spirit of understanding, the spirit of the fear of God . . ." Yes, it was this fear that he had seen in her large gray eyes; and he had pushed his way through the dense crowd toward this strong young girl in the fur coat covered with blue velvet, first of all astonished and then delighted by her obvious pleasure in the hymn, and the fear that glowed through her tears. Though not pious by nature, she had been completely absorbed in the prayers. He discovered this the evening of that same day as they were riding in a sleigh down the Kameno-Ostrovski Prospekt. The knowledge pleased him, but not because he himself was an unbeliever (though his father, Ilija Stanković, was a priest in Belgrade) , and not because he felt sympathetic toward atheists in principle. On the contrary, from the time he had gained any knowledge of women, he had known that women who had no strong faith also lacked strong passion. Masha had swept him off his feet by the subtlety and depth of her emotion, a quality which he prized in women above all else, placing it above beauty in his lover's scale of values. Yes, this unique power of hers had indeed made him happy: from start to finish he had known complete happiness in their love.

Maria Denisovich Rayevska, known as Masha—a student who for some reason concealed her origin, told everyone she was born in the Caucasus, and gave no further information about herself—had insisted to him and all other people that her only relative in the world was the man she was in love with. For three years he had indeed been her sole kin, and he had sincerely convinced her that she was all he had in the world. It was not just a lover's lie; that was how he felt. He had to conceal from her that he wrote regularly to his mother and received long, anxious letters from her every week. He was deeply in love with this extremely jealous girl with meek, gray eyes and a sweet, childlike face that changed with every new thought and feeling. The moment he absent-mindedly said something about the women he had loved before he met her, her gentle submissiveness would be transformed into something insulted and menacing, for she wanted to be everything to him, the one single thing in his life. "You know, Grisha, I'm jealous of your shirt, of your watch because you keep it warm, of every single thing that touches you," she had said to him even on that final night, just before their last visit to the fair in the Imperial Meadow.

At that fair, full of the confidence of love, he had allowed himself to relax for a few moments, had permitted himself the liberty of not following her, and that had been fatal. Or so he had believed, and for years had sought to convince himself of this, to comfort himself; but in fact it wasn't so. The reality was quite different; what had vanquished him was the inexorable law which prevails even among the deer in the woods: that what is most beautiful belongs to youth.

They had been eating some hazelnut cakes bought at a stall and could scarcely push their way along over the frozen, well-trodden snow through the drunken, laughing crowd, wholly absorbed in their fun; every now and then they stopped in their tracks, enjoying the coarse jokes of a quaint old man. At last they came to an enormous whirligig with four wings to which small painted boxes had been attached, placed so that they could whirl around on their own axles. Couples were getting into them. An accordion player gave the word of command to make the whirligig start whirling. There was a frenzied shrieking of men and women as the painted boxes began to revolve.

"Come on, Grisha!" she said, aflame with enthusiasm at the sight, as if calling him to bed.

"Over my dead body! I'm not going to let myself be whirled around in a painted box," he said, without a moment's reflection.

She was taken aback; flushed and angry, she looked him straight in the face. "So you won't come with me, is that it, Grisha?"

"I don't want to go on the whirligig!"

"But, Grisha . . ." she stammered, hurt and disappointed.

"Only children enjoy themselves on a whirligig. Children and . . ." He had no time to say who else; he was cut short by the expression on her face, and by her gaze fixed on something behind his back. Her stare remained fixed for some minutes, which made him angry, and not only because of their disagreement. He saw quite clearly—he could not forget that moment, which often roused him from sleep—that the anger and disappointment had suddenly fallen from her face like a heavy veil, and that face was suddenly lit up by a look of gentleness and rapture which broadened into a smile. He quickly turned around to see the cause of the transformation.

A young man, a mere boy, said with a triumphant smile (he had never before or since seen a man with such large and irregular teeth): "I'll go with you on the whirligig! My name is Seryozha Zubov."

"Come on!" she said, quickly and decisively, without looking at Gavrilo.

From the painted box she shouted, "I'm going to fly!" and his masculine pride had been wounded: they were contemporaries, and for them he was almost an old man. But his feeling was something more than this; after nearly seven years, he still couldn't decide exactly what he had felt. He couldn't bear to look at them; instead, he walked away from the whirligig and stood in front of a booth, where an old buffoon was shouting: "A battle and a defeat! A performance and a fine view! A battle and a defeat!"

Behind him, the whirligig whirled around, to the accompaniment of the accordion and women's screams; but in that general clamor he could hear quite clearly Masha's scream stifled in her throat, the sound she made when she was most excited. That cut him to the quick. In spite of the passage of seven years, including three years of fighting, the pain was still there. Tonight he felt it more hopelessly than ever before.

If a snowstorm hadn't come whirling over the fairground, who knows how long they would have gone on flying toward the sky in the whirligig. He had had a second and better look at Seryozha Zubov that evening at the restaurant on Karpovka where he and Masha had had her favorite dish for supper, the special carnival pancakes; but the carnival had ended both for her and for him at the whirligig in the Imperial Meadow. Afterward she had walked alongside him without a smile, without curiosity. She had said she was tired and wanted to go home, but he had insisted that they go out to dinner; he didn't want to leave her alone that night for a single moment. Later he regretted his persistence. If they had gone straight to his room, if they hadn't again encountered that idiotic young man with tousled hair and ugly teeth, then perhaps that fatal incident wouldn't have occurred. While they were having supper, not even his most persistent efforts succeeded in changing her mood; but Seryozha Zubov achieved this by just walking into the restaurant.

How her face lit up! How her eyes glistened, her lips trembled! She looked straight across Gavrilo at him, quite openly, as though she were alone.

He paid the bill before they had finished; without a word, she got up and followed him to the door. There, standing by the hatrack, was Seryozha Zubov; with obvious pleasure, as if Gavrilo had not been at her side, he said, "So long, Mashenka!" Mashenka, indeed! He wanted to strike him for such insolence. He hadn't said a word to her as they drove home in a sleigh; he was thinking what he would say to her in his room. A few doors down from where she lived she had jumped off the sleigh and said, "Good-by." He had jumped off after her, but she was running over the snow toward her house, obviously trying to escape. Why hadn't he caught up with her? Why hadn't he tried to explain things and demanded an explanation from her? Why hadn't he promised her anything she wanted? He had never been able to answer these questions. In fact, however, he couldn't have done anything; everything had been decided out there by the merry-go-round. When he went to her house the next evening after a sleepless night, to take her first to his room and then out to supper as was their custom, Masha wasn't there. Her landlady told him crossly that Masha had left for the Crimea by the evening train. "Alone?" he stammered despairingly.

"She was with that poet."

"What poet?"

"Surely you've met Seryozha Zubov?"

He had no memory of what he said to the landlady, whose swollen face and squeaky voice he remembered whenever he thought of Seryozha Zubov.

The spring came and went unnoticed without Masha, and his only recollection of the smelly St. Petersburg summer was of a long, somnolent period of waiting for Masha, or for a letter from her.

Ever since his return from Russia his life had been waging war and waiting. He had sent his address to all his friends, to all their mutual acquaintances, and to the landlady. Every day he waited for her letter. After the mail arrived at the battalion he would go out to an observation post and smoke his pipe. Even when he was taken prisoner, he still thought that a letter from Masha might reach him by way of Vienna and the military mail. Then he would bite his lower lip, but his self-contempt wouldn't last long: he had ceased to rebel against his suffering, aware that once it was over he would be left without love. Perhaps Masha's infatuation with the whirligig and that silly poet would come to an end; perhaps his pretense of lofty emotions would begin to bore her. Ah, that "sacred" lie! My God, Gavrilo Stanković, what have you reduced yourself to? The first rival, the first pang of jealousy—and also the last! As soon as the war was over he'd go back to St. Petersburg. He knew from experience that there was no greater joy than that of a humiliated lover, when the woman who has betrayed him at the very peak of their love comes back to him, crushed and conscious of her sin. No embrace can compare with the embrace of a repentant mistress, one who loves in repentance and gives herself for her own salvation.

Then he would find his friends in St. Petersburg; Shishkin and Platonov would have returned from Siberia to continue their old arguments, punctuated by silence: What was Spartacus thinking when he was stoned by the slaves, his former followers? Why did Robespierre and Saint-Just remain silent on the way to their execution? Had something snapped in Bakunin's soul, causing him to write his repentant letter to the Czar? Why had the Bolsheviks no less hatred for Bakunin than they had for Solovyev and Stolipin? Why must one believe in God, if one has no faith in eternity?

"Let me see your leg, Major," said Sergeev. He drew back the eiderdown and undid the bandage. "It's no good, Gavrilo. We'll wait till morning, then we must decide."

"What are you going to decide, Nikolay Maksimovich?"

"As I told you this morning, your wound is bad, very bad indeed."

Tola Dačić had no money for overnight lodging in a house in Valjevo, and all the other places where he might have kept dry until daybreak were occupied by sick and wounded men from both armies. So at dusk he left the town and started walking along the Kolubara, hoping to find a hut in the fields or a pile of corn stalks. He came upon some fires beside carts and wheelbarrows containing empty coffins; fathers and mothers were staring mutely at the fires, waiting for the middle of the night, when they would go to the cemeteries and remove the bodies of their sons who had died of wounds or disease, and take them to the cemeteries in their villages. Tola did not stop beside their fires, though he was cold and wet through. He could not share in the silence of these people, who in his opinion were doing something that shamed both the living and the dead. The young men had died for their country; the country should take care of their graves. He walked past these fathers who did not think as he did and wandered through the meadows and gardens by the Kolubara in the murky darkness, but found no hut or haystack. He turned back and walked toward the fires, which cast a whitish gleam on the empty coffins. He selected a fire where some walking wounded were warming themselves. Tola introduced himself, told them how many sons he had sent off to the war and what had happened to them, then took out a bottle of strong brandy and offered it around. He also brought out some cornbread and a piece of bacon and began to tell them how he had looked everywhere for his son Miloje but hadn't found him. He told them everything from start to finish, beginning with the preparations for his journey and the great difficulty he had had in obtaining wax for Miloje's wound and for the souls of the dead.

"You're a wise old bird! How much wax do you have with you?" asked a soldier with a wounded arm, who had come up to him because of his brandy and bacon.

"I've got two good-sized rings of wax and about a hundred candles."

"God bless you for taking so much thought for the soldiers," said another wounded man, with a large moustache, nodding his head as he spoke.

Tola offered him some brandy and bacon, then started to tell his tale. He knew that behind the army that had chased the Austrians across the Drina there were many graves without crosses and lighted candles, and it just wasn't right that those souls which had expired in the darkness shouldn't have some light to guide them. Tola had walked the length and breadth of Prerovo, stopping wherever he saw a hive or heard that someone kept bees. So with a bit of money borrowed from George Katić, but more by means of lies and whining, he had collected enough wax for them to melt a whole cauldron. Andja and her daughter-in-law had made the hundred candles and put the two big rings of wax at the bottom of his bag, then on top of them a piece of bacon to keep his strength up, a string of onions to ward off all kinds of illness, some pastries prepared by his sister-in-law, a bottle of red wine, two bottles of strong brandy, and some pretty buttons for Uncle Miloje from his nephew. He counted all the things in his bag, feeling sad that he hadn't found Miloje. The wounded man with the moustache reproached him for not having first looked in the Valjevo hospitals, but Tola insisted that he had been to all the hospitals, schools, restaurants, and warehouses in Valjevo where there were sick and wounded men and hadn't found the name of Miloje T. Dačić on a single list. First thing the next morning he'd go from hospital to hospital, peer into every corner, and lift up every tent flap.

It was snowing lightly, the Kolubara roared, and dogs barked; Tola fell silent. The fathers and mothers who knew where their sons were got up, harnessed their oxen, and set off toward the graveyard. The wounded listened sadly to the sound of spades and shovels banging against the empty coffins and went on drinking Tola's brandy. The man with the moustache suggested that Tola get a bit of sleep. Tola lay down on a bundle of straw, without removing his bag from his shoulder, and the man with the moustache covered him with his own overcoat, as if he were his son. That is what Aleksa would have done, thought Tola sadly, and with that thought he fell asleep.

Feeling cold and wet he woke up: it was pitch dark, the fire had gone out, though a few twigs still smoldered; there was no one around. He was frightened and jumped up. Only three fires were burning nearby; the rest had gone out. They've gone off to the graveyards, he said to himself, and shook his wet, cold shoulders: that was better, much better. What about his bag? Where's my bag? He thought, My bag's gone! He bent down and rummaged through the straw, crawled around the remnants of the fire, poked it; but there was no sign of his bag.

"Where's my bag, folks?" he wailed.

The Kolubara roared away, heavy with its burden of water.

"Better ask where your head is!" cried someone from a nearby fire.

The wax, the precious wax! The presents for Miloje! Where had those wounded gone to? Where was the man with the moustache, that cunning bastard? May God melt him in boiling wax! He hurried toward a fire where some peasants were dozing, lying down with bags on their backs, just as he had lain down and gone to sleep the night before. Then he halted in his tracks: not everybody had been asleep last night in Valjevo; but some people with brimful bags had slept, and during the night they were robbed. Necessity knows no law! But he couldn't go to Miloje empty-handed.

"What's the matter, old man? Did you find your bag?" asked a peasant sitting under a wheelbarrow with two coffins.

"I didn't lose it, thank heaven. I dreamed that I lost it, and started in my sleep as if someone had stuck me with a bayonet. Will it soon be daylight?"

"Who can tell? Many won't live long enough to see it."

Tola made sure his knife was in his belt.

Doctor Paun Aleksić, the hospital director, was awakened by the sound of discreet coughing in front of the door of his office, which also served as his sleeping quarters.

Only Doctor Pantelić would do such a thing, but it wasn't Pantelić. No, it couldn't be Srećko, the accountant. As for Toma, his orderly, he wouldn't dare cough while waiting in front of the door to be summoned. He must go back to sleep. His shoulders and neck felt cold; if he took his hand out from under the eiderdown to cover himself up, his sleep would be finished; so he slid down under the covers and curled up.

Outside there was a sound of buckets banging and people swearing.

Remember, gentlemen, a good hospital is at one and the same time a cloister and the kingdom of Frederick the Great: a cloister in the quietness of voices and movements—*Die stillste Stille*—and Frederick the Great's kingdom in its order and hierarchy; the ruler, of course, is the head of the hospital. That was what Professor Liebermann had said; the romantic old fellow had no idea what a military hospital was like, nor of the conditions now prevailing in Serbia. One day, when he was a professor, or minister of health, or head of the Army Medical Services (yes, that was it), when he addressed the young doctors, he would say something like this: A good hospital, gentlemen, is so quiet that nothing can be heard except the director's footsteps. A good hospital is like a perfectly run state. A hospital is a realm of quiet where the subjects have no cause to groan, and the ruler avoids any semblance of cruelty—that's better. All trace of vanity must be hidden. No, forget vanity. But why? Wherever death establishes itself, vanity rules. Such thoughts blew one's sleep to smithereens. Go on coughing, you idiot, I'm not getting up for you. Who dared spoil his sweetest moment? A time when everything was soft, gentle, blurred. The true measure and affirmation of order in the world, and of human well-being: the peace of being in bed and the morning quiet must be saved by every means possible.

Outside a dog yelped and a man was singing, or perhaps crying for help; and again that coughing in front of the door.

He simply must resist by military methods, by force if necessary, this primitive behavior, this disgusting lack of consideration so typical of the Serbs, this facility for making such a row in the morning, something unheard of among cultivated people; he must protect his morning sleep, and the experiences he shared with her. How she crept out of bed before dawn silent as a cat, how his weary body was free from soft yet burning touches which banished sleep and once more inflamed desire. There was nothing sweeter than lying just a little longer in a clean, warm bed, lazy and relaxed, but in a cold room. The contrast made it even more pleasant. When his nose felt cold, as it did now, he must cover up his whole face with the eiderdown. This was not so pleasant after every encounter with a woman. There were very few women—far too few in this damned war—whose presence in bed one could still enjoy after they had gone. Here in Valjevo there wasn't a single one whose skin had the same fragrance as Katya's—not one had skin like hers; not one left behind such an exciting scent on the sheets and pillows; not one induced in him such blessed weariness as the absent-minded, wanton Katya—not Ružica, and not that shameless bitch Janette. With them it was the same old thing. Physical power and a vulgar rhythm. With Katya he would have continued where they had left off the previous night. He wouldn't have minded a bit of fun with that stupid Ružica either. He experienced that marvelous feeling only in the morning in bed, when he didn't desire any one particular woman, but several, and someone new as well who had a bit of each of the others. He would have liked to have them all at the same time. Really there was nothing in our Christian civilization more stupid and criminal than monogamy—but enough of women. He wanted to sleep, to sink back into himself.

Outside there was groaning and banging—someone was being chased away. Then those damned noisy crows, and that angry coughing outside the door.

Here he was, the director of a reserve hospital in Valjevo during a typhus epidemic. Not much to advance a medical career in wartime, with his life at risk. A miserable and stupid situation; at the first opportunity he must get closer to the High Command, get himself exposed to the great. People were always the same; right now they were dying one after another, while those who were hand in glove with the powerful got on. Would people suffer so much without the prospect of promotion and decorations if they were not striving toward peace in time of war? He must get to Kragujevac, make contact with the medical service, get out of this hole as soon as possible. These days a doctor was worth more than a general, and sensible people could advance themselves. That shit went on coughing. All right, you bastard, cough your guts up. He would doze a little, withdraw into his own skin, into warmth and sweetness.

What time was it? If he looked at his watch he'd be wide awake. Go on, cough to your heart's content. As for people—they were envious animals, evil and spiteful creatures. If I can't sleep, I won't let anybody else sleep either. Let them rot in their weakness. The envy of underlings was a strange sort of envy—quite irrational. The more removed people were from the object of their envy, the less was their envy; but when they were close to the person they envied, then they hated him with a bestial, paranoiac hatred and could scarcely wait for revenge. Any man in a position of power had to fight seriously only with those closest to him, with his so-called collaborators, assistants, deputies. The person coughing so grossly and shaking the snow off his boots on the staircase wasn't his orderly, Toma; it could only be Pantelić or that Russian bear Sergeev. He would doze a little longer and breathe in the scent of Katya's fabulous skin. Still, she was a whore, she'd been with some expert since their last night together. It was that idiot Sanya, of course—a medical student, a nobody who had learned his job in Paris. I'm a greenhorn, he thought—a fool, no doubt! It was all over with sleep. But I'll bring some order into this chaos if it kills me.

"Come in, Toma!" he called. His orderly, who was carrying a bucket of hot water, and the third-draft man, Brka, whose whole body was twisted around his armful of wood, were not alone; with them was Srećko, the hospital accountant. He was angry and frowning, something quite unusual.

"Have you been coughing out there since dawn, Srećko? I got no rest, you know."

"Forgive me, sir, but an urgent letter has arrived from the medical section of the First Army."

"That's why you've been coughing since midnight?" He propped himself on his elbows; he could have shot Srećko right through the forehead. "Get out of my sight this minute! Why are you staring like that?"

Taken aback, Srećko left the room.

Doctor Aleksić sank down onto his pillow. It was his own fault for permitting a certain social intimacy; subordinates should always be kept in their place.

His orderly put down a bowl of water beside the bed; the fire was burning in the stove. From a small table he took a bottle of alcohol, poured some into the water, got up, wrapped himself in the eiderdown, sat on the edge of the bed, and put his feet in the bowl, then immediately jerked them out.

"This water's cold as ice!"

"It only seems that way, sir. It's cooled off a little, there's been a bit of snow, and you've slept late this morning."

"Brka, clear those dishes and glasses from the table, and bring some more dry wood." He got back into bed with wet feet. Nothing could spoil a man's morning as much as his orderly, his accountant, servants of any kind; these insolent creatures transformed a pleasant, enjoyable experience into misery and raging fury. Surely there was nothing more unpleasant than putting one's warm feet, fresh from bed, into tepid water. If only it were really cold, fresh, and stimulating! But tepid water—it was slimy and repulsive. This letter which had made that scoundrel Srećko cough like that? If it had good news, he'd have called out from the door. God knows what frightful things may be in store for me today.

Toma brought in a bucket of water from which the steam was rising.

Now that idiot's going to scald me, he thought, and told him to pour half the water from the bowl, then carefully pour in the hot water. He remembered Katya and some of their experiences the previous night, which set his heart on fire. That very day he would put that good-for-nothing Sanya from Paris under Vinaver's orders. He lowered his feet into the bowl once more; the water was hotter than he would have liked, but one couldn't expect tact from a peasant, not even with hot water. He poured in a little more alcohol, wrapped the eiderdown more closely around him, told Toma to bring in his breakfast, then gave himself up to enjoyment, gently wriggling his toes, breathing in the alcohol with the steam from the bowl, and feeling his toe tips swell and his veins dilate. A sense of well-being crept up from his shinbones to his knees; he felt a draft somewhere, but this made the warmth around his feet and limbs even more agreeable. How disgusting this war was—and to top it all, a typhus epidemic!

His orderly brought in some cheese, two fried eggs, and toast, setting the tray down on his knees.

"Bring me a pot of black coffee in ten minutes," he said, "but put another log in the stove first." Only when he was alone did he begin to eat; he could not endure anyone looking at him while he was chewing.

He ate slowly, until the water in the bowl got cold, and while he was eating made every effort not to think about the tasks awaiting him, or indeed about anything unpleasant. His orderly arrived promptly with his coffee; he let him give his feet a good rub with a cold linen towel, then bring him his breeches and his boots, which had been cleaned and polished the night before. He did not address a single word more to the orderly; he would never repeat the mistake of the previous morning, when he had allowed him to babble on about the complaints of the sick and wounded. Authority was undermined by showing confidence in underlings; they must not know what their master is thinking about and what interests him.

"Why isn't the barber here?" he asked when he was dressed and sitting beside the warm stove, waiting for his customary shave.

"It seems that Ramiz has fallen ill, sir. I called him, but his eyes were all bloodshot."

"Well, what did you do then?"

"I asked that man Grčić, but he said that he had to shave someone for an operation."

"So now I have to wait for Grčić?"

"You needn't wait, sir, I'll go fetch him at once."

That means Ramiz shaved me when he was already infected, he thought, as he lit his first cigarette, and the day before yesterday he cut me. My God, I'm already infected myself! He got up, paced back and forth in the room, and drank his coffee. Would his wife and children ever find out? (Who knows whom she was mixed up with last night!) Would all these thieves behind the lines, all these refugees from Belgrade, disporting themselves with grass widows and real ones in provincial towns, discussing winter preserves and victory (much they cared that an epidemic was raging like wildfire, mowing down everyone in turn)—would his descendants, the medical students, the younger doctors of tomorrow, have any inkling in peacetime of what the doctors of today had suffered, fighting valiantly for human lives in Valjevo, a handful of doctors in a sea of patients? No one tomorrow would either know or remember. Humans were more selfish than wolves, or any other beast. Women most of all—Schopenhauer was no fool for despising them. There's Slavka, fussing about with war relief committees, spending more money while I sacrifice myself! Then at night writhing under some shirker who got out of military service because of *Vitium cordisa*. She hasn't written to me for a week, the bitch. I must burst in on her one night, the sooner the better, right now while this disease is spreading, and she's sure I can't come! I'll take her by surprise just before midnight . . .

"Doctor Sergeev won't let Grčić leave the operating room. He has to shave someone's head for an operation," his orderly reported.

Doctor Aleksić frowned: since the beginning of the war there had been only one day when he hadn't been shaved. But that Russian was always pulling him by the nose. If he hadn't been a Russian, an ally, he'd have cut him down to size long ago, but what could a wretched Serb do today? He had to put up with any kind of slob, if he was an Ally.

"Make the bed and tell Srećko to come," he said in a spiritless voice. He combed his moustache, twirled the ends, and sat down at his desk, listening to the quarreling and bawling in the hospital. Yes, it was a pity you couldn't take the stick to people any more.

Srećko, the accountant, saluted, making no attempt to conceal the fact that he was offended. "Here's the letter, sir."

Doctor Aleksić took the open envelope and read that an Allied medical mission would arrive soon in Valjevo; hospital chiefs were advised to take all necessary measures to welcome the Allied doctors in a fitting manner; the day of the mission's arrival would be communicated in due course. He didn't raise his eyes from the letter, which he read twice; before he listened to what Srećko had to say, he wanted to think carefully what those words "take all necessary measures" meant. All he said to Srećko was: "I'll think it over and send for you. Tell Doctor Pantelić that I'm waiting for him."

The entire human race, to say nothing of Serbia, will be ruined by administrative machinery—what the Germans call bureaucracy, he thought as he smoked. It's as if paper and ink, seals and protocol were fashioned from an essence of stupidity which simply vaporizes in offices and intoxicates like morphia the minor officials who write directives, official letters, regulations, and reports. What preparations could possibly be made in this primeval wartime chaos, in this desperate struggle with typhus?

Doctor Pantelić came in on tiptoe as if not to wake him; Aleksić didn't even hear his greeting. He had wound some rubberized cotton around his leggings and fastened a belt around his coat tightly, because he believed that typhus was transmitted by lice. He stank of sulfur, carbolic, and naphthalene. Yesterday he had waited in vain for his wife, consumed by the pangs of love; consumed too by remorse, because his "Serbian conscience" had made him send his brother, who had been wounded at Cer, back to the front before he was ready, and after three days he had been killed. Pantelić was a coward, keeping his mouth covered with gauze like that.

"Report only the most important changes," said Aleksić sternly.

"Well," he said, looking at a piece of paper, "in the six rooms I managed to make rounds in last night there were twenty-seven deaths. Among the staff one orderly has died, and two are sick; and I'm told that one of the volunteer nurses has a high temperature. I'll make rounds of the other sections before noon. However, sir, the worst thing of all is that fifty cartloads of new patients arrived last night."

"Fifty?"

"I didn't count them, but there'll be fifty or more. They're still arriving. I've no idea what we'll do with them. This morning some of the wounded—about a hundred, I'd say, including officers—were up in arms. They'd have torn me to pieces if I hadn't gotten out of the way."

"Why were they rebelling?"

"The intolerable conditions here. No heat, no medicines, dreadful food. Well, you know all about it."

"Doctor Pantelić, you must realize that all these unpleasant incidents, which seem to be more and more frequent, are a matter of faulty propaganda. There are about six thousand Austrian prisoners of war in Valjevo, and one hundred spies are enough to upset the entire Balkan peninsula, let alone a single town like Valjevo."

"What can *I* do about it?"

"Summon the hospital platoon and tell them to take some of those loudmouths outside and listen to their complaints in the storeroom with a stick. Not for nothing was court-martial invented."

From outside came sounds of screaming, of calls for help. Aleksić went up to the window: the baggage men were attacking two orderlies.

"Come with me, Doctor Pantelić." Fully dressed and carrying his cane, he walked slowly up to the crowd of baggage men, who were fighting the orderlies with their bare hands. "What's going on, soldiers?" he asked. The baggage men let the orderlies go and retreated, giving frightened and menacing looks. "Answer my question: what's going on here?"

"We've been waiting out here all night, sir."

"All night?"

"Yes, sir, all night; and I've been here since noon yesterday."

"So have I."

"It's a disgrace! Poor men," said Aleksić, speaking softly as if to himself, but he could see that they were all listening; some of the sick in the carts propped themselves up and stared at him. "You certainly didn't deserve this; but what can we do when all the fine folk have crowded behind the lines and settled comfortably in warm rooms? Niš is full of shirkers and army suppliers, and the peasants are dying like animals. You know who's to blame for the fact that right now I have nowhere to put you but the attics." They looked at him grimly, dumbfounded by his words. "What staff have I got to treat you? What medicines have I got? I have a handful of orderlies and three doctors —well, you can see for yourselves. Today every man looks after himself!"

While they were still silent he hurried back into the hospital full of protective power and the pleasure arising from it. "Where are the orderlies?" he cried as he stepped into the corridor. "Why aren't the rooms heated? Why are these unfortunate men lying on the bare brick? Why haven't you brought straw for them? It's ten o'clock, and they haven't had their breakfast. Where are those fine ladies, the volunteer nurses? Why are these delirious patients naked? Nobody here cares about the sick and wounded!" He stepped over the patients in the corridor and stopped in the middle, where he could be heard in all the rooms: "Every day I ask for beds, blankets, and sheets. Every day I complain to the authorities and ask for more food and medicines, and the only answer I get is: 'We have no money. We didn't anticipate the need.' So what am I to do now? Put a bullet through my forehead?" All fell silent, except those who were unaware of anything and went on raving, shouting, and waving their arms wildly. "Now which of you soldiers would like to go home?" A number expressed the wish to do so. "Anyone who wants to go home and is able to should go get his clearance papers from Srećko, the accountant. As soon as you've recovered, report to the Regional Command." He turned to Doctor Pantelić. "Give their places to those who've been waiting all night, and prescribe the maximum dose of aspirin for everybody."

"We have only a few aspirin left, for the most serious cases and the officers."

"There must be some aspirin. Tell Belić to give you some. You're only too happy to say we're out of something," he shouted. Should he go see that Major Stanković, a pigheaded creature typical of the military? After his display of insolence yesterday, that fool didn't deserve special attention; he'd see him when he made his general round of visits. He hurried along to his office, full of anxious thoughts as to what measures he should take to receive the Allied mission.

In his office he found his friend Milan Belić, the pharmacist and chief of medical supplies for all the Valjevo hospitals, who looked as though he were about to burst into tears.

"You've come just at the right moment!" exclaimed Aleksić joyfully. "But you look a bit tired, Milan. Toma, pour us each a glass of cognac, then you can go. The evolution of our species, my dear friend, is the evolution of the instinct for enjoyment; and that means, among other things, the need for drugs. Now why are you grinning?"

"Last night at Mrs. Predolac's I lost my last cent at cards. I even wagered my watch and my wedding ring. If Olivera knew, she'd hang herself. It was incredible—almost funny—what rotten cards I had last night! It's not a matter of chance either. Our fate stalks us through a game of cards, naked and unashamed, like a whore."

"I must say I find that rather difficult to believe."

"Really? There's no law in the universe so inflexible as bad luck at cards. It's not a matter of chance that gambling is the passion that produces the greatest number of suicides."

"Don't worry, I'll pull you out of it somehow. Listen, I want ten boxes of aspirin for some important patients in town, and if you've brought some diagalen, you can have three nights of bad luck at cards with an easy mind."

"I can't accept yesterday's price. If this epidemic in Valjevo goes on another ten days, one antipyretic tablet is going to cost a ducat. And Mišić's adjutant told me that the Austrians and Germans are concentrating all their forces for a new attack. That'll be the end of us. I give you my solemn word, I won't live a day under enemy occupation. I swear it in the name of my children!"

Aleksić looked at him with naked disbelief: of all lies, he found those inspired by patriotism the most disgusting.

"That's Vojvoda Mišić's concern," he said seriously. "Did you know that there's an Allied medical mission coming here?" He still felt angry that the Serbs would be disgraced in the eyes of Europe.

"Any change since yesterday?" asked Gavrilo Stanković caustically, as he lay on the surgical table in the operating room, irritated by Sergeev's prolonged poking about his thigh and probing his wound with tweezers—not to mention his portentous silence, knitted eyebrows, and frowning forehead. On Milena Katić's face there was expression akin to terror.

Sergeev remained silent for a few more moments, then walked to the window and back, and finally spoke, looking sternly at the major: "It's gangrene. I don't want to deceive you. I must operate."

Milena dropped her instruments on the table and hurried out of the room. The two men followed her with their eyes, but with different expressions. Then their eyes met; they were alone now, to face what must be faced.

"You're going to cut off my leg?"

"There's no alternative."

"What do you mean, no alternative?"

"It's to save your life."

"So I'm to live the rest of my life as a cripple?" Gavrilo exclaimed, staring at Sergeev, who was drumming the rigid, outstretched fingers of both his hands together, and looking at the major with an expression devoid of pity. "What if you had changed the bandages the night before last, when we arrived here, Doctor? What would have happened then?"

"I don't know. I'm inclined to think it was already too late. Anyway, the state of this hospital is the business of you Serbs. I'm just a surgeon working here." He spoke slowly, in a mixture of Russian and Serbian.

"You're quite sure that this is the only thing you can do?"

"How old are you, Major?"

"Forty-one," Gavrilo replied, dropping his head onto something hard and metallic.

"Then why do you hesitate?"

Once again Gavrilo stared at Sergeev's hands, which were suddenly still, with the tips of his long, bony fingers pressed together. Bloodless fingers. They'll cut off my leg with a saw. What does that saw look like? His leg began to throb violently, the whole room was full of it.

"You think I've lived long enough?"

"You're fortunate in having lived long enough to get through the second half of your life on the experiences of the first forty years."

"So I'm to live on memories?"

"You'll live the true life, Major. Life's very essence, which is what we remember."

"So that's what I'm to live on?" His glance lighted on a pile of bloodstained bandages spilling out of a bucket in the corner; a livid, rigid fist peeped out of the bucket—the hand of the man the orderlies had carried out a while back, unconscious. "My wretched leg won't fit into any garbage can."

"Our present life is a stream of filth. A sewer flowing through a human settlement. Only in what is dead and gone can we find something of what was great and just. If man makes any sense at all, only the past can reveal and confirm it. Why are you frowning?"

"Because what you're saying is contrary to all sense and reason! You're talking against yourself!"

"If the gangrene had attacked your head, I'd let you die. One cannot afford to lose anything at all from one's head."

Suddenly Sergeev pulled apart his interlocking fingers. Gavrilo could hear the table shaking underneath him. "How long will I live if you don't cut my leg off?"

Sergeev didn't reply and looked at him as if he hadn't understood; he was again drumming his fingers together.

Gavrilo couldn't bear to look at them: how many arms and legs had they amputated in the name of that "purpose" which would finally be revealed?

"What did you say?" he asked in Russian.

Sergeev gave a quick smile, then put his hands in the pocket of his white coat.

"With your constitution, you'd last a few days. Yes, perhaps a few days. Your gangrene is not the fulminating type."

"Well, bandage it. I'll think it over."

"You've no time for that."

"Nonsense, Doctor. Never in my life have I had so much time for important decisions. But clean up this rotting, stinking flesh. I can't breathe for the smell of my own putrefaction—and your iodine."

With great misfortunes, the hardest thing of all is to know their origin. When cities and enormous forests have been reduced to ashes by mighty conflagrations, the person who ignited the first spark usually remains unknown. No one can testify with certainty how plague and other dread Diseases entered into towns and spread there. The credulous tell stories about this which they don't really believe themselves.

As regards this Epidemic in Serbia, we still don't know the real cause, the place where it originated, or who was its first victim.

My head aches intolerably, and I hear all sorts of things: that the Sickness is airborne; that it is transmitted exclusively by contact; that it is spread by Austrian spies and witches; that it is carried by the wind like pollen, the fragrance of meadows, the stench of dunghills; that it is something from Outer Space, something which has fallen on the earth instead of snow; that it is part and parcel of this damp, chill, dreary, putrefying weather, this frostless, unhealthy winter; that the Sickness is the scourge of God, the punishment for our impiety, the vengeance exacted by the Great Evil for our human stubbornness, the price of our national folie de grandeur, the fate of our poverty-stricken people, sunk deep in the mire.

Everyone of us Sick who is still alive blames somebody. The Opposition blame Pašić and his government, while the soldiers castigate the High Command, which did not provide them with winter clothing and the most essential food; the civilians blame the army because the Sickness first appeared there and was spread by them behind the lines; and all Serbs, men and women alike, curse the Austrian prisoners of war because wherever they are, there the Sickness is, too. *The Patients, for their part, consider the doctors to be the main culprits, regarding them as ignorant men who simply deceive them, while the doctors shift the responsibility to the medical service of the High Command, the State, and our ingrained national propensity to uncleanliness; when the Sickness appears in a house, the women blame their menfolk, who frequent cafés and all other places where there is plague and pestilence. In short, when Sick people think about their Sickness, their very thoughts are Sick.*

In Latin our Sickness has the resounding name of Typhus exanthematicus, while in Serbian it is called Spotted Fever, which sounds gay, derisive, almost mocking.

A young man who studied medicine in Paris, who has treated more than two hundred people here (or so they say), told me last night in confidence that the white louse is the carrier of our Sickness—the white louse!

Mankind's longstanding and excellent acquaintance, which has participated in all important historical events—wars, migrations, revolutions, changes of emperor and pope—a creature that has been a domestic pet ever since man first inhabited the earth: a living organism ever present during the winter season to tickle and amuse the soldiers and the poor under all rulers and all flags, from Alexander the Great and Hannibal to Franz Josef and Vojvoda Putnik—can it really be this creature, the louse, that is killing us now? This in spite of our historical interrelationship, or just because of it—that organic similarity, that climatic and geographical identity, that spiritual interdependence between man and louse? That small, stunted, manyfooted, mournful, dirty little creature, which the Romans called Pediculus vestimenti, threatens to spread disease throughout Serbia! The louse? When I look at it I simply can't believe it, and I understand all my compatriots who refuse to. We have broken the power of the centuries-old Turkish Empire and driven it back into Asia; we have defeated Bulgaria totally, and just a month ago we smashed the Balkan army of the Austro-Hungarian Empire. Yet now it seems the louse, this tiny, insignificant creature, is going to conquer us! What divine anger can this portend?

Man can resist death in human form. But what will happen to mankind and to Serbia when the advancing enemy is this rotund, whitish, bloodthirsty creature no bigger than a tiny grain of wheat?

What can we do in the face of a killer armed only with its millimeter-long proboscis which is nevertheless hard enough to pierce a man's skin and suck and drink a drop of his blood, whether he be hero or coward, and to leave an invisible seed of Sickness within this human monster or on his body? Surely our historic destiny will be ordained by something larger, stronger, and more dignified than the louse? Really, one must laugh with all one's might!

The louse crawls over people, over their ragged clothing in houses and hospitals, on the roads and railways; sucks only human bood and copulates on the bodies of its victims, on their hairy parts, and in their clothing leaves its tiny glistening eggs, which the next day hatch out and become its hungry progeny. Sometimes they die, bursting and leaving a trail of blood between our nails. However, these are insignificant losses in a force that can never be annihilated. I myself have surrendered to the lice. I no longer defend myself against them, no longer scratch myself. I feel that my nonresistance pleases them, and they crawl over me and copulate, staying indefinitely.

Judging from the experience I have acquired by observing people during the Epidemic, a man shows more determination in resisting the first lice, when they begin to infest him and the world around him, but resistance weakens as the number increases. We get used to them and gradually surrender to these creatures of filth. People resist least of all just before they die, and become indifferent to their insignificant killers. By then they have covered our bodies and heads, our eyebrows and moustaches. Chains and necklaces of eggs have filled to bursting the hems of our shirts and tunics. Our clothes, our beds, the whole room is full of lice. We know that the lice have vanquished our country, for which we have made such sacrifices. I hear that public institutions and families, friendships, and love affairs are all in ruins. All kinds of evil swirl around us and within us. Folly is rampant; selfishness and every kind of baseness run riot; all human feeling is stifled or burned out. The horror which grips some souls at the onset of the Sickness changes to a tormented melancholy as soon as the Sickness acquires a serious grip. The patients sink into despair without a sigh, without a spark of resistance. Nothing can rouse them any more, or spur them to any kind of effort.

From time immemorial we have known that the most crushing defeats have always been inflicted by a worthless opponent. Historians have simply failed to perceive this truth: the more insignificant the foe, the more final the defeat. Because only a serious and powerful opponent can arouse in man the desire to resist and create the will to rebel. There has never been a tyranny against which men have not revolted. They have killed emperors and kings, brought down Napoleons and one Louis after another, sent Dantons and Robespierres to the guillotine. Men have been fortunate because of their anger, dreaming of vengeance against the oppressors. But against the rule of the louse, raised up and seated on its throne, men have rarely revolted; they have submitted to it as soon as it begins its attack. The reason is simply this: they do not fear the louse, it inspires no hatred. It wins its victories just by sucking, by bites which do not appear dangerous, by means of dirt that is hardly noticed; and by their sheer numbers, by which people are at first disconcerted, but to which they soon grow accustomed. If the bite of a louse really hurt, if it had a foul smell, then great epidemics would never get under way. But man has not the sense to grasp that the most insignificant foes are in fact the most dangerous, but they rarely offer resistance to a frivolous or worthless oppressor, or to a false and corrupt ruler. A land where lice and dirt reign supreme always has false and corrupt rulers, because such rulers outdo their subjects in cunning and baseness, and please the prevailing nature of the majority.

Such a man, the director, rules over this Hospital: a lazy and incapable man, dishonest and pleasure-loving, a lecher and a liar. Outwardly he is pleasing; he is handsome and has a wide, ready smile for everybody and every occasion. Is it possible that someone can smile in this stinking place? But our amazement doesn't last long. After that we are grateful that he is pleased with life, that he is healthy, that in our Hospital he at least is happy.

Never is it he himself, the director, but always others who are responsible for all the horrors of the Hospital, for our intolerable situation. He scolds and curses the doctors and orderlies with such passion that we have no reason to add one iota to his dissatisfaction; in his words and anger he is always on our side.

Thus the same laws prevail in our Hospital as outside it: rulers without virtues are the most popular. In general, people like those who like what they like, who do what they would do if they were in a position of power—grab everything they can. The rabble hate those who love justice and truth, people who respect the law and work honorably. Here in the Hospital I have observed that the lower *classes show particular devotion to those in power who do not know the truth, because only deception awakens hope in the multitude. Truth leads them to gloom, even despair. When our ruler lies he gives us, his subjects, the right to lie, too. Since he lives without exertion, without any sense of responsibility, without knowledge or conscience, we have an even greater right to live in the same way. If in addition the ruler is a gourmand and full of fun—if he likes meat, song, and a good joke, as our director does—then you have some inkling of the prestige of Doctor Paun Aleksić. The majority of the patients like to hear about his orgies with the volunteer nurses, his nocturnal merry-making. People enjoy seeing and hearing how their lord and master enjoys life; somebody at least should do so amid this Epidemic. If those of us with a high temperature haven't had our memories burned away, we know that corrupt, pleasure-loving, lying rulers have rarely been toppled by revolts. Such men fill the hearts of their subjects with sweet and easy yearnings, quenching anger and the will to resist.*

As in any administration where the director is pleasure-loving and untruthful, not a single division in our Hospital functions properly. Where there is no respect for law or conscience, dirt reigns supreme. Cleanliness and order go with love of truth and respect. In our Hospital the dirt is such as to defy comparison. This suits the Patients admirably, because truth and virtue, cleanliness and order require sustained, unremitting, conscious effort, of which very few people are capable.

I still have the right to put my trust in frost and snow. Only the snow can slightly lessen the impact of dirt, at least as far as our eyes are concerned. Only frost, perhaps, could stifle this ever-present stench. However, here we are in the middle of winter, and there is neither snow nor frost—just slush, rain, and raw cold: damp and gloom everywhere. When day dawned this morning on a light cover of snow, and when we caught sight of something white and clean, some of us felt deeply troubled. Our rooms, our beasts' lairs, our torn and dirty bed-clothes seemed repulsive. Some people, probably those already convalescent, took their blankets and went outside to sit down at least for a moment on something white and clean. The rest of us regarded them with pity and scorn. But that little bit of snow was already gone by midday, so it was easier on our eyes.

If things were not as they are, I would keep silent; I would endure my pains and watch the lice crawling along my veins, trying to climb up the hairs on my forearm, and always falling down. When my temperature drops and the pain in my head subsides and the cramps in my stomach turn into nausea, then I believe that the time has come for astonishment and lies. Whoever survives it, if he is not overcome by shame, will strive to forget it.

3

FROM *Giornale D'Italia:*

THE AUSTRIAN OFFENSIVE IN SERBIA, WHICH ACCORDING TO PUBLISHED REPORTS WAS TO HAVE BEEN A RAPID CAMPAIGN, HAS TURNED INTO A TERRIBLE ROUT. THE SMALL SERBIAN ARMY, THOUGH CONSIDERABLY RE-DUCED IN NUMBERS AFTER TWO BALKAN WARS AND FOUR MONTHS OF CEASELESS FIGHTING ON THE SAVA AND THE DRINA, HAS NEVERTHELESS SUCCEEDED IN FORCING THE AUSTRIANS INTO A RETREAT. JUDGING BY THE NUMBER OF ABANDONED STANDARDS AND CANNON, THAT RETREAT SEEMS TO HAVE BEEN CARRIED OUT WITH GREAT SPEED.

PARIS

FROM *Le Matin:*

THE SMALL STATE OF SERBIA, IN A SINGLE HEROIC GESTURE, HAS SO SMARTLY BOXED THE EARS OF THE OLD EMPEROR IN VIENNA THAT HE HAS SEEN THE THREEFOLD CROWN OF HUNGARY, AUSTRIA, AND BOHEMIA WOBBLING ABOUT ON HIS FOREHEAD, ALMOST READY TO FALL OFF. FOR SERBIA THIS VICTORY MEANS NOT ONLY THE LIBERATION OF HER PEOPLE, BUT ALSO THE UNIFICATION OF THE SERBS, CROATS, AND SLOVENES. WHEN OUR ENEMIES ASK FOR PEACE, SERBIA WILL HAVE THE RIGHT TO PARTICI-PATE IN THE PRELIMINARY DISCUSSIONS ON AN EQUAL FOOTING.

BERLIN

GENERAL VON BLUM, IN *Tägliche Rundschau:*

ONCE AGAIN WE SEE THE STATEMENTS WE HAVE FREQUENTLY MADE IN CONNECTION WITH THE OPINION, TAKEN FROM CURRENT SATIRE, THAT THE

SERBS ARE PIGS. BUT IN OUR VIEW THE SERBIAN ARMY SHOULD BE TAKEN VERY SERIOUSLY AND REGARDED AS A DANGEROUS FOE OF AUSTRIA-HUNGARY.

ST. PETERSBURG

FROM *Novoe Zveno*:

IT WOULD BE EXTREMELY DIFFICULT TO FIND ANOTHER ARMY IN EUROPE WHICH, IN SUCH CIRCUMSTANCES AND WITH SUCH RESOURCES, HAS NOT ONLY REPULSED THE ENEMY BUT ALSO DESTROYED THEIR MILITARY SELF-CONFIDENCE, BEATING THEM TO THEIR KNEES. THIS THE SERBS HAVE DONE, AND IN SO DOING HAVE DEMONSTRATED ONCE AGAIN THE TRUTHFULNESS OF NAPOLEON'S DICTUM THAT VICTORY DEPENDS THREE QUARTERS ON SPIRIT, AND ONLY ONE QUARTER ON MATERIAL RESOURCES.

THE VOJVODAS AND GENERALS AT THE HEAD OF THE SERBIAN ARMY RANK AMONG THE GREAT MILITARY GENIUSES OF ALL AGES.

BUDAPEST

FROM *Vilag*:

SERBIA IS THE GRAVEYARD OF THE HUNGARIAN REGIMENTS. THE COUNTRY THAT IN OUR CAFÉS WE HAVE CALLED "THE DEGENERATE STATE OF KING PETER" HAS PROVED OUR GRAVEYARD. YET WE SAID OF THIS SERBIAN ARMY, "THEY'RE JUST POOR WRETCHES WITHOUT AMMUNITION, AND WITHOUT ANYTHING ELSE EITHER, AND HUNGARY IN THE BARGAIN." THOSE WHO TALKED LIKE THIS ARE NOW GAPING WITH ASTONISHMENT. "A POVERTY-STRICKEN, RAGGED GROUP OF MEN"—THAT'S HOW PEOPLE HAVE ALWAYS SPOKEN AND WRITTEN ABOUT THE SERBIAN ARMY.

BERLIN

FROM *Staatszeitung*:

SERBIA IS NOT SUITABLE TERRAIN FOR FIGHTING, BUT THE SERBS ARE EXCELLENT SOLDIERS, COURAGEOUS, AND WITH EXCEPTIONAL POWERS OF ENDURANCE; THEY FIGHT LIKE HEROES AND SHOW DESPERATE DETERMINATION. PEOPLE WHOSE OPINION CARRIES WEIGHT NO LONGER LABOR UNDER THE ILLUSION THAT THEY WILL EASILY DISPOSE OF SERBIA.

SOFIA

FROM *Mir*:

THE SERBIAN ARMY HAS REDUCED TO DUST AND ASHES AN AUSTRIAN ARMY WHICH GLORIED IN ITS MILITARY LAURELS. THE MILITARY AMBITION OF

AUSTRIA HAS BEEN DEALT A POWERFUL BLOW. THIS WILL OPEN THE EYES OF THAT HANDFUL OF WRETCHED BULGARIANS WHO HAVE BASED THEIR POLITICAL SYSTEM ON AUSTRIA, AND THEY WILL SEE THE FUTURE OF BULGARIA WHEN THEY LOOK AT AUSTRIA.

IT IS POSSIBLE THAT THE SERBIAN SUCCESS WILL NOT LAST, AND THAT NUMBERS AND RESOURCES WILL PROVE STRONGER THAN COURAGE; WHAT MORE CAN BE ASKED OF THE SMALL, EXHAUSTED NATION OF SERBIA? WE ADD OUR SYMPATHY TO THAT OF THE ENTIRE WORLD. THE RECENT SERBIAN SUCCESSES MUST EVOKE A RESPONSE IN EVERY WARLIKE BULGARIAN; FROM PRACTICALLY ALL PARTS OF OUR COUNTRY YOU WILL HEAR THE CRY: WELL DONE, SERBIA!

PARIS

FROM *L'Homme Libre:*
CLEMENCEAU HAS PRAISED THE HEROISM OF THE SERBS AND THE LOYALTY OF THE ALLIES, AND THE REJECTION OF THE AUSTRIAN OFFER TO NEGOTIATE. HE SAYS THE THREE MAJOR ALLIED POWERS MUST RENDER SERBIA ALL POSSIBLE MORAL AND MATERIAL ASSISTANCE.

FROM *Petit Journal:*
WHILE THE SERBS HAVE CROWNED THEMSELVES WITH GLORY IN THE DEFENSE OF THEIR COUNTRY, THE AUSTRIANS CONTINUE TO BRING SHAME ON THEMSELVES BY THEIR BRUTAL ACTIONS ON SERBIAN TERRITORY. HOUSES ARE BEING PLUNDERED, GIRLS AND WOMEN RAPED, OLD PEOPLE AND CHILDREN SHOT. LOATHSOME CRIMINALS HAVE STAINED THE BOSNIAN LAND WITH BLOOD. THE SLAV INHABITANTS EAGERLY AWAIT THEIR LIBERATION.

FROM *Figaro:*
HISTORY OFFERS NO MORE HEROIC SPECTACLE THAN THIS SMALL, COURAGEOUS NATION WHICH HAS STRUGGLED FOR FIVE MONTHS AGAINST AN ENEMY VASTLY SUPERIOR IN NUMBERS, AND INFLICTED ON THEM A CRUSHING DEFEAT AT THE VERY MOMENT WHEN THEY MIGHT HAVE FEARED THE WORST. WHEN THE TIME COMES TO EVALUATE THE CONTRIBUTION OF EACH OF THE ALLIES TO OUR COMMON STRUGGLE, SERBIA'S CONTRIBUTION WILL BE SEEN IN ITS TRUE MAGNITUDE.

To live on one leg, walking with crutches, or not to exist at all? To be a victim of death in war, or a victim of life in peace? Was this the problem that he, Gavrilo Stanković, must ponder, tormenting himself to the breaking point?

Ever since he had been aware of his existence, he had always enjoyed life to the full, always been a whole man, bringing his various desires into harmony, never striving to exalt the spiritual side of his nature over the physical; he never lied to his father, who in his very first words to him had tried to convince him, in a manner peculiarly his own and not altogether in keeping with his priestly calling, that human happiness was to be found in purity of soul, "in superiority over people in general, and in keeping as far removed as possible from many of their affairs." With the best will in the world, he couldn't believe his father, but he never opposed him in word or deed in an offensive way. His father never tried to frighten him with the idea of God; he spoke of Him as he spoke of the universe and nature—as something eternal, invisible, and incomprehensible. "Don't believe in anything founded on fear," he once said to him. Meanwhile, at his father's request, he had read heroic national poems with great excitement, learning Njegoš's *Mountain Wreath* by heart, and also a number of Latin proverbs—one for each day of the week—which his father wrote down in a notebook every Sunday, when he would question him and test his knowledge. He felt in some way ashamed of these Latin proverbs, and as far as he could remember he never used them outside school—except in St. Petersburg. Yes, he had used them in his conversations with Shishkin, who had loved to use his knowledge of classics to confound "stupid dialecticians."

He was sixteen when his father died, on the verge of being irrevocably disappointed in his son. Or was this just how it appeared to him now? If his father were still alive, perhaps his own life would be different; perhaps he would have followed some other path. He didn't really think so. His father's death had brought him so much freedom that he never again had felt restrained by fear or moral precept from the fulfillment of any desire or pleasure. His mother had always faithfully accepted what he did, even when he refused to fulfill his father's wish that he should enter the priesthood. Thanks to her, his acquisition of knowledge and success in schoolwork had not interfered with games and pleasant outings on the Sava and in the Deer Park; at school he learned as much as was essential, but for himself he wanted to know all the things that his contemporaries didn't know, things they didn't learn at school. So in the twelfth grade of high school he could recite from Victor Hugo for an hour at a time and declaim Robespierre's speech on the Republic in French; but that same summer he was one of the five best swimmers on the Sava, and the lover of two distinguished widows—a lover who neither boasted of his success nor concealed it. He wanted to linger in memory over those first joys of manhood, especially over Katarina, who by the force of her surrender had implanted in him a lasting desire and capacity for the cruder aspects of sexual experience. Now, however, his leg would not allow it, his wound would not permit him to stop a while in her entrance hall cluttered with sofas and cushions, where she would wait for him drenched with perfume.

Then when all his childhood, youth, and the first years of manhood fused into a single glance, a single upsurge of recollection, he saw that everything had combined to give him the maximum enjoyment of life. He had been an outstanding athlete, the second-best runner in the military academy, the best rider in his regiment, and an excellent skater in St. Petersburg. He had had physical strength for every kind of effort, and courage whenever he needed it; strength and skill in his fists, to defend his pride and punish insults; and feet to take him wherever he wanted to go, and to flee with from shame, or from those stronger than himself. As a schoolboy, a student at the academy, and an officer, right down to the time when he became a lieutenant, he had never bowed even under the heaviest blows. There had been some, from dishonorable causes, which had filled him with shame; but of course there had been other things in his life, too. How respectfully he had listened to anyone who knew more than he did himself! All those nights when he had sat until daybreak over some good rare book!

So what was it that he should protect most from this gangrene? What did he love most? He loved precisely what others loved and esteemed in him so highly: his strength and his harmony, his beliefs and his voice, his glance and his steps, his carriage and his words. He had consciously striven to acquire and cultivate this harmony, sparing no effort. It was this inner harmony, and not any special gifts, that distinguished him among his contemporaries. He was aware of this, and rarely attempted to do anything beyond his powers; he was quick to flee from "strange forests," as he called circumstances that made heavy demands on him. It had not always been a glorious victory.

Faced now with gangrene, he didn't feel he could respect what he once regarded as his wisdom. No, he couldn't respect it.

The liking which people felt for him, he knew, was founded on his special qualities and abilities as much as on his handsome appearance, his strength, and his health. It was in this makeup of his character and the ideas he advanced, most of which were superior to those of his acquaintances, that he found some compensation for his unsuccessful career as an officer. The fact that he had not suffered too much because of the scorn of his fellow-conspirators, whom he had abandoned two months before the assassination of King Alexander Obrenović; that he had borne without too much trouble their sense of superiority and the vengeance exacted on him as a "traitor"; that no one had ever noticed the wound to his pride because he was only a battalion commander while his classmates commanded divisions— all these things could be explained by his satisfaction with himself and everything that made him what he was. Nor did he have any regrets for his fatal mistakes; he had always felt, and still felt now, that even these brought their own recompense and justification. Not even his sufferings in love, his wild and stormy sorrow for Masha— the defeat that had brought the greatest suffering in his life—had destroyed his faith in himself. This was because he loved everything that was part of himself—everything, even defeats and disgrace.

His health? He had never even had a toothache. The only physical pains he had known were those from bruises received in a fight, corns caused by long marches in ill-fitting boots, and a few falls from his horse. He had had the usual childhood ailments, and had caught a cold three or four times during his carousals in St. Petersburg. Illness had been for him "a state of uncleanliness," and he had never for one moment thought that he would die as a result of it. Once he had decided on a career as an army officer, believing that in this way he could most directly serve the cause of freedom, he had also decided that he would die in battle. Freedom and death were for him inseparable. Dying for freedom gave to freedom the greatest significance; at the same time it was for him the easiest of deaths. Since he believed that wars were looming on the horizon, he believed that he would die young in battle. This feeling was like a sediment in his soul that he often stirred up in moments of solitude. From high school on he was prepared for a short life, and this thought governed all his actions.

During his campaigns and battles, from Kumanovo to Suvobor, it was death that he had feared, not wounds; if a bullet hit him, he firmly believed he would die. He had convinced himself of this, and in so doing had deceived himself. After being wounded on Suvobor, as soon as he regained consciousness and realized that the bullet had blown away half his thigh, for days he had believed the wound would prove fatal. To have been wounded on Previje in the divisional rearguard was the greatest, most momentous disappointment he had ever experienced. His anger had seemed stronger than the pain. So he had felt right up to the time of the Serbian victory, to that early morning in the inn when, lying beside Hans Koegner, he had lit his pipe and slapped Radojko's face because Radojko had been beaten in the wrestling match with Pepi. It was in hopes that he would survive his wound that he had lit his pipe, the pipe which had been disgraced by the Austrian's arrogance and avenged by Bogdan's boldness.

He felt a constant pity for his right leg, as if he had lost his entire body, as if every part of it had been bitten off by that bullet; he felt like this because he knew and loved every part of himself, and because he was hypersensitively aware of the special qualities of every part of his body; from his toenails to his ears, from his fingernails to his hair, he felt a conscious pleasure in himself. There were those who regarded this as narcissism, but such people didn't like him. He for his part had always considered the scorn of Narcissus to be one of the lowest and most stupid manifestations of human hatred. He did not hide his pleasure in himself; he was always spotlessly clean, always dressed in the best linen, suits, and shoes, ate the best food, and drank the best drinks; he looked after himself carefully, rested thoroughly whenever tired, and spent everything he had on himself. His wants were by no means small. A bed in which he felt comfortable, in which he could relax completely and sleep, had given him the greatest trouble. This ideal bed existed only in his old home: it was the bed that had belonged to his father, with bed linen chosen, sewn, and laundered by his mother. He had such respect for his body that he didn't like to make love with women who were not exceptionally beautiful and in love with him. In view of such requirements, he could seldom really be happy; it was even rare for him to laugh. There was no one he despised more than people who laughed easily. As a result, apart from his pain over Masha, he hadn't suffered much in his life. He had never given anything of himself without a price and recompense that he himself determined, and did not consider as lost those things which had been taken away from him.

Being wounded, therefore, had suddenly threatened his whole being; that Austrian bullet had smashed and distorted his life. During those nights on Suvobor, and then as a prisoner, it had seemed to him that he had been wounded long ago, when he parted with Apis and the other conspirators in front of that whirligig at the fair in the Imperial Meadow; thereafter, his self-esteem had simply made him blind to the wound, but he had easily mastered such feelings—or had he?

Perhaps the most painful moment since being wounded and taken prisoner was the last time Doctor Vojtekh had bandaged him, when he had smelled the thick, sweet smell from his wound, a smell so strong that Vojtekh had given a start and Bogdan had turned his head away. "So I'm rotting away, am I—I'm turning into a piece of carrion? Is that it, Doctor?" he had cried, disgusted with himself. He had felt the same repulsion when he saw the first louse on his chest, and was disgusted now by his louse-ridden state. Later, while he was being transported to Valjevo, he had often twisted himself up so that he could sniff at his wound like an animal, in spite of the intense pain this caused him; and he regretted that he didn't have the strength to bite through his wounded leg like a wolf. He lacked strength enough because he didn't care all that much about his life; but was this really true? As revenge for that moment of uncertainty and the stench from his own body he had pressed his wound to make it hurt, pressed until it began to bleed, in his desire to wash away that sweet rotting flesh with blood.

What he found particularly humiliating was being helpless, being unable to see to his own personal needs. How was it that in his reflections about human failure and suffering, about which he had talked so much, he had never given a thought to what a man suffers when he is unable to attend to himself, never thought of the repulsiveness of this situation, of shitting and pissing like an animal? What government can inflict such humiliation as illness? What social injustice could cause such pain as this disgust with oneself and one's body? How had it happened that all philanthropists, reformers, and revolutionaries believed that hunger, poverty, injustice, bondage, and ignorance were the sources of the deepest human suffering, the greatest evils in the world? All the ideologies and religious faiths concerned with human suffering gave little thought or none to the sick and the maimed, to those millions of unfortunates who existed even before wars broke out, and in still greater numbers after them. He himself had considered justice the foundation of everything good in society, an ideal for which no sacrifice was too great; but how could he have foreseen the great injustice which divides the sick from the healthy, the maimed from the whole? He had pondered the humiliations men suffer ever since he was in high school. Countless times he had sat up until the small hours in St. Petersburg, listening to Platonov, Zharov, Shishkin, and Nedzhinov talking about all possible human humiliations, thinking them up with a wild inventiveness that was typically Russian. He had reacted with dilated eyes, his senses aflame at all the insults and offenses which could be inflicted on a man, but never had he given a single thought to how a cripple felt, a man lying helpless on a stretcher.

He had always had strong reasons for not wanting to live as a cripple, and they were still with him now; but they were no longer the only reasons. This horror of impending darkness which he now sensed, a darkness in which everything that formed part of himself would be extinguished—was this the ultimate fear, which had the power to change the significance of everything that made him what he was?

All night long the pains in the shoulder of his amputated arm alternated with dreams from the front and from Prerovo, so that Miloje Dačić couldn't distinguish between dream and reality; Austrian attacks and retreats ended in scything the fields on the banks of the Morava, or playing tiddlywinks in Prerovo, with shells falling in the midst of the games. Perhaps it was the barking of the dogs around the hospital that brought him back to Prerovo, while the sudden silence transported him to the battlefield; or maybe for most of last night he had been lying at the bottom of an old rowboat, being pounded by some strangers and crushed by sacks of maize; in this state he sailed down the Morava, hit the floodgates, and smashed the wheel of the watermill, until he finally sank beneath the water; now he was being rescued from this muddy whirlpool by the hubbub around him and the voice of Vukajlo, his corporal, whispering in his ear: "Dačić, shove this into your corner and cover it up with straw!"

Miloje gripped the edge of his blanket with his left hand, so that Vukajlo couldn't see him; he was wondering whether he should go on hiding the watches, tins of tobacco, and pocket knives which Corporal Vukajlo had stolen during the night from dead or badly wounded men. That old thief had enough now, either in his bag or stashed with Miloje, to stock a small shop. It was true that they had both been wounded at the same time, and that he owed his life to the corporal, but never again would Vukajlo order him to fix his bayonet, or swear at him for being a hick. Now that he had lost an arm, Miloje Dačić was not dependent on any general, or on Vojvoda Mišić, or even on the King. His life and his remaining arm were no longer at the disposal of the State and the Fatherland. The oath was not valid for men with only one arm, so to hell with the King, the Fatherland, and Vukajlo!

With a curse Vukajlo pulled the blanket away from his face; Miloje began to resist, but the pain in his right shoulder broke his stubbornness.

"Why are you so grumpy? Hide this away someplace and don't open it, or I'll split your guts."

Miloje took a small parcel and shoved it under the straw against the wall. "Well now, let's see what you copped last night!"

"You try, and I'll break your other arm!"

Vukajlo, who had been wounded in the buttocks by a piece of shrapnel, rolled over onto his own place, accompanied by curses from Miloje, who felt a strong desire to unwrap the stolen parcel and show it to everyone in the room.

"Miloje, just look at that thing in the corner!" said Sibin quietly, lying on his stomach. "Is that a bed, or is the fever making me see things?"

"You're seeing things! That's a carriage drawn by two fine horses," said Miloje, without looking at the major's bed; then he again covered his head with his blanket, so as not to see the sick and wounded men as they pressed around the slop pail and urinated, even though he had to listen to the muttering and whispering that marked the beginning of another day.

Look here, gang, is that a real bed? Where do you think it was made? In Germany—there's lots of counts and fine folk there. But how did it get to Valjevo? Why couldn't the Russians make a bed like that, if they made the biggest bell in the world? The Russians just don't have people who know that trade. Anyone seen those flowers on the bed, almost real, like? It's a rose all right, and yet it isn't. What do you mean, a rose, you must have a fever. Maybe I have, but you just tell me what those flowers are. Those are flowers of paradise, you old peasant, and the birds are birds of paradise. Orderly, bring me some water, or I'll rip you open with a bayonet! And what do you think your wife's doing now, Mika? Milking the cows and putting out the hay for the cattle, I suppose. More likely some rotter is milking *her,* you idiot. He's singing again—hit him in the teeth! Well, let him, it's the last time he'll do it. Look, gang, that guy next to me has shitted again! Who'd like to have a bet with me that the knobs and casters on that bed are made of real gold? My God, is this place supposed to be a hospital? I'll bet you ten dinars that those flowers aren't roses! Can't you see how many leaves there are, you fool? You might as well go on babbling, you won't do it much longer. Has anyone ever seen a bird of paradise, you stupid bastard? Now how could a bed like that belong to a king or an emperor, when there's one like it here in this stinking hole? What do you say to that, gang? Why haven't they given it to Vojvoda Mišić instead of to an ordinary major? Oh, shut up, I want to go to sleep, I didn't sleep a wink last night. It's already daylight, stop making such a row. My God, is this really our country? It's high time someone lit the stove, we'll all freeze to death. I'm rotting away anyhow. What am I going to light the stove with? Well, you can at least piss into it. Stick it out, after all, you're a Serb. Whoops, there's my old cock straightened up again! As soon as I see somebody worse than me, I feel better. Same here. Quiet, all of you! The doctor's coming on his rounds.

Miloje Dačić removed the blanket from his face: a doctor was standing in the open doorway, with two orderlies carrying an empty stretcher.

"Did anyone in this bunch kick the bucket last night?"

"Yes, Doctor, the man next to me. I heard his rattle a while back."

"The Holy Archangel took off my neighbor last night, too."

"And the guy next to me. I never even heard him."

"Take them away at once," said the doctor to the orderlies, and went out.

"Doctor," someone pleaded, "if you won't give us an injection, can't you at least give us a powder?"

"The visit is over," said the orderlies, setting down the stretcher next to a dead man.

Miloje Dačić covered his head with his blanket. If I survive, he thought, and get out of this hospital, I'm not going back to Prerovo, or any place where there are people. I'll build myself a hut on the top of Kopaonik and stay there alone with the animals. I don't want any neighbors, no one to hear when I lie down and I get up, no one to know when I'm miserable or I'm happy. I don't want to ask anybody for anything, or to give anything to anybody. I don't want to hear any human voice, or even the sound of any man's rooster or dog.

"It's time now, Major. You've slept well; you're rested. The best possible preparation for an operation," said Doctor Sergeev in Russian.

He couldn't open his eyes: they'd cut off his leg. All he wanted to do was go on lying in his bed, in its clean, white bedclothes, for a whole month. Then to sleep in his own bed at home, to look at the Sava and its island, to watch the sun set over the woods of Srem from his father's armchair on the porch of the house. Now the sun would set over *our* woods, and disappear over *our* horizon. The sun would no longer shed its warmth over the Austro-Hungarian Empire after midday, something which had annoyed him intensely all his life. The entire sky above Belgrade would be Serbian. One of the aims of his life would be realized. His sacrifice would not be in vain. What else would not be in vain? What would come of it all? Freedom, the unification of all the Serbs, the union of the South Slavs, a great state. What about justice? Yes, there would be justice, too. Why was he a cripple? Why? Because of everything that had caused him to go to the military academy, to don an officer's boots and uniform. Surely there must be more reasons for justification and hope?

He opened his eyes: those hands! Doctor Sergeev's long, bony fingers, rhythmically drumming against each other. Unbearable!

"No, Doctor, you're not going to operate on me!" He could feel his cheeks burning and sweat breaking out on his temples.

Sergeev quickly put his hands into the pockets of his white coat. "Listen, Stanković, let's be sensible. I'm not a doctor because I like medicine. I'm not a surgeon because I enjoy cutting up the human body with a scalpel while a man is lying helpless. I find such work disgusting. I can't think of anything worse. But a man must be saved from a stupid and messy death. That's essential! Are you listening to me, Major?" said Sergeev in Russian, so slowly that Gavrilo felt irritated.

"Speak up—talk in a normal voice!"

Sergeev sat down on the edge of the bed. "I came to Serbia a month after the war broke out," he continued. "I came for humanitarian reasons, and because I'm a Slav. I had no idea that you Serbs were such an unfortunate people! Everyone here encourages suffering, prolonged suffering."

"What makes you think I'm that way?"

"Don't bite my head off! We're both Slavs. Our stories don't begin where Westerners think human stories begin."

"What has all this to do with my leg?"

"It's important spiritually. To tell you the truth, only half of what you Serbs suffer is genuine suffering for which you can't be blamed. The other half is something you should be ashamed of. Have I offended you?"

"What are we to be blamed for?"

"In Russia, too, there are people who have a passion for defiling every kind of pain, but only a few. With you Serbs, it's the majority. Many of you transform suffering into something ugly. Yes, something ugly and unclean. I've never yet met a Serb who was ashamed of his suffering."

"But we feel much more shame than you Russians do. Don't talk to me about these things; I know you."

"Yes, what you say is true. We're not ashamed of suffering either, but we're not so arrogant about it as you Serbs. Yes, Gavrilo Stanković, you Serbs are arrogant. Believe me, it's difficult to be a faithful friend to you."

"What are you trying to tell me?"

Sergeev lit a cigarette and inhaled a few puffs of smoke. "I want to tell you, like a brother, that the death which hangs over you is not the sort of death you should die."

Gavrilo propped himself on his elbows, his face contorted with pain. "Are you trying to tell me that I should die a heroic death—on the battlefield, at the head of a battalion or a regiment, or in a cavalry charge? Is that it, Nikolay Maksimovich? I should die from a saber cut, or be blown to pieces by a shell?"

"No, my dear Major, it's not that. I have no reverence for the kind of death that any fool may deserve. It's just that I think a man should have the kind of death which he has chosen, of which he is worthy. One must think about such a death, and work for it. That's a man's real task in life, perhaps the greatest. It requires intelligence, willpower, special gifts. Do you follow me?"

"Well, I'm not contradicting you," Gavrilo said quietly, sinking back on his pillow. He was silent for a few moments, then raised himself once more. "Listen, every insect, every fly, has the will to survive, and man more than most; but to exist doesn't mean to live under *all* conditions."

"I don't believe it's the strong who have thought up such sayings."

"You mean it's cowardly to run away from pain and humiliation, don't you? How many people have done this, and still do it?"

Sergeev leaned forward. "I am summoning you to do something greater."

Gavrilo couldn't endure the expression in his eyes, so he looked at the crack in the ceiling. Sergeev continued brusquely: "Really, Gavrilo Stanković, there's no sense in dying a stupid, pointless death —in dying from the *anaerobe bacteria,* as modern science calls it. One of the most common and ordinary infections."

Gavrilo felt irritated by this professional talk about something outside the range of his knowledge, something for which there were no alternative words and concepts; he was offended by this superiority, this didactic tone, this concern for his life. Was it worth so little that it depended on proofs of its value? This was a typically Russian disease: to turn every mortal thing into words!

"So what do you consider the right kind of death, the death one deserves?" he asked sharply, trying to smile.

"It's the kind of death which helps to create us, or completes our being. That's what I mean."

"Well, perhaps I've chosen just such a death. I mean death from gangrene," said the major in a challenging tone.

Sergeev raised his eyebrows in amazement, leaving the cigarette still in his mouth. Then he folded his hands over his chest: "You haven't much time to choose your fate."

"Have you no stronger proof than that of the value of life, Doctor?"

Sergeev remained silent for a few moments, then stammered in embarrassment, "Would you like me to give you an injection of morphia?"

"No, thank you. I prefer to endure the pain in my leg," said Gavrilo in Serbian, and turned his face to the wall.

If only he could fall asleep again! All he wanted was to sleep, and not to see and hear those who thought they knew more about his life than he did. The thick, sweet odor of his wound, and the smell of iodine and gauze, filled his nostrils; he pressed the eiderdown to his face to breathe in the scent of clean bed linen, that familiar scent of his mother's linen—a mixture of soap, ironing, and his mother's fingers. A redolence of love and anxiety, of her tireless concentration on the well-being of her son. The dark acts of devotion bestowed on linen, typical of widows. He ought to write a letter to his mother before nightfall, while his brain was still clear. But what could he say to her in this last letter? Should he tell her that he had no wish to live as a cripple, though he knew very well that he would never be a cripple for her, even without both legs? Or should he write: Mother, I've decided to die. Could he really say that to her, when she had grieved so long because her only son had given up his army career after breaking with Apis and his fellow-conspirators, and gone into voluntary exile in St. Petersburg, deceiving her by saying that he was attending the highest military academy there, and in this way justifying the money he spent? During those six years in Russia he had spent all her inheritance from her father, several hundred ducats, and all she could spare from her widow's pension, from her own food. Yet never in a single letter had she asked about his studies, nor had she said a word about it when he came back. I don't want to live with only one leg: how could he say that to his mother, who, just before he rejoined the army, had implored him to get married and leave her a daughter-in-law who would bear grandchildren? This had been her entreaty when he had returned home after midnight, as was his custom, and she was waiting for him, as she always did, to offer him a cup of cold milk. He had remained silent. He couldn't tell her that he was deeply in love with a young Russian girl, Masha, who had abandoned him just when he was convinced that she loved him most—abandoned him because of her desire to swing and whirl through the air, because of a game. He had pushed his mother away, left her as he would leave his overcoat on the bench on the porch. When they parted, just before he left for the frontier, his mother had again said, weeping: "Please, my darling, choose the prettiest of your girls! I hear you've got plenty. Choose the prettiest, and tell her to come here and live with me. I'll obey her and look after her as I look after you, and wait for her to give me grandchildren. But don't go away to war until you've brought her here." Then he sat down on the seat beside her and told her; she had taken both his hands and placed them in her lap. It was the first time he had confided his sufferings to anyone outside Russia; the first time he had admitted the fact of Masha's existence to anyone since his return to Serbia. It was moonlight, and he couldn't help seeing her eyes; she had dropped his hands and gasped. He had got up and gone to his room, taken off his boots, and lain down on his bed without undressing. When she had wakened him to leave for the barracks, he saw the linen sheet over him, and had shuddered from a feeling of horror, some kind of premonition.

"I've brought you a cup of milk, Major." He heard the husky voice of Milena Katić, and the thumping of his own heart. How did that gentle, fragile girl come to have such a deep voice? What woman in his life had had such a voice? He turned around and stared at her with astonishment, and also with entreaty: perhaps it was she, not Sergeev, who could convince him that he should go on living with only one leg, that life was worthwhile, even as a cripple. But he couldn't see this in her eyes. Her lips were trembling, too. She was saying something hesitantly.

"I can't hear you, Miss Katić."

"Please call me Milena."

"Thank you, Milena."

"Bogdan is delirious. Doctor Pantelić won't let his mother take him home. If his temperature doesn't go down by tonight . . ."

"Bogdan!" he exclaimed, and fixed his eyes on the crack in the ceiling. He had forgotten all about Bogdan! Since the morning he hadn't looked at him or spoken to him. But she must surely know that he was more seriously ill than Bogdan, that his crisis—a crisis which had only one solution—was not the same as Bogdan's. Here we are again in front of the whirligig, he thought; and once again he was looking at a youthful face over his shoulder.

"Major Stanković, why don't you do as Doctor Sergeev says?" she said quietly, bending over him.

"Doctor Sergeev? Do you think the same as he does?"

"Yes, of course I do."

It seemed to him that the mattress was beginning to creak from the tremors that shook his body, so he gripped the iron rods of the head-board with both hands. He didn't know what to do, the way she was looking at him. Yet she was just a child—she could be his daughter. Where did she get this superiority, this confidence?

"Listen, Milena, since you feel so strongly about a certain matter—like human life, my life, let's say—answer this one question. Mind you, I'm sure that you're your father's daughter, that you have his character. Why are you frowning? Of all politicians, apart from Tucović and two or three other socialists, I respect your father most of all, but that really isn't important. Forgive me, my mind is confused. Do you really think that I value my life so highly that I would permit others to support it when it has already begun to decline?"

"It's your leg I'm thinking of. Your wound."

"All right, my leg, Would you mind moving it a little to the left?" She did so deftly, but it was no use: the huge, burning, dead weight almost dragged him down.

"You must have the operation!"

"Why must I?"

"Because you're a brave man, and a brave man loves life."

"So a brave man loves life, does he? Where have you heard that, or read it? That a brave man doesn't commit suicide?"

"Here in the hospital, Major Stanković. I've learned everything I know about courage here."

He looked at her in astonishment. "What else have you learned here?"

"Please don't cross-examine me like my father!"

"All right, I won't; but tell me one more reason why I should consent to have my leg amputated."

"Major Stanković, surely you don't need me to convince you that you must go on living? You must," she added, confirming the words by a movement of her head.

He could see her fingers were trembling. He held his breath in order to listen to what she would say, and watched carefully every flicker of expression on her face, so as to distinguish between compassion and the kind of love that isn't capable of compassion—Masha's kind of love. Milena grew confused and looked timidly at the wounded men, who had stopped talking to listen. Gavrilo felt sure that she could hear him trembling, and with his eyes he asked the unspoken question: Do you realize, my girl, that you are the only person here who knows the facts and has the power to convince me that life is worth living, even as a cripple? Her eyes, her face, and her hands showed that she knew this, but she was struck speechless, and would have liked to run away. He raised himself up, plunging into the very depths of the pain in his leg, to see that silence in her eyes.

With a groan, Bogdan called her; she escaped from Gavrilo's gaze and turned toward him. Gavrilo fell back on his pillow.

Tola Dačić, carrying a sack over his shoulders, searched all the hospitals, corridors, and sheds—everyplace where there were sick and wounded men. "Is there anyone here by the name of Miloje Dačić?" he cried. "He's quiet, not the kind you'd notice easily. Wouldn't hurt a fly. A bit on the rough side, my Miloje, but you can see his cap head and shoulders above other folks in a crowd." All he got in response were crude jokes.

Although he had already once called out Miloje's name from the door of a room in which he had seen an exceptionally large and beautiful bed, he paused once more in the doorway to gaze at that marvelous object, where a man with a beard lay; he must be a colonel or a general. Tola looked at this ornate white bed and couldn't help wondering what it was doing there among all those unfortunate creatures lying on the floor; the bed seemed so inconceivable that it didn't arouse in him any resentment or envy toward the man who was in it. The craftsman who made it must have had golden fingers, he said to himself as he turned to go into the next room. He collided with Milena Katić. "Ah, my girl! You must be Vukašin's daughter."

"Yes, I am. And you must be from Prerovo," she said, pausing on her way to Bogdan Dragović with some tea and aspirin.

"My name's Tola Dačić, and I live right next door to your grandfather. You saw me in the autumn with your Uncle George. Do you remember?"

"Yes, I remember very well. How's my grandfather?"

"Oh, he's all right, and in good health," said Tola, putting down his sack, "but he worries a lot about you and your brother. God grant that he's alive and well. He sends you his greetings and some quince; and he says you're to come to Prerovo as soon as you get leave."

Milena felt both pleased and sad: she had never yet seen her grandfather. What terrible thing could have happened between him and her father? She wanted to ask Tola, but she was in a hurry to get to Bogdan; she'd talk to Tola when she had a little time to spare.

"Are you going to stay here with your son for a few days?" she asked him.

"You mean Miloje? Where is he?"

"Over there in the corner. He's all right now, don't worry."

"Why couldn't he answer me, the silly fool? I called his name out twice when I came into this room this morning," he muttered, overwhelmed by joy. He followed Milena to where Miloje lay with a blanket over his head.

"Miloje, your father's here."

Tola put down his sack and bent over Miloje, afraid to remove the blanket from his face. "Were you hit in the head, my boy, so you can't see or hear me?" he whispered.

Slowly and hesitantly Miloje removed the blanket from his face, staring at the ceiling as he did so. Tola bent down lower, but didn't dare to touch Miloje's forehead or his hand; he was so thin and pale, unshaven too, poor boy, but he was *alive!*

"Yes, I can see you and hear you all right, but I don't want you to look at me any more," said Miloje slowly

"Why do you feel like that, Miloje?"

Miloje bit his lip and turned his head to the wall. What was one son to a father who had four, three of them still alive? Even if he'd been an only son, his father wouldn't sacrifice his life for him. When he saw that he'd lost an arm, he'd pretend to feel sorry, but he'd be thinking: What will he do at home, who's going to feed him? I'll have him around my neck till the end of my days. Since the bullet hit him, why didn't it go a bit higher up, a bit to the left, so that I could take a good swig of brandy and shout out to the folks at Prerovo: "Two of my sons have lost their lives! Show me another man who's lost two sons!"

Tears welled up in Tola's eyes, and he turned to Sibin, who was lying on his stomach. "Is he badly wounded?"

"They've cut off his arm," whispered Sibin.

"Is that all?" exclaimed Tola, with a mixture of happiness and despair as he turned toward Miloje. "Well, my boy, you're in luck! There is a God in heaven, no doubt about it! Just think where the bullet might have hit you, and what those doctors might have cut off! But now nobody can do anything to us any more!"

Miloje turned his face still further toward the wall.

"Did they take it all off?" Tola asked Sibin.

"Yes."

Tola bent his head, then whispered to Sibin: "Do you know what they did with it?"

"I've no idea, old man."

"How can I find out?"

"Sergeev would know, and that nurse Milena, who helps him."

"When did they do it?"

"On Wednesday."

"I'm alive, you needn't whisper!" interrupted Miloje crossly, his face still turned away.

"I'm glad you're alive, boy! I can come see you and help you until your wound heals up. Then we'll go to Prerovo, God willing. The winter will pass, and spring will come. Sunshine and green leaves heal all wounds. I'm not worried about you any more. If only I had news of Blagoje and Aleksa, I'd be on top of the world. Now, my boy, just look at what your mother and sisters-in-law and nephews have sent you. See what I've brought for you and your friends." He removed the bag from his sack, and took out first of all a large loaf of bread.

That lump was making itself felt as Sergeev's injection began to lose effect; the burning pain of his wound throbbed and pulled at the bandages. Let it hurt! If it didn't hurt, he wouldn't have to torment himself over the last decision. The pain of his wound alone wasn't enough for that decision. But why did he have to die with all this pain? Just sleep, Gavrilo Stanković, sleep in this royal bed, the most comfortable you've ever slept in, a bed worthy of your last sleep. It's not a matter of chance you're in this bed; you've done something to deserve it.

His mother, who had had a stroke, would soon follow him. He had no sisters, so he would leave no sorrow behind him. His uncles and other relatives had their own families to grieve over. Masha would perhaps never know that he was dead. He had written to her many times, until he could stand it no longer. Anyway, her tears would merely be a sign of pity. As for other people whom he had loved, he hadn't loved them so much that he could feel sorry for them, or that their grief could mean very much to him now. They would see him go with a sigh, perhaps a brief expression of regret, usually that most stupid one of all: he was a marvelous man, he was a silly fool, he didn't belong to this world, he was . . . Not a single tear would be shed for him. What a bitch is vanity!

His friends—Apis and those others . . . Friendships founded on ideas and on the loyalty of conspirators enjoyed the fate of those ideas and of that particular conspiracy. The objective for which he had risked his life had brought a victory rewarded by stars and epaulets. A disastrous friendship, indeed! Then those friendships in St. Petersburg with the revolutionaries, especially fanatics like Platonov and Shishkin—these would have dissolved into hatred if after 1905 he had had the courage to speak his mind, to tell them that after the destruction of an unjust order there is an even harder task—to change oneself, to introduce a rational order inside one's own skin, running through one's own veins and bones; to attain freedom in one's heart and establish justice in one's head; to finish with one's own selfish-ness and subdue one's own vanity. That's right, one must first of all cut out evil at its root, without killing and destruction. If he had admitted to them that in his heart of hearts he was not prepared to submit himself completely to the "higher purposes" of a secret organi-zation, in which an unknown leader would decide when and for what he should give up his life, he would have been despised as a coward. He hadn't dared remark even to Raguzin that these revolutionaries, in their passion for justice, created injustices where there had been none before. How those idealists would have kicked him and trampled him if he had confessed that he was no longer capable of fighting for an objective, any objective, that justified all possible means. Yet these people were the best he had ever known.

As for the boyhood friendships that he had tried to renew after his return from Russia, they continued only for sentimental reasons. The friendships of wartime, forged at the front, were nourished on suf-fering and the remembrance of unpleasant experiences; a man could not commit himself wholly to them. Could it be true that he hadn't loved anyone that much, that he himself didn't mean that much to anybody, so that it didn't matter to the rest of the world whether Gavrilo Stanković was dead or a cripple? Vanity again! Make no excuses! You're alone now. If it wasn't for your orderly Radojko and Bogdan, who's delirious now, you'd be quite alone. Where had he set out for, but not arrived?

Even when he had believed that the liberation and unification of all the Serbs was the mission of his generation, when he had broken his promise to his father and entered the military academy instead of going to Kiev to study theology—his life had been twisted and broken: while studying military tactics and strategy, at first secretly and with a sense of guilt, he was reading everything he could lay his hands on about the French Revolution, and studying the works of Herzen, Chernyshevsky, and Svetozar Marković. So for him national liberation and social justice became fused into a single ideal, for which it was necessary to fight in a different way from that taught in the military academy, and to use different strategy and tactics. But this conviction was very dangerous; it could exist only deep in the heart and demanded courage of the highest order. Even then he had understood clearly that no power except love brought such undiluted enjoyment as courage. If there was a God, then He must be a God of courage. To dare to do everything he could think of, to dare even to oppose death, to put it to the test, to do what others could not and dared not do—this was what had tormented and excited him all his life, and still did tonight.

When as an army officer with the rank of captain he had violated his oath to King Alexander Obrenović without any pang of conscience, and had sworn with Apis to rid Serbia of the Obrenović dynasty, then broken with the conspirators because he couldn't agree to kill one king so that another might rule Serbia—that had been the turning point in his fate. So as not to be a traitor, he had parted from Apis three months after the plot had been carried out, resigned his commission, and gone to Russia, telling his mother that he would pursue advanced military studies in St. Petersburg. Instead, he had continued to study the teachings of Herzen and Kropotkin, Lizogub and Kravinsky; he had become the friend of the St. Petersburg revolutionaries, the brother of Slav rebels in Prague and Vienna. Every day he had written and received letters, all of them dealing with the fate and future of the Balkans, the Slavs, and mankind.

How dark and serious had been his passion for ideals during those years of his life! How strong had been his desire for destruction, how powerful his dreams of a new world! It was all an illusion, but of all illusions, it was the least. Well, he had no regrets about his sins, his illusions, or indeed about anything. No, he had no regrets about his evil deeds! Everything I have done—all my life experience—is *mine,* he thought.

What a life it had been! The years in St. Petersburg he considered a prolonged luxury, a rare privilege. He had devoted himself entirely to his passions and his ideas, to Masha and his friends; it never occurred to him in those days that he could lose some of these things or grow old, nor had he pondered what would happen once he had spent the last of his mother's money. He had lived as he pleased and nothing had been lacking in his life, not even his native country. He had tried hard to learn as little about it as possible, had avoided meeting his compatriots, and read only headlines about Serbia in the newspapers. Not that he felt offended in any way; after all, he had left his country of his own free will. He let the future decide about his return, entrusting it to fate, and yet he knew the return was inevitable.

The morning he read that Austria-Hungary had occupied Bosnia and Hercegovina, his blood had boiled at the great wrong done to his people. In that moment he remembered the porch of his house in Belgrade, the window of his room which overlooked the Sava and the imprisoned sky. Suddenly St. Petersburg and everything he had experienced there lost meaning. He sat down and wrote a letter to General Putnik, asking him to take him back into the army and assign him whatever rank and place of service he thought fit. Putnik had replied more quickly than he expected, telling him to come home immediately and present himself to the General Staff for further orders. Three days later he finished his packing; then, suddenly struck by grief, he began to drink and carouse with his friends, and by the time he had sobered up he was in the train, hurrying away from St. Petersburg through the first snowdrifts of the approaching Russian winter. He remembered Masha and realized that he was leaving her forever. That thought was like a bullet piercing his breast, and he wanted to jump off the train at the next station. Even if he had left the train then, however, he would surely have taken it again in 1912. Everything had happened as it had to. The shell that hit him on Suvobor had been fired at him long ago, perhaps the day of his birth. Had the short span of his life been too long? Had the gangrene entrenched itself in his skin as soon as he learned to walk, as soon as he began to run? Was it already there when he embraced Katarina, when he went skating with Masha on the frozen Neva?

The burning pain reached to the top of his thigh. Radojko was standing sleepily next to his bed, looking at him sadly.

He tried to curl up under the eiderdown, but the thick stench of his wound filled his nostrils.

The sick and wounded men were scolding the orderlies for waiting till dusk to bring wood to light the stove. He hadn't noticed that the room was unheated, or if they had had anything to eat, or if the doctor had come through on a visit. The men who were cursing the orderlies and the director—those discontented men who envied him and hated him because of the bed—would all survive their wounds and sickness. The quiet and courteous would not. He heard Radojko cough. Radojko was standing by the bed; he would stand there all day long, looking at him, waiting for him to open his eyes and give some orders, waiting to obey him, to carry out his every wish. Really, his life had not been entirely in vain if he deserved such devotion from a single soldier.

"Radojko, is there anything I can do for you now?" he asked softly. "Why are you silent, Radojko? Tell me, the way you would a buddy."

"I'd like you to have your supper, sir. I've got a roast chicken here."

Gavrilo relapsed into silence. Should he go on living just because of Radojko, to receive his kindness, which sought no return?

"If you don't want it cold, should I warm it up, sir?"

"By all means, Radojko, warm it up." But the thought of food was so repugnant that he knew he'd vomit the first mouthful.

Radojko was hurt and saddened by the few mouthfuls the major managed to swallow. All his effort had been in vain. Why had the major chosen that evening to ask if there were anything he could do for him? He was sorry because he had slapped Radojko—that was why. He ought to have said, Just watch me when I wrestle with Pepi next—I'll throw him to the ground!

"Are you thirsty, sir?" asked Radojko, still standing in his place.

"No, I'm not. You go off to bed."

"I'll get all the sleep I want, sir, don't worry."

"But I can't get off to sleep while you're standing there. Go away now, and come at daybreak. I'll have made up my mind by then."

Under the eaves of the hospital roof Radojko ate half the chicken, stuffed the rest into his bag, then went out into Valjevo in search of Pepi. The prisoners would be gathered around the pot, so he should be able to find him. All day he had been looking for Pepi in every hospital, but there was no sign of him; it was as if he had disappeared into the earth, yet he knew for sure that Pepi had been sent to Valjevo. Those two wrestling defeats bothered him terribly, especially the last one, after the Serbian victory. The shame and disgrace he had experienced in front of the major and the wounded men refused to go away. His cheek still smarted from that blow; while he was thinking about the major or doing something for him, he would suddenly remember the burning sensation in his right cheek and, after the blow, that shrill cry in his ears before he went to sleep. Since his disgrace, the major's words and the look in his eyes hadn't been the same. Everything in their relationship was upset. The major didn't give him orders the way he used to, nor did he feel the same pleasure in carrying them out. Not even the bed had dispelled the dark look in the major's eyes, nor the reproachful edge in his voice when he tried to say something pleasant in his usual way. Bogdan was different, too, though Bogdan had never forgiven the major for punishing Radojko in front of all those people, including Pepi and the Austrians, just when our army had broken through to the Drina.

As he hurried along the main road into town, suddenly he stopped in the darkness and felt his face, felt his cheek marked by the major's thick fingers. Why hadn't he hit him at night, when no one could see? How could he go back to his village and face people there once it got around that he, a famous wrestler, had been thrown into a puddle by a one-legged Austrian? No one would bother to mention that this Austrian was the champion of all Vienna, of a great empire. People forget everything except your shame—that's what they love to remember! Worst of all, the major wouldn't forget his disgrace. He was the kind who remembered what was best forgotten. There was no way out: he must find Pepi. He would turn Valjevo upside down! He hurried down the road, floundering in the mud.

In the streets he peeped into every group of Austrians lying on boards, small piles of straw, or torn-up fences laid on the pavement, since such was their hospital. He went into every room where he heard people speaking German and called Pepi's name. He asked about him among the Croat and Serb prisoners from across the Danube, told them what Pepi looked like, and offered them tobacco and brandy if they would find him. The Austrians nudged each other and muttered in their own language. Radojko was angry because they couldn't understand him, and swore at them. But there was no sign of Pepi, and Radojko grew threatening. He wouldn't sleep a wink that night; he'd go on looking for Pepi until daybreak, when he must make tea for the major and bring him cold compresses. He'd search attics, cellars, sheds, and henhouses. He'd leave no stone unturned in Valjevo, because now he knew exactly how Pepi had been able to trick him and throw him—how Pepi had deceived him by evading his blow, then taken a flying leap at his side and crushed his spleen, so that his arm grew limp and he felt a pricking sensation under his heart, as though he'd been caught on the tip of a bayonet. This time he wouldn't wrestle with him in front of the sick and wounded soldiers; he'd wrestle in the marketplace, where the women would smile at him and some old man egg him on. The major would burst out laughing; after all, he was a real man, he'd have to say, "Well done, Radojko," when he told him that he had bounced Pepi on the cobblestones. Or should he throw him in a mud puddle? If only the major would agree to that operation, or his wound will carry him off before then!

"Pepi. Pepi! Where are you? It's me, Radojko! Damn you, you Fritzies! What good's your language if you can't understand a simple question?"

Gavrilo Stanković wriggled himself to the side of his bed and placed his hand on Bogdan's head.

"Are you better now, Bogdan? Yes, I think you are. You're less feverish than last night. Now we can talk. There's something I must tell you—something I must ask you. You must answer me truthfully. I know you're not afraid to speak the truth."

Bogdan Dragović was immersed in a sizzling, nauseous darkness in which dogs growled and tore at each other. With a great effort he extricated himself from it and raised his head: above gleamed the white bed, looming right up to the ceiling, the major's bed, Radojko's bed. The light bulb in the corridor had burned out. An old man lit a candle; it would set fire to his beard.

"Bogdan, would you let them cut off your leg?" whispered the major, grasping the headboard rods and propping himself up so that he could see Bogdan's face in the darkness.

Bogdan didn't reply.

Gavrilo sank back on his pillow and lit his pipe. The tobacco was bitter and smelled unpleasant—his blood was spreading the poison from the gangrene through all his senses, but he was determined to smoke the pipe to the end.

What should he say to Bogdan tonight? What should he confide to him from his own life's experience, how should he advise and instruct him—this young man who could have been his son, who resembled him in many ways, and who faced the same fate? For Bogdan too would see that victory belonged to those who loved power and honor, and that his victory would not give birth to what he called the "future." Gavrilo had great fondness for Bogdan, especially since the time Bogdan had risked his life for the major's pipe. That was what he wanted to talk to him about tonight. Should he try to convince him that it was pointless to risk one's life for a pipe? At Bogdan's age one didn't realize that defeat gives greatness to justice and right, and bestows its true value on freedom. Did Gavrilo have the right to draw such bitter conclusions on the basis of his own defeat, which had not been of any great significance, and which hadn't really cost him much? No, indeed, defeat was no excuse. Had the moment come when he should say something to his "son"? Perhaps these were his last hours, when he could still think about things and remember them, before the gangrene poisoned his brain. What about his decision? He'd do something about that next morning at daybreak; he'd suddenly say, "Cut it off!"—as if giving his battalion the order to charge. Was there anything at all in which a young man should firmly believe? Any advice or experience that could do him some good? Bogdan might not survive his wound and his pneumonia, but he was the one person Gavrilo could talk to tonight and so postpone his decision. He hadn't seen Milena for some time, and she was too young to understand. He would ask that pretty girl if she could love a cripple. Don't kid yourself, Gavrilo! You got your answer in front of that whirligig, resounding with Masha's and Zubov's laughter. You knew then and you know now that there's no creature more wretched than an aging lover. Now you must find other means to justify what life has taught you. Still, he must pass on some small truths to this young socialist, this enthusiastic and ambitious young man. Certainly those truths wouldn't bring him much pleasure. Had he nothing more significant to tell him tonight?

The light from the candle lit up Bogdan's face; the major met his damp, feverish gaze. There was something sad in his expression. He had always been aware of this in Bogdan, despite his physical strength and self-confidence. Suddenly Bogdan whispered, "Why did you hit Radojko, sir? Why?"

Gavrilo recoiled, transfixed by this new blow. When the pain subsided a little, he leaned over and said, "Because, my boy, I can't stand humiliating defeats."

"Are there defeats that people can be proud of?"

Gavrilo pondered for a few moments: Should he tell him what he really thought about defeat and humiliation? There was no time for that. He sank back onto his pillow once more, surrendering to the pain. He must say something that Bogdan would remember. He was the only one who would remember—if he survived, that is, and if he could hear in his delirium.

"Do you remember that night on Suvobor, when you said you were sure that love was something exceptional? Everything that is great is exceptional, you said, but I told you there is nothing exceptional about a great love except its end. I advised you not to mix women with ideas, or friends with principles. Never turn love into an abstraction. If you do, you'll be left without love and without principles, too. Can you hear me, Bogdan? You also said that you considered loyalty a greater virtue than courage. But loyalty can exist only among equals, and equality between lovers is an exceedingly rare phenomenon, a miracle. Among people in general, too. The fact is, we're not equal. That's why we strike each other. That's why we betray, abandon, and offend others.

"Take Apis and myself. We were among the first seven conspirators. At that time the destruction of the Obrenović dynasty was the most dangerous objective possible for an army officer. It was a great thing to destroy the moral decadence of the government—the ruling family's brazen pursuit of pleasure while the people lived in poverty. You know, the destruction of tyranny is the most exciting work on earth. For that you need a perfectly calculated, exact kind of courage, which is the finest thing about all conspiracies. Apis and I were intoxicated with it. Those meetings, those midnight walks, those dangerous secrets . . . You could hear Apis's footsteps at a distance. He had a most unusual step, that man. I can hear it now when everything is quiet. Are you listening, Bogdan?"

Bogdan groaned.

Gavrilo lay back on his pillow. He ought to take some morphia tonight, then he would sleep, sleep right through his next-to-last night. Or was it? What stronger pain could he summon to quiet that putrid leg, for which even this bed was too small, and the eiderdown as heavy as the roof of the hospital? He would think about Apis. No, about Masha *and* Apis.

Had it really been necessary to destroy that friendship, which meant more in his life than the ideals in whose name it had been broken? It had been ruined by folly and error, by Apis's arrogance and his own vanity—by fate. The break had come when the conspirators were deciding who should seize power after Alexander Obrenović, and he, Gavrilo, had yelled that he wasn't about to kill or be killed just to put the crown on another head, and that Serbia should become a republic. "After Napoleon Bonaparte, no one in Europe has the right to be a monarch any more!" he had shouted. "The French Revolution has put an end to the history of kings. Louis XVI was the last king who considered himself ruler by divine right. Napoleon Bonaparte was the last historical figure to become a ruler by virtue of his personal gifts and trickery. From now on no one should be given any kind of permanent power to which all citizens do not have an equal right."

"For what country is this historical precedent valid?" asked Apis, seizing him by the shoulders.

"For every country that knows the meaning of freedom, and for which freedom is a necessity. No human being deserves such trust that he should rule till the end of his life! Never mind what ideas he represents, or how wise or virtuous he may be. These things make no difference!"

"It all depends on the man, Gavrilo. On his character."

"No, it doesn't! Man is a dangerous and vicious creature! A man in power is even more dangerous and corrupt, especially if we have faith in him. Can't you see this, Dragutin?" he said, on the verge of tears.

"Even if I do, Gavrilo, the people we serve don't. We have no right to go against them."

"Yes, we *do* have the right! Our love for the people gives us the right. Freedom gives us the right. The sacrifices we make will justify our cause."

"I don't agree. We're army officers. We're servants of the nation, not of our personal values. I don't like crowned heads either, Gavrilo. But our people still don't hate the crown so much as the person who brings shame upon it."

"So you think, Dragutin, that we should sacrifice ourselves for this so-called *realpolitik?*"

"I'm not risking my life for any political cause or person. I'm doing it for my country, without any thought of reward. Surely you know that!"

After that night he began to lie awake until reveille. During those sleepless hours their friendship smoldered away. Their disagreements smarted, grew larger. Nocturnal meetings produced no reconciliation; all they remembered were their angry words. They felt hostile and avoided each other.

Why was he thinking about him tonight? Why, at this moment, did he wish to open his heart to him, to justify and explain? Vanity again! No, this time it was love that tormented him. It was still alive. But love is a coward, it protects life. Could this be just an illusion, like so many others? Since his return from Russia six years ago, Apis had made no attempt to greet him in the street. He had even pretended not to see him in cafés, and never mentioned his name in the presence of mutual friends. Yes, this famous leader of the conspirators, now victorious, had never wavered in his contempt for him, a renegade and traitor. For surely that was how he thought of him, damn him!

How can I live with only one leg? What'll I do, hop about on crutches? Live on memories, talk to people? Who'll be interested in my disappointments? Who needs my truths, my self-deceptions? What time is it? He took his watch out and looked at it: twenty past eleven. He couldn't sleep for the pain and the lice; he hadn't been able to sleep since daybreak.

Bogdan seized his hand. He couldn't quiet his heart at the contact of that hot hand. He'd agree to the amputation; he'd call Sergeev first thing in the morning. There were people with whom one could live, even as a cripple. One could survive in this beastly world with a single friend and have some happiness. Why not? He'd always known that the basis of human happiness is to bring your desires into harmony with your abilities; and he had sense enough for that.

"He risked his life for you, and you hit him. . . . You brought shame on your victory," muttered Bogdan, letting go of his hand.

"I disgraced our—*your* victory?" Gavrilo exclaimed.

The wounded groaned in their sleep. Some called to the orderlies for a drink of water. Outside the hospital, dogs barked.

Gavrilo trembled. "What victory hasn't been shamed?" He lit his pipe again, inhaled a few puffs of smoke, then let the pipe go out. He gripped the pipe hard and stroked it, feeling every pattern and incision in the wood. Should he give it to Radojko or to Bogdan? Anatole Zharov's pipe.

"Do you know who this pipe belonged to, Bogdan—this beautiful pipe for which you risked your life on Suvobor? It belonged to Anatole Zharov, an aristocrat and a revolutionary, a friend and pupil of Dmitri Lizogub, a man with a mission, who refused the Czar's pardon and went to his death with a gentle smile. He sold all his estates, used the money to support illegal activities, and lived like a pauper in St. Petersburg; only now and again would he consent to have a meal with a rich man like me. He was tall and pale, with a long beard. He had strange eyes with thick eyelashes, like a woman. He used to wear a black cloak, and underneath it a short linen jacket with large wooden buttons, and a black vest, buttoned right up to his neck, and a leather cap, of course. He'd have been an ideal man, Bogdan, if he had loved women, but he couldn't bear them anywhere near him. Otherwise there was nothing any man could do to frighten him. Among the revolutionaries it was said that the only thing Zharov feared was cockroaches. He'd run up and down stairs and along the passages at night, because the houses in St. Petersburg were full of them. 'Why are you so scared of cockroaches, Anatole?' I asked him once. 'Because they live on dirt,' he answered. Well, Bogdan, the only thing he kept from his days as an aristocrat was this pipe. I'll tell you all about it after my operation. You'd like to hear about it now? Right. Even if I survive the operation, who knows whether I'll want to tell you then?

"It was during the St. Petersburg uprising of 1905. That's a long story. That I really will tell you after my operation. Only now I'll tell you about Zharov. A few of us who had escaped the machine guns were fleeing from the mounted police. We tried to hide in the cellars and hovels where the poorest people in Russia live. My God, those people! They didn't want to hide us. If you knew, Bogdan, what a risky business it is to trust the poor . . ."

"I don't believe you, I can't!" muttered Bogdan.

"I must finish the story about the pipe, even if you don't believe me. We were running along the Karpovka River. Zharov and I ran the farthest; the others either stopped in their tracks in the snow when they couldn't go on or were hit by bullets. We got to the point when we couldn't move, so we ran into the courtyard of the Peter and Paul Hospital, where the orderlies chased us away with sticks. We just didn't know where to turn, so we rushed down by the canal that carried the hospital sewage into the Karpovka. Then one of the mounted police noticed us and rode toward us with his saber drawn. We were trapped! I got out my knife and waited. Zharov grabbed me by the chest and said, 'This man is going to kill me! Here's my pipe. Good-by, Gavrilo!' Then he pushed me into the canal. Fortunately there was snow there and I didn't get hurt. I clung to the side, fell into the snow, and waited. I couldn't see what was going on above me, but I could hear every word. I want you to remember these words.

" 'So it's you, Anatole Kirillovich. How delightful to see you!' our pursuer said, and I began to hope we might escape after all. 'God has indeed rewarded me, if I'm to accompany Your Excellency to heaven,' he continued in the same high-pitched, happy tone. I was baffled.

" 'Who are you, soldier?' asked Zharov.

" 'Don't you recognize me, Anatole Kirillovich? You've forgotten Mishka Shchepkin, the son of your best coachman and faithful servant, Vasili Shchepkin? The boy to whom your mother used to give your worn-out shoes and coats! But look at me now, Your Excellency! Now you see Mishka Shchepkin carrying the Czar's saber!'

" 'Is it really you, you poor idiot?'

" 'Yes, and I mean business!'

"I counted fifteen blows from his saber before I lost consciousness."

"You son of a bitch!" exclaimed one of the wounded men on the floor. Gavrilo had forgotten himself and was talking too loudly. Never mind, he thought: at least someone has heard it. He wanted to explain to the soldiers just why it was the poor and his own followers who drove the nails into Christ's feet, why slaves kill rebellious slaves, servants torment rebellious servants, and the police cut down those who are fighting for justice—the police, and not the kings and emperors! And why in this war, he thought, we're being killed by our brother Slavs—Croats, Serbs from across the Danube, Slovenes, and Czechs, the people for whose liberation we're giving our lives. There's never any conflict face to face with those responsible for evil and injustice. That's because the world has been so created, and man so fashioned, that he's at one and the same time a servant, a tyrant, and a rebel. This trinity, together with numerous variations, dwells inside the same man, always in ceaseless conflict. None of them ever achieves permanent dominance. Evil is in all of us. Poverty is in our very bones. When we're fighting for freedom and justice, we kill ourselves and our own people—don't you understand? Of course you don't—you never will! Maybe it's just as well.

His leg, that lump of carrion, seemed to strain through the mattress, then plunge to the floor and up the walls of the hospital; next pulled him back with it into the bed; then at last was quiet and offered no further resistance. Lying back on his pillow, he gripped his pipe firmly and surrendered to the pain, sank into it for a long time. Why hadn't Doctor Sergeev come? He had left him to die like a dog. Where was Radojko? If only Milena would bring him some tea. Tea, indeed! What he really wanted was to look at a beautiful woman's face just one more time, a face over which he would never bend his head.

Bogdan Dragović was wakened by his thirst. "Bring me some water," he called to an orderly. His voice grew louder and echoed as from a stone cave. The multitoned reverberations frightened him. He raised himself on his elbows and looked around: the room was empty and huge—it was impossible to see its walls. Where was Major Stanković, and his bed? I want a drink of water!

Rista the Clown lifted his head and offered him a mug of milk, his clown's smile branded on his face like a mask.

"Take this aspirin first," whispered Milena Katić, raising his head. "Don't be frightened, Bogdan; your temperature will go down. Then we'll send you home."

"Life has no less force than death, sometimes more. You must believe that, Bogdan," said Gavrilo, who turned to Milena and added, "Don't take him away from here until he's feeling better."

"But at least he'd be warm and clean, and his mother would look after him, Major."

"Let him stay here today and tonight. Then you can take him away tomorrow. Not before tomorrow, though—please, Milena!"

He touched the muscles near his knee; they were so cold that he could scarcely feel them. He moved his foot, but couldn't feel it. Then he lifted the eiderdown and shuddered: his leg looked gray as ash. Was it from the gangrene, or from the feeble smoky light in the corridor? How deformed his knee had become! And those repulsive lumps of hair on the lower part of his leg, full of lice and their eggs, which no longer bothered him. His leg: now a dull, pulsating lump of pain and tension around his smashed thigh, encased in tight, torn skin. He had the feeling that his leg was desperate for space: it wanted to tread on the ground, to run over it and annihilate it, to jump over bushes and streams, to climb up steep slopes and rush down them, to get wet, to skate on a frozen river, to make its imprint on virgin snow. His leg wanted the feel of a soft boot, and the warm cruppers of a horse as it stretched itself over them and thrust into a stirrup, while the horse galloped swiftly through a meadow. His leg longed to have Masha's thigh, tender and restless, beside it, longed to press hard against her hip, to curl up and rest in the white hollows of her lap. This swollen knee dreamed that it would once more, only once, sink into the thick warmth of Masha's lightly pressed legs and feel her desire. Meanwhile his foot, spreading its livid toes, had fallen asleep, remembering the sound of grass and the crackle of autumn leaves beneath it, remembering the grip of skates, the feel of ice and cobblestones, his mother's soft, warm sheets at home, marches along rough roads and through deep mud, the bitter cold on Suvobor . . .

Yes, that leg. He could remember the time he first noticed the fine down on his thigh and calf while having a bath in a large wooden tub, pouring in the hot water himself while his mother passed his underwear through the door that stood slightly ajar. After that, whenever he undressed and before he got up in the morning he would take a long look at his legs, following the transformation of the pale gray down into strong black hairs. At first he was displeased with his bony knees and the poorly developed muscle of his calf. He could remember all that jumping, running, and swimming to fill his slender legs with strength and endurance. Then there were those victories in races at the military academy; the first time his legs appeared completely bare in front of a woman; the first time he put on his officer's uniform, and his dissatisfaction with the floppy trousers; that numb, dull feeling in his feet and hips after drill and exhausting marches. He had tormented his feet so often! That leg gave him his height, distinguished him from other people, enabled him to be seen from a distance and to see far ahead. It gave him strength, skill, and a fine appearance; it made him self-confident and brave, proud and honored. That leg was now dying of gangrene.

What sort of person would he be without his right leg? He would be deprived of dancing, love, and warfare, and of his friends Apis and Masha. As for freedom and justice, they weren't so important to him as they had once been. He would be deprived of everything that made life worthwhile and gave it joy, deprived of its beauty and its pain. His existence was unthinkable without that right leg.

So what could he do without it? What kind of life could he live without that leg, strong, beautiful, and untamed? What if he sacrificed it and went on living as a cripple, bearing within him the bitterness and glory, the rancor and envy of his sacrifice? What about his suffering because of lack of recognition from the world in general? He would feel continually offended, full of scorn and hatred for those who were healthy and successful. He'd be a retired major, a lieutenant-colonel maybe, while his friends would be generals, and Apis lord of Serbia. Life would be without joy. He'd disturb those around him with his forced gaiety, he'd be an ugly imitation of a man. Saddened and humiliated, he'd live through peace and victory until he joined Ilija Stanković in the cemetery.

Even without his leg, though, he could look at women, at trees, books, and rivers, and listen to jokes, songs, and words of wisdom. He'd be able to think. Surely that was most important of all! He'd read, and talk to people about justice, about joys they knew nothing about. He'd enjoy food and drink, and have his wartime friends. He might even marry and embrace a woman. How many women had loved him! There would be others. Couldn't he find pleasure in at least some of the many joys life offered? He'd still find plenty to worry about! He'd be sad, and suffer as a man who has lived through great trials. Bogdan Dragović would surely want to have him as an older friend, a protector, someone he could trust. A little while ago Bogdan had wished with all his heart that the major was his father. Even as a cripple he wouldn't lack significance. He'd have good reason for pride, and a right to his vanity. He might even meet Masha again. He'd go to St. Petersburg. After the war that dangerous, secret life which he and his revolutionary friends had lived would reach a climax; there'd be long, turbid confessions. It was still a good world!

He must somehow move this damn leg; it was tramping through his brain. He shoved it to the edge of the bed, but it was no use.

He'd be only half a man, a monster, a hulk on crutches. Tap, tap! The whole street would know when he passed by. Yes, he'd be alive, but never again able to jump and run, to ride a horse, to embrace a woman as a man should. He'd be repulsive to a woman. The gnarled, dead skin across his sawn-off thigh would touch her hip, his tenderness would make her shudder. He'd force her to lie, torment her with his longing, with the insatiable passion of an offended, disappointed lover.

Surely he couldn't allow his body, his senses, his time to be used only for the consumption of food and drink? No, he couldn't lower himself to that, or curtail his being. It was easier once, and once only, not to be a coward. I can't live a life that isn't whole. I don't want to regret that on one occasion only I was a coward.

"How do you feel, Major?" said Doctor Sergeev, speaking softly in Russian as he sat on the edge of the bed.

Gavrilo hastily covered himself and replied, "You disturb me, Doctor."

"We're ready for the operation. Why don't you smoke a cigarette? Here, take one of these."

"I smoke a pipe."

"All right. Light your pipe."

"It's a drug of no importance. Like a habitual lie."

"Then shall I call the orderlies to take you now?"

Hit in the center of his being by a fearful pain, Gavrilo felt himself on the brink of something unknown but enthralling: had the moment really come?

Shadows were twisting around him, one of them was smiling. The shadows put something on the bed, lifted up his leg. His wound made things clear to him. The orderlies set down the stretcher and removed the eiderdown. Radojko smiled at him, so did Milena, while Sergeev waved his hands and said something to the orderlies.

"Wait! Who told you to come here?" Gavrilo said, covering his legs with the eiderdown. "Take that stretcher out of my sight! What are you waiting for, Radojko?"

Sergeev leaned over the bed. "Listen, Gavrilo Stanković, tomorrow may be too late."

He was seized by a feeling of dull horror which drew him irresistibly into the darkness. In a voice not his own, he said: "No, Doctor, it won't be too late." The eerie hoot of an owl filled the room. "It won't, I tell you!" he added with hatred in his voice. He was bathed in sweat, tears, and burning heat. "It won't be too late! Radojko, get the towel out of my knapsack and wipe my head and chest." He blinked his eyes as if he now felt better.

Milena wiped his face tenderly; he could feel her soft fingers and hear her sigh. Perhaps it really would be too late. He looked at her: what had happened to her beautiful face and ardent eyes?

"Give me a cigarette, Doctor. Thank you, Milena. Now go to bed. You too, Radojko. For breakfast get me some milk and toast. Sit next to me, Doctor. Let's talk about St. Petersburg."

Sergeev sat down and lit a cigarette for him. Gavrilo forced himself to smoke. What had he decided, in fact? Had he simply postponed the amputation to some unspecified day?

"Why do you torment yourself like this, Gavrilo?"

"Why? Because I love life, love it in a way you couldn't begin to understand."

"Your logic is standing on its head, Major."

"Oh, no, it isn't! A man who doesn't feel a desire for death doesn't know why he lives."

"I don't believe that one lives for something that is only a matter of words."

"One lives for some definite reason. Or because one fears death. One or the other, Nikolay Maksimovich."

"You don't believe in yourself, you don't believe in your own spirit. That's why you're tormenting yourself."

"That's not true. I *do* believe in my own spirit; but my legs, and my clenched fists, make up my spirit. Give me an injection, Doctor, then we can talk some more. My spirit has served my body honorably and gladly. What I'm trying to say is that my legs and my head have worked together perfectly, and all my other organs have worked with my soul. As you see, I'm quite a healthy man."

"Why are you so afraid of pain?"

"I won't agree to just any kind of life. That's not fear of pain."

"Do you want to live just for pleasure?"

"I want to live in my own way and as a free man. A cripple isn't free. Now give me an injection; go on, jab it in. You know I'm sorry, really sorry, that I didn't feel any pain from the needle."

"Is there someone that you love, Gavrilo?"

"There's little to be said against me on that score, Doctor."

"On the contrary. That's where the evidence against you is strongest."

Gavrilo fixed his eyes on the ceiling; then, without looking at Sergeev, he said: "Since you're so kind as to ask, and since the girl is Russian—well, she left me! Her name was Maria Rayevska."

"You're a lucky man. You'll never forget her."

"I don't wish to."

"Is your mother still alive?"

"Yes, but we aren't indebted to anybody in the world for our life. Nobody at all. We're not indebted to mother, children, friends, or any ideal whatsoever. My life is *mine*, I have a right to it. How I use it, what I do with it, is my own affair."

For some time neither of them spoke.

"Have you some good, sensible friends? Or do you like to have only servants around you?" whispered Sergeev.

"Statesmen need sensible friends, as do leaders of gangs of criminals; and probably great artists as well."

"You know, the only people I really can't stand are cynics and nihilists, especially nihilists. They're stupid creatures and cruel, too. Don't you want to smoke any more?"

"Nihilists are brave people, but sad. They're the only people who really know what faith is all about. What made you think of nihilists?"

"Because in some ways you remind me of the army of negators who are spreading through the world like a disease."

"I'm not one of them. Nor am I a pessimist, though I may seem like one."

"In that case, why can't you believe that there's some point in living without a leg or an arm?"

"My dear Doctor, I think there are many reasons for living—but not at all times and not for everybody. Sometimes life itself makes living pointless. But one can't argue about such matters with any conviction. All these big questions are purely personal. One must keep quiet about them. The thicker the darkness that covers them, the better."

"Gavrilo, you have no idea what fabulous worlds there are, worlds you've never dreamed of! Life is an endless succession of truths, se-crets, and joys, as long as one can think. All we need do is think, and then there's no such thing as a hopeless situation."

"How happy I'd be, if you could convince me of that now! But the Russian language doesn't have the right words to describe the ampu-tation of one's entire right leg. Still, your injection is beginning to work."

"You know, Gavrilo, only small things can be proved, and some-times they're not even true. Great truths can't be proved. Life itself defies proof—you're right about that." Sergeev fell silent.

"Go on, Doctor, I'm listening."

Sergeev brought his face close to Gavrilo. "Major, you're a terrible coward!"

Gavrilo felt depressed: was that how his struggle for life really appeared?

"Don't be angry," said Sergeev. "Would you like some brandy? That won't do you any harm." Sergeev got up and walked out of the room.

The wounded men were sleeping. There was a heavy, tepid stench, pungent with tobacco smoke. In the corridor someone dropped a bucket; outside the dogs barked, a wind was blowing. He pulled him-self out of the bed to see Bogdan. "Are you asleep, Bogdan?"

"My head aches terribly. I'm shivering."

"Do you think Sergeev is right?"

"I'd let them cut off both my legs if it would save my life."

"Would you really?"

Gavrilo lay down again. What was going to happen tonight? Or had it already happened?

Sergeev came back and handed him a bottle of brandy. "Don't you know, Gavrilo, that Beethoven went deaf at the height of his creative power? Stone deaf, but he didn't hang himself. Dostoevsky had epi-lepsy, but never even complained about it. Did you know that? Phi-losophers advise us to accept our fate, Gavrilo, to accept it willingly!"

"But that means to love torment and suffering! I'm not capable of that kind of love. I know I'm not, Doctor."

"Are you sure? Don't answer right away! Think!"

Gavrilo took another swig of brandy. It didn't taste like it used to. He said nothing as he listened to the gurgling sound from the bottle and watched Sergeev drinking. The doctor wiped his beard, then leaned over toward him. "I want to tell you something as a man who understands a bit how sick people feel. You know, a sick man does not know the truth. He just doesn't."

"You're probably right, Doctor; but tonight don't think of me as your opponent, and please don't force me to contradict you, since you're trying your hardest to help me."

"Your knowledge of human nature is superficial if you believe that sick people and invalids are incapable of happiness. You simply have no idea of all the things that can bring joy into people's lives."

"That's a lie inspired by your magnanimity—comfort offered by a compassionate man."

Sergeev spread out the fingers of both hands and slowly pressed his fingertips together. If he starts to drum I'll be rude to him, thought Gavrilo, I'll make him leave the room.

But the doctor's fingers remained still. He looked at the major for some time, and the long silence became unpleasant. Finally he spoke: "For you, Gavrilo, ideas are as easily expendable as stolen money is for a thief."

"You don't understand," stammered the major, fully aware that as he said these words he was setting his course in another direction, with no chance of return. He wiped the sweat from his face with both hands.

Sergeev got up. "I'll be waiting for you in the operating room at daybreak. See you then."

Gavrilo couldn't say another word. He fixed his eyes on the crack in the ceiling and stared at the long, twisting crevice that gaped above him, echoing the barking of dogs and a roaring sound from the outside.

Dr. Paun Aleksić, the hospital director, was lying on his bed with his boots on, smoking in the darkness. He lay in a pile of ruins, on a building site. Everything smelled of plaster and lime. His orderly, Toma, had not removed his boots, and the fire in the stove had gone out. Everything in his life had changed because of preparations for the reception of the Allied mission.

His worries had curtailed—indeed ruined—his sweetest moments: his dreams when on the point of waking, and soaking his feet in warm water and pure alcohol—a special ritual that he had missed only about ten times since the beginning of the war. Yesterday he had only moistened his feet, and that just to avoid disturbing the routine of his orderly. This morning, however, when Toma brought in the bowl of warm water, he had said with a sigh, "Pour it out, Toma." He had eaten his breakfast without any pleasure in his food, voraciously snatching a few bites like an apprentice, and drank his coffee standing up while talking with the accountant Srećko and a Hungarian prisoner, an engineer who was helping enlarge his office so that he would have a *salon* where he could receive the Allied mission in a manner worthy of Serbia.

As if anyone would be grateful to him for such sacrifices! It would never occur to his superiors to promote him or give him a decoration. To hell with them! He wouldn't get a word of thanks from anybody. No one would think of saying, Well done, old man! On the contrary, the patients would curse him because he had squeezed them even closer together, and reduced their rations on account of the expenses incurred in receiving the mission. One day, because he had spent the hospital's money without authorization, Vukašin Katić's Opposition press would denounce him for embezzling hospital funds. Such was life in the Balkans, among these mean and evil-minded people. They humiliated and spat on their best men, those who sacrificed themselves for their country, who did all they could to enhance its prestige in the eyes of the world.

Was there anything he still hadn't done for the reception? The work on his office would be completed by tomorrow; in the reception room the rug from Pirot would be replaced by a Persian carpet, and all the rickety chairs by elegant armchairs borrowed from Mrs. Predolac.

There would be corresponding rearrangements in the hospital. He had selected two rooms, had them cleaned and whitewashed according to regulations, then brought into them practically all the beds the hospital had. He had acquired pillows and straw mattresses, sheets and blankets, and had placed in these rooms those patients who could represent Serbia most fittingly. Likewise he had picked the best nurses and orderlies, and had relieved Doctor Pantelić from all other responsibilities and put him in charge of these rooms. He must make it impossible for the foreigners to see the entire hospital and anything he didn't want them to see.

He had put the sick and wounded prisoners in a separate ward and provided beds for most of them, and straw mattresses and blankets for them all. He had put Doctor Dobi, a Hungarian, in charge of them, and given him the two orderlies he asked for, since, being a count, he was allowed two servants even as a prisoner. His biggest headache, and the thing that took up most of his time, was what to give the mission to eat and drink. He wouldn't allow these people to be made sick by Serbian food on their very first day.

New caps and aprons had been made for the doctors, orderlies, and nurses; they were here in his office, ironed and ready to be distributed as soon as he learned by telegram that the mission was on its way. Naturally he had had a new uniform made for himself; it had cost him half his salary. The accountant had insisted that he could get the money back out of general expenses, but he still wasn't sure whether he would do this. A man in a position of power, as he could now see, was a martyr to temptation.

What else was still to be done? Was there anything he hadn't foreseen? He had instructed Milena Katić to get some flowers and say a few well-chosen words of welcome in French when the mission arrived, and to escort the French members; Mileva, who knew Russian, would go with the Russians. He himself would look after the English; with his knowledge of German, there was no danger of creating a bad impression. The china and cutlery for the meals had been borrowed from the best houses in Valjevo. There was no reason for any feelings of inferiority on that account. He had even given careful thought to the after-dinner conversation, when the foreigners would be in a good mood and feel confident in their hosts. He would say that life is a miracle—but in a philsophical way.

He hadn't forgotten about photographs: there was a Czech prisoner who was a professional photographer. Everybody in a position of authority must have photographs; they were even more necessary in wartime than in peace. He must take care that he wasn't caught with his face in profile.

He lit one cigarette after another. But the patients—they were unpredictable! He had sweated blood to get them into the right mood and raise their national consciousness. Their behavior in front of the Allied mission would be crucial.

Outside, the dogs barked, and peasants coughed under the eaves in the darkness. What could he do about the dogs? They were certainly an unpleasant sight. How could he get rid of those packs that had been swarming around the hospital the last few days, rushing up at the orderlies and the wounded? He must chase them off or kill them. An even worse problem: what should he do about the peasants? How could he remove from the highway and the hospital precincts those crowds with bags and wheelbarrows who came to take their sons away from the hospital if they were still alive, and from the cemetery if they were dead? Those famished dogs and unhappy peasants would spoil the good impression he wanted to make on the foreigners—so vital to the national interest.

He put on his overcoat and went out into the night: now the staff and the patients would know that he wasn't asleep, that he was really worried. Peasants and dogs, peasants and dogs, he repeated to himself as he walked along, then paused: peasants and dogs—yes, it was a catchphrase, a fateful Serbian catchphrase. He would bring this into the conversation sometime—when he was drunk.

"May I have a word with you, sir?" asked Doctor Sergeev.

"Of course, Doctor. What is it?"

"It's about Major Stanković—you know who I mean."

"Oh, yes, that man who was complaining that we have no Swiss sanatoria in Serbia."

"He's an extremely interesting man, but that's of no consequence now. He's got gangrene in his right leg. It's not fulminating, but definitely fatal. He won't consent to surgery."

"You've warned him of the consequences?"

"Yes, I have, and not only the medical ones; but unfortunately he—"

"He's a grown man, Doctor Sergeev, a responsible adult. We dare not go beyond our legal authority in this matter."

"But we must save him, sir! Get in touch with his friends, ask them to come convince him that he ought to go on living, even with one leg. I beg you, sir, do it tonight."

"This evening Colonel Kajafa, his division commander, was asking about him again, and I told him what his condition was. Very well, I'll telephone the Staff at once and tell them that Serbian majors set less value on their own lives than on their grooms!"

Tola Dačić emerged out of the darkness. "While on that subject, Doctor, I'd like to ask you, and also this Russian gentleman, why you don't show proper respect for ordinary people?"

"Why are you hanging around the hospital?"

"I'm asking why you don't give folks a decent burial. You pile them up like slaughtered chickens. You throw chopped-off arms onto the dunghill as if they were chickens' feet instead of human arms. You've no heart at all."

"Go to hell, you silly old fool! We'll throw you on the shit heap, too!" said Paun Aleksić, hurrying off to his office.

Radojko Veselinović bent over the headboard and whispered to Major Stanković, "Shall I ask the Russian to come and clean that up, to ease the pain a little?"

"You mean my soul, not my leg, Radojko."

"Folks go on living on account of other people, sir. On account of other people a man has to put up with everything. He's even got to do wicked things and deny God Himself. What's walking with crutches? Nothing!"

"I can't hear you. Come sit here."

"I'll dirty the bed, sir."

"Who cares? Go on, tell me what you had in mind."

"Well, I look at things this way: even if a man has no legs, he can have a friend, a horse, and a cane to support him, like—"

"Do you know anyone in that situation?"

"In the village of Jabukovac there's a man who had both his legs crushed by a beech tree when he was quite young, and to save his life the doctor cut them off. Well, that man's got a nice wife—he's the envy of the village—and two sons. Good healthy boys, and real nice-looking. He's head of the household, and his wife obeys him and looks after him. He's always merry and full of jokes. To hear him sing at weddings and patron saint feasts, you'd think he had four legs!"

"Tell me everything you know about people who have only one leg."

"There's quite a few of them in my region, sir. People think that those that have only one leg, or one arm, are extra strong in the head. They say their strength goes into their heads and their you-know-whats. There are some folks with one leg that are village mayors. They deal with people honestly and make fair judgments, because they're not afraid to be strong and just."

"What else do you know about people with only one leg?"

"I know they live a long time."

"Is that right?"

"Yes, sir. They don't wear themselves out."

"Go on, Radojko."

"Well, sir, spring's coming. The grass will be green, and the flowers will bloom. There'll be a nice, gentle breeze, and the days will be long. Everything will look brighter, and all difficulties and troubles will seem easier. Let's go to my village. My mother and my wife will fatten you up on milk and honey. Your wound will be healed before the cherries ripen. Then bit by bit you'll start to walk about the meadow with your crutches."

"What will I do when I come back from the meadow?"

"Then you'll talk to people in that nice way you have. There'll always be someone who's got time enough to listen, someone who likes to hear a good story."

"So I'm to live from one story to another? Is that enough for a man, Radojko?"

"Of course it is, sir! You'll ride a horse again, just like you used to. Until I get back from the war to help you to mount, I'll fix a place where they'll bring the horse to you. I've got a tree stump, and I'll dig that in behind the horse, so that all you have to do is get yourself into the saddle."

"Where will I go on the horse, Radojko?"

"You can go to the village. There's plenty to see—fields, vineyards, all sorts of things."

"You go to bed, Radojko."

"The Russian doctor is waiting for you, with that pretty nurse. Shall I take you to the operating room, sir?"

"You go to bed, you're tired. You have to be up early to get me some milk."

"I won't fall asleep before you do."

"Then stop talking."

"Tell me why you did so much studying. Why did you spend so many years in Russia, putting up with those blizzards? Why have you told people all those stories, sir?"

"That's enough, Radojko."

"I stabbed myself in the arm so that I wouldn't have to leave you at the mercy of hospital orderlies. The Austrians took me prisoner with you, I risked my life as you saw yourself; and I've stayed next to you in this epidemic, though I've got a house and family of my own. I didn't expect you to behave like this."

"Be quiet, Radojko! You know I can't bear sob stories from men! I'll sleep while the injection is working. I want to sleep."

"Shall I wake you up in an hour, sir?"

"I'll wake up myself. You go to bed and get some sleep."

"Well, just in case you want me, I'll be in the corridor."

Gavrilo struggled hard to fall asleep, so that he need no longer think, or listen to the dogs that had been growling outside since dusk. The pain pierced his pelvic bones, then wrenched away from them and lay like a dead weight on his moribund leg; then it rushed forth from the bed and filled the room, the hospital, Suvobor, and Belgrade. After that it retreated to his forehead, dug into his temple, and left its metallic imprint inside his head as it returned under the eiderdown next to his emaciated left leg and forced it into movement.

The sergeant whose leg had been amputated up to the knee groaned louder. Gavrilo had shouted at him several times already and would have to again. The dogs growled and snapped at each other right in the back of his head. Fearful of the dogs, the room had grown silent; all was quiet in the corridor; the hospital had surrendered itself to the dogs. He *must* fall asleep once more. He could feel himself dropping off. What a blessed, happy state! No, it was more than that, it was salvation.

He could hear footsteps—unusual footsteps, strong and heavy, with a special rhythm. A powerful, dominating kind of step. Or perhaps that was just how it seemed to him, because since last night footsteps had sounded especially distinct and clear to him, alongside the barking of the dogs. During a short spell of sleep he had dreamed that he was marching by himself through the yard of the military academy. But these footsteps sounded familiar. Who in his life had walked like that? Intimidated by those footsteps, the dogs had stopped barking. Even the sergeant had stopped moaning. Apis used to walk like that. Apis! Could it really be he? They hadn't spoken since his return from St. Petersburg, they had avoided each other. When mutual friends had tried to bring about a reconciliation, he had said without reflection, "Apis and I were friends when there was reason for it, but no longer." He didn't know what Apis had said to them.

He was drenched with sweat. In front of the door the footsteps stopped, or did they? He could hear whispering. Why did he imagine that he was hearing Apis's footsteps? He wiped the sweat from his forehead with the palms of his hands. There was no one he less wanted to see. The hospital director, that bastard, was standing in the open doorway, talking to someone: "But why? I'll show you where he is. No trouble at all, Colonel. He's in that bed. The only bed in the room. Yes, Colonel, I'll be waiting for you in my office."

The director went away. There was no one standing in the doorway; all was quiet. So it wasn't Apis after all. Why was he thinking about that proud, conceited, dominating leader? The past was tormenting him with ghosts. He must be dying. Sweat poured over his eyes, and he didn't move his hands for fear he would be caught in that movement. He blinked, clenched his jaws, and didn't try to resist the pain. In the corridor the footsteps suddenly stopped. He wouldn't look at him. The sound of boots resounded through the room. He shut his eyes.

The newcomer stood over him, sighed, and touched the clenched hand that lay across his eyes. It was he! He sat down on the edge of the bed. Gavrilo jerked his wounded leg away so that they wouldn't touch each other. A spasm of pain shot through his spine and he groaned. Still he didn't remove his hand from his eyes. What was happening tonight?

The visitor lit a cigarette, breathing asthmatically. He too had been crippled by an infected wound at Kosovo, but he was alive. The sergeant whose leg had been amputated moaned. The sick and wounded squirmed on the floor. They must have seen him in the doorway—the man whom so many in Serbia worshiped, though some also hated him with a passion. He for his part was equally unaffected by love and hatred. Gavrilo had loved him more than anyone in the world, except his mother and Masha.

"Don't sit on the bed, I'm full of lice," he said, frightened by the sound of his own voice.

"They won't touch me."

Had he said this because of his overweening confidence, or because of some flaw in him? Gavrilo opened his eyes and saw Apis's bent head and the spark of his cigarette under his moustache; he was gazing down at him intently, his legs widespread. Perhaps his long illness had softened him? A sick, rotting hulk of a man, but alive—Apis, the god!

"You know that I'm done for?" Gavrilo whispered.

Apis remained silent and motionless. Only his cigarette crackled faintly.

"So you've come to say farewell to the traitor?" The caustic tone of his own words made him pinch his dead thigh.

"All that is over and done with, Gavrilo."

"Dead and buried, you mean?"

Apis slowly turned toward Gavrilo full face. He was in the shadow and his eyes weren't visible, but his lips and moustache were lit up by the glowing spark of his cigarette. His shadow stretched across the sick and wounded men, and his head climbed up the wall.

Now I must tell him everything, Gavrilo decided; but first he wanted to lift up his gangrenous leg and bend it at the knee. The sharp pain blacked out his consciousness, and he wasn't sure he could hear Apis clearly.

"I'm unhappy, Gavrilo."

"Are you really?" he exclaimed, grinding his teeth from pain. "Is it because you're ill?"

"That's the least of it."

"So you're unhappy! You killed a king and toppled a dynasty. You deprived one heir to the throne of his inheritance and made his brother the king. You killed Ferdinand, the future emperor of Austria-Hungary. What have you failed to achieve?"

"I accomplished far too little; but that's not why I'm unhappy."

"Are Pašić and Prince Alexander bothering you now?"

Apis leaned toward him as if he couldn't hear properly. He was silent for a moment, then said in a whisper: "The price paid for Serbia's freedom has been too high, Gavrilo. My friends have been killed. Do you know how many of them have been killed, and the war has only just started?"

"Is that what's making you unhappy, Dragutin?"

"I keep asking myself, How could I believe that we should all die for our cause? What is freedom, Gavrilo, without those for whose sake we wanted it?"

Gavrilo moved slightly and his head fell back on the pillow. After the pain subsided, he whispered, "Are you afraid of the future, Dragutin?"

"The cowards and jackals will come out on top. The future belongs to the worst elements."

He's trying to play on my emotions, thought Gavrilo; he's heard from the doctors what I've decided. Or is he trying to uphold and comfort me in that decision? Even when they were as close as brothers, it hadn't always been easy for him to guess Apis's real intentions.

"That's the law of all idealistic struggles," he said.

"I have no patience with these laws, Gavrilo. I've no patience with any laws. They're all man-made."

"Yes, that's true," said Gavrilo. He stopped speaking because of the tremor in Apis's voice.

When Gavrilo was a captain in the second class he had succeeded in convincing Apis, then a lieutenant, that they belonged to a generation whose mission it was to change all the laws in Serbia and to establish justice. Justice, however, couldn't exist where there were kings and policemen. He had also convinced him that being enslaved by one's own people was the most humiliating form of slavery; and that those who acted as avengers of justice and fighters for freedom would not die or perish. He had explained at length Seneca's idea, and said that there was always a way out of any kind of slavery, that a man could end his misery and his life at any moment. This was what Apis had found most difficult to grasp. They had walked up and down the Deer Park until early morning. But what must he try to convince him of now? That all that agonizing over freedom and justice was but a trifle in the face of eternity. How a man should step forward into eternity, take that one step which put him beyond human laws, beyond all laws and boundaries. Apis was capable of taking that step. He had demonstrated it when, wounded in the doorway of the palace, he had ordered the guard to shoot at him, using the bullet which could have hit his companion who was on the point of achieving his aim. And Anatole Zharov had thrown him, Gavrilo, into the canal, but himself had waited on the bank to face the mounted policeman. So even now he had no right to talk to Apis about such things. He pulled himself up on the pillow, leaned his head and shoulders against the head of the bed, and lay pressed there by the pain in his leg. "Give me a cigarette."

Apis lit a cigarette for him, then said in a whisper: "Did you change your opinions while you were in Russia? I mean your ideas about a revolution in Serbia?"

"I haven't changed the ideas that made us part company. Certainly not. What about you? Are you intending to put an end to another king, or do you want to get rid of Pašić first?"

Apis lowered his head, but said nothing.

"What will the situation be in Serbia then—out there, where all I hear is dogs barking?"

Apis turned toward him. "I've come to ask you to work with me in the Information Section of the High Command. It's very important work." Apis bent over so low that Gavrilo could feel his breath on his sweating face. "One of our Croats could get within a few steps of Franz Josef. You know what that could mean for Serbia and this war."

"He's an old man. We'd only make him a victim."

"At one time you said that kings and emperors couldn't be victims."

"I was exaggerating to steady your hands in the palace when you were face to face with Alexander Obrenović. I never congratulated you on the order you gave the guard to fire on you when you were wounded. Well done, Dragutin!"

For a while neither spoke.

"We could get Ferdinand of Bulgaria with a thrust of a knife. In the back, though. That's how we must do it to him. I know a Macedonian whom we could train for the job together."

"I couldn't do that as a cripple."

"Why not?"

"I never ask other people to do what I can't do myself. Put my cigarette out," he said, then fell silent. Apis was testing his power on an emperor and a king, playing the game of removing crowns, yet he lived under one. He wanted to have a place in history as an activist or victim, it didn't matter which. Or is he challenging me to change my decision? he thought. Or have the doctors told him that all isn't lost?

Apis took hold of his arm and whispered: "Let's have one more go at something really big. Perhaps fate will be merciful and turn the wheel in our favor. There are fearful paths waiting for us; and humiliations too, Gavrilo."

"There's nothing that can humiliate us as much as our beliefs, Dragutin; and nothing can enslave us as much as our longing for freedom."

"I know that. Just because of that, Gavrilo, we mustn't surrender. For our own sakes."

Gavrilo waited for him to say something more, something ordinary and personal; he waited for him to say something about his leg, which he hadn't mentioned so far. Under the windows the dogs yelped. Apis gave a hoarse, broken sigh and lit another cigarette. For a long time they were silent, then Gavrilo cried out: "I'm right! We must not give ourselves up to just any kind of life! I've made my decision, Dragutin! I won't betray myself."

Apis gave a start and looked him straight in the eyes. "What have you decided?"

"That I won't be a cripple."

"So you've surrendered?"

"I haven't betrayed myself!"

"I know you well enough, that's you all over."

Apis looked down at the floor between his outstretched legs. Even his breathing was inaudible.

"I'm no longer afraid of the future. I have no fear at all, Dragutin."

Apis came up to him and asked, "Any news of your mother?"

"She's had a stroke."

"I know."

"Then you know as much as I do."

"I'm off to Belgrade tomorrow. I'll go see her. What shall I tell her?"

"That you haven't seen me."

"But I have, Gavrilo!"

Both of them fell silent.

Apis got up slowly. The mattress creaked. He thrust both his hands into the pockets of his overcoat and took out a bottle of wine and a pouch of tobacco. "Our special red wine," he whispered as he put the presents at the foot of the bed. "I've only one more bottle left. I'm keeping it to celebrate the liberation of Bosnia and Hercegovina."

"Thank you, Dragutin."

Apis walked over to the window and stared into the darkness. Then he sat down again and muttered: "Do you remember that Christmas Eve when we ate two suppers, first with your mother and then with mine? Afterward we took a walk in Kalemegdan—you could hear the snow drifting. You asked me what my last wish would be if our conspiracy was discovered and we were sentenced to death."

"Yes, I remember."

"I said I'd ask a military band to play while I was being led away to execution, but you said . . ."

"That's right, I said that my last wish would be to punch a king. I'd be quite happy if it was the king of Serbia, Alexander Obrenović."

"What would be your last wish now, Gavrilo?"

"To see a woman."

"Can I bring her to you?"

"I'm afraid not, Dragutin. Would you still want to go to your death to the sound of a military band?"

For a long time Apis didn't reply. "Now my wish would be to have dug for me the deepest grave in which a man was ever buried, so as to be as far away as possible from people."

"When did you get that idea, Dragutin?"

Apis simply pressed his hand, perhaps a little more warmly than on his arrival, then got up from the bed and went away. His heavy, rhythmic footsteps reverberated through the room. Gavrilo pressed both hands over his eyes.

At daybreak Tola Dačić, shaking with cold, came down from the attic, returned the ladder to the shed, and hurried off to see Miloje.

"Water, give me water! Where are those orderlies? Damn them!"

"When I see that doctor, I'll go for him with my teeth! This place is a dump!"

The sick and wounded men groaned and raved, but Miloje, his head covered with his blanket, was trying to figure out why he felt pain in the elbow of his amputated arm. Could it be from the dream he had had last night, in which he had been wrestling with Adam Katić on the bank of the Morava? They often used to wrestle, in the hayfield or the meadows, but never on the riverbank; Adam had trampled him, then suddenly pushed him into the Morava; falling, he had banged his elbow on a willow stump, saw sparks, and just before he fell headfirst into the water the pain woke him up, damp from head to foot. Last night wasn't the first time he dreamed that he had fallen, or that someone had hit him, or that he had cut himself on a scythe or a plow. He had had all sorts of dreams about Prerovo, but never before had something hurt him after he awoke. It did now, though—he wanted to gnash his teeth from pain. Perhaps he had typhus, and everything was upside down in his head. He could ask Sibin if you could feel pain where you had felt it in a dream, but Sibin would laugh at him. His elbow hurt all right—there's no pain worse than a blow on the bone. But how could something hurt which had been cut off and thrown in the trash can? Something which has been gnawed by the dogs? With his left hand he felt the bandages on his shoulder and chest: there was no arm, it had been cut off. Then why did it hurt so much, damn it?

"How did you sleep, my boy?" asked Tola, bending over him.

"A lot you care what I did last night!"

"If I didn't care I wouldn't have shivered all night next to that cold chimney, with the rats scuttling and squeaking around me like they wanted to bite my ears! Are you feeling better?"

"I wasn't in pain last night, and I'm not now. I feel like whistling, as if something great had happened to me."

"Then whistle, my boy, if you feel like it. Thank God you do. You'd feel even better if you'd let me put a bit of warm wax on your wound. There's no better medicine in the world. This gift the bees give us can heal all wounds and cure everything."

"I wouldn't let you stick it on my ass, let alone on my arm!" said Miloje from under the blanket.

It was daylight. Gavrilo gripped the iron rods of the headboard with both his hands and felt like crying out: Sergeev!

There was no one whom he could send for the Russian doctor with the malevolent fingers, not Milena or any of the orderlies. He must have fallen asleep, or else abandoned the major to his gangrene. He couldn't call Sergeev because of the people on the floor, his own soldiers. He groaned from the depths of his chest: he just didn't have the courage to draw back before the last step, it wasn't in his power.

When his head cleared a bit he lifted up the eiderdown to look at his rotting leg, which was beginning to swell into his pelvic bone, into the mattress, the walls, and the floor, even the foundations of the hospital, flooding them with burning, throbbing pain. He felt his wound with his fingers: it hissed more audibly than on the previous night. The swelling was now paler, but there were spots everywhere. His thigh was cold under the wound and the swelling, and there was no feeling in it or in his foot. His leg was dying. What about those spots? They were spreading, growing numb. Or, was he seeing things? The gangrene had affected his vision, too.

"Bogdan, sit up and take a look."

Bogdan was breathing hoarsely. Gavrilo leaned over and called his name, remembering that since daybreak he had been delirious. He couldn't bring him back to his senses. Did he have typhus? Would this young man follow him to the grave? He put his hand on Bogdan's hot, sweating forehead: he had a high fever. He wiped his temples and caressed him, feeling close to tears. Bogdan's groans grew louder and he sighed as if having a terrible dream.

Gavrilo covered himself with the eiderdown and stared at the ceiling. Was it really impossible to change anything now? The early morning noises of the hospital were growing louder, and streaks of murky light began to appear in the door and the window.

"Well, how are you, Major?" asked Doctor Paun Aleksić.

"What's that to you, Doctor? Radojko, wipe my forehead."

"I've been ordered to inform you that Colonel Hadžić, chief of staff of the First Army, has been asking after you."

"Tell him I haven't collapsed in the slush. Now get out of my sight."

"Serbia isn't to blame because we have no Swiss sanatoria, and because every place that has a roof has been turned into a hospital. Anyway, you can discuss that with Colonel Kajafa."

"Kajafa?"

"Colonel Kajafa will be here any minute."

Why was Kajafa here? His former friend and companion, who had called him a traitor and avoided him in the street; that Prussian-style officer who considered severity a virtue. When he had been lieutenant and Kajafa a captain in the second class, on a number of occasions Kajafa had grossly humiliated him at cards, taking all his pay, and removing his boots and cap in the presence of other officers. These incidents in the Officers' Club had been the talk of the entire Belgrade garrison; not until they became fellow-conspirators in the plot against King Alexander had they been reconciled. Kajafa was his commanding officer, but he had never sent greetings even through his orderly. What could he want here now? This was indeed the last joke of fate.

"Is that the whistle of a train, Radojko? What do you mean, you can't hear it? Now wipe my chest with a dry towel. Bring me a bucket of snow; you'll find it somewhere. There's plenty on Suvobor. But first tell Milena Katić to come here. Tell her that Bogdan is worse this morning. Is that you, Kajafa? In person! I'll never again be able to stand at attention in your presence, even though you're the division commander. I can't hear you. Sit down on the bed, if you're not afraid of lice."

The hubbub suddenly died down and was followed by a tense, burning silence.

Kajafa took Gavrilo's hand in both of his and held it for a long time, looking straight into his eyes with an expression of mingled irony and sadness. He couldn't endure that look, or the friendly hand-clasp—Kajafa would feel him trembling. He withdrew his hand and lowered his eyes to Kajafa's revolver.

"I'm glad, Gavrilo, very glad indeed, to be able to tell you personally that you've been recommended for promotion to lieutenant colonel. You've been put in command of the Eighth Regiment. Mišić has given me his approval by telephone."

"I don't understand," stammered Gavrilo, still staring at the revolver.

Kajafa sat down on the bed and leaned toward him. His overcoat had a cold, damp, horsy smell. "You've been put in command of the Eighth Regiment and promoted to lieutenant colonel. A short time ago Mišić recommended you for the Karageorge Star, for the defense of Suvobor."

"So, you've already buried me! Don't mind me—I appreciate your generosity. In Serbia it's rare now for a man to die as a traitor, thank God!" His eyes once more fixed themselves on Kajafa's revolver, which hung from his belt.

"Don't make a fool of me, Gavrilo. You know I don't like jokes. I came to help. What are you doing to yourself?"

"You mean, what am I doing about the gangrene?"

"I've issued orders that the doctors start the operation in ten minutes."

"You've given them orders to cut off my leg?"

"I've told them to do what's necessary to save your life."

"So the division commander has ordered my leg amputated!" For some time he was unable to speak; then, frightened by the long silence, he cried out, "I'm sorry, Colonel, you've exceeded your authority in relation to a subordinate officer!"

"I'm simply taking advantage of my privilege, Gavrilo. I understand cowards well enough, but I have no use at all for fools."

Gavrilo looked at Kajafa with tears in his eyes and despair in his heart: so Kajafa didn't know the real reason for his decision, for his life?

"So you think I'm a fool?" he stammered.

"A man who doesn't value his own life doesn't value the cause we are fighting for."

"That's what I think, too, Kajafa."

"Then everything's all right. Want to smoke?"

"Everything is *not* all right. We've come to different conclusions. I don't feel like smoking any more. It's as if you've slapped my face."

"That's wounded vanity!"

"You don't understand; I'm sorry."

"I'm sorry, too. But we can talk about that when you're well again."

"No, we'll do it now. I'm glad we're talking again after twenty years. We were born on the same street, went to the same school. I learned a lot of tricks from you. There's only one man who could give me greater pleasure—but that's another story."

"I sent him a telegram. I hear he was here last night."

For some time neither of them spoke.

"Are you afraid of the operation?"

"It's life that I'm afraid of, Kajafa."

"Why are you so faint-hearted?"

"I'm grateful to you, Kajafa. Your presence has clarified so many things in my head. But I must tell you, as an old friend, that I don't want to live as a cripple. I can't!"

"Who gave you the right to live only as long as you want to, Gavrilo?"

"My mother gave me that right. It's my inalienable right. Two thousand years ago people knew that there was no need to live simply out of necessity."

"There are eleven of us left from our class. Not one of us has made his own decision about his life. We've dedicated our lives to the Serbian cause. And that's how we've got to go on."

"Sorry to disappoint you, but I see things differently. Ever since I can remember, I've lived my way, followed my star. You know how much my father wanted me to study at the Kiev Theological Seminary. You know how I hated the barracks and military discipline, and how I despised the uniform and the saber. I put up with it all because I'd decided of my own free will to work for the liberation and unification of the Serbs. You know too that in our conspiracy I couldn't submit to Apis's will and yours, and so we parted ways. I was the one who paid the price, and yet you regard me as a traitor."

"Nobody thinks that any more. People expected a lot of you. We saw you as our leader. No man was more popular than you before you resigned your commission and went off to Russia."

"You're consoling me, Kajafa; I'm grateful. But I had to capture two batteries at Kumanovo, lead a battalion against the Bulgarians at Kočan, and do what I did on Suvobor. All that is unimportant now. I simply wanted to say that I've lived for the things I wanted. I can't change now."

"That's pure self-indulgence. Selfish philosophizing. People of our generation have no right to that. No man of honor can allow himself such a right."

Such ruthless and ironic words aroused in him a desire to disagree for the sake of disagreeing; he almost felt hatred for this man who was driving him *there* by arguing from another stage of his life.

"Now you listen to me, Kajafa! I'm prepared to stand on the banks of the Drina with no legs at all. I'm ready to be a stump on the banks of the Sava, for the Austrians to stumble over. I can do all that. But I love nothing in the world more than myself. I'm ready to die for Šumadija, but not to walk about it on crutches. I've risked my life for the Drina and the Sava, but I want to swim in them. You're the sort of man who can understand that."

"I understand but I don't approve, Gavrilo."

"So you think there's some point in living without acts of courage? Not to be able to strike at a thief or scoundrel, or fight for a beautiful woman? Always to be at the mercy of other people's cruelty and compassion, to wait for illness to put an end to eating and shitting? You can eat and drink easily enough, God knows, but to piss and shit is a humiliating business, it takes effort. To arouse pity, to become a butt of ridicule—not me, Kajafa! Nothing in the world would induce me to place restrictions on my life!"

"You're deceiving yourself badly if you think this wisdom and courage. If you think it heroic to refuse this operation."

"Maybe it isn't wise or courageous."

"It isn't even honorable!"

"I accept your verdict. It isn't honorable, but that's how I want it! And I can do it! To do the last thing you want to do, when it's no longer possible to change or repeat anything, sometimes that's all a man can do. Don't frown, Kajafa!"

Kajafa sighed and averted his eyes.

What if he doesn't reply? thought Gavrilo, and felt afraid. The room was quiet. Not even Kajafa could advance stronger arguments than those he had already uttered! He fought so bravely and passionately, and was no less proud than Gavrilo Stanković. Why had he given up so easily—he who couldn't endure defeat?

Staring at the window, Kajafa began to speak softly, almost inaudibly: "When we were at the academy, and later during the conspiracy, we used to talk all night long about sacrifice and the need to be prepared for it. We talked about sacrifice as something immortal."

"Yes, I remember."

"Have you changed your mind?"

"I never shared your views about sacrificing oneself for national ideals. I had the same arguments in St. Petersburg with people even more fanatical than we were. I've argued more about sacrifice and the need for it than about anything else in my life. Sacrifice is the most fatal word in the human vocabulary, Kajafa. A base, degrading, vicious word."

Kajafa turned around suddenly and Gavrilo caught that familiar, youthful expression in his large, sad eyes. His moustache was turning gray now, and there were wrinkles on his forehead and around his eyes. Still, he and his division had accomplished a breakthrough on the Suvobor front and had smashed one of Potiorek's army corps.

"I'm sorry we differ so much. I haven't felt so sorry for a long time, not since the beginning of the war," Kajafa whispered; his lips were trembling.

"I feel the same, Kajafa."

"Well, then, have the operation, Gavrilo!"

Gavrilo avoided looking at him and fixed his eyes on the crack in the ceiling. Kajafa was saying something else, but he couldn't hear him. He felt a keen pain in his thigh. He would have groaned aloud, but he felt ashamed.

"When the Austrians took me prisoner," Gavrilo said, "they took my revolver. I've got used to having a weapon, and I can't manage without it. I'd be grateful if you'd give me your revolver."

The pupils of Kajafa's eyes contracted and his gaze narrowed. He asked him a question with his eyes. Gavrilo answered in kind: let him see what he wants to know. Was he nodding in agreement or refusal?

Yes or no, it didn't matter now.

Did Kajafa whisper something to him? There was no reply in his faraway expression. Still he did say something, and he pressed his hand. Then he walked away slowly, dragging his feet. He hadn't given him his revolver. He stood in the doorway.

With a supreme effort Gavrilo propped himself up, gripped the iron rods of the bed, and stared at Kajafa's back; he would have liked to call out, Why have you stopped? But he had no voice.

Kajafa turned around, his face distorted, and their eyes met; he came back even more slowly, stood beside the bed, and stared at him. Gavrilo was looking at Kajafa's revolver. Kajafa slowly unfastened his belt, removed the revolver from its case, and placed it under the pillow.

"Now we think the same, Kajafa," whispered Gavrilo.

Kajafa stood at attention, saluted, then turned around and walked quickly out of the room, passing Sergeev, accompanied by two orderlies with a stretcher.

"Thank you, Kajafa!" cried Gavrilo as Kajafa turned into the corridor. "What are you doing with that stretcher, Sergeev? Take it away!"

Paun Aleksić, the hospital director, sat on his bed and stared at the telegram.

His feeling of a special occasion, his pride in doing a job of national importance, his self-satisfaction on account of so many tasks completed for the common good, and his flights of fancy when he thought of himself as a man with a mission, especially when proposing toasts—all this had been shattered by a telegram. "An Allied medical mission will arrive in Valjevo tomorrow or within the next few days. Prepare the best reception possible. Place yourself at their disposal. Instructions to follow. Colonel Genčić."

His hands shook as he read it for the tenth time. What was he supposed to do now anyway? Was he to go to the station every morning at six o'clock to meet the train with a volunteer nurse and a bunch of flowers, and stand lined up with delegations from the other hospitals, gaping at the train until the last old woman and cripple had gotten off? Do this for a whole week? Here was all this food and drink prepared, the hospital mobilized, the dogs and peasants chased off into the town and fields every morning, and for nothing!

He summoned Doctor Pantelić and the accountant Srećko, and informed them that the mission was due to arrive the next morning.

They were to be ready to leave for the station at half past five. They received the news of this long-awaited event in silence, without visible emotion. This indifference annoyed Aleksić. He dismissed them brusquely and then gave himself up to self-pity, recalling Belić's warnings: "For goodness' sake take care of yourself, Paun. Don't forget that after the war we'll be living in a madhouse!" To which he had replied in a childish way: "I'm a fatalist, dear friend. That means I'm an optimist." But I'm just a tragi-comic buffoon, he'd thought to himself that night. Meanwhile the dogs barked and growled around the hospital as if it were a slaughterhouse. Last night he'd forgotten to tell the commander of the hospital platoon to scatter that bloodthirsty pack at daybreak with shots. He didn't regret this: let the gentlemen from Europe reach the hospital through the din of the dogs' barking. He wouldn't drive the peasants away either: let the Allies see the fathers and mothers of the boys who twice in the last four months had routed the Austro-Hungarian army.

Quickly he put on his new overcoat, lit a cigarette, stepped into the chilly dawn, weighed down by an unfamiliar feeling of hopelessness and anxiety. He hadn't felt like this even when the Austrians had been about to enter Valjevo and he had fled to Mionica. He looked at the dark, blurred outline of the hospital, which seemed to tremble and sway from its own heavy burdens and turmoil. Temperatures would now be falling from the level of the previous night; patients would be lifting their jackets and shirts to see whether typhus had appeared; tormented by thirst they'd curse the orderlies and him, too—particularly him. The sick and wounded and all his subordinates felt that the man in authority had been unjust to them. Well, he could put up with this injustice, this perpetual envy and malevolence. Much those patients cared for the fate of Serbia and her reputation in the world! Their skin, their guts—that was all the rabble ever bothered about!

He went back into his room, ordered a mug of black coffee, and began to pace back and forth, repeating to himself his speech of welcome in German, which now he didn't like at all. He wanted to change it, but couldn't find the right words. He was furious. It was now half past five, and they simply had to start: the carriage had arrived.

He climbed into the carriage and called to the two volunteer nurses to join him, then shouted to Srećko the accountant: "If everything isn't done right, I'll have you court-martialed! Tell the platoon commander that before he hears the train whistle, all those peasants are to be driven off the hospital grounds at gunpoint!"

Only when he was on the platform did he remember that he hadn't said a word to Srećko about the dogs! His worry was interrupted by the stationmaster, who called out from the window of his office, "The train will be an hour and a half late!"

He felt better. With his hands behind his back, he walked up and down beside the tracks, whispering his welcome speech and modulating his accents. When at last the train whistle sounded from the forest, he gave a start and hurried toward the hospital delegations lined up behind the flustered Doctor Vinaver.

Then in a split second crowds of people poured out of the train, but no sign of the mission; the train filled up with passengers leaving Valjevo, and he stood there, cold and defeated. Aleksić noted in Milena Katić's hands a rather modest bunch of privet, which always reminded him of old women and winter poverty. He couldn't restrain himself: "Miss Katić, I told you to find some real flowers. It's all right to greet your father with privet, but . . ."

"Then why didn't you order some camellias from Nice, Doctor?"

He looked around to see whether his colleagues had heard this impudent reply; he was afraid of this arrogant schoolgirl who played the same opposition role in the hospital as her father did in the country. He would take his revenge by making her walk back to the hospital.

Kajafa's revolver under the pillow tore at the pillowcase and dug into the feathers. It pressed against the nape of Stanković's neck like a stump. It would tear his head to pieces—that pitiful, comic spasm of anguish that was his brain, that haze of resistance and doubt. Well, let his brain agonize a little longer over the final decision. He would shut his eyes and listen to the rain dripping from the eaves, and to the ticking of his watch. Perhaps tomorrow he wouldn't hear the water dripping; he found it exciting to listen to that headlong flight of the raindrops, soft and noisy. This was the last experience in his life: a tiny particle, a short moment of the infinite. How was it that he had never fully enjoyed all this? What within him had always drowned out the sound of the rain, of water dripping from the eaves in the twilight? Wishes and hopes. Those conversations and arguments with his friends, most of all with Masha and Apis. Then his insatiable longing always to have people around him—mostly women. He had never been alone. Loneliness was the one thing in life he hadn't the strength to face. And now? He was at last alone.

What had Kajafa been thinking as he stood in the doorway? He had unfastened his belt, removed his revolver, and winced with a mixture of sadness and approbation. He was trembling when he shoved the revolver under the pillow. After saluting, he had gone away quickly, his back bent, as if waiting for the sound of a shot. Perhaps he had sat in the director's office drinking coffee and waiting for the shot. Or was he waiting for news of it at Headquarters? Had he told Hadžić and Mišić that he had given Stanković his revolver? It didn't matter. Well, let him wait a little longer. Let him feel doubt and regret. Would he come back? No, he wouldn't. Everything that he, Gavrilo, could do, Kajafa could do; he remembered that from the days of the conspiracy. Apis would not come back either. Poor Apis! Apis had tried to persuade him that planning the assassination of Franz Josef would make up for the loss of his right leg—that a cripple could be happy if he was bringing about the death of kings. Obviously he had nothing better to offer by way of consolation.

He would listen to the rain dripping from the eaves a little longer. He would savor the pain in his leg, which was pressing upon the room and the hospital, and taking its throbbing flight to Suvobor and Belgrade, to the valley of the Kolubara, as far as Povlen. Was that the crackle of a fire in the stove?

Whenever he thought of death, he thought of how to die with dignity. The peasants have the right idea: "to die beautifully," they say. Was it really so important to him that his last moments should be dignified? Or was it vanity and self-indulgence—a melancholy, stupid romanticism?

It would please him no end if Radojko were now waiting for him in front of the hospital steps with a good horse, already saddled. He would mount and ride slowly at first, until he had left the hospital grounds, then cross the highway and gallop through the fields beside the Kolubara—no, he'd turn off toward the foothills of Suvobor where he had retreated with his battalion, and rush through the gathering darkness, breathing in the clouds, the wetness of the streams, the fragrance of damp oaks and conifers, while the earth grasped at his horse's hooves, obstructing them with streams and slopes; and so he'd rush along until the horse collapsed from exhaustion. Then he'd pick himself up and continue on foot, hopping on one leg like a wounded bird, going forward all the time; finally he'd fall, coughing up that little whiff of intelligence, that tiny drop of his soul, in some meadow or orchard; he'd fall into a clear stream with clean black pebbles . . .

A dull burning raced through his thigh and pelvic bone, then struck at his spine. Tomorrow his stomach would be blue and swollen, and would begin to rumble. The purulent blood, that poisonous swill coursing through his body, would pour over his brain. His last thought would have that sweetish stench of putrefaction. What thought, what memory, would it be?

If he had believed in a life after death, he would have yielded without self-torment. If he had had God within himself, then nothing would be done in fear. Nothing at all? No, not quite, because of those still alive. He was unable to believe, because his father had tried too hard to convince him. At that period in his life he had easily re-placed the little belief in God that he did possess with the idea of justice; for him all divine laws were subject to the law of this world. Had he lived according to this law? He had tried to. Hardly a fitting conclusion for a faith that had sustained him right up to Suvobor and gangrene. While his thoughts were still free from the poison, he had not a moment of regret or justification. All his ideas and ideals were out there, outside the walls of the hospital where the dogs were growling. Would his last thoughts be of love and friendship, of past experience which had been the most important thing in his life? He would die pitying himself, would be powerless to carry out his decision. If he didn't pity himself, there was no meaning in his decision.

Should he think about the good and beautiful things in his life, recall his own deeds of bravery, his victories, his greatest joys? It wasn't true that there hadn't been any joy.

How then should he live the last part of his life? What should be his final experience? It was pointless to think about it. Yet if he really believed that his present mental torment was pointless, then he would yield to fear and die a victim, incapable of reasoning. For all those who knew him now, the revolver under his pillow would be proof of his misery and helplessness, confirmation of his last defeat, the one defeat which people would remember. What was the point of all his serious thinking, all his plans and dreams for himself, all he had hoped and struggled for, when he hadn't prepared himself for this moment? He had never given any thought to how he should live his last hours so that they would encompass everything in his life.

Someone opened a window: the chilly, damp night crept in, the night air of those outside. A distant breeze smelled of the corpses. The air trembled; it was alien, menacing. No, it was simply indifferent. If only they'd stop moaning and groaning just for a few minutes, and the dogs stop barking! Then once again he could hear the midnight quiet by the Kolubara, and feel the pulsating breath of his country, of everything which he felt to be his country. Then he could be deafened by the silence from the undulating mountains, from Suvobor and the foothills around Valjevo. How good it would be if the wretches on the floor didn't hear his shot. He felt a shudder spread right through to the last sinew of memory, to the utmost limit of thought. It wasn't a shudder of terror, but that unknown in life, its end.

What of that January night in St. Petersburg in 1905, the night before the uprising, when they had been anxious to see whether they would all come to the rendezvous? That night when some of them had lingered on the bridge over the Neva, looking at the frozen river in the moonlight? A good thing he remembered that night. He'd think about it until he thrust his hand under the pillow.

"Radojko, soak some towels in rain water and bring them to me."
"Yes, sir."

It was that night that he had made his most solemn promise. Radojko placed a cold, wet towel on his forehead.

"Thank you, Radojko. Now go to bed."
"There's something I want to tell you, sir."
"It can wait till tomorrow."

Platonov and Shishkin had been trying to convince him that there could no longer be room for tyranny in any honest heart. Suddenly he had felt an overwhelming desire to go down to the frozen river and skate, to skate on the Neva in the moonlight until dawn, to skate to his heart's content, and then go rest. The next day he must set out on a dangerous task in the cause of justice, in a foreign land which had that night become his own because of that task. He spoke of this urge to his friends. They might all have gone down to the icebound Neva with him if Zharov hadn't cried out: "Dostoevsky was right! No doubt about it!"

"Why is he right tonight?" asked Rodinov.

"Yes, it's true, what he said! There's no feeling more vital for a man than to be able to bow down to the infinite. That's right, my friends. Look at the cosmos, and tell me if it isn't so!"

"Well," said Katushev, "I'd change one word in that idea of Dostoevsky's. In the face of the infinite one should *not* bow down—all you have to do is think honestly."

"One must hate the infinite—that's our duty!" said Shishkin, banging his fist on the snow-covered support of the bridge. "I hate it. With all my heart I hate the cosmos, eternity, the infinite. The infinite is death!"

"That's not true!" said Platonov. "This compulsive need to put everything into words is a disease! In the face of the infinite a normal, healthy man remains silent. Just that. Don't you agree, Gavrilo?"

"You have to step forward into the infinite, somehow. You've got to take just one step," Gavrilo said hesitantly.

"Why?" asked Zharov angrily.

"Why? Because of life! And something else, too," he had replied with conviction.

"Nonsense!" said Rodinov, laughing.

"I agree with you, Gavrilo," said Shishkin, clapping him on the shoulder. "You're more modest than Kirillov, and once you make the decision, it'll be easier for you than for him. Now let's go skate."

However, at that point nobody felt like skating. They went on arguing about the infinite. He listened to them in silence, feeling that what he had said shouldn't be explained further; in fact, he sensed that what he believed in was in no way more modest than Kirillov's faith that by means of freedom one became a god. He hadn't slept a wink that night; he had some doubts about what he had said so easily above the frozen river. Still, he had set off punctually for the beginning of the great rebellion.

Well, now the time had come for that one step, the only possible step. He had to kill death itself—death, not life. He had to do it because of his love for life. He had to fire that shot. Out of love for himself, and to show that life was more powerful than death. The monstrosity was slowly rotting away, but it was still capable of thought.

Not now, at midnight. No, he'd do it at daybreak, lest Bogdan interpret it as an act of despair. Until then he would live with his unshakable decision, like a corpse that still had the power to think. He would live for a few moments like a man who has his murderer on his knees. Like someone who has defeated death, and lingers a while above fear.

He removed the revolver from under the pillow, took it out of its case, and threw the case away. The revolver was cool, unpleasantly so. He warmed it with both hands. Suddenly he felt horribly sick. He would soil the clean bedclothes, make a mess of the bed. So his last experience would be vomit! He must postpone pulling the trigger.

Someone sat down on the bed. The major didn't recognize him.

"I see you're not asleep, sir. I have some new cards—my war booty. Shall I turn the light on, so we can have a hand? This bed's just made for gambling."

"What's this all about?" Gavrilo asked, placing the revolver next to his dead, cold leg.

"Cards are the only thing that'll give you any pleasure tonight, sir. Gambling can save you in this madhouse."

"What can a game of cards do for me?"

"Win, sir. Your only victory tonight can be at cards."

He looked at the thin, dry fingers rapidly shuffling the cards like a magician. "Are you wounded, or sick?"

"I'm an optimist, and I love gambling more than bread, women, or freedom."

"Your leg's been amputated at the knee?"

"But my hands are all right, and they feel like playing cards."

"Why have you picked on me as your partner?"

"Because it would give me the greatest pleasure to win a game with a major. If I licked some peasant tonight, there'd be a bad taste in my mouth in the morning."

"Leave me alone! There are thirty men in this room. Why me?"

"Don't be angry, sir. I told you it gives me no pleasure to play with men of lower rank. There's no risk. Without risk, it's no fun."

"Get off my bed, Sergeant!"

"It would make me feel real good tonight if I could win against Gavrilo Stanković, who's been visited by Apis and Kajafa. Don't be cross—I'm a cripple."

The sound of the cards mingled with his laughter—or was it his weeping?

"Radojko, I'm going to be sick! Call the orderly!"

He wiped the cold sweat off his face with the edge of the eiderdown.

The noise of the cards being shuffled, mingled with the sergeant's crying or laughter, grew louder. It was becoming more and more unbearable, and he was powerless to do anything about it.

"Where are you, Radojko?"

Radojko Veselinović took a swig from his bottle of brandy, then left it under the bed. Leaning over the major, he whispered: "I have something to report, sir! Today I wrestled with Pepi, in front of a whole regiment of soldiers. There were people from the town there, too, and the priest stopped on his way back from the cemetery. We wrestled right in the middle of Valjevo, in the cattle market."

"Go on."

"We got hold of each other, right there on the bare cobblestones, with the soldiers and people standing around. The Austrians cheered for Pepi, though not all of them. As for the Czechs and our boys from Bosnia and Croatia, I could see from their eyes that they were enjoying it, though a bit scared."

"What happened?"

"Pepi grabbed hold of me and punched me in the groin. I fell down on the cobbles, just as on Suvobor, but I got up again. I said to him, 'You may be the champion of Vienna, but I'm the best wrestler in Podrinje, you bastard!' I stood there like an elm tree, and we fought on the cobbles. I just held him in my arms, and my arms are strong now, thank God—I've been eating, sir."

"Then what?"

"Pepi groaned, I groaned, and we went for each other like wolves! We were waiting to see who'd collapse first. The children cheered for me, and the women, too. I like it, sir, when women watch me wrestle. I've never liked wrestling without women there to watch."

"Go on, Radojko."

"It was a wrestling match that nobody'd seen the like of before. The priest was crossing himself. Vojvoda Mišić's adjutant was watching, and he was amazed. All I thought was, Why isn't the major here to see what Radojko can do? To see the feathers flying from the champion of all Vienna!"

Radojko crouched down, took a swig from the bottle, swallowed slowly, then moved closer to Gavrilo to convince him of his lie. "I'd give a meadow by the Drina for you to have seen me, sir. There was I, your orderly and an ordinary Serb, taking on the strongest wrestler in the Austrian Empire. I'm sorry, I was just waiting for you to turn up on your horse. We went on wrestling, I tell you, from twilight till sunset. I was wet through, like I'd fallen into the Drina. Then it grew dark and I couldn't see his eyes. You've got to look an Austrian in the eyes. Then when it got dark all sorts of things happened. Can you hear me, sir? Pepi collapsed like a balloon! All his innards squirted out, and him the best wrestler in all the Austrian Empire! I'm just a peasant from Šljivica, but I licked Pepi, sir; I threw that bastard into a puddle like a torn sack! Can you hear me, sir?"

Gavrilo's bed seemed to be carried away and pinned against the wall: plaster poured over him as he fell. He was anxious about the revolver under his pillow.

Where's this letter from? Russia. Too late. Was it really necessary for him to wait for so many years? This was his third war, and he could have been dead a hundred times. But here it was: Grisha, my dearest. I'm on my way; wait for me and I'll explain everything. I embrace you, Masha. But do you realize, Masha, that they've cut off my right leg, up to the thigh? Cripples can't embrace. It's too late. Forget about me. Then just his signature.

What's this, Radojko, another telegram? For me you're not a cripple; I'm in Niš already and will be in Valjevo tomorrow morning. Maria Rayevska. What can this mean, Maria Rayevska? Why so sad, Radojko? You're a soldier. Get a horse ready for me. Saddle it and bring it to the hospital steps. What do you mean, will I be able to mount a horse and not just a nag? It would be a sorry sight for you to be holding me as I go through Valjevo—people would laugh! For me you're not a cripple. Of course not!

If that's the sparrows twittering and it's morning, it's time for me to get dressed—with Radojko's help, of course. All right, Radojko, but why only one boot? Yes, I know my leg's been amputated, and I can't step out into the infinite. In their heart of hearts people like cowards. But you're to bring me both boots every morning properly polished. Now bring the other one. For heaven's sake, Milena, why do you need such a big mirror? He'd got very thin, and there were dark circles under his eyes. Why were his nose and ears that dark blue color? And why those spots on his eyelids? Why did he look so repulsive? Who are you talking about? Anyway, who am I, Miss Katić? My suit has been properly ironed, but it's loose, just hanging on me, nothing inside. A typical convalescent. Can't be helped—we must accept our fate. Anyway, I'll work with Apis, plotting assassinations of kings and emperors. I'll live a secluded life, in a little house by quince trees, and look at the Srem and the Sava while the sun is setting —until she comes. But she won't deceive me this time; the moment I feel so much as a trace of pity, I'll say: Good-by, Maria Rayevska, here's the money for your journey. The carnival is over; you can sit in the little box, but the whirligig has stopped.

Don't hold me, Radojko, I can manage. Going about on crutches isn't so bad after all. One can get about quickly, very quickly— especially on the floor in an empty room, and at night when everything is quiet. Yes, Kajafa, you're right, it's horrible. The košava roars through Belgrade for several months, but on a hot day you can just sit on the porch and look across the Sava. I'll be waiting for you on the steps; bring the horse there. It's a marvelous morning, as it should be. The plum trees are in blossom, and the apricot trees; you're right, Radojko, I'll look at the fields and the orchards. I'll listen to the bees. It's plants that bring us the greatest joy, Bogdan, and plum trees. I must confess I've had a gloomy, self-absorbed outlook on life. I've completely gone to pieces, poisoned and festering in my self-loving obstinacy. You're asking me to help kill kings, but I wanted to kill death. Don't hold on to me, Radojko! We're on an official footing now, and you know where the groom's place is. What's the horse's name? Putko? It's a long time since I felt a horse's skin so tense in my hand, it's like a tissue of tremors. Let me stroke him a little. I like a horse with a heavy mane. My heart's beating so loud I'll wake up the entire hospital. Don't hold on to me! Don't you remember how I threw myself into the saddle? Now I mustn't take risks; the entire hospital has come out to see if I can mount. Now listen, Nikolay Maksimovich, in my heart—in my soul—I have both legs. You'll never be able to cut them off—never! A man lives whole to the end of his life, he does *not* die a cripple. Do you hear me, Doctor?

Radojko, calm that horse down! A horse can't stand any but healthy hands on it, and a good horse can't take babbling. Why are the patients quarreling? They're making bets that I can't mount the horse. That I'll fall down like a log. All right then, make your bets! As soon as you're done, I'm getting on that horse! Bogdan, my boy, there's nothing sillier than people's laughter. The hospital is echoing with the shouts of the wounded and crippled. But he's riding just as he used to! He can jump over hurdles! He's flying out the gate and onto the highway! Why so many people in the street, pressed up against the walls and fences? They're shouting, clapping, wild with excitement! He's spurring his horse, galloping through Valjevo! Townspeople, soldiers, prisoners of war—they're all clapping. He must be a famous cripple. Long live Major Gavrilo Stanković! Where's the road? How can there be no road out of town? You have to go through the plum orchards. That tree is big—thick, too. Its branches will throw him from the saddle. They're scratching his face; never mind—they're green. The horse can't stop. The green branches have crowded around him, the horse is floating. Someone's calling to him. It's Kajafa! But the division staff mustn't catch up with him. Kajafa and his escort have overtaken him. How did you get here, Gavrilo?

"So it's you, Nikolay Maksimovich."

"I've given you an injection. As soon as you feel any pain, call me."

"I won't."

The train was only an hour late; from it some ten women wearing tropical helmets and carrying olive-green bags with the sign of the Red Cross, huge knapsacks, and folded tents descended into the wet snow.

Dr. Paun Aleksić looked at them with incredulity and a trace of scorn. So this was the Allied medical mission! There was only one man with the ladies; he was wearing a beret and had a pipe in his mouth. Major Avram Vinaver went up to the women and their escort, a second lieutenant in the medical corps, and introduced himself. Only one of the women shook hands with Vinaver, while the rest busied themselves with their luggage, casting inquisitive glances at the town as they did so. With a gesture Major Vinaver summoned his colleagues, and with his eyes signaled to Paun Aleksić to proceed. Doctor Aleksić then delivered his speech of welcome, smiling slightly and speaking with faultless diction and carefully chosen phrases; but it was clear that nobody was listening, except Vinaver and the Serbian officer acting as escort to the Scotswomen. They were still busy with their knapsacks and tents; their leader, Miss Inglis, who was standing between Vinaver and the escort, was staring at something beyond the station. Having spoken the last sentence of his speech of welcome—pronounced in the name of Valjevo, "where at this moment only human compassion is waging a tragic struggle with death"—Aleksić bowed deeply and kissed the outstretched hand of Miss Inglis, whose glove smelled so strongly of chloroform that Aleksić felt affronted. Milena Katić handed her the bouquet of privet, but without her speech of welcome in French; to punish her for this spiteful behavior, Aleksić vowed that as soon as the mission's visit was over he'd have her transferred to a reception center in town. His anger quickly disappeared when the man with the pipe and beret introduced himself in German: "My name is Doctor Hunter; I'm a bacteriologist."

Paun Aleksić introduced himself.

"So your name is Paul! That's easy to remember. Thank goodness there's one Serbian name I can immediately remember."

Paun Aleksić was unmoved by this blunder. As they walked toward the carriages, they discussed the epidemic and conditions in Valjevo; Doctor Hunter puffed at his pipe and slowed his steps as he listened, forcing Aleksić to be absolutely precise in the information he gave him.

Two of the Scotswomen joined them in the carriage without waiting for an invitation. They smiled at him wearily. They hardly understood a word of German. What a pity, said Aleksić to himself, as he gazed at the unusually sweet and gentle face of the younger one. He watched all three closely to see how they would react to the street, packed with sick and wounded men and with prisoners lying in the snow. When they passed two short funeral processions, the Scotswomen asked Hunter something; as far as Aleksić could understand, he replied that the Serbs belonged to the Orthodox Church. The young women arched their eyebrows in surprise.

"I've spent four nights in Serbia," said Hunter, "three in Niš and one in Kragujevac, and I'm exhausted. Can you explain to me, Paul, why people in Serbia get up at such a disgustingly early hour?"

"Because they are peasants, Mr. Hunter. The earth and the animals make early rising necessary."

"I wouldn't have thought that was the reason. I have relatives who are peasants, and I've visited them several times. I haven't noticed that Welsh peasants get up so early."

Aleksić changed the subject, talked about the epidemic and its victims, and pointed out the scenes in the street. Once again Hunter interrupted him: "You know, Paul, I'm most impressed by the generosity of your nation toward the enemy. You must be a very religious people. Just look!" he said to the Scotswomen, pointing to two wounded men on the pavement who were cutting bread and handing it out to prisoners. "Do you see what they're doing?"

The Scotswomen were staring at some children lugging a coffin from a workshop; two typhus patients were sitting on the step, waving their arms about as if warding off a hornet. An old woman appeared behind the coffin, which the children set down on the pavement. She was carrying a mug with some lighted candles inside, and bent over the mug to protect the candles from the wet snow. The carriage stopped to let the funeral procession pass. Doctor Hunter got up to have a better look at the Serbian wounded, who were cutting up pieces of hardtack for the Austrian prisoners; he continued to express his enthusiasm for the Serbs' kindness. This pleased Aleksić, but he warned the soldier driving the carriage to move on, so that Hunter wouldn't see that the bread was being paid for with money or sugar. As the carriage continued on its way toward the Grand Hotel, the Englishman could find no words to express his enthusiasm.

In the Grand Hotel, which had been emptied of sick and wounded in order to receive the mission, stod two rows of tables loaded with hot meat pie, cheese, bread, roast suckling pig and turkey, and little flasks of hot brandy. The Scotswomen shook the rain off their capes and looked in amazement at the quantity of food on the tables. In spite of all Vinaver's entreaties and persuasion, they would take only a piece of bread and some cheese; they asked for tea, resolutely refusing to have hot brandy instead—which only Hunter drank with pleasure as he argued with Aleksić about Christian morality, asserting that only a profound understanding of Christ's sacrifice and a sincere return to his teaching could bring about the moral and spiritual regeneration of the world after the present war. Naturally Aleksić didn't believe this, but as a good host he contradicted the Englishman only just enough to keep the conversation going; he was in fact displeased by it, and by the almost pointed refusal of the Scotswomen to eat anything at all except bread and cheese.

Miss Inglis abruptly terminated this display of hospitality: she asked that the young women immediately be taken to their rooms. After four hours' sleep they would begin their work. They would visit Doctor Aleksić's hospital at noon the next day. He said good-by to the young women whom he had brought in his carriage, and only just managed to kiss the hand of Miss Inglis. As he was leaving, Hunter overtook him. "Could I see you this evening, Paul?"

"I'm at your disposal, Doctor."

"I'll be waiting for you here in the hotel at eight o'clock. Do come. You know, Paul, you're the only Serb who hasn't clapped me on the shoulder during a conversation. I really do find you congenial."

Aleksić gave him a withering look.

"You must explain this curious habit to me: why is it that you Serbs hit the person you're talking to on the shoulder?"

"We do that as an expression of strong affection," he said curtly. He gave a slight bow and went out into the street, distinctly annoyed.

He spent the rest of that January day, shortened by thick, soft snow and cloud which engulfed the hills around Valjevo, sitting in his office, drinking cognac, and smoking; he felt thoroughly disheartened by the day's events.

Everything was losing its meaning, even pain. He didn't want to end like this. He didn't want to die without pain. He didn't want death to destroy him, to stop the beating of his heart in this rotting flesh. Now when he felt like it after so much torment, and when everything had lost the last vestige of meaning, he ought to do something really very easy: press his finger into that little circle which was revolving ever more slowly. He would stop it with his own finger, by his own act of will. Surely that was a heroic deed? His existence had begun by chance, but wouldn't end so. First of all he would kill death itself. That was power—the vital step and the longest. He would leave his tracks in the stone. Straight through the heart. That throbbing organ was a garbage heap. He would fire at his head; his head *was* him. It was the fault of his head that he hadn't enjoyed life more, that he didn't believe in God or in life after death. But that's a lie; his head was innocent, and so was his father. What was he waiting for? For the cocks to crow? Yes, he was waiting for daybreak. When day showed its first light, then he'd thrust his hand under the pillow; first of all he'd remove the catch and grip it firmly, for his hands were now very weak.

Don't destroy yourself, Gavrilo! Don't surrender! Don't, Gavrilo, don't! He raised his voice and cried out his own name: let the whole hospital hear.

He'd have to summon all his strength to end in a convenient position. To look like a real corpse. What should he do with his hands? What, indeed?

"He's moribund," said Doctor Pantelić to an orderly. "What are you laughing at, Major?"

"At the word *moribund*, Doctor."

"So you know Latin?"

"Am I smiling at you, Milena? Please answer, it's important. Sit down on the bed, Milena. You're a fine girl! He's a lucky fellow . . ."

Doctor Pantelić didn't believe that Bogdan would pull through.

"At daybreak, when I leave this garbage dump, move Bogdan into my bed. You and Radojko."

The night roared, the dogs barked and growled.

He felt his revolver. It was infected with gangrene. No, it still wasn't daylight. He'd do it at dawn, when the cocks began to crow. Utterly pointless. The final act of stupidity in this garbage dump.

"Radojko, tell Milena to come."

"I'm here, Major Stanković."

"Call me Gavrilo."

"Would you like some tea, Gavrilo?"

"Pronounce my name in a whisper—louder, I can't hear you. That's better. Now let's finish the job. Milena, you hold my head, and you, Radojko, take hold of my thighs and put me down on the floor. On the straw where Bogdan is lying. Then lift Bogdan onto my bed and cover him with the eiderdown. What are you waiting for, Radojko?"

"But it's your bed, sir!"

"Get out!"

The night was slowly dying away, and the sound of the dogs, too.

I've been far too ordinary. I regret it now. The thought fills me with despair. My life has been a tyranny of all that's ordinary, and I have been its slave. That's enough, Gavrilo!

He pulled himself out of the bed, bent over toward Bogdan, and placed his hand on his forehead. Gently and affectionately, he removed his eiderdown and covered Bogdan with it.

"Here's the pipe, Bogdan. Your inheritance."

He leaned back against the pillow and aimed the revolver at his gangrenous leg, ready to kill it. With a feeling of disgust he fired at it, and yet with some kind of pleasure, too, which confirmed for him something important—and yet quite insignificant when he brought the revolver close to his heart.

Miloje Dačić didn't remove the blanket from his head, although he was awake when startled by the sound of two shots. From what the orderlies were saying, he gathered that the major had fired one bullet into his wounded leg, and another at his head. Once he had decided to do this, his major's rank availed him little, and that bed even less. Well, maybe the major got tired of seeing and hearing so much foul talk around him, and since he couldn't run away, he'd taken care of it the best way he could. Too bad he hadn't thrown two or three grenades first, to make mincemeat of the worst of these thieves. If by any chance he, Miloje, had to squeal in his corner, if he began to bleat and gasp like those typhus patients next to Sibin, he wouldn't do it alone! His neighbors wouldn't outlive him—though they didn't know what they were in for. He'd give everything he owned for just one grenade.

He heard quarreling and removed the blanket from his face. It was already daylight, and Sergeant Žabarac was sitting on the major's bed, holding on to the rods with both hands. Lieutenant Simić, who was gripping the headboard with his one sound hand, shouted: "Get off that bed, Sergeant! The major's bed belongs to me now, because of my rank."

"Rank doesn't mean anything now, Lieutenant! It's our wounds that give us seniority."

"To hell with your wounds! Get off!"

"Over my dead body!"

Two captains, accompanied by orderlies, entered the room and ordered the sergeant and lieutenant away from the bed.

"Over my dead body!" repeated Žabarac, still gripping the iron rods.

"Throw him off!" said one of the captains to the orderlies.

Žabarac took a revolver from his belt and aimed it at the orderlies, who stepped back. The captain shouted, cursed, and pulled at the headboard. The orderlies took hold of the bed and pulled it toward the door, with Žabarac still sitting on it with his drawn revolver. "Over my dead body! Over my dead body!" he shouted.

"Then shoot!" shouted Miloje Dačić, as he covered his head with his blanket.

Milena Katić sat on the edge of her bed and stared in front of her, transfixed. The volunteer nurses were returning from the night shift, waking up those in whose beds they must sleep, undressing, and talking about the previous night.

I was just going to light a candle for a student when the shooting started. I thought to myself: The Austrians are back again! I was half asleep on my feet by the main door. Some old gaffer lit the stove last night, and there was a funny smell. Was that major married? Does he have any family? When that idiot fired the shots I thought I must be dreaming. What do you think, girls: was Stanković a hero or a coward? A coward! What do you mean, a coward? I think he was a coward, too. That's just a superficial view, you silly goose! I'm sorry I never knew him. He had a wonderful black beard. If I'd known him I'd have fallen in love with him. Take Jennie's temperature— you can see she's delirious. Milena, this is the second time I've asked you whether the major was married.

Milena jumped.

"Pull yourself together and get dressed," said Dušanka, bringing her a clean apron and veil. "You're to be ready in five minutes. The director's gone crazy since yesterday. Come on now, get off the bed. I'll help you to dress. The major was a very interesting man, even though he was old. Exciting eyes and really beautiful hands. What will become of Serbia if all the wounded begin to kill themselves?"

Milena grew rigid as she remembered Gavrilo's face covered with blood, and Bogdan kissing Gavrilo's dangling hand, and Bogdan's groan when the orderlies jerked the hand away in order to place Gavrilo's dead body on a stretcher and carry it out. She was reminded of Vladimir's cry that night she had tried to say to him, "It's snowing, Vladimir."

Dušanka continued to talk: "I really envy you! You'll be enjoying yourself all day with that Englishman. Is he blond? He must be a real gentleman! Why are you so stiff? You really are an idiot! Up till now you've been crazy about Vladimir. Now suddenly you're mad for the major. Pull yourself together, Milena, or I'll hit you, I really will!"

"Tell the director I'm ill. I can't go with those people just now."

"What's the matter with you, Milena? You're the only one who knows French."

"I've forgotten it all."

Dušanka removed her bloodstained apron and shook Milena as she scolded her. "Milena, there's something I forgot to tell you last night. Nadežda Petrović has arrived."

"Nadežda Petrović? My teacher?"

"Yes, the painter."

"Where is she?"

"I don't know where she's working."

Milena pushed Dušanka aside, put on her coat, and set off for town to look for Nadežda.

Paun Aleksić got up very late and made his orderly change the foot bath twice. By prolonging this enjoyment, he was attempting to restore the self-esteem destroyed by the sleepless night; he was going to need it badly that day. He ate his breakfast, ordered more coffee, and just barely heard the morning report submitted by Doctor Pantelić.

"All I'm interested in is whether everything is in order in the rooms to be visited by the Allied mission," he said, as soon as Pantelić had saluted.

"I'm sure everything is all right, but I'll double-check. However, in addition to the forty-three deaths reported last night, we've had one suicide. Major Gavrilo Stanković shot himself twice with a revolver."

"To be expected. An aggressive personality, hypomanic." He got up and gripped the edge of the table. It *would* have to happen today, damn him! Now Apis will scream and Kajafa, too—the staff will intervene. "You'll see, Pantelić! There'll be an investigation, interviews, a post mortem. This we didn't need! Doctor, make a thorough search of all wards and remove all weapons, particularly from the officers. I don't want any more trouble from the sick and wounded. The suicides will really start when they're in a state of raving delirium."

"It's impossible to remove the soldiers' knives. They hide them, sir."

"Oh, no, it isn't! Tell the orderlies to strip them to the skin; and let me have a detailed report of this idiot's suicide by noon!"

Srećko opened the door without knocking and shouted, "Only two of them have come!"

"What do you mean, only two?"

"Two ladies wearing those hats, with Major Vinaver. They're in a carriage."

"Where's Milena Katić? And Mrs. Stefanović?" he shouted as he buttoned up his jacket and put on his overcoat.

"Mrs. Stefanović is here, but not Milena. Someone saw her going down the main road a while back, and she hasn't returned."

"Going down the main road? Where could that impudent bitch have gone off to?"

"I'm afraid I don't know, sir."

There was no time for argument; he could hear the carriage in the courtyard. He set out to meet it, accompanied by Doctor Pantelić and Mrs. Stefanović in spotless hospital coats. He was still struggling to master his irritation when he greeted them and gallantly kissed the hand of Miss Inglis. He then introduced his colleagues and asked the visitors into his office. The Scotswomen made it quite clear that they wished to go around the hospital immediately. Sensing the danger in their strictly official attitude, he gave Doctor Pantelić a warning look and led them and Major Vinaver to those parts of the hospital reserved for the visit.

The hospital reverberated with banging and shouting, as if the whole place was up in arms. With a withering look, Aleksić ordered Srećko to quiet things down, without even interrupting his conversation with Miss Inglis about his trouble in obtaining medical supplies and accommodations for the patients. Right in front of the entrance to the specially prepared wards, however, something went amiss: the other Scotswoman hurried off after Srećko toward the main entrance. Aleksić stopped talking and cast a despairing glance at Pantelić. Pantelić then hurried after the curious Scotswoman, but Aleksić ordered him back in such a tone that Major Vinaver was startled. "What happened, Doctor Aleksić?" he asked anxiously.

"You don't understand?"

"No, I don't."

"Then everything is all right. Please follow me."

After that everything happened precisely the way he didn't want it to: Miss Inglis merely glanced from the doorway at the carefully prepared rooms, and paying no attention to his frenzied explanations and attempts to detain her, set off to go around the entire hospital; she asked no further questions. She walked quickly, pausing only to write in her notebook. Aleksić accompanied her, silent and indifferent.

"You know, Doctor, you've played a nice trick here, a real dirty trick, in front of these visitors!" said Doctor Vinaver.

A typhus patient at his last gasp ripped off his undershorts and gripped his scrotum, then collapsed before an orderly could get to him. Miss Inglis gave no sign of any embarrassment; she didn't even look at a patient who was singing Menelaus's aria from *The Fair Helen*, and gave no start when a patient right in front of her removed a thermometer from under his arm, put it in his mouth, crushed it with his teeth, chewed it, and spat out the bloodstained fragments.

In the drawing room, when the Scotswomen refused to eat or drink anything but tea, Aleksić's anger overflowed into a sweet and vengeful enjoyment of his defeat; he stopped offering them anything and lapsed into silence with a slightly cynical smile, making it quite clear that he wished them to leave as soon as possible. When they did so, he ordered the food prepared for the reception to be distributed among the sick and wounded, got into his carriage and set out for the medical supply depot to see Milan Belić, and then called on Mrs. Predolac.

After such an undeserved defeat, what could a man in a position of authority do, he asked himself; only gambling and whores could offer any consolation. Yes, that's it, he said to himself with conviction, as the wheels of the carriage sliced through the mud and rattled over the snow-covered cobblestones.

My body is possessed by lice: it's their lair, their feeding ground, their breeding place. They have reproduced to such an extent that it's too crowded for them on my skin. I can feel them fighting for a place, for a pore into which they can dig their snout and suck— suck blood, and the sap of my dissolving skin and muscles. Now they're rushing to pierce my veins, to course through them and breed in them. They'll plant their eggs in my blood. It will become hard for my blood to seep through the slopes and curves of my veins. They'll clog the capillaries. They'll fill my heart with the sediment of their progeny, until it's completely overrun by lice and their eggs. A struggle will ensue between my heart and the louse for primeval victory; but we've always known who the victor is in that struggle.

Nevertheless, some curious descendants may ask: How could these insects, which don't even fly, overcome an entire nation so swiftly and easily?

To understand this historical event, we must grasp the fact that in nature and among men there is a reciprocal relationship between spatial areas and the creatures that inhabit them. We know which areas are inhabited by elephants and bears, and which by lice and bugs. It has always been the same—large creatures in large spaces, tiny creatures in tiny spaces. Furthermore, History has its periods and phases, so we can understand easily enough when a particular disease, wild beast, insect, or misfortune attacks mankind. As for the louse, this little creature has a reciprocal relationship with those in positions of authority. It's not always clear who causes what—whether those in authority are the cause and the louse the effect, or the other way around; or whether the louse and our rulers are both cause and effect at one and the same time. In this Serbian epidemic our rulers have done their best not to threaten the freedom of the lice in any way, and to create the most favorable conditions for their multiplication and nourishment. Thus we have a total occupation of Serbia by lice—something never heard of before.

Among the people around me, the Healthy are distinguished from the Sick only by their brutality, by the sheer force of their evil and stupidity. In the last resort, there is less and less difference between the dead and the living. The most significant difference, of course, is that the dead don't have lice. They flee from their victim and killer in the wake of his soul. They fear absolute peace beneath human skin, feel cold on a dead body. This is no small matter: in this one instance, the louse is afraid of man. However, we can no longer feel proud because of this, since if we had within us a ray of light, we'd have crawled away from this stinking hole. In this world, nothing good can be accomplished and nothing changed for the better without self-respect—nothing!

Sickness degrades a man more than any other misfortune, far worse than jealousy, more painfully than any vice. Sickness deprives us of all self-respect, strikes us down as citizens and human beings; Sickness enables us and indeed forces us to reveal our worst personal and national characteristics. A Sick Man has no capacity for dissimulation or cunning; in Sickness the man can be seen whole. In fact, a man is what he is when he is Sick.

Sickness reveals the ugly face of our country. It requires an exceptional imagination to see one's country outside the walls of the Hospital. National aims and ideals, solidarity and zeal—all these have turned sour. On the battlefield men die in a split second; in Sickness the whole world dies a lingering Death. In this Epidemic our past has perished, our great men are destroyed, as is our hope in Europe, in all great ideas, in the progress of the world.

Whatever the Sickness, Death from it is always accompanied by suffering. In our particular Sickness, people die disgusted with themselves and the entire human race. Only one who has been ill in the Hospital with this Disease and survives has the right to talk about human virtues; future generations should believe only in his knowledge, moral values, and patriotism. Why this ridiculous and melancholy concern about the future? In the entire spectrum of human anxieties and ambitions, there are none more groundless than those arising from lofty feelings for one's nation and mankind.

After a night of silence, however, while the lice crawled over my eyelids and scaled my lashes, I must confess that there is nothing more disgusting than hatred of one's country and the human race. Perhaps my Sickness hasn't yet reached the stage when I can see myself and the world clearly, and dare to say what I have seen.

At this time, the hardest thing for me to face is the disappearance of human love. Sickness deprives us of the illusion of friendship and many of our loves. Those who are alive and well see their salvation in our death. This Sickness deprives the Healthy of the need to lie to us; no one here has enough compassion to lie, to deceive us by saying we'll get well. True sincerity is cruel!

I have to recognize that there is no respect for great suffering. A man respects suffering only to the extent that he himself is prepared to suffer. Here human intelligence doesn't err: it values what it wishes to achieve. As for compassion and consolation, they are only convincing if they come to me from those who have suffered in equal measure with me—that is, from other Sick People. The compassion of the Healthy is often humiliating and makes one melancholy.

History teaches us that there are certain salutary and unchanging truths. I can see now that there are also salutary lies, indispensable to man. For man's survival among his fellow men, for our human souls, not to mention our tranquillity or happiness, these lies are of greater value than many of the truths on which men pride themselves, and on which their intellectual power rests. What virtue is to be found in a really good lie! A convincing, pleasing, beautiful lie! Without the slightest hesitation, I'd say: Even if you don't love some-

one, say that you do. No god, no human law, will judge you guilty or consign you to hell for that untruth. At this late hour, amid the raving which echoes through the Hospital, I have one hopeless wish —that someone, anyone, in the Hospital would utter the lie that he loves me a little. Why are people so honest, so sincere, and so bold that they won't tell this lie? I have a great longing for someone to smile at me, to whisper something pleasant, to caress my hand. How can I die without this illusion of love, this false kindness, this touch from a fellow creature? Of all forms of Death, this is the most unjust, the most cruel. Why, then, has one lived at all, and endured so much?

I'm delirious.

Why have I kept silent about the real truth for so long? The worst thing about this Sickness is that I'm not alone and that sometimes I weep.

It is only in solitude that a man can live according to his real desires, be what he really is, and even become perfect—without vice or hatred, without envy or stupidity, without injustice, customs, or laws.

To be alone means to be pure.

To be alone means to be immune to defeat or victory, to be free from vanity and ambition.

To be alone means liberation from torment, to be open to happiness.

To be alone means to be eternal.

Oh, if only I had a grenade to wipe out this Hospital, and so be alone one day and night in peace.

Then I'd tell everything, without shame or fear. After that—silence.

TO THE AMBASSADORS OF THE KINGDOM OF SERBIA IN ST. PETERSBURG PARIS
LONDON:
INFORM GOVERNMENTS FRIENDLY TO US THAT AN UNPRECEDENTED OUT-
BREAK OF DISEASE IS SPREADING THROUGH SERBIA. A GREAT DANGER CON-
FRONTS US. IT MAY PROVE CATASTROPHIC IF WE DO NOT CRUSH IT IN TIME.
WE HAVE MANY WOUNDED AND PRISONERS. OUR ARMY LACKS THE BAREST
NECESSITIES. DOCTORS MEDICINES FOOD EQUIPMENT BLANKETS LINEN ARE
ESSENTIAL. WE ARE NAKED BAREFOOT AND EXHAUSTED. HELP URGENTLY
NEEDED.

PAŠIĆ

TO PAŠIĆ, NIŠ:
THE HOLY SYNOD HAS DECIDED THAT A DAY OF PRAYER FOR SERBIA SHOULD
BE HELD IN THE CHURCHES OF THE EMPIRE AND DONATIONS BE COLLECTED.
A COLLECTION WILL BE MADE FOR SERBIA AT THE SUNDAY SERVICE.

SPALAJKOVIĆ, SERBIAN
AMBASSADOR TO RUSSIA,
ST. PETERSBURG

ST. PETERSBURG
AFTER A SERVICE OF THANKSGIVING IN THE CHURCH OF THE SERBIAN
EMBASSY THREE THOUSAND VOLUNTEERS HAVE BEEN DISPATCHED THROUGH-
OUT THE CITY TO COLLECT DONATIONS FOR SERBIA AND MONTENEGRO.

FROM *La Nation:*

A COMMITTEE HAS BEEN SET UP IN PARIS TO HELP THE SERBIAN PEOPLE
AND THE WONDERFUL FIGHTERS OF THIS HEROIC NATION. MAY FRANCE
OPEN HER HEART TO HER DISTANT BROTHERS, NEEDY AND UNFORTUNATE,
WHO ARE STOICALLY ENDURING THEIR FATE.

MOSCOW

TODAY A RED CROSS MEDICAL UNIT NAMED FOR THE CITY OF MOSCOW
SET OUT FOR SERBIA. THIS UNIT INCLUDES A FIELD HOSPITAL WITH TWO
HUNDRED BEDS.

NIŠ

FROM *News:*

EVERYTHING IS TOPSY-TURVY!
THE BOOKSELLERS ARE SELLING EGGS AND RUM.
THE BARBERS ARE SELLING BREAD.
GROCERS ARE SELLING SOLDIERS' CAPS.
CONFECTIONERS ARE REPAIRING WATCHES.
CARPENTERS ARE SELLING ONIONS AND BLACK CLOTH.
ACTORS HAVE BECOME AGENTS FOR SECURING "GOOD FEMALE SERVANTS."

ZAGREB

FROM *Horizon:*

ZAGREB IS PREPARING A FORMAL BIRTHDAY CELEBRATION FOR OUR CRO-
ATIAN KING, OUR BELOVED RULER AND FATHER, FRANZ JOSEF. THIS WAY
WE WILL ONCE MORE BEAR WITNESS TO OUR LOYALTY TO THE ILLUSTRIOUS
HOUSE OF HAPSBURG.

TO PRIME MINISTER NIKOLA PAŠIĆ, NIŠ:

IF THE STATEMENT ABOUT THE LIBERATION OF OPPRESSED AND SUBJU-
GATED PEOPLES WITH WHICH THE ALLIED GOVERNMENTS HAVE JUSTIFIED
THEIR ENTRY INTO THE WAR IS NOT TO REMAIN AN EMPTY PHRASE, WE
HAVE THE RIGHT TO HOPE THAT ON THE TERRITORY OF THE SOUTH SLAVS
A SINGLE STATE WILL BE ESTABLISHED INCLUDING ALL LANDS CONTAINING
SERBS, CROATS, AND SLOVENES. TO BE PRECISE, UNDER PRESENT CONDI-
TIONS AND ACCORDING TO THE CLEARLY EXPRESSED WILL OF THE PEOPLE,

SUCH A STATE WOULD INCLUDE THE KINGDOM OF SERBIA AND THE SOUTH-
EAST BORDER REGIONS OF THE AUSTRO-HUNGARIAN MONARCHY INHABITED
BY CROATS, SERBS, AND SLOVENES: BOSNIA-HERCEGOVINA, DALMATIA WITH
ITS ISLANDS, BAČKA, BANAT, CROATIAN SLAVONIA, MEDJUMURJE, ISTRIA
AND ITS ISLANDS, GORICA, GRADIŠKA AND TRIESTE, KRANJ, SOUTH ŠTAJER
AND KORUŠKA.

ALL THESE REGIONS SHOULD BE UNITED ON THE BASIS OF NATIONALITY
AND SHOULD COMPRISE A SINGLE UNIT.

THIS STATE NEEDS TO BE CREATED ACCORDING TO THE PRINCIPLE OF
NATIONAL UNIFICATION. THE BASIS OF SUCH A CREATION IS THE SELF-
EVIDENT TRUTH THAT THE SLOVENES, SERBS, AND CROATS ARE ONE AND THE
SAME PEOPLE.

FRAN POTOČNJAK [CROATIAN POLITICIAN]

FROM *Figaro:*
THE "SERBIAN DAY" TO BE CELEBRATED TOMORROW IN ALL FRENCH
SCHOOLS BEGAN THIS AFTERNOON WITH A FORMAL MEETING AT THE SOR-
BONNE, WITH THE MINISTER OF EDUCATION IN THE CHAIR.

FROM *Paris Midi:*
NEVER HAS ANY NATION RECEIVED SUCH A TRIBUTE OF SYMPATHY AND
ADMIRATION! THE WHOLE OF FRANCE HAS ACCLAIMED THIS NATION.
YESTERDAY THREE MILLION PEOPLE CHEERED THIS HEROIC PEOPLE IN
THE BALKANS, WHERE THE FATE OF EUROPE WILL BE DECIDED, A NATION
WHICH HAS SET THE WORLD A MAGNIFICENT EXAMPLE.

In the office of the Medical Section of the High Command in
Kragujevac, Dr. Mihajlo Radić was looking attentively at the elderly
colonel in the medical service who, seated at the table and noisily
sipping his coffee, was informing him of his transfer from a division
first-aid station to service behind the lines.

"You can choose your own graveyard, Captain," he said.

"Where are the best prospects for that, sir?"

"Niš, Kragujevac, Valjevo . . . It's hell everywhere."

"I assume the Medical Section of the High Command has been
informed of the places where hell has no doors."

Loudly spitting out a grain of coffee, the colonel stared at him
with his opaque, sleepy eyes, for the first time showing a slight

curiosity, though still speaking in a superior way: "You're a cynic, aren't you?"

"I don't know how to be cynical, unfortunately."

"A suicidal type, then? Something quite rare in wartime."

"I have the greatest respect for suicides."

The colonel continued to sip his coffee as he looked through the window at the crows. "Well, the choice is yours."

"Which place is really the worst?"

"Valjevo. It's the Kossovo* of this century."

"In that case, transfer me to Valjevo."

In the crowded waiting room at the Kragujevac station, Mihajlo Radić kept a firm grip on his medical bag filled with medicines obtained "under the counter," and his suitcase full of new white shirts and handkerchiefs. He waited for the train to be assembled, and for the first infected louse to bite him. Thus infected, he would still have two weeks in which to convince his superiors in the medical service that it was the louse that carried the typhus infection; then he would fall into the terminal delirium of *Typhus exanthematicus* and quickly die, like any other lice-infected creature. But in this world, at least, he would never succeed in changing the ideas of that elderly colonel, a conceited surgeon decorated with orders bestowed by his country because he believed in Linnaeus, the great eighteenth-century biologist, and so believed that man would never discover the truth about microbes. The colonel placed his faith in the scientific authorities of the eighteenth century! Not even the new graveyards would prove to such people that the errors of science were more fatal than the ignorance of any peasant, and that among all the powerful people in the land, the most powerful would continue in ignorance. He turned around to view the faces near him, and to try to recognize those that were carriers of death; but the eyes of all seemed dull and fever-ridden. He felt that lice were already biting him around his backbone, under his arm, and along his shinbone, but he couldn't scratch himself; there was now no defense against them. Why was he silent? Why didn't he tell these people, lunging forward into an infectious disease as if possessed, that some were carrying and some receiving death itself?

Men and women were pushing their way into the waiting room and

* In the battle of Kossovo (1389) the Serbs were disastrously defeated by the Turks and lost their independence for over four centuries.

sticking close together, so the louse could spread more quickly; they seemed fearless to the point of stupidity in the face of this form of death. Why didn't he tell them what was in store for them? Why didn't he shout as if the roof of the railway station were on fire, as if the Austrians had mined the train?

A soldier opened the door of the waiting room and yelled something. The human torrent pressed toward the exit, carrying Radić through the door and thrusting him onto the platform in front of the train, which was now assembled. He didn't even try to resist; the rabble threw him forward and deposited him a long way from the train, right next to the lavatory. He made no attempt to move toward the train, but kept a firm hold on his medical bag.

Women and soldiers, peasants and townspeople, old men and walking wounded were surging toward the train, as if there were a raging conflagration behind them and this was the last train to safety; they stepped on each other, pulled each other off the steps of the cars, bit the hands of those who had somehow grabbed the iron bars on the doors. The whole place resounded with cries, curses, and groans.

They're sick, every single one of them, he thought, as he put his suitcase and medical bag down beside him. He lit a cigarette and through the large, thick snowflakes watched the bitter struggle of soldiers and civilians to get on the train. What impelled them to travel, to get into a train in which they would either leave lice or acquire them, become infected and fall ill, and many die? Which of these wretches was already lice-ridden and a carrier of death? Perhaps the most ruthless among them, those two men who were pushing some peasant women off the steps of a coach. It was his duty to tell them what would befall them on the train, but they wouldn't hear him. This was a time when people destroyed even those who were trying to save them. The wet snow extinguished his cigarette; he lit it again and turned up the collar of his overcoat to prevent his neck from getting wet.

In their struggle to get into the train, people were now getting in through the windows by climbing on each other's shoulders; they were being pushed away by those already inside who wanted to make room for friends of their own. Women were shrieking and men laughing at the sight of the women's bare bottoms bending over the windows. The engine began to whistle.

Now he must do the impossible.

He tossed away his cigarette, climbed onto a large crate in front of the warehouse, spread out his arms, and shouted: "Don't rush headlong to your death! Don't travel! The train is full of lice, and the louse is a carrier of typhus. I'm a doctor—I know what I'm talking about!"

No one heard him, no one even looked at him. The engine whistled. Desperately he sought the eyes of another human being—somebody, anybody! For a moment he thought he had caught the attention of a woman, but she was carried away by the crowd. He stood on the crate with his arms outstretched, bewildered, humiliated, helpless. They aren't at all afraid, he said to himself. No, people were not afraid— that was their trouble. How could he make them afraid?

He took his bags, pushed his way through the crowd to the official carriage, which was guarded by soldiers with bayonets, and climbed into the train.

Amid cries from those who hadn't made it into the train and the constant whistling of the engine, the train began moving off between bare trees toward the snow-covered hills. Radić felt better; fortunately, a man can sometimes be alone, and that was no small thing. He stared at the muddy fields flecked with snow, and the deserted villages dotted with black flags flying from the doors and eaves. How could these people be made to fear the unseen world, he wondered.

As the darkness enveloped the unlighted train, these same people poured in and filled the corridor of the official coach, forcing him into the compartment and his seat; then, moving silently in the darkness, they came into the compartments and sat on the floor, crowding between the legs of the officers and officials. Happy to be on the train, they began to pass brandy around, to eat, smoke, tell jokes. They were living their wartime life, traveling in search of medicine, sugar, and gas, or buying food, trading, and speculating, going to visit sick and wounded relatives, or to carry back their dead and bury them in their own cemeteries. Some were weeping and lamenting their lost ones; some were teasing women, courting widows, and telling lies— all sorts of lies. They sold typhus cures—powders from England, drops from Germany, teas from Asia; they sold coffins, medical certificates, official letters guaranteeing preferential treatment. By candlelight they told fortunes with cards, interpreted dreams, and talked about Austrian spies who were poisoning the wells with typhus and cholera germs. They spoke with pride of the medals and promotions won by their sons, husbands, and brothers, and whispered about how they had fooled the draft boards.

He couldn't see their faces, and felt more threatened than ever; if he could at least see their hands, he'd know what sort of people they were. Eyes and hands reveal what pain a man fears, and in that fear lies his essential human quality, his character and power. All these people around him were sick—sick with passion and grief, and most of all with war.

The train stopped in a wet, sick station; in rushed more people destined to be sick, determined to get on the train at any price and go somewhere, to a hospital or a cemetery. Even the switchman's lamps, flickering specter-like in the darkness, looked sick, and some primeval sickness seemed to afflict the very darkness that engulfed the valley where the engine was fighting its way through the wet snow, belching out fire in its death rattle, panting under a load that grew continually heavier. He lit a cigarette; for a moment its glowing spark illuminated an expression of unusually acute suffering on a woman's face. Was she in mourning? He didn't think so. He wanted to see her again, but it seemed a heartless wish.

The carriage was full of noise, the stench of war, and the common people. A woman sitting on the floor complained that her head ached, and she was shivering. She's ill, he concluded, and squeezed himself up into the space above his suitcase and medical bag, so that no louse could thrust its snout into his skin. From time to time he felt disgust and anger for the people around him, in fact for all people, sick or well; but he fought against these feelings. As a doctor, he had never felt disgust for any man or for any human condition, least of all suffering. If there was one thing in a man that he had always respected, it was his pain. But whom was he trying to convince tonight? Why were his thoughts now going around in that old vicious circle—the pointlessness of sacrifice? Was he afraid for his life? Perhaps this was his last journey. In Valjevo a doctor died every day. He should have spent the night in Kragujevac gambling away all his money and staying with some quiet, gentle woman till dawn. Even now, if in this tense darkness inside this chilly, clanking mass of iron, there should be a woman with a timid heart and a small hand who desired his protection, perhaps some rather different purpose would become apparent in this journey, a purpose of which he hadn't even dreamed.

He struck a match to light another cigarette: in the doorway of the compartment that beautiful, suffering face was illuminated for a moment, then extinguished. It was such a beautiful face that for a long time he was afraid to strike another match; he held it between his fingers until it grew damp, threw it away, and took another, but didn't strike it at once. Perhaps he was experiencing a hallucination from prolonged fatigue. He struck the match too hard and broke it. At once he took a third one and struck it carefully: the light flickered over the suffering which had gathered in the woman's face and given it form, but not disfigured it. On the contrary. What was the cause of this suffering? Not bereavement, for she wasn't in mourning. She was totally absorbed by her pain, but in a manner that was superior and noble. Clearly she didn't want to be comforted. The flame died away before he managed to light his cigarette. She was a middle-aged woman, and exceptionally elegant for this train and these days. Where had he seen this woman? He resisted a sudden trembling by concentrating on the reason for her pain. He postponed lighting his cigarette; the light would have added to her suffering, and his curiosity would be humiliating to her. His curiosity? The old trouble again. When other people lit cigarettes, he looked straight at her. He had never seen such pain on a woman's face. This woman must have a capacity for suffering which left no room in her heart for lies and pretense. In the love of such women, respect occupies a place no lower than passion. But what was such a woman doing tonight in this disease-ridden train, on its way to the very heart of the epidemic? Perhaps it was all hallucination, typical of his sort of mental state. The same old troubles. No, it wasn't that; it was the beginning of his illness. What a beginning!

Before striking another match, he waited for the train to stop in a station. The woman was leaning against the compartment doorway, her head wrapped in a dark scarf with an Oriental pattern, an elegant traveling bag in her hand. Her expression was still the same: absorbed in her pain, indifferent to the pushing and shoving of others. She doesn't see or hear anything, he thought with a feeling of envy. He quietly offered her his seat, indicating it by the light of the match. She sat down at once, without a word of thanks.

Until daybreak, by which time the train was approaching Valjevo, he lit cigarettes with increasing frequency and stared at the woman's face, preoccupied by the pain in it. And not only on her face. No, it wasn't like his own wife's pain, which he hadn't understood, and which he had underestimated till the day of her sudden death. Her silence had taken away everything, that silence to which he had paid no heed, to which he had been impervious. He had behaved cruelly and would never be able to make amends. Every time he had an opportunity to fall in love with a woman, he was prevented by his sin toward a woman whose love and suffering he hadn't understood.

The woman to whom he had given his seat never once closed her eyes. All night long her suffering kept her awake. The dawn made that pain seem more severe and somehow final. There was no fatigue in those greenish eyes and the network of wrinkles around them. She was sitting motionless, looking out the window, staring at the snowy hills around Valjevo, but not with the ordinary curiosity of a traveler. Was she returning home or visiting someone? The other passengers were preparing to get off; Valjevo was the last stop. She alone didn't move, but remained staring toward Suvobor, as if she had every intention of staying on the train.

The engine whistled angrily, then braked: luggage fell down, passengers collided with each other, everybody was up and pushing toward the exit. Carried along by the crowd, he moved toward the steps, although he wanted to wait for her. The woman was still sitting in the compartment, still staring at the mountains. He paused on the steps: the people in front of him couldn't get off because of the crowd surging into the train. It was as if all Valjevo was migrating, fleeing from the epidemic. A woman screamed. The train came to a stop; he heard frenzied shouting: He's dead! Why was he running? He was ill. It cut him in two, like a cucumber. Let me off! I've got to get on! Why? The train won't leave till noon. Everybody's dying in Valjevo. I'm getting out of this place. I want to see my son. He's dead. You folks are murderers. Get out of the way or I'll jump on your head!

The crowd in the corridor of the coach swept into the mob on the platform. Mihajlo fell headlong over some women and sacks and dropped his medical bag. He gathered his last ounce of strength to extricate himself and grab hold of the bag, and was then pushed into a puddle near the station pump. He turned around to see what had happened to the woman. He couldn't see her in the crowd spilling onto the platform from the train. How could he have left her like that? He waited for her to appear, as the train emptied with convulsive spasms. Some were silently making their way into town, while others crowded onto the train, but there was no sign of her.

He walked back to the coach he'd traveled in and saw the torso of a soldier who had been run over; people were jumping over it as they climbed onto the train. He caught sight of the woman trying helplessly to push her way toward the exit. She was indeed beautiful— exceptionally so. Only in times of great misfortune could one meet such a woman. He stretched out his hand to help her down the steps; she gave him her hand at once, without looking at him, without saying a word. She descended, then withdrew her hand from his. He walked alongside her, embarrassed, waiting for her to speak, but she was silent, as if quite alone. This excited him and made him accompany her further, though he knew this was crude and importunate, and not at all like him. She stopped in front of the station entrance; inside sat sick people wrapped in rugs, blankets, and tent flaps, some simply staring in front of them, others delirious. One whistled, another rushed out of the station, charging at Austrians. She opened her bag, took out a handkerchief, and wiped her eyes, as if she couldn't see well. This gave him an excuse to speak.

"Madam, my name is Mihajlo Radić. I'm a doctor. Should you need assistance, you'll find me at the hospital."

She looked at him with an inscrutable expression, whispered something which he didn't catch, then moved off slowly, walking around the sick people on the steps to the waiting room. He didn't venture to accompany her any farther. Perhaps she'd been infected on the train. Yes, it was all hallucination. It didn't matter.

Only when he felt sure she was sufficiently far away that he couldn't catch up with her did he set out toward the town. He was suddenly overcome by fatigue. He paused at the corner and saw coming toward him a cart full of the dead bodies of prisoners of war, escorted by an Austrian, who was sitting on top of them. A soldier, with a bayonet in his belt, was trudging along beside some sweating horses, their skin steaming in the raw, sunless morning. They clattered on the cobbles; there was no other sound.

He looked down the street toward the center: on both sides of the street, sitting or crouching on the narrow paving stones against the walls of the shops and houses, or lying on straw, were little groups of sick people.

The corridor in front of the office of Major Avram Vinaver, the superintendent of the Valjevo hospitals, was so crowded with civilians, medical officers, and captured doctors that Mihajlo had to wait in line for some time before he could enter. Suddenly overwhelmed by fatigue, he moved back from the impatient crowd and leaned against the wall.

What he had seen in the street between the railway station and Vinaver's office reminded him of descriptions of the plague in Milan at the end of the seventeenth century. Then the friars and followers of Christ had been the doctors and nurses; Christian compassion had made up for lack of knowledge, and somehow these sacrifices in the name of God had saved Milan. By what faith could unbelievers such as we, he thought, make up for our lack of knowledge and conscience, and save Valjevo? Could this be accomplished by patriotism, our one effective virtue? Patriotism enables us to die honorably for our country, and to achieve something in public life; but such a faith lacks the depth and dimension necessary to save the people from a misfortune such as this. In the present circumstances what was vitally necessary was a faith that would arouse great fear—a life-saving fear of the invisible world and of dirt; a faith that demanded both virtue and knowledge, that would give birth to strength and the need for cleanliness, that most rare and venal strength among humans.

From Vinaver's office he heard a voice: "Anyone here from the High Command?"

That must be me, he said to himself, and pushed his way toward the door, provoking grumbling and fierce looks. He found himself in front of Major Avram Vinaver, along with a lieutenant from the Serbian medical service and a captain from the Austro-Hungarian medical corps. Vinaver stood up to greet them, through his pince-nez looked slantwise in some confusion at the prisoner, then moved away from the table, revealing his crumpled, bloodstained jacket. In a hoarse voice with a strong Polish accent, he asked, "Are you from the High Command, Captain?"

"No, sir, I'm from Varaždin. I'm a Croat, a doctor from Zagreb. I was called up in July, unfortunately, and since then I've been assistant to the hospital director of the Thirteenth Corps of the Fifth Army, the army commanded by Potiorek." He smiled.

"Well, what about it?" said Vinaver, stroking his reddish beard.

"I was counting on your understanding, sir. From the bottom of my heart I'm a Yugoslav. I want to offer you a modest gift of four hundred thousand crowns for the Serbian wounded, and to beg you to let me work in a Serbian hospital. I want to help you. I hate the Austrians and Hungarians as much as you do. I am your brother, and as a brother I ask you to let me get rid of this shameful uniform immediately."

"Of course—congratulations! You're a true Croat, a Slav. I'll do all I can. At last, some good news this morning! Sorry, Doctor, I didn't catch your name."

"Doctor Antun Mihalčić."

"Would you wait outside, Doctor Mihalčić, while I talk to this other gentleman? I'll call you back in a moment."

"Thank you. But do take my gift now, Major," he said, taking an envelope out of his pocket and handing it to Vinaver.

Doctor Vinaver thanked him with some embarrassment. As soon as the door shut behind the Croat, he banged the envelope on the table. "Our Slav cause, our Serbian cause, is winning! They have freedom in their hearts! Gentlemen, yesterday two Czechs and one Slovenian came to me, all doctors, offering to work in our hospitals. And this is the second Croatian doctor to remove his uniform since the liberation of Valjevo."

"Unfortunately, we expected much more," said Mihajlo quietly. Vinaver was frowning. "Still, these cases give us grounds for hope," he added.

"I beg your pardon; with whom have I the pleasure of speaking?"

"My name is Mihajlo Radić. I was serving with the Timok Division. The Medical Section of the High Command has transferred me to serve under you. Here is the letter."

"And you, Lieutenant?"

"Philip Simić. You'll find the rest of the particulars in the official letter."

"Are you a doctor? That's all I'm interested in at the moment. We're all dying."

"I graduated in medicine."

"Where?"

"In Berlin. Then I worked in Heidelberg with Professor Friedmann."

"Very good, very good indeed."

Mihajlo stared at this young, exceptionally handsome man with the angry expression.

Doctor Vinaver asked them to sit down, then returned to the table to read both their letters. "Simić, you will take over the duties of director of a reserve hospital, which is in a terrible state. The director became ill three days ago, and two doctors have already died. I assume there's no need for me to tell you what your duties are."

"Sir, I don't want to be a director."

"Why not?"

"I studied medicine, not law."

"That's why you are able to perform administrative duties in a hospital."

"I detest all forms of authority. Most of all over the sick and wounded."

"What on earth are you talking about, young man?"

"I'm not prepared to perform the duties of a police clerk."

"Well, I'm not the district chief in Valjevo."

"That's up to you, sir; but please let me do some kind of medical work, as an orderly if I can't work as a doctor."

"Do you mean to say that today, when people are suffering as never before in living memory—when typhus is mowing down our doctors one after another—that you, a doctor and a Serb, are refusing to do your duty, to do what the country requires of you?" He rose from the table.

"Sir, I'm immune to ideas about submission to the people and the State, or anything like that."

Vinaver looked at him in amazement. "One shock after another! Then why did you study medicine if you aren't prepared to serve people? What do the people mean to you, Doctor?"

"Either a political concept or a rabble. Neither of these stands close to my heart."

"You haven't answered my question. What led you to study medicine, if you have such a low opinion of humanity?"

"Health."

"You mean the protection of people's health?"

"No, I don't. I mean the joy that health generates. Its power and beauty."

"What are you talking about, young man?"

"From the scientific point of view, I'm interested in blood groups, and in immunity chains in plasma."

Mihajlo stared at him with curiosity. Lucky fellow! He for his part had devoted himself to medicine out of love for a tubercular sister, to try to cure her—but without success; she would die.

"Where were you born, and what was your father?" Vinaver asked Simić.

"In Pirot, sir. My father was a judge."

"So now I have to tell you how to behave? That's sad. One shock after another!"

"Don't bother, sir. I'm not going to accept an administrative job. I'll work as a doctor or an orderly during the epidemic. If you don't agree to that, have me court-martialed."

Vinaver looked at him with some embarrassment, but said nothing.

Mihajlo asked if he might smoke. He sympathized with Simić, on account of both his bold opinions and his behavior in the present circumstances. The young man was probably suffering, he thought, and struggling hard to find happiness outside human beings. How foolish.

"No, I won't have you court-martialed," said Vinaver, speaking more calmly. "Do you realize, young man, that there are over seven thousand sick people in Valjevo today? At the beginning of the war Valjevo had three thousand inhabitants. Today Valjevo is the only town in the world with two or three times as many sick and wounded as healthy inhabitants. The Austrians left behind over twenty-five hundred wounded, and for these several thousand patients, ours and the Austrians, we have only sixteen doctors. They are dying too, after performing superhuman feats of endurance. Yesterday more than a hundred and twenty people died in Valjevo. In two weeks everybody in the place will be ill!"

"Let's not waste time, sir."

Vinaver nodded his head despondently, fell silent, then asked in an agitated voice, "Who is going to organize this chaos of death into something resembling a hospital?"

"Good, energetic sergeants. Or, better still, some notorious pen-pushing policemen. There's no shortage of them in Serbia."

"What did you say?"

"Like all people in authority, a hospital director must be impervious to bribes and not afraid to use a big stick. This epidemic is not a medical problem."

"What is it, then?"

"A problem for the government and the police. For the State."

"That's right!" said Mihajlo, unable to restrain himself; but Vinaver continued to listen to Simić.

"We've got to use force to crush this invasion of lice-ridden people. The lice must be annihilated by the State, and measures taken to prevent them from being carried from one person to another. Forgive me for speaking so freely."

"Take a walk around Valjevo and look at all those sick people in the streets," said Vinaver. "Be sure to go into one of the hospitals. Then we'll talk about it."

"I've seen all I need to see."

"Maybe, but take another look. Those are my orders!" he said, raising his voice and trembling. Simić saluted and left the room. "Did you hear that young idiot?" he said, turning to Radić.

He's suffering from ambition and from migraine, too, thought Mihajlo, as he looked at Vinaver. "He's a strange fellow. But it's crucial for our future for such eccentrics to survive. I'd like to work with him."

"I'd like to see what his father would do if he were in my shoes."

"As for his ideas about preventive measures, I agree with him. Without the big stick, of course."

"What could you possibly mean by that?" asked Vinaver in alarm.

"We can't expect any success in fighting the epidemic until those in authority make it clear to the public that typhus is carried by the louse. I'm convinced, sir, that this should be our approach."

"If that alone would save us, I'd agree with you; but the causes and carriers of *Typhus exanthematicus* are many, and the factors which produce an epidemic are complex."

"Still, the fact remains that the louse is a carrier of typhus, and that is only partially a medical problem, sir."

"What are you trying to tell me?"

"In my opinion, an epidemic represents a more acute phase of a state of sickness present in society, a sickness that is moral and spiritual, and also organizational. So the society must be treated."

"The total sum of what you're saying is that Serbia is sick. Serbia, which has won the admiration of Europe and the world for her moral health and heroic spirit? Serbia, the pride of the entire Slavic world?"

"It's painful for me to talk about what's wrong with us; believe me, I don't like people who can see nothing else. But all you have to do is spend one night on the train from Kragujevac to Valjevo. There is something stupid and suicidal in our communal spirit—something irretrievably unfortunate."

"What will I hear next this morning? No, Doctor, it can't be so!"

"I don't want to contradict you, Major. I simply ventured to assert that we'll experience a real catastrophe if we don't immediately abandon our prevailing misconceptions."

Vinaver slumped over the table and remained silent for some time. Then he said in a resolute tone: "We must do our duty conscientiously. We doctors, I mean."

"That's not enough now, sir, I'm afraid."

"What else can we do?"

"Make people fear the world they can't see. Fill them with a consuming fear of lice and dirt—far stronger than the fear they feel for the Austrians and enslavement."

"Fear? What next?"

"Only by instilling fear into the people can we make them work for life, sir. The danger is so great that we must all, without exception, work for life. Be afraid for the sake of life." Even as he spoke he regretted his display of self-confidence.

Vinaver stroked his beard and looked at Mihajlo, stared at him just like the gray-haired captain in the medical service when he came before the recruiting board. Mihajlo found it unpleasant; it made him feel ashamed, as if he really were before the recruiting board, where for the first time in his life he had stood naked in someone else's presence. It was the first time he had felt humiliated by his own naked body. And it was the first time he had felt such hatred for people, because of their indifference to the shame of a fellow creature. He had vowed then that he'd be the kind of doctor in front of whom people would never feel ashamed.

"I'm appointing you director of the Second Reserve Hospital. I'll get a soldier to take you there. You'll take over immediately from Doctor Aleksić. He's a good surgeon, but a bad director. You can count on my sympathy, but don't ask me for money or supplies—I don't have any. We're on a desert island, Doctor. If we're to stay alive, we must be as resourceful as Robinson Crusoe. Good-by!"

"May I ask something?"

"I don't like words that precede actions."

"I understand. Would you assign Lieutenant Simić to my hospital, unless you have some other spot where he's vitally necessary?"

Vinaver squinted and ignored the request.

In front of the hospital gates Mihajlo Radić was confronted by a pack of twenty dogs that looked threatening. The soldier carrying his suitcase said: "You needn't be afraid, sir. Valjevo is full of them. The villages are empty, the people have fled or been killed. The dogs are hungry and have come down into town. Right now Valjevo is a kingdom of dogs, but they don't attack the living."

"Whom do they attack?"

"Those behind the gates."

"You mean the patients?"

"I mean the dead bodies, sir."

"You can't be serious."

"Take a look at that heap behind the fence. There's no one to bury them. For days now they've been lying in the rain, bitten by the dogs."

Hesitantly, Mihajlo walked through the pack of dogs. They made no attempt to get out of his way, but stiffened their tails and looked at him with hungry eyes. Mysterious. They growled as if wanting to say something. What was that strange look in their eyes? He reached the gatepost and stood transfixed in front of a heap of dead bodies, most of them unshaven and wearing torn and dirty underwear, their tongues hanging out, their eyes wide open. He studied them attentively, without horror. What should be his first step against such contempt for life? Shouldn't he first bury the dead?

He clenched his fists and pushed on. So this, he thought, is my hospital: a long, low building painted yellow, surrounded by stables, storehouses, and sheds. In front of the main building was a small, narrow one painted white, with several doors and flights of steps. The two buildings were separated by an empty space with a large acacia tree. The smaller building must be the administrative headquarters, from which he would wage his war against lice and dirt. The dogs prowled behind his back. He pressed forward, strained like a taut bow.

"Before the war this was a barracks, sir."

He gave a start. "I know. Put my bag down and get back to your duties."

Several young boys walked past him, carrying cats in their arms and bundles of candles. Were his eyes playing him tricks?

"Where are you taking those cats?"

The boys looked at him, broke into a run, and hid behind some oxcarts in the yard.

The dogs were yelping at someone. He turned around: an old man was driving the dogs away from the entrance with an ax handle. Catching sight of Mihajlo, he walked up to him and said: "A man with any heart wouldn't wish this on a criminal. Have you heard that oath, sir: may a dog strike your dead flesh with its teeth? That oath has now come true among us Serbs."

"What are you doing here, old man?"

"My name is Tola Dačić and I come from Prerovo. I'm looking after my sick son. He was wounded at the front, brought here to this damned hospital, but all they've done to him, thank God, is cut off his right arm. As for this hospital, the Fritzies couldn't have done anything worse to us. It's damp and freezing cold. There's no wood —not even a stove in all those rooms. No orderlies to speak of; they're running away. Not a soul to light a fire for these poor bastards. So I'm cutting what wood I can find and bringing it in to make a fire."

"So you're keeping the hospital supplied with wood?"

"Well, if the State can't do it, a father has to, Captain. And what government could supply all the hospitals now? I don't chop down the trees of poor people, and I don't pull up fence posts where I see a black flag. What brought you here, Captain?"

"I've come to work here. I'm a doctor."

Tola Dačić looked at him with amazement and delight. "Do you have some powder to stop the typhus fever, Doctor?"

"I don't have any medicines with me."

"I can't pay you in money, but I have a good memory. I can remember longer and better than God Himself."

"I'll have a look at your son today and give him some medicine."

A column of prisoners came in through the gates, carrying chunks of bread inside tent flaps and pots full of steaming liquid. A soldier was running alongside the prisoners with his gun cocked, shrieking, "I'll kill you, do you hear?"

"Why is he threatening them?" asked Mihajlo.

"They're stealing the patients' rations. These Fritzies steal bread like skunks, then sell it; and if a bit of meat finds its way into the food, they fish it out. Between the kitchen and the hospital, they manage to fill their pockets."

"Why are you making up these stories?"

"It's true, Doctor, and there's worse. I'm real pleased when foreigners and prisoners of war find things good here in Serbia, but it turns my stomach when I see these Fritzies take the last morsel from our sick and wounded."

"Where do they get the food?"

"From another hospital. Here the kitchen only serves the doctors and the staff. Do you see them sneaking away?"

The pack of dogs again filled the open gateway; Mihajlo stepped back.

"You must look them straight in the eyes without moving an inch, Doctor."

"Whom must I look straight in the eyes?"

"A wild dog; and today I say a man, too."

What's tormenting this strange old man, wondered Mihajlo. "How many people would you need to supply the hospital with wood and keep everyone warm from now on?"

"Five healthy men."

"Come to the director's office at noon."

"When will you have a look at my son, Doctor?"

"Before nightfall."

"It won't be too late then?"

"No. Bring in the wood and get fires going in the wards."

He left the old man and walked toward the pile of dead bodies; as he did so he caught sight of a hand moving in the snow. He bent down and felt the pulse: the man was alive! He couldn't see his face, which was covered with corpses. He took hold of the hand and pulled the man out. When the crown of his head fell onto the snow the young man gave a groan: he had a long, handsome face with a black moustache.

"You're safe now!" said Mihajlo softly. His eyes sought out Tola Dačić, to tell him to bring some orderlies with a stretcher.

"Every day they throw out someone who's still alive," said Tola as he hurried back to the hospital.

The living man looked at Mihajlo with bloodshot eyes and whispered, "I'm thirsty."

"We'll get you into bed first. Then you can have some tea."

"Where am I?"

"Among the bodies."

The man winced, more from surprise than fear. He grabbed a handful of snow as if to make sure he was alive, then dropped it; he brought his wet hands close to his face and stared at them.

"What's your name, soldier?"

"What's the difference?"

"Your teeth are chattering. That's a good sign."

The young man struggled to get onto his feet, supporting himself against the dead bodies. Mihajlo tried to help him.

"Captain!"

Mihajlo turned around and caught sight of the woman he had met on the train. He began to tremble. What could she be doing here?

"Please, Doctor, get rid of these dogs!"

Confused and hesitant, he walked toward the animals, then stopped: between the woman and himself was the pack of growling dogs, and he had nothing to drive them off with. He turned away helplessly.

"For heaven's sake, do something!"

Clumsily, he began pelting the dogs with lumps of wet snow; they crowded together defensively.

The woman spotted the corpses and covered her face with both her hands. She remained so for a few moments, then resolutely stepped forward through the pack of dogs and hurried toward the hospital. Tola Dačić arrived with an orderly; they put the living man on a stretcher, and Mihajlo set off behind him.

Only when he announced that he was the new director did the orderly timidly point out the director's office, adding that Doctor Aleksić was still asleep. Mihajlo tapped politely on the door, then grew angry.

"Don't bang like that!" shouted someone from inside.

He opened the door: on the table in the office was a dish of meat, some dirty plates, some wine bottles and glasses—and a bunch of privet!

"What do you want?"

He was startled by the question, and by the sound of a mattress creaking. In the bed a woman's head ducked under the blanket, while a man raised himself up and covered the woman's naked shoulders.

"It's dark in here. Why don't you open the curtains?" stammered Mihajlo.

"Who let you in? I'm not up yet!"

"There's a horrible smell. Who are you, anyway?"

"I'd like to ask you the same question!"

"For the past hour I've been the director of this hospital. I've come to take over my duties."

"What has that to do with me? There must be someone in this world who knows how to do things properly."

"You're right about that. It's now nine o'clock. By ten precisely this pigsty is to be cleaned up and turned into an office where you'll hand over your job to me."

"I have nothing to hand over. Everything here is at your disposal."

"No, it isn't, Doctor. Wait for me at ten o'clock, alone." Slowly he shut the door behind him.

Outside, the woman from the train was standing beside the acacia tree. He walked past her with his head bent, went into the hospital, and stood by the door: the corridor was full of sick people lying on straw and rags, their faces sweating and feverish, their swollen tongues protruding; they were delirious. In a doorway some people were fighting over a white iron bedstead: The major killed himself here, and his bed stays with us! That bed isn't your property! I have orders to carry it into the officers' ward! Over our dead bodies! What do you peasants want with a bed? You're cattle!

A patient at his feet stood up and urinated on another patient, who stared at the ceiling with deathlike eyes. What was the meaning of so much suffering? Mihajlo asked himself. Was it for their country, for liberation and unification of the Serbs, Croats, and Slovenes? Was that worth so much suffering and evil?

"Get out of here, you goddamn thieves!" someone shouted at him. A mess kit flew past his head and landed on the steps. "Get out!"

Mihajlo didn't know what to do, he felt so ashamed. He walked on through the corridor, taking care not to tread on anyone. He walked past the group squabbling over the bed, peeped into two more rooms, and stopped dumbfounded at the threshold of a third: Auguste the Clown—a real clown wearing a false nose, top hat, and checkered coat—was performing one of his numbers in the middle of the room;

sick and wounded men were sitting around him, some laughing, but most of them silent.

"Get out, you goddamn thieves! Get out!" a patient behind him shouted. The white iron bedstead, now almost in the corridor, was suddenly pulled back, throwing down the crowd in its wake.

Like a sleepwalker, he moved on aimlessly. In this chaos was it possible to fulfill his duty in any way whatsoever?

Never before had he embarked on any significant enterprise with less hope or more fear. There seemed to be no sense at all in sacrifice. What he wanted to accomplish didn't seem a heroic deed or duty. It would mean giving his life in order to confirm once more that human beings were helpless when confronted with such an insane situation where all good intentions—anything beyond saving one's own skin— were utterly meaningless. If he had ever deceived himself that he could alleviate human pain, be it only a headache, he couldn't believe it now. Sickness had attacked human beings at their roots. He too would fall prey to this sickness.

Outside he selected a patch of untrodden snow, picked some up, and rubbed first his hands, then his forehead.

The fifty-odd paces between the pack of dogs, the pile of corpses, and the large acacia tree seemed an eternity to Olga Katić. Her life before she reached the hospital gates had become a distant blur, like a story someone had told her long ago. She stood by the acacia tree with her suitcase at her feet, not knowing what she could or would dare to do in this place, or what would happen when she met Milena. She didn't think she had ever been as horrified by the miseries of war as before she came here; it was as if she had suddenly grown old. She looked around her in expectation; what she saw in her field of vision was a building emerging from a murky sky, a building which didn't resemble any she had ever seen. Some ragged, unshaven soldiers were pottering about near the main entrance; they looked like people who had suffered their final defeat.

"Are you waiting for someone, madam?"

"My daughter works here."

The lame nurse moved away; Olga wanted to have her send for Milena, but felt it would be inappropriate. So she simply tensed up her body, wishing to make herself smaller, invisible.

In the operating room Milena was looking at the lobe of a lung swaying under the scalpel of Doctor Sergeev; her glance strayed to the window. "Mother!" she cried out. The surgical instruments dropped with a clatter in the tray.

"What is it, Milena?" asked Sergeev in Russian, his eyes on the wound.

"My mother's out there."

"Give me the iodine and gauze. Just another minute, please—now go and embrace your mother, Milena."

She ran out of the hospital.

"My darling!" sobbed Olga.

Milena rushed to embrace her, but at the sight of her mother's face her hands fell limply to her sides. "What's happened, Mother?"

Olga couldn't hold back her tears, which dissolved everything. Then she pulled Milena convulsively toward her. She would take her away from this place and never be parted from her again.

Wrapped in her mother's arms, Milena felt, even more than joy, the protective power of Olga's trembling.

"Where are you living, my pet?" she asked as their hold on each other relaxed.

"Any news about Ivan, Mother?"

"He's a prisoner of war. That's what your father was told. We're trying to find out more through the Red Cross. Najdan has asked one of his friends in Geneva to locate him."

Both of them felt the need to say something more about Ivan, and each waited for the other to do so.

"Mother, I have a feeling that Ivan is alive; I'm sure of it," said Milena.

"If I didn't believe that . . ."

"Bogdan Dragović, Ivan's best friend, is here in the hospital."

"I want to see him, Milena."

"Later. He was seriously wounded in the chest, and he's got typhus, too. He may not live."

"Take me to him at once!"

"He's unconscious, Mother. You can see him when his temperature comes down a little. Right now you and I must spend some time together alone."

"You and I will never be separated again. We'll talk about it tomorrow on the train. But I must see Bogdan right away." She picked up her suitcase.

"How are you going to manage with that bag? We'd better leave it in the nurses' room," said Milena, taking her mother's arm; but Olga pulled her toward the door of the hospital. Milena went reluctantly with her.

Milena's resistance made Olga anxious. Bogdan Dragović must know something about Ivan. Milena stopped her on the steps.

"Mother, this isn't an ordinary hospital. There's an epidemic, and everybody's been crammed in here. All Valjevo is one big hospital."

They stepped into the corridor, and Milena was immediately assailed by cries: Nurse, give me a drink of water! Bring me water, or I'll kill you with my bare teeth! When will you bandage me? Nursie, I'm hungry—bring me some nice clean dirt! Don't be so stand-offish, honey!

Olga paused, then stepped hesitantly into the corridor, with its thick stench of sick and wounded men who lay pressed close together, or crawled about on crushed straw and rags.

So this is where Milena was while I held meetings of the Serbian Nurses' Association in Niš, where people recited patriotic poems and played Schubert!

Pale with anger, Milena shouted: "I'm not giving you water or medicine, when you swear like this! You should be ashamed!"

Did she dare talk like this here? Olga couldn't bring herself to go on.

"Come on, Mother!"

She moved ahead, stumbling over legs, bags, and stretchers. She caught up with Milena, took hold of her apron, and feeling slightly protected against the looks of the patients, followed along behind her daughter. They entered a room where the men were packed in even tighter on the floor, and the stench was more stifling, the requests more insistent.

"This is Bogdan Dragović," said Milena, bending down.

His eyes were closed and he was breathing heavily. He hadn't regained consciousness since the dead body of Gavrilo Stanković had been carried out. How he had wept then, and embraced the wounded leg into which Gavrilo had fired his first shot!

So this is the boy Ivan would have liked to have as his brother,

Olga thought to herself. A boy with an older man's moustache. Handsome, too. She bent down, knelt beside his pillow, and took his hands to caress and kiss them. There was some dried blood on his fingers; she gave a start but didn't let go of his hands. That hand had touched Ivan, given him something, helped him jump across a stream. She wanted to see his eyes, to hear his voice.

Milena looked at her mother, kneeling there devoutly like a penitent, and trembled all over.

"The night before last Major Gavrilo Stanković killed himself. He was Ivan's and Bogdan's commanding officer," said Milena, then immediately regretted having spoken.

Olga let go of Bogdan's hand, but remained kneeling. "Why did he do that?"

"He had gangrene. He was a most unusual man. Have you heard about him?"

"I knew him. He was one of the conspirators. He lived in Russia for a long time. What did he say about Ivan?"

"That he was brave, and like his father. Nothing else." Milena wanted to get her mother out of there as quickly as possible. The sick and wounded men were now listening carefully to what the two of them were saying. "Come along, Mother. You can visit Bogdan again this afternoon."

"I can't leave him." She took a handkerchief out of her bag and gently wiped Bogdan's sweating face. "My poor boy, my poor boy," she whispered.

Bogdan groaned and raised his hand as if to defend himself.

"He's been delirious since last night. Don't be afraid, ma'am," said the wounded man lying next to Bogdan.

Olga looked at Bogdan and saw his heavy, confused eyes gaze imploringly at her. She looked at them all in turn: deathly pale faces and blue, cracked lips; men panting, gasping, raving, suffocated by their sore, swollen tongues, and with livid, dark blue spots scattered over their hairy chests. Some gnashed their teeth, one giggled, another beat the wall with bloodstained fists. Two others in a corner were fighting over a pile of straw.

"Mother, you'll get covered with lice here!"

She couldn't get away from their eyes—imploring, begging, threatening eyes. They filled her with shame for the life she had lived in

Niš, for the glib talk about them behind the lines, for the contributions she had collected at performances.

"Please, Mother! I'll bring you back when his temperature has dropped!"

Could she get up, turn her back on them, go away? How could she live with the memory of these people?

Milena lifted her up, then picked up her suitcase and pulled her toward the door. Olga wanted to say, I'll be back, I just want to leave my things, but she had no voice. She walked uncertainly behind Milena, weighed down by their glances. At the bottom of the steps she stopped, looked around the hospital to make certain that they were alone, then asked in a whisper:

"Did Vukašin come into the hospital? Did he see them?"

"Even if he had seen them, how could he change anything?"

"What do you mean, how could he change anything?"

"There are eight thousand sick and wounded men here in Valjevo. It's the same all over Serbia," said Milena, hurrying toward the nurses' room.

"Now I understand why you didn't come home. Now I understand everything. Forgive me, my dear," she said, and stroked Milena's face.

"People are dying here, Mother," said Milena, her eyes focused on a puddle that was freezing over.

Mihajlo Radić didn't know what to say to the man who until that morning had been the hospital director. Mihajlo sat by the window, smoking, and thought: He has the hands of an exceptionally sensitive man, and fingers made for some delicate craft, but his lips are lascivious, his expression restless and scornful. He is a man of flawed character, a typical egotist who could suffer only from hunger or perhaps jealousy.

"I'm at your disposal, Captain," said Doctor Aleksić for the second time, seated behind his desk.

"How many patients do you have here, Doctor?" asked Mihajlo hesitantly.

"Between nine hundred and a thousand."

"What do you mean—between?"

"Well, that's how it is. During the last few days there have been from forty to fifty deaths each day, and more new arrivals."

"You don't have an official record?"

"The office isn't functioning. The bookkeeper is ill, and the orderlies don't do that sort of work properly; and who bothers about written records now?"

"Then how do you order food and medication?"

"What's the use of my placing an order, when they give as much as they have? There's no budget. No arrangements were made for it—that's what those in authority say."

"Where is the bath?"

"Something's wrong with the boiler."

"You mean this hospital has no bath?"

"Even if we had one, we've no fuel for hot water."

"What about the laundry and the disinfection center? How do you delouse the patients and wash their linen?"

"Who's going to wash and clean them when we have only eight volunteer nurses, all fine ladies from Belgrade, and ten orderlies? We did have three barbers, but two fell sick and the third ran away yesterday."

Mihajlo lit a cigarette. What could he say to this man?

"I have three doctors and one medical student," continued Aleksić. "You've seen for yourself how things are. This is a hell from which neither you nor I will emerge alive. We shall be victims, Doctor Radić."

"Only fools are victims," said Mihajlo, meeting Aleksić's scornful glance. "By the way, do you believe in a living, invisible world?"

"I believe that the world is corrupt beyond hope of redemption."

"Is that all you believe?"

"Yes, I'm a sincere man."

"How do I strike you?"

"You strike me as an optimist."

The sound of a coarse masculine voice singing in the hospital added to Mihajlo's confusion. He got up and looked out the window, unable to believe his ears. "Is that really someone singing?"

"The wounded sing when they're drunk."

"When they're drunk?"

"Some believe disease won't attack you if you're drunk. So they swig brandy from morning till night."

"Why don't you stop them?"

"How can I? They buy it, or their families bring it. All sorts of things go on here. It has its funny side as well. You'll have a tough time if you can't appreciate it."

Mihajlo looked hard at Aleksić, who now violently attacked the government and the High Command for the spread of the epidemic. He could hear no facts, only Aleksić's vehemence and fury. Was he the only sane person in this place?

"Please summon all the doctors," he said quietly.

A soldier appeared at the door, carrying an armful of wood.

"Take that wood into one of the wards! I don't want a fire in my office until all the wards are well heated."

The soldier withdrew in amazement. Mihajlo walked over to the window. When a suitable occasion arose, he'd apologize to the soldier for a reproach he hadn't deserved. Under the acacia tree two boys were selling cats to some walking wounded. So the wounded were buying cats! Was it to have something alive and healthy, or a memory of home and family life? Poor bastards! The words of Hippocrates were eternally valid: Man is wholly sick—*L'homme est tout malade*. The entire man must be treated; but how, under present conditions?

He saw Lieutenant Philip Simić walking across the yard. He opened the door for him and said: "I am glad we'll be working together. I count on your support, on your conscience, Doctor. The conditions here are unbelievably bad—incredible."

"Conscience can only operate in a man who's slept well, Captain."

Mihajlo was taken aback. He said in a different tone, "That attitude is inappropriate here, believe me."

"It's hard for a man who's overworked to be considerate. High moral standards express health and strength."

"Sit down, Doctor. If what you say were true, life would soon become extinct on this planet. In any case typhus will demolish Serbia, no doubt about it."

"There's no direct connection here between cause and effect."

"Yes, there is. Just as human intelligence has a direct connection with time and place."

"An antiquated concept, Captain. It belongs way back in ancient times."

"It's truth is all the more convincing for that, Doctor."

"Let me have just two hours' sleep and I'll place myself under your command. Don't think for a moment that I'm sensitive about being in a subordinate position."

"You can go to sleep after we've discussed what should be done here. I guess you've seen that pack of dogs and the pile of bodies by the gate?" He turned and stared at the hospital yard, and saw the woman from the train with one of the volunteer nurses. Could it be her daughter? Or her younger sister?

Aleksić came into the room, followed by three doctors in dirty, blood-spattered medical coats. They saluted, then introduced themselves. Mihajlo shook hands with them and asked them to sit down. He spoke at once: "Gentlemen, I've been sent here to help. Naturally, first of all I want to hear your opinion about the state of the hospital. I consider truth the first step toward health." They looked at him wearily, and more sternly than the occasion demanded.

"This isn't an examination for promotion, is it?" asked the most tired-looking of them all.

"No. Simply a confirmation of your medical knowledge, Doctor."

They remained silent, lit cigarettes; one of them cracked his fingers. He must be a surgeon, Mihajlo thought.

"To work together successfully we must be in agreement over the cause of the prevalent disease and the manner in which it's transmitted," he said. "I assume you believe that the louse is the carrier of typhus."

"That's hardly crucial under the circumstances, Captain."

"I think it is, Doctor."

"Gentlemen, let me tell you something," said Philip Simić sternly, "so we don't waste our time talking hot air. Two days ago I took a louse from a seriously ill patient—moribund in fact—and put it on my chest. Ten seconds later it bit me. Now I'm counting the days. It'll take eleven more days at most to confirm Nicol's hypothesis."

"What hypothesis? What is there to confirm?" cried Mihajlo, jumping up from his chair.

"What hypothesis? Nothing permanent is known about man. Everything must be proved over and over again. That's what I'm trying to say."

"That's ridiculous! Ambitious, adolescent nonsense!"

Simić smiled gently. "By all means, Captain. Mankind is a close-knit community of fools. Stupidity is the foundation of our world. Forgive me for saying so."

Mihajlo looked at him, but without his usual assurance. He didn't know how to continue the conversation in the presence of this strange young man.

"Even if the louse is the sole carrier, would that entail an important change in our procedures?" asked a doctor with a weak, unpleasant face.

"It vitally changes the way in which we perform our duties," said Mihajlo quietly. "I'm requesting you to act in this hospital from now on as if the High Command had issued a directive stating that the louse is the carrier of typhus. Now tell me what you think about the hospital."

He listened to them carefully: their remarks revealed violent exasperation with the government and the higher authorities. No genuine fear or human grief, no vestige of hope in their despair. He looked at their hands: only one had fingers that could detect pain, the silent one with the beard. But perhaps he was the Russian and a surgeon. He found his colleagues' violent language intolerable: "Gentlemen, there's no profession which requires a greater precision in expression than ours. To know and respect man, we must have a respect for words." The ex-director gave him a pitying smile. "Gentlemen, a doctor should have a better knowledge of language than a poet. If we don't speak precisely about pain, we can't alleviate it."

"Very good! Very good!" exclaimed the doctor with the hands of a real physician, speaking in Russian. There was a sudden silence.

"Are you Russian?" asked Mihajlo.

"Yes. My name is Nikolay Maksimovich Sergeev."

"I'd be extremely interested to hear your point of view on the conditions in the hospital," said Mihajlo in Russian.

"My point of view? My dear doctor, my view of the conditions here derives from my view of any human condition. I believe there are only two questions worth serious consideration."

"Only two?" said Mihajlo in a challenging tone, encouraged by his words.

"Yes. Our conception of death and our understanding of women."

Philip Simić laughed aloud, then tittered insolently. "Let me tell you this," he said. "A nation that respects death doesn't value life, and a nation that doesn't value life has no future. That's us Serbs. As for women, this is not the time or place to discuss them."

"You're right, Doctor Sergeev!" said Mihajlo firmly. "How we regard death is the vital question for our survival. I consider that respect for man as a human being begins with our understanding of and respect for death."

"That's an old Christian delusion! Life has nothing in common with death—nothing at all!" said Simić defensively.

"You understand what I have in mind," Mihajlo continued. "First we must bury the dead properly and restore dignity to the patients."

"There's nothing we can do about the dead," interrupted his predecessor.

"Who can, then?"

"The Valjevo municipal office, which hasn't yet decided on a place for the military cemetery; and the priest, who hasn't been able to perform the funeral rites. I've asked him personally three times."

"I'll ask him again today."

"What we need are lavatories!" said Simić caustically. "That magnificent edifice, nonexistent in Serbia! The sacred temple of the healthy. The historical differentiation between man and the lower animals!" His words provoked a smile only in Sergeev.

"Go get some sleep at once!" said Mihajlo sternly; then he continued: "From now on, gentlemen, I want us all to wear clean, freshly ironed medical coats. The nurses, orderlies, everybody. And it's our duty to see to it that within a week there isn't a single louse in this hospital."

"Within a week?" exclaimed Aleksić.

"Yes, within a week. The bathrooms, disinfection centers, laundries, and other services must be in good working order."

"What do we wash our coats with? There isn't a bar of soap on the premises. We requested soap three weeks ago and it still hasn't arrived."

"Then we must buy soap out of our own pockets."

"You can't get it in Valjevo, not even under the counter."

For a moment only the cracking of Sergeev's fingers could be heard.

"Then we must do like Robinson Crusoe!" Mihajlo suddenly bellowed.

He wanted to meet one understanding glance—one at least.

Olga's sleep was brief, if that fleeting darkness which cut across her thoughts about Bogdan could indeed be called sleep. She felt his heavy, tormented, imploring eyes upon her—those death-stricken eyes from which she could no longer escape. She crawled into bed only so as to keep silent about the purpose of her visit. But surely she had already made her decision—when she knelt down next to Bogdan and took his hot, bony, boyish hand in hers, when she wiped the sweat off his flushed and emaciated face, when she looked at the faces and eyes of other sick men and suddenly felt that she couldn't run away from their suffering. She felt frightened of herself, of something that would disrupt her life and pull her toward the unknown, perhaps death; so she quickly lay down half undressed in the warm bed, from which a nice young girl with a gentle smile got up.

What about Milena? How her lips had trembled when she had stammered out the words, "People are dying here, Mother." The stench, the groans, and the curses would have killed a wild beast, let alone a delicate girl on whom so much love had been lavished; but she had endured it all for four months without a word of complaint in her letters. Where did she get that strength? She's my child. That strength comes from me. From *me*? But I've come to save her, to take her away! I must save her. How can I think of anything else?

The hospital stench had soaked into the bed in which she was lying; it streamed out from the walls, and from the very words and movements of the nurses behind her back. Who are they? What women could live beside a pile of corpses and a pack of dogs, waiting for sickness and death? She heard them talking: Listen girls, the new director has arrived! Is he kind? He's tall and thin, rather ugly. Feverish blue eyes, as if he'd been crying all night. Where's he from? A captain. Well, no one can save us now, dear girl.

Olga thought about the officer who had given her his seat on the train. She couldn't remember his name. She might have remembered him only as one of those high-class officers who consider it their duty to pay court to younger women, not crudely but persistently, thus making their behavior the more disagreeable. She had met him again at the hospital beside that pile of corpses, looking confused and frightened.

He must be someone special to have come to Valjevo today, or he hasn't any influence with the High Command. The only person this hospital needs now is a priest. I'd just like to see the last of Aleksić before I drop dead here. It's all the same for us, with or without Aleksić.

There was something coarse and despairing about these girls, Olga thought, something she hadn't expected. She continued to listen attentively.

I can't stand it any more. You've been watching someone dying again. Why do you do that, Danica? Well, last night that old man made me promise that I'd light a candle for him. If we can't offer them hot milk and tea, if we can't provide beds for them, we should at least light a candle on their deathbeds. This morning a delirious patient in Ward Seven stuck his head in a lighted stove; he burned his skin and howled. In Ward Two yesterday one of the boys stuck himself on his bayonet; he died while Sergeev was operating on him. Has the mail come? The mailmen are sick. So the mail's infected, too! Oh, shut up, I've been on duty for two nights.

I have to look those girls in the eyes and tell them why I'm taking Milena home, thought Olga Katić. What could she say to them? My son's a prisoner, she's all I have now. What if they had brothers who had died or were prisoners? What could she say to them? They must run off without saying good-by to anyone. Was this the only way she could save her child? She could hear Milena whispering, "Is my mother still asleep?"

Let her sleep. Traveling from Niš to Valjevo these days is harder than being on duty. Lie down next to her, Milena. I'd love to have my mother with me! Me, too. When I go home, if I ever do, I'll lie down beside my mother for two whole days and nights! You'll get your wish, Vera—in the next world.

Olga could feel the undercurrent of sadness in their whispering. Suddenly they stopped talking. They were listening to her, to hear what she was thinking. Well, let them. There was nothing she wouldn't do to save Milena, even if it were shameful or dishonorable. She was not Vukašin. Milena was not liable for military service. She had volunteered to work as a nurse. She had stuck to it for four months—no small achievement for a girl of eighteen. Who would blame her for saving her daughter? Quickly she dressed and put her shoes on. The girls were looking at her with tense expectation.

"Have you had a bad dream, Mother?" asked Milena.

"I was very tired. Forgive me."

"Do tell us what it's like in Niš now, Mrs. Katić," asked a girl with beautiful dark hair.

"I don't really know," she said, confused by the look in the girl's eyes. Then she bent down, opened her suitcase, and took out some cookies, chocolate, sugar, and coffee. "Help yourselves," she said. "Milena, distribute these few things among the nurses, and make some coffee, if there's anywhere you can do it. I'm going to see Bogdan."

"Mother, he's delirious."

"Never mind," she said, then left the room in order to compose herself, to allow the confusion and an unexpected feeling of nausea to settle, and to still the trembling of her body. What would Ivan say to me now? she wondered, walking slowly toward the entrance of the hospital.

Milena divided the provisions her mother had brought among her companions, leaving only some cookie crumbs for herself. She didn't feel like making coffee. Sitting on the bed she shared with Dušanka, she began to eat the crumbs from the bag, but without savoring the taste of those with hazelnuts, her favorite.

She had felt overwhelming joy when her mother embraced her. What was in her mother's mind when she said, "Now I understand why you didn't come home with your father"? Did she understand? Even after entering the hospital, thought Milena, she knew why I'm staying here to die.

"Why so sad, Milena? Sorry you're leaving us?" said Ruška with her mouth full of cookies.

From their first meeting this girl, the ex-director's mistress, had disliked Milena and offended her on every possible occasion; Milena gave back as good as she got. Now she didn't reply.

"Aren't you sorry you're leaving us to die here without you? I meant to ask you to light a candle for my soul."

One of the girls laughed. Milena flushed.

"Why are you so bitchy, Ruška? Milena and Dušanka were the only ones who stayed here with the wounded when the Austrians entered Valjevo."

"My dear Mrs. Stefanović, every fool knows why Milena stayed with the wounded. She's been written about in her father's newspapers."

"You ought to be ashamed of yourself! You and Paun Aleksić fled to Mionica in a carriage the minute you heard the first cannon firing."

"That was war, which is quite different; but now people are dying and our hearts are on trial. Tell me, Milena, isn't it true that your mother is taking you to Niš tomorrow?"

Milena's eyes dilated with anger; she could find no adequate reply. Then suddenly the door opened and Toma, Paun Aleksić's orderly, shouted: "Excuse me, ladies, but you're all ordered to the office to meet the new director. All of you!"

"Well, now we'll get a chance to size him up," said Ruška, getting out of bed.

Milena waited for them all to leave; Dušanka led her away. "Why are you so pale, Milena? To hell with Ruška! Your mother's a lovely woman. Do you know what? If I could be born again, I'd like to have green eyes like your mother's. I've seen the new director only in profile, but I can tell he's interesting. Milena, I can't let him see you in this state."

Only when the new director looked hard at Milena did she pull herself together.

"How old are you, Nurse?"

"Eighteen."

"Only one of us here has had more nursing experience, Captain," said Mrs. Stefanović.

"Indeed. Young people are capable of the greatest sacrifice. A sign we're born to do good. Please sit down, ladies. My name is Mihajlo Radić. I've been appointed director of this hospital. I've just come from the front. I'm not a surgeon, just an ordinary doctor."

Milena withdrew into a corner, sat on a bench, and looked at him.

"Captain, you just said we're born to do good. That's true, but not of everybody, I'm afraid," said Mrs. Stefanović.

"You're right. If we're to protect ourselves from dirt and death, we must have a better opinion of ourselves. We must value and respect ourselves."

"Right now we can only pity ourselves, Captain."

He stood up, leaned against the wall, folded his arms, and began to speak quietly, looking at the floor. "If we're prepared to sacrifice ourselves for people, then we must respect something in them. There's a spark of goodness in every heart."

"There are very few such people, Doctor," said Milena firmly.

"You haven't had much experience of life, Nurse. Young people know only those they love."

"Maybe. But since the beginning of the war I've been looking after the sick and wounded. Among them, probably one in ten has the spark you're referring to." She felt better for having said it.

"Then, Nurse, you haven't sacrificed yourself in vain. If you've saved two good people, that's a great achievement. Greater than if you'd given birth to them."

"Aren't you being too magnanimous, Captain?" cried Ruška coquettishly.

Milena resented Ruška's support. She raised herself a little, in order to get a better view of the doctor's face above Ruška's head: it was tired and anxious, and yet there was something superior about it with its high, lined forehead. Their eyes met.

"Tell me, now that we're on this subject, why did you become a volunteer nurse?"

"Because I love our country and freedom. As all of us here do," Milena said, dissatisfied with her answer.

"Except that I love Serbia, but not the Serbs," interrupted Ruška.

"But you *do* love the Serbs!"

"The Serbs? My dear Mrs. Stefanović, I wouldn't stain my hands with carbolic for their sake. I wouldn't cross the threshold of the hospital."

They all jumped on Ruška. Mihajlo smoked in silence until they calmed down, then said: "There are people who can sacrifice themselves for humanity, their nation, and high ideals. Those who can't rise to such heights have a duty to sacrifice themselves for any man who's suffering. They can alleviate his pain, arouse his hope, stimulate his will. That's within our competence and power, and it's no small matter. If we don't have this, we condemn ourselves to death."

His words sent a warm shudder through Milena.

Dušanka pinched her on the thigh and whispered: "I told you he was interesting! How beautifully we'll die!"

"How many of you nurses are there?"

"Seven."

"Not enough for the work ahead of us. But maybe it is. Yes, I think so."

"How can you think that, Doctor? There's one nurse and two orderlies for every two hundred patients."

"For every three hundred, Mrs. Stefanović!"

"We're on our feet twelve hours at a time. Now we're getting sick. Three nurses have already come down with typhus. The orderlies are running back to the army. One glance inside the door of the hospital, and you can see the state it's in."

"I've seen. But I'm sure we can clean up this filth and awaken some hope in the patients. If it weren't for you ladies, I'd cut out right now."

"A real new broom! He'll sweep us all over the place," whispered Katya.

"He must have some physical defect," said Ruška, while Milena listened with excitement to words she hadn't heard before in the hospital. This tired-looking man was talking quietly, with long pauses, as if to himself: "With so much suffering around us, it's difficult to believe in God. We're left with a less common and more uncertain faith, one that's easily extinguished." He paused. "I mean faith in oneself. Again, I say it's fortunate you ladies are here. The patients can believe in their mothers and sisters—their mothers most of all. That means in the love least likely to wear out, and which will find no task distasteful in the interests of life."

Mihajlo Radić was about to say more, but turned pale. Milena turned and saw her mother in the doorway. Olga sat down at the end of the bench, right by the door. Mihajlo brought his chair over to her, but she refused it. Their eyes met, each trying to guess the other's thoughts. Milena walked over and sat beside her mother.

"Forgive me for coming in without permission," said Olga Katić. "I'll leave if I'm in the way."

"Please don't! You can help, in fact," he said too loudly. "This country will experience a catastrophe if you women don't work for our sick people. We need your strength to clean up our homes and hospitals, and to make our suffering more bearable."

"Do you know this man?" Milena whispered to her mother.

"No, I don't."

"To save our lives, we must obliterate the louse, and we must arouse hope in the patients through kindness. That's my program."

"How, Doctor?" cried Mrs. Stefanović.

Milena seized her mother's hand. She expected him to confirm what he had already said—something she felt inside herself, too. He looked thoughtfully at Milena. She let go of her mother's hand. He said in a quiet voice: "Only God knows how one man saves another. Nurses, you know what we have to do in this hospital."

He promised to let them know the following morning what their duties would be. The nurses filed out, silent and perplexed.

Milena led her mother out of the hospital and onto the road, where they could talk by themselves for a while. In a meadow on the other side of the road, several women in tropical helmets were putting up a large tent.

"Who are these women, Milena?"

"The Scotswomen. They're setting up their own hospital."

Olga stared at the women, about ten of them, who were exerting all their strength to pull the ropes and stretch out the tent.

"They're from Scotland?"

"Yes, they arrived a few days ago, and yesterday some Swiss people arrived as well."

"How did you live through the occupation of Valjevo," asked Olga, "and what happened to Vladimir?"

Standing on the bank of the Kolubara not far from a wooden bridge, a wounded soldier showed Mihajlo Radić the cemetery. On a hillock directly above the town, in a ray of light from the sun setting over the mountain, he saw a group of mounds with tombstones. Two carts bearing coffins, followed by small groups of mourners, were winding up the road. The cemetery stood poised above Valjevo and dominated the region around it. Whoever looked toward the setting sun, whoever turned to face the winds, whoever gazed on the storm clouds heavy with rain, whoever came into the town from an easterly direction, could not fail to see the cemetery. Its dark shape loomed above roofs and chimneys, hearths and dining tables; above beds, childbirths, and weddings; above the sick and the healthy; above the embraces of love and the blows of hate; above quarrels and burglaries. It represented the unknown which must surely be faced, the end of all journeys, the certain outcome of all intentions and troubles. There, for him too, this day had to come to an end.

He set off toward the bridge and the even, somnolent murmur of the river. In the middle of the bridge, from a crevice in the wooden piles, a dog appeared. Was it barring his way or following him? Mihajlo Radić leaned against the wooden balustrade and stared unblinkingly into the dog's eyes. That same dog had been waiting for him with the same expression when he left Vinaver's office. The same mud-spattered dog had been waiting for him later in front of the shops, where he had tried to buy some soap. It had disappeared when he stopped to ask where he could find wooden boards and nails to make coffins. An old man had said to him: "You'll have to steal a few doors, my boy; but that won't be difficult—there's plenty of empty houses in Valjevo." That same dog had blinked at him from behind a corner when he had gone into the district office to demand that a plot of land for a new cemetery be designated at once, and carpenters mobilized to make coffins for his hospital. The policeman had told him right off that there were only two carpenters in all Valjevo who worked for the townspeople. And now here was that same dog staring at him. What was that strange light in its eyes?

The noisy flow of the river tempted him: he wanted to jump in, to plunge headlong into oblivion. He would have wonderful images of this dog, convincing yet improbable, as in a dream. An infected louse may have bitten him last night on the train, as he was looking at the face of that woman—the same one who had upset his conversation with the nurses. What if the louse had bitten him even as he had been trying to solve her secret? Well, at least he would meet his end working for the sick, doing what he could for people: he'd be following his conscience.

The dog continued to follow him at a distance. The road in front of him rose steeply and wound among bare trees. A strong, biting wind blew from the mountains, turning the mud and wet snow into ice. His hesitant footsteps were further slowed by the sound of a powerful, coarse voice singing "God most Holy," more like a shout of anger than a prayer; it came from up above. It must be the priest, he thought. He walked past several wheelbarrows with empty coffins, next to which old peasant women were sitting, their heads swathed in black scarves; the men, smoking as they leaned against the wheelbarrows, watched him with a scorn that made him shorten his steps. He knew what they were there for: as soon as darkness fell they'd dash in, dig up the graves, and take their sons away to their own villages.

At the entrance to the cemetery he stopped, unable to believe his eyes: in a ditch running alongside the cemetery fence stood a pack of dogs, staring at him. Could they be the same dogs he had seen at the hospital that morning? They looked menacing. He turned around to look for his own dog, but he wasn't there.

"Don't be afraid, sir. They don't attack the living, not yet at any rate," said someone inside the cemetery. The voice sounded like that of Major Vinaver's orderly, who had said the same thing that morning.

Mihajlo buttoned up his overcoat, clenched his fists, and walked into the cemetery. Rows of wax candles, incense, and small bags were set on benches and chairs. Old women crouched over their wares, offering him candles, medicine and hot brandy, a shroud and sprigs of privet, and charms against sickness, bullets, and shrapnel.

"How about soap?" he asked.

"What do you need soap for nowadays? Look after your head, and your skin can look after itself."

He hurried past them and stopped again in front of some fifteen coffins, which were closed up and scattered over the mud and snow; above them stood bent old men and women holding lighted candles they were shielding against the wind. The good and the wicked, the respected and the despised, all finally arrived at the same place. Weren't the differences between the living really of no significance— mere vanity? thought Mihajlo Radić. He stared at the dead bodies inside the wooden coffins. He recognized them, knew all the pains they had endured except the last. All suffering human faces are alike. There was no difference between the pain of that beautiful, enigmatic woman and the pain of this wrinkled peasant woman biting her lips as she gazed at a coffin. That everything ultimately rots away is both the hardest and the easiest thing to grasp. When one has grasped it, what then? What use is that knowledge?

Beggars, cripples, and gypsies were milling around him, while in the plum orchard above the cemetery some children were throwing snowballs, sliding, and harnessing dogs to a sled.

He too had played in the churchyard while his grandfather Marko had performed the services in the church, officiated at christenings and funerals. Throughout his childhood he had spent his holidays reading and playing in the vicinity of the church near Lazarica and Prince Lazar's Tower, climbing over its ruins with the lizards, while huge flocks of jackdaws and ravens croaked overhead and bats came out at dusk. At night, walking between Lazarica and the Tower, firmly clasping his grandfather Marko's hand, he would listen to the corncockles and the owls, which to him were something different: in the wind he heard the neighing of horses and the tread of their hoofs; in his mind's eye he saw heroes from epic poems. "What can you see, Grandpa?" he would ask. "Everything that you can see, Mihajlo." Then he would snuggle inside his grandfather's mantle, trembling with a delicious fear, a kind of excitement he never experienced again, and beg him to stay out in the dark as long as possible and tell him again what the devil looked like, since his grandfather had come upon the devil several times in the belfry at midnight, swinging on the bell rope, bleating, and biting his own tail. But the Evil One described by his grandfather wasn't terrifying enough; soon he was sure his grandfather had made the stories up. This doubt may well have been the beginning of many others, from the attempt to check whether the holy things in the altar reliquaries and the wafers and wine were really covered with blood, to that great and painful doubt in the existence of God, which had been aroused in him by his first reading of Darwin in his last year of high school, a doubt which had cast a shadow over the whole of his childhood and lowered his grandfather in his eyes. Yes, he had played in the churchyard just like these children, while his grandfather had sung the funeral office; but he had played in a different way, and his grandfather had sung the office differently. He had played by himself, silently and seriously; he couldn't stand noise and merriment, challenges and victories in his games; he had loved silence and solitude, which his imagination filled with scenes from books and stories told by his grandfather. The church bells had invested all his games with a certain solemnity, and the christenings and funerals in the church had given them a greater seriousness than any kind of work or study. Perhaps there was no period in his life when he had been so serious or thoughtful as in those childhood days around the church at Kruševac. The things he hadn't understood then he still couldn't grasp; all his serious doubts had first sprouted among the ruins of Kruševac. Time and experience had merely deepened their roots, thrust them into the depths of his being. Those doubts had even made him old. At their very onset, as he lay on the grass near Lazarica, gazing at the depths of the sky, he had often experienced doubt in his own experience. Such moments had enthralled him and made him feel happy. That dying for an idea, and within it.

He walked slowly toward the children, avoiding the fresh mounds, but as he listened to the singing of the funeral service, he had no strength to go on. For the first time the singing of this office, which he had heard hundreds of times, sent a shudder of horror through him. The priest Božidar was shouting and threatening as he sang. He loathed death and was angry with the person for whom he prayed. Mihajlo's grandfather Marko had been carried away by the same song the priest sang. He could remember well his grandfather's face when he sang "God most Holy": both his voice and his eyes expressed something bright and healthy, some deep-seated gaiety; no death had ever seemed terrible to him. This childhood experience of death hadn't been disfigured even by his first dissections as a student in Moscow. Later, as a doctor, when he stood over dead bodies and those on the point of death, his feelings couldn't be described as fright and horror; and when he stood over the body of his grandfather Marko, lying on a large table in the guest room with candles and sprigs of privet on either side of his head, he had listened to "God most Holy" sung over him without shedding a single tear, though his grief was real and sincere. Even when he had kissed his dead father he hadn't wept, nor had that death held any terror for him. He still heard his grandfather's bright and cheerful singing of the office.

A sudden weariness forced him to sit down on a fallen tombstone. All over the cemetery little clusters of candles were struggling to keep alight. Their flames kindled his weariness. The cemetery seemed like a cloud swaying over Valjevo, far above its roofs and chimneys and the smoke of its evening fires. He felt that its mounds and tombstones would sweep down upon the town and put an end to its disease. The people would be saved, all of them in one fell swoop; the cries of the children at play would be heard no more, nor the voice of the priest Božidar: "No, Milorad, you didn't deserve to be punished by this sickness. With the blessed skill of your hands you made fine shoes for poor people, shoes fit for the rich! Nobody can count how many people you've made happy by your honorable handiwork. Remember this, Milorad, Christ didn't deserve His punishment either. If your long hours of work as a shoemaker didn't allow you to show yourself a believer in Christ in the church, still in death you have become His brother. You are a lucky man! Amen."

Mihajlo opened his eyes: the priest, a tall, thin man wearing a yellow stole, crossed himself and went over to a newly dug pit and coffin, beside which three childen and two old women were standing. As he walked past, the priest shouted to the children playing in the plum orchard by the cemetery: "Mića! Nadežda! You've let the fire go out! Light it again and get yourselves warm; you've done enough sledding. You're wet through, like drowned rats. I'll be along in a few minutes."

The wind stirred the candle flames; the crosses would catch fire and fall down upon the roofs of Valjevo; nothing would matter any more. The priest Božidar continued to shout his prayer in angry and threatening tones.

Mihajlo folded his overcoat under him. He felt cramped, sitting on the cold stone, but it was all to the good; he wouldn't be able to sleep long, just to rest his eyes a little from the flames twisting above the smoke of Valjevo.

"Nor did you, Dostana, deserve such a devilish punishment. You were a clean, hard-working housewife—none better in Valjevo. You left your children warmly dressed and well shod for the winter, and a pure image for your husband at the front. Just this morning I noticed that your windows were full of muscats. All credit to you, Dostana! When your tasks permitted, you managed to say a prayer to the Mother of God, and now in death you have become her daughter. You're a lucky woman! Amen—Nadežda! Mića! Where are you? Go gather some dry twigs from the underbrush and make a fire! I'll be with you soon!—God most holy, firm and enduring, holy and eternal . . . Yes, you walked this earth like an ant, Anastasius, although you were the head man of Valjevo. Though you were the right hand of the government, your fist and nails were not against the people. You left the peasants a dry market and an accurate scale, you put down cobblestones in three lanes for the townsfolk and travelers; for this we give you thanks. You didn't often get to church because you had so much to do for the people, but you didn't go to the tavern often either. You always carried Christ in your heart, and so went to your death to remain His brother. You're a lucky man! Amen—Mića, you've played long enough; it's dark. Get yourselves around the fire, I'll be along soon—May the Lord God remember His servant. Amen!"

"Forgive me, Officer, I can't see your rank. You'll catch cold sitting on that stone. Are you asleep, or is it the beginning of the sickness?"

Mihajlo raised his head and saw a smallish man with a bag and a lighted candle in his hand. With a great effort, he stood up; his legs were numb and stiff. He lit a cigarette.

"Whom have you buried, sir?"

"I'm waiting for the priest."

"We can wait together. My name's Jevrem. I'm the baker here. The people are dying like flies, as you can see. There isn't a man or woman in Valjevo I haven't baked bread for these thirty-two years."

'And now your customers are dying."

"I'm not lighting candles for my customers but for my brothers. Those with whom I've sworn brotherhood here on earth made up a large family."

"I don't follow you."

"Today people struggle along on their own, a lot of them without kith or kin. So you've got to seek them out and gather them into one big family. There isn't a murderer who doesn't need love, and no evil-doer who doesn't want a brother. Not one!"

"Are you religious?"

"I wouldn't say that. I try to spread brotherhood. If tomorrow morning a hundred people in Europe made a vow of Brotherhod with ten people each, and those with ten more, and they went on like that, just figure out what would happen in the world, brother. Before spring the human race would become one big family. The war would be changed into a great feast. The kings and emperors would become brothers, too."

Mihajlo continued to puff on his cigarette.

"Surely you know at least ten people worthy of becoming your sworn brothers?"

"No, I don't. Really and truly. Good-by!"

Mihajlo hurried off toward the cemetery exit, where the people from beside the coffins were now gathered around the priest.

"Father, I've been waiting for you since this morning."

"I've been here since noon. I've got a temperature, I'm ill."

"I can't sing the service in the dark. I'll be here early in the morning. Mića! Nadežda! We're leaving now."

"How can we sit in the cemetery all night, Father? It's cold, and the dogs are just waiting for us to move. Don't you see?"

"Well, then, keep watch. Two at a time. Good evening, Jevrem. I haven't seen you all day."

"I spent the day talking with the prisoners, Father. I found three really good Czechs—better men, believe me, Father, than the best of the Serbs. We've arranged to swear brotherhood in the church."

"The Czechs are not of the Orthodox faith, Jevrem!"

"I asked them about that. They say we all have one God."

"That's true, but I can't do anything before Sunday. Come with them to the morning service. What brings you to me, Officer?"

"I've been appointed director of the Second Reserve Hospital, Father. I'm here to ask you to sing the funeral service for our dead in the morning. We must bury them before noon."

"I won't perform the last office over corpses, only over people. Three times I told your predecessor, Mr. Aleksić, that he must make a list of the dead, so I know where they came from, how they earned their living, and what their rank was. Are you frozen, my pets?"

Several little boys and girls appeared, carrying a cage with a jay inside and dragging a sled. The priest gave his censer to the sexton, took off his stole, then took out some wafers and gave three to each child. "There's two for supper, and you're to keep one for breakfast. Come on, children, it's getting dark."

His grandfather used to bring him wafers, Mihajlo remembered, on his way from the cemetery. Each one had a different taste, but they had all smelled of wax and incense; and the pears and apples which his grandfather brought back when he went around the villages to bless the holy water had smelled of the wafers. He could hardly restrain himself from asking the priest for just one wafer. He hadn't had anything that day except coffee and tobacco. The vendors were packing up their wares and leaving the cemetery. A sound of stifled sobbing was in the air. A cold wind blew from the mountains, bringing with it darkness and frost.

"Would you like to join us, Director?" called the priest as he came down the hill with the children.

The invitation both startled and pleased him; he caught up with the priest. "Are these your grandchildren?" he asked.

"Two of them, but not the rest. They're orphans. I'm now grandfather to all of them. The Austrians killed their fathers, the sickness took their mothers, and their relatives are either refugees or sick. So I've brought them to live with me in the church rectory. I take them out to play in the morning, and give them something to eat while I perform the services in the cemetery. In the evening I bring them back. That's how it is."

"You take care of them yourself?"

"Yes, with some help from the sexton. We must try to save the living, Doctor, and give them faith in life. There's only one misfortune from which there's no hope of being saved—lack of faith."

"You mean lack of faith in people?"

"Lack of faith in God, first and foremost; but in people, too, and in dogs, Doctor. There comes a time when even faith in a wolf is not in vain."

They clambered down the slope, thin ice crunching under their feet. Down below in the town, lights appeared in the dark blue dusk. The children skipped and chattered cheerfully; Mihajlo envied them.

"You have been busy burying these good people since dawn, Father?" he said, to make conversation.

"They deserved a few kind words, both for the way they lived and for the way they suffered, which they didn't deserve."

"No, Father, we are to blame for our suffering. This isn't God's punishment, but man's doing."

"I've never believed, Doctor, that our Creator metes out punishment. If I believed that, I'd lose my faith. Every man alive possesses the evil power to punish. In that respect, God doesn't resemble men, but people in general resemble God."

"Then it's impossible to have faith."

"In God and in people?"

"What does the word *people* mean, and what kind of people are we? We perish and destroy in the name of freedom, but we're conquered by the louse! We fight for great national and democratic ideals, yet never has there been so much lying and stealing. When has there ever been so much evil and stupidity in Serbia as right now, when so many people have lost their lives fighting for our survival? And this after a military victory which won the admiration of the world! Can't you see how many thieves, profiteers, and shirkers there are in the land? And how much dirt? That's your human race!"

The priest turned to look at Mihajlo. "Where do you get the courage to think so badly of our people, Doctor? Especially now that they're suffering so much."

"We aren't suffering because of wind, water, cold, or earthquakes. We ourselves are responsible for our suffering! Our worst misfortunes are our own fault!"

The priest stroked his beard and asked gently: "Are your parents alive, young man? Do you have a wife and children?"

"I have no wife or children, but I have a mother, two brothers, and a sister. My grandfather was a priest in Kruševac; my father was a schoolmaster."

"Do you have any friends?"

"Yes, I suppose I do."

"You don't think much of our people?"

"I have a poor opinion of every nation in the world, Father."

"You think you can heal with such ideas in your head? You're in charge of a hospital? What good can you do them, Doctor?"

Mihajlo wanted to tell him some of the things he had said to the doctors and nurses earlier in the day, but the priest was walking briskly behind the children, who were scrambling down the hill. When they reached the bridge over the Kolubara, the priest's voice rose above the cold, dark clamor of the river: "Just make me a list of those who have died, to make them seem like human beings. You can expect me at daybreak!"

Mihajlo stayed on the bridge, leaning against a beam, until his feeling of hopelessness gave way to a conviction that he had done something significant that day. Perhaps the very thing he ought to have done on his first day in Valjevo.

Mihajlo entered the staff headquarters of the First Army, introduced himself to the officer on duty, and requested an urgent interview with Vojvoda Mišić, to whom he had to communicate some information of exceptional military importance.

"Couldn't you give it to the chief of staff, Captain?"

"No, I can't."

The lieutenant gave him a long, suspicious look and disappeared.

I haven't said anything that isn't true, Mihajlo told himself as he lit a cigarette. Anyway, I have the right to tell a lie at such a time.

The officer returned, accompanied by an angry-looking major. "You may rest assured that I'll communicate everything you say to the general."

"I'm not going to tell you anything."

The major didn't argue. He left, but soon came back to take Mihajlo down a long, dim corridor. The man who worked a miracle on Suvobor must believe in the unseen world, thought Mihajlo; he was dissatisfied with his own hesitation as he entered the office of the First Army commander.

The general sat at a table in his overcoat, his head in his hands, his cap covering his eyes. On the table was a box of tobacco and a telephone. He got up slowly and said, "Well, Doctor, what do you have to tell me that's so strictly confidential?"

Mihajlo was disconcerted by the sharp, unexpectedly shrill voice of

Vojvoda Mišić. He couldn't see his eyes because of his cap, but he felt, indeed knew, that Mišić was watching him closely.

"Please sit down, Doctor. There's a chair behind you."

Mihajlo's eyes sought the chair but couldn't see it. "I wanted to tell you personally, Vojvoda, that Serbia will be conquered by lice."

Mišić lifted his cap from his eyes: "Conquered by lice?"

"Yes. We've succeeded in resisting death while it took the form of an enemy in an Austrian uniform. We resisted death with great courage and self-sacrifice, as you yourself know all too well." He fumbled for a cigarette, but there were none in either of his pockets.

"We have also resisted death with intelligence and endurance. Especially endurance, Doctor. The person who can hold out longest survives great misfortunes. Do you smoke?"

"Yes, Vojvoda, but I left my cigarettes in the reception room. It's much easier for us to lose our heads than to use them to understand obvious truths. Some absolutely simple, obvious truths."

Mišić offered him some tobacco from his wooden box. "Would you like me to roll you a cigarette?"

"No, thank you. I prefer to make my own," he said untruthfully, which made his hands tremble so that he spilled the tobacco. I've never been afraid of any man before, he thought, as he looked into the eyes of the general who had beaten Potiorek: an elderly man with a peasant moustache, sitting at a table in his overcoat. Probably he suffered from rheumatism, and certainly from glory. What sort of pain did such a man experience? It must be terrible—bad enough to rob him of his sleep.

"You're the director of a hospital in Valjevo?"

"The Second Reserve Hospital, sir."

"Tell me what's being done. How can I save my army?"

Mihajlo still couldn't bring himself to roll a cigarette. "I speak as a man of science. Typhus is carried by the louse, that dirty, blood-sucking insect whose belly contains the invisible cause of the disease that's killing us. Yet we don't believe in the invisible world, we're not afraid of it."

"What makes you think that?"

"We must all, without exception, be afraid of this invisible force that's attacking us."

"Go on, Doctor."

"First of all we must believe in it. Only fear can save Serbia now."

"Fear?"

"Yes, a great fear. Then, cleanliness and conscience."

Mišić got up, walked over to Mihajlo, rolled cigarettes for the two of them, lit them, then returned to the table. "So you'd put fear in the place of the will to live. That's unhealthy."

Mihajlo thought about this last word. Why had the general concluded his remarks with the concept of health and its opposite, sickness? He drew a few deep puffs. "There are circumstances in which only great fear can promote the will to live in all people. In any case, Vojvoda, the whole of human life—our very existence in the face of so many threats—is based on fear. We continue to live, thanks to the intelligence and cunning born of that fear. That's how I see it."

"I'm not so sure about that, but go on."

"Only fear that can generate the strength and need for cleanliness. Otherwise the epidemic will destroy Serbia. It will decimate the country before spring."

"Quite honestly, Doctor, I don't like people who prophesy evil. I respect truth and facts, and the ability to look straight at them."

Mihajlo frowned at the brusque tone of the Vojvoda's voice. One should speak differently with generals. But how? How could one instill fear in them? How could one frighten this bravest of generals?

"Tell me, Doctor, what factors have caused this epidemic?"

"We've captured some Austrian field hospitals. We've taken sick people prisoner, and they've infected us."

"You mean we've made sickness one of our prisoners?"

"Yes, Vojvoda."

Mišić remained silent, then asked quietly, "I presume you wish to make some observations on the work of our medical authorities?"

"I do, Vojvoda. All our medical authorities, indeed all those in authority, military and civil, are going about things the wrong way. They're acting as if under orders from the Austrians."

Mišić got up quickly, extinguished his cigarette, and placed his hands on the table. Mihajlo also rose.

"As of tonight you must strictly forbid all traffic, all movement from place to place, all gatherings of civilians or soldiers. You must cancel soldiers' leaves and forbid them to go home. Remove the soldiers from inhabited areas. Those should be the first measures."

Mišić sat down again and stared out the window. After a long pause he said, "Why is it that so many doctors, and such excellent doctors as we have in the Medical Section of the High Command, don't agree?"

"The errors of so-called science are more fatal to the human race than the ignorance of any peasant or shepherd boy."

"You're right there, Doctor!" said Mišić, still staring out the window.

Outside there was a strange commotion: moaning, doors banging, raucous laughter.

"Vojvoda, you have the power to control the chaos caused by this epidemic. Death reigns supreme in dirt and disorder."

Mišić looked at him in a way that made him think he understood.

"It's the women who can save our country! The women!" Then, as if he'd seen a smile on the Vojvoda's face, he added, "Those who give birth to us can also save us from our present misfortunes."

"What must we do, Doctor?"

"Tell the truth; and of course perform our duties conscientiously."

"It seems to me, Doctor, that merely doing our duty isn't enough in the present circumstances. We must do something much more difficult. I'll think over all you've told me. You may go now, Captain."

No sooner had the door closed behind Radić than Mišić regretted having let him go. Why had he parted so quickly from this slightly confused but deeply worried man, who believed that fear and women could now save Serbia? It was a long time since he had had before him such an anxious face, or heard such convincing words. The doctors talked about the epidemic in a different way, using technical language and expressing a different kind of fear. This man was undoubtedly both brave and resolute, but he saw salvation in fear. Had he understood him properly? He had come to frighten him by saying that lice would conquer Serbia. Lice! Was this doctor the man who appears in all great misfortunes, the unknown man whom every nation has within it, who appears unexpectedly and does the one thing necessary for survival? Fear, conscience, cleanliness—and women! Women?

He opened the door but couldn't see him in the corridor; the officer on duty and the sentries were standing at attention against the walls. "What happened to that doctor who left my office just now?"

"He's gone, sir."

"Bring him back!"

He shut the door and waited. It was disease that had destroyed Napoleon's army in 1812. And the Russians had likewise been decimated in the Crimean War. History hushed these things up. Not all wars were won or lost on the battlefield, but this was forgotten. He had submitted the fate of his army to medical advisers, doctors, and disease. He had dispersed it among towns and villages to rest and recover its strength, but it had fallen sick. It had won its victory, then fallen sick. It had captured lice and disease, and its own death. Had this happened in accordance with that higher law of fate about which he had begun to worry from the first moment of victory on Suvobor? Was there something vital that he had failed to do when they had all been overwhelmed by fatigue and victory? He had pottered about with the staff in the district court in Valjevo, brought his wife and children there, listened to Louisa's chatter, and read Press Bureau telegrams repeating English and French eulogies of the Serbian army. He had read these things with pleasure, but he knew that Europe was far too lavish with its praise and glorification, which would do no good to Serbia. For one thing, he thought, our people don't know how to bear praise and glorification, and our Allies aren't so generous that they won't make us pay dearly for such things. They're already submitting bills.

The officer on duty reported that the captain had already disappeared, and that Mrs. Mišić had sent a message that the general was expected home for the dinner they were giving for Olga Katić.

"Tell the head of the medical service to come here, and send a message to my wife not to wait for me for dinner."

He went up to the stove and threw some logs in, but didn't shut the doors. He stared at the fire. Could fear save our nation? No! Fear has never saved any nation. Fear could save a man from sin, from some minor danger, or from trivial wrongdoing; but it couldn't save anyone from a great calamity. That doctor had things a bit mixed up in his head, but everything else he said was very sensible.

The chief of the medical service entered the room, clicking his heels a bit too loudly for a medical officer.

"Major, will you give me the latest medical reports?"

"According to the reports I received before six o'clock, seven thousand one hundred and fourteen officers and men have fallen sick. During the last two days three hundred and nineteen soldiers have died, three noncommissioned officers, and three commissioned officers. That's not counting suicides."

"Seven thousand—that's almost a third of my army! Two regiments! A whole battalion dead within two days! Do you realize what a defeat that is?"

"Two days ago, Vojvoda, I submitted to Colonel Hadžić a detailed report on the army, plus measures to be taken to build it up again."

"Are you convinced that typhus is carried by the louse?"

"Everything points to it, though I'm sure it's not the only cause."

"If *I* am convinced that the louse is the carrier, what measures would you take?"

"I'd continue with all the measures taken so far, and I'd ask you to see that the civilian authorities fulfill their responsibilities."

"If you doctors take no other measures than what you've been doing so far, in ten days the whole of the First Army will be stricken. You certainly haven't done all you could, Doctor!"

Colonel Hadžić, the chief of staff, walked into the room. "Here are some telegrams from the High Command, Vojvoda."

Mišić didn't pick them up. Looking sternly at the doctor, and mastering the irritation caused by his dry and pedantic way of speaking, he said: "Will you please reflect on all these matters before evening, Major? Right now you bear a heavier responsibility for the fate of the First Army and this part of Serbia than I do. I hope you realize, Doctor, how much trust I'm placing in you."

"Vojvoda, I hope I haven't been unworthy of your confidence."

"We have not done our duty! Neither you nor I! Please report to me tomorrow morning at seven o'clock; and I don't want to hear what I already know."

"May I take this opportunity of informing you of a suicide? Since suicides are rare in wartime, it's my duty to report it. Major Gavrilo Stanković killed himself two days ago, in the final stage of gangrene."

Mišić frowned, then said in a strained voice: "I despise suicides—they're murderers. You may return to your duties." When the door closed behind the chief of the medical staff, he turned to Colonel Hadžić. "Gavrilo Stanković! I'd proposed to put him in command of a regiment, and recommended him for the Karageorge Star. He was one of the most intelligent Serbian officers, wasn't he, Hadžić? If he hadn't been carried away by revolutionary ideas in his younger days, he'd have commanded a division by now. A strong, handsome man; he had everything."

"Yes, Vojvoda. I knew him very well. He was one class ahead of me. Unfortunately, he liked to philosophize and indulge in fantasies. He chose the wrong profession."

"Stanković made a mess of his life. That's why he shot himself. What a pity! Please prepare another recommendation for the command of the Eighth Regiment. Now read me those telegrams."

Hadžić stood under the feeble light bulb and read the telegrams word by word, in an indifferent tone: "Our Allies continue to exert strong pressure on our government to order the Serbian army to cross the Drina and Sava and advance on Budapest and Zagreb with the minimum delay. They believe this offensive would exploit our victory and hasten the Russian penetration into the Hungarian plain. Our government requests the High Command to give serious consideration to the Allies' demands, and to take appropriate measures to fulfill them. I wish the army commanders and the commander of the Belgrade garrison to consider this demand in relation to our situation. During the next few days you will be summoned to the High Command for consultation. Vojvoda Putnik."

Mišić spilled the tobacco; carefully he gathered it up and put it in the box. "Read it once more."

Hadžić did so, but more rapidly, in the same monotone.

"Impossible. How can heads of governments and the general staffs of the largest armies in the world attach so little value to a whole nation? A small nation which has defeated the Balkan army of the Austro-Hungarian Empire. Do we have to destroy ourselves completely to save other people's skins? For the strategy of those frauds, the Great Powers? I can't believe it! Hadžić, they must think us morons or murderers! They treat us as if we had no brains at all. Incredible!"

"I'm surprised at our government, too. I'm surprised at Pašić," said Hadžić, who then fell silent.

Mišić felt numb and empty. He was brought back to his senses by the shrill cries of some children nearby, and the wailing of a woman in a house across the street. "Read me the other telegram."

"It's also from Vojvoda Putnik: 'To the army commanders and the commander of the Belgrade garrison. According to all reports the enemy is rapidly recouping his losses. There is a strong possibility that he will resume hostilities soon. I order appropriate measures—' "

Mišić interrupted: "Do you believe that the Austrians will attack soon, Hadžić?"

"Judging by the situation on the Russian front, I don't believe they're capable of a strong attack on Serbia at present."

Mišić rolled another cigarette. "That's both logical and sensible, Hadžić; but so far our enemies have confronted us only with surprises —and so far, to their own undoing. However, our present situation provides them with their best opportunity since the beginning of the war. Do you think we're doing all we can to fight this epidemic?"

"No, sir. The government is responsible for the present situation, and the Allies are giving us very little help."

"I'd like you to think again this evening about what we, as soldiers, can do."

"I will, sir. Yesterday evening the Quartermaster Corps informed me that within the next few days the daily ration of bread and all other commodities will have to be reduced by half; and today on my way back from the hospital I saw ditches full of oxen and horses that had died of hunger."

"For such starvation of men and animals, all members of the army staffs, beginning with you and me, ought to be court-martialed and shot for treason!"

Hadžić fell silent for a moment, then said, "I was told that General Dračić, the commander of the Užice army, died of typhus today."

"Vukoman Dračić died of typhus? An army commander killed by a louse! So they've invaded the staff headquarters, too. You may go, Hadžić."

When Hadžić had gone out, Mišić opened the window and listened to the sounds of the night. The wind carried the smell of carbolic and putrefaction. Women were sobbing quietly and dogs were barking.

He called his adjutant and ordered him to get horses ready for him and his orderly Dragutin, who then helped him to mount. Refusing any other escort, he rode slowly down the street. On either side, on the sidewalk and against the walls of buildings, fires were burning; around them the walking wounded and sick were sitting, or lying on straw, on planks, or on doors that had been torn loose. He noticed some Austrian prisoners among the sick and wounded. He regretted that the rattling of the horses' hooves on the cobblestones prevented him from hearing what the members of two warring armies were saying to one another. He stopped his horse and listened: they were quarreling about tobacco, buying and selling bread and sugar, squabbling over medicines. How little they cared that he was watching them and listening! Sickness reigned supreme, and want dictated their actions. Here in Valjevo the Serbian and Austro-Hungarian armies sojourned in a kind of truce, with hatred diminishing between them. The victors and the vanquished warmed themselves around the same fires, united by cold, poverty, and a common fear. Prisoners and free men alike were powerless against the lice; their blood and sweat mingled in the burning, shivering fever of typhus. Death, the same for all, made them brothers. Did this extinguish differences, hates, ideas, all the causes of war? The war criminals were now suffering alongside their victims, and the heroes had stooped so low that in their own country they begged their prisoners for sugar, hardtack, and coffee! They swapped and traded. Heroism had become an impossibility; cowardice was neither a vice nor a disgrace. How could he launch an offensive? How could he defend the Sava and the Drina? What could he do in the midst of these men incapable of killing or pursuing, in this silent place under the sway of the lice, during a calm without joy or hope?

He pressed forward through the shadows and summoned Dragutin to ride alongside him. "Are you afraid, Dragutin?"

"To tell the truth, sir, there's a great fear in the army and among the people. If the Fritzies come against us again, what can we do with so many people sick and all of us in such bad shape?"

"What else are you worried about, Dragutin?"

"About the spring, sir."

"The spring?"

"The soldiers are wondering whether there'll be any healthy folks in Serbia to plow and sow the wheat, and where they'll find animals for plowing. They're dying of hunger one after another."

Mišić jerked the reins to make his horse go faster, past the fires, then past the hospital. The north wind stung his ears. If only it would snow. The snow would clean up the air and the earth. He looked at the sky: it was dark and overcast; a damp chill emanated from it.

"O God, grant at least snow and frost to Serbia—at least that," he whispered, and crossed himself.

Dragutin also crossed himself three times with broad, sweeping movements.

In the room that Louisa had put at her disposal in Vojvoda Mišić's rented apartment, Olga Katić sat on the bed fully dressed, waiting for daylight so that she could go off to the hospital. She felt a weariness full of premonition. From the day she was born she had lived in complete security. In all her forty-three years she hadn't made a single decision independently, had taken no serious risks, and until the war she had known no pain. She ought to have been happy, and all who knew her believed that she was; out of pride she had played the role of a happy woman—her one and only lie and deception. She acted the part of a happy woman, and her deception was the more dishonorable in that there was no need for it. She pretended she was happy through persistent silence, rather than through any insistence on her carefree state, or any visible pleasure in herself and her children, her wealth, and Vukašin's reputation. However, as she saw her children growing up and rejoicing less and less in her tenderness toward them, and as Vukašin's political anxieties came to be the only ones he ever expressed in her presence, she began to feel ever more strongly that her own life was a failure. The children and her love for Vukašin, which were the only things in her life, no longer seemed to be what she wished. The love that surrounded her seemed to be imperceptibly and inexorably slipping away—from the house, the nursery, and the marriage bed. Everything was there, yet no longer there; they were all hers, yet she no longer belonged to them in the way she wanted to; they all loved her, but not as she wished to be loved.

On this downward slope of her life into a dark and restless state, she devoted herself to meaningless occupations: she embroidered tapestries, collected small silver objects, sought to convince herself that her life was in the best possible order. She didn't succeed in these efforts; they only brought her new disappointments. Then she decided to fill the house with guests, with interesting people, especially poets and actors. She argued passionately about art and politics. With some bitterness she concluded that after the noise and excitement of the guests, the silence in the house was even more painful. Fear of the future settled in her soul like a sediment, a fear she couldn't define. Yet in these restless moments she was intoxicated by a desire to do something great and unexpected, to risk everything for the sake of some change, however unpredictable or dangerous. Many times she wanted to experience a genuine defeat and thought about doing all sorts of things; but she soon understood that she couldn't do it, that she wasn't capable of taking a real risk by changing the course of her life. Crushed by her own weakness, she thought of gambling: at least she'd lose money; but she couldn't find strength for that either—and not because of the money: she was afraid of what people would say about her. There was hardly anything she hadn't thought of doing, in order to change something by her own decision.

Then last night it had happened, and it would happen today: she would take Milena's place in the hospital and send her to Vukašin in Niš. She would save her, and honorably.

In the bed behind her, little Branka was talking in her sleep. Olga remembered how night after night she had watched over Milena's bed and listened to her playing and quarreling in her sleep, while Olga was waiting for Vukašin. When the children were small—when they needed her, and had loved only her, their father, and their toys—then she had been happy, only then. To bear and rear children, to live for them and their joys, to live on their love and loyalty, that was the only thing in life that lasted, the only thing that could never be destroyed, the thing one ought to live for. Why had she borne only two children? Why not seven, nine? But if she had, what suffering she'd be enduring today! How many of them would be dead or prisoners? She might have been suffering for three sons, for five. She would have been driven out of her mind, she would have died for her children. That was real life.

She could hear Louisa and Živojin talking in the kitchen; it was still dark. She would have liked to slip away unnoticed, without explanation. She had said nothing to them the previous night about her decision, not because she feared she wouldn't carry it out, but because she didn't want anyone's arguments to enter into a decision entirely her own. She could hear the wailing of a woman nearby; someone had died. Olga got up, put on her coat, picked up her handbag, bent over little Andja, and remained there for some time. She kissed her little hands and then, fighting back her tears, went into the kitchen.

Vojvoda Mišić was sitting on a chair pulling on his boots. Louisa was lighting the stove.

"Where are you off to so early, Olga?" said Louisa. "Have some breakfast with us first."

"No, really, I must be going. Milena goes on duty at six." But they persuaded her to have some coffee.

"Last night, Olga, one of our doctors convinced me that typhus is carried by the louse. Be careful. Don't stay too long in enclosed spaces. I'm afraid for Milena, very much afraid." Mišić accompanied her to the door.

"Your daughter is also a nurse."

"Yes, I know. Still, I'd get Milena out of this place. That's what I'd advise you."

Perplexed by this unexpected advice, Olga thanked him. Then she hurried off toward the hospital through the murky dawn, feeling a certain excitement and power, like the tranquillity of a person doing something that must be done. She stopped for a moment beside the tents marked with the Red Cross, watching three Scotswomen dig drainage canals from the tents with pickaxes. At the hospital gates she found doctors, nurses, orderlies, and a group of soldiers with a tall, thin priest beside the bodies. She caught sight of Milena and went up to her.

"I'm glad you're here in time for the funeral service," whispered Milena.

Olga wanted to tell Milena of her decision immediately, but the priest, wearing a stole over his cassock and carrying a lighted censer, said, "Give me the list of the dead, Director."

Mihajlo Radić handed him a sheaf of papers.

The priest looked at the list. Everyone waited in silence for the priest to speak. Slowly he raised his eyes and looked closely at the pile of bodies.

"While they were alive, many of them hid their faces—some from fear, some from shame, many because of undeserved injustice. In peace and war, they got in each other's way. That's how it was. Now, Director, stretch them out on the ground; let them lie comfortably, so that I can see every man's forehead. A dead man doesn't feel cold on the ground."

"Well spoken, Father!" exclaimed Tola Dačić, as he moved forward with the orderlies to remove the rigid corpses from the pile and arrange them beside the wire fence.

Olga pressed Milena's hand. "I've decided to stay here and become a nurse," she said. "You can join your father in Niš tomorrow."

Milena seized both her mother's hands. Her eyes were wide with fear and sadness, anger and gratitude, as she gazed absently into the cold, murky dawn.

"Who is he, and why is he the only one in a coffin?" asked the priest angrily and in too loud a voice.

Mihajlo cast an inquiring glance at the soldier standing at attention beside a blue-painted coffin.

Radojko Veselinović drew himself up even straighter and replied, "Major Gavrilo Stanković, commander of the First Battalion, Eighth Regiment."

"Did he die of disease or of wounds?"

"He died by his own hand, Father. By his own orders."

"You mean he killed himself?"

"He didn't want to hop on one leg."

"So he violated his own life?"

"He was born to command. The poor man couldn't live like that. He just couldn't."

The priest moved up to the coffin, raised the shroud, and looked hard at Gavrilo Stanković. He replaced the shroud brusquely, moved away, and began to intone the service even more angrily than in the cemetery the day before. After he had completed the prayers, he took the list and began slowly and clearly to read the names of the dead, giving the surname and Christian name of each some special significance. He proclaimed every soldier to be a hero; thought up some good deed or special merit for each; promoted them from private to corporal, corporal to sergeant, sergeant to lieutenant, giving all a higher rank in death, and even awarded them the Obilić Gold Medal. He acknowledged that they were all "worthy descendants of their great and glorious ancestors," asserted that their children and their country would remember them forever. But he removed the officer's rank from Major Stanković and denied him any merit, proclaiming his "an unworthy descendant of his heroic forebears, a man who lost his life because he was a lost soul; people will forget that he has lived, and if anyone mentions him, he will regret having done so."

"Shame, Father!" muttered Radojko, and burst out sobbing.

Milena pressed against her mother and whispered, "I'm going to stay here with you."

Olga shook her head.

"Don't tell me to leave, Mother. And don't cry."

"You must go to your father," Olga said, as she caught sight of

Mihajlo Radić in front of her. He paused, moved his lips as if to speak, but she spoke first: "My name is Olga Katić, Doctor. Will you let me work in the hospital? I'll do everything a woman can."

"You want to work here?"

"Yes, Doctor."

Olga was at first annoyed by his surprise, then embarrassed by the joy in his eyes, which lit his whole face and made him look younger.

"Thank you, Mrs. Katić. Come to my office so we can discuss it," he said, then walked away ahead of them.

After a brief conversation with Mihajlo Radić about her duties in the hospital, Olga wrote the following letter:

Dear Vukašin,

I'm sure there'll be no need to explain to you why I've decided to stay here in the hospital with Milena and do what I feel is a mother's duty. You understand better than I the feeling that one mustn't try to save oneself from human suffering. Something told me last night (when I was with Louisa and Živojin Mišić) that it's here in the hospital that I'll be closest to Ivan. Milena and I pray that God will look after you.

Your loving wife,
Olga

Milena Katić found Nadežda Petrović in the hospital laundry room. She was standing among some volunteer nurses at a large wooden tub, enveloped in steam from boiling hot lye, washing the hospital linen.

"Miss Petrović!" Milena exclaimed from behind Nadežda, expecting her to turn around and embrace her; after her family there was no one she adored as much as Nadežda.

Nadežda continued to rub the dirty and bloodstained rags against the ribbed board, then turned her head slightly, caught sight of Milena out of the corner of her eye, and said in a weary voice: "It's you, my dear. Let me finish washing this underwear. A piece of shrapnel has taken a bite out of it and it's falling to pieces like a spider web."

Milena remained motionless behind Nadežda, a little disappointed. She's lost the sister she loved most, she thought to herself; perhaps sorrow has changed her. She looked at Nadežda's wet hands, swollen from the lye, and at her fingers, which were rumpling and squeezing the bloodstained rags. Surely she wasn't painting any more. Would those stained and swollen fingers ever again be able to hold a pen or paintbrush and produce those pictures which were so strange and ugly at close quarters, but so excitingly beautiful when seen from a distance?

The laundresses were working away, absorbed by the nimble movements of their own hands; the linen soaking in the steaming water splashed about. Everything here was damp and smelled of lye, of soldiers and the hospital. Even if spring did eventually come, bringing sunshine, flowering trees, leaves, and grass, the soldier-hospital smell would persist. It would be with her the rest of her life.

"Wait outside, Milena. You'll suffocate in this steam."

Milena merely withdrew toward the wall and leaned lightly against it, her eyes still on Nadežda's hands. She thought of her first drawing lesson with Nadežda: "Now, children, I want you to remember this from now on: nature, freedom, and our people constitute the inspiration and content of art, and of everything noble and worthy created by man." Someone had cried out, "Say that again, Miss Petrović, so we can write it down." "I don't want you to write down what I say. In my class I want you to draw and to think about what is beautiful." Nevertheless, Milena had written down the first sentence at the top of her sketch pad, and at lunch she had read it out enthusiastically to her father and mother and Ivan. Her father had nodded in approval, her mother suggested that the word *people* should be replaced by *man,* while Ivan proposed that *nature* and *people* should both be crossed out, leaving only *freedom.* During Nadežda's classes, which in spring and autumn were held in the woods of the Deer Park, there was more talk about the liberation and unification of the Serbs and South Slavs than about painting. Nadežda talked about the emancipation and equality of women with more passion than she did about modern art. Nadežda's classes had begun two years before and had lasted until the previous summer; but many things had happened between that first drawing class and this hospital laundry. Milena decided she must ask Nadežda why no one—not she or her father or the books she had read—had ever mentioned the terrible truth she had learned as a hospital nurse: that few people are prepared to do good, or to show gratitude in return for kindness and love.

A soldier poured a kettle of boiling lye into the tub, and Nadežda's head and hands were hidden in the steam.

"War is a dirty business run by men. Let's go into my room, Milena," she said, wiping her hands on her apron. "I hear your mother's here. Why didn't you bring her along? I can't wait to see her."

"She's having instruction all day. On how to bandage wounds and all the other essentials. She sends you her love."

"Your mother's good at surprises; but to come here and work as a nurse, and now of all times . . ."

Milena walked behind her teacher in silence. In Nadežda's room she was stunned by the paintings and drawings on the wall above the bed, which was covered with a beautiful rug. Her eyes lighted on a bunch of vivid purple irises, broken and already faded, gathered in the darkness, snatched away from somebody.

Nadežda washed her hands with brandy from a bottle; only when she had rubbed her fingers well and dried them with a white linen towel did she come up to Milena, take her face in both hands, and look intently into her eyes. "I asked you to come, my dear, because I wanted to have a look at you. How pale and thin you are! You look like Andja, my favorite niece, who died." She stroked Milena's cheek.

Milena trembled, struggling to restrain her sobs. Nadežda stared into her eyes even more intently and whispered something with quivering lips. Milena's hands shook, and her face remained rigid under the caress of those rough fingers; she wanted to stay forever looking into Nadežda's eyes, once fiery and aggressive, now gentle and unhappy.

"Sit down on the bed and have a quince," said Nadežda quietly, taking the bottle and pouring herself some brandy. Then she sat down at the table, on which lay a sketch pad, paints, painting brush, and some snowdrops in a glass.

Milena sat on the edge of the bed and took the smallest quince from the basket in front of her. She took a bite, then held it in her lips until she had calmed down a bit. She wondered whether Nadežda had known Gavrilo Stanković.

"First of all, tell me where your brother is."

"Father thinks he's a prisoner of war."

"A prisoner? Well, I can't think of anything worse than going off to war wearing glasses. Eat that quince. Fruit's good for you."

Milena was staring at the irises on the wall: the flowers were rotting and dissolving in a deep purple.

"I'm proud of you, Milena, for staying with the wounded when the

Austrians took Valjevo. For an action like that, courage isn't enough. You need a really deep love."

"Love? I don't know what love is. I'm disappointed in people, Miss Petrović."

"I'm no longer your teacher, so don't call me 'Miss Petrović.' Now I'm your elder sister, Nadežda. As for feeling disappointment, who wouldn't in your shoes?"

"People are wicked! Wicked and crude and selfish. Not the way you and my father said they were."

"That's true. I deceived you children a bit, to make you love our country and be willing to sacrifice yourselves for our people. Where would we be without a few illusions—and some disappointments?"

"But these aren't just small illusions and disappointments. I didn't expect insults, except from our enemies. I've gone without sleep for two nights running. I do everything I can to help. I rush over every time I hear a groan. But they curse and insult me. Why?"

"Because they're unhappy, and because you're a pretty young girl, my dear."

"That makes it even worse!"

"Are you still working in the operating room with that Russian surgeon?"

"Yes. I'll stay with him as long as I'm in the hospital. If he hadn't been here when the Austrians came, and Vladimir ran away and died . . ."

"Your young man. Your handsome lieutenant." Nadežda whispered and gently patted her head. "Do you still faint at the sight of bad wounds?"

"Rarely. Sometimes at an amputation."

"Why don't you ask to be moved from the operating room?"

"I can't do that. When I came to the hospital, I chose the hardest job. Anyway, it'd be the same everywhere, except when a man shoots himself."

"A wound is something I'll never be able to paint."

"Sometimes it's harder to look into some people's eyes and listen to words than to look at torn intestines."

"When I was at the front I saw a living heart on a torn thorax. I saw it twitching and spurting out blood. I couldn't take my eyes from its quivering. I actually heard a heart vibrating. It was a quiet spot by a stream." She shut her eyes. "I can hear it now, that peasant heart.

I can see that knot in the oak tree, the clod of earth, and the black pebbles. I wouldn't have painted it red. Look at the black and green on that rug. Those are the colors I'd have used. Now eat your quince!"

Milena struggled to find words for the question she wanted to ask Nadežda: Was she to blame for Vladimir's death, because she had come to him even after he told her that for her he was dead?

"I've been disappointed in people, too," said Nadežda. "They've hurt me, insulted me. . . . People—not our nation. No, that's something different, something complete in itself and eternal, like the land we live in, like the universe around us—something that lives forever."

Milena took a bite from the quince. She's talking like this to comfort me, she thought, but she doesn't really believe it.

"As you know, Milena, I've devoted my life to painting and to the liberation of our people. You remember how your father and I talked night after night in your house; and your mother used to listen, but not say anything. I felt nervous, as if I were addressing a thousand people."

"Mother loves you and has great respect for you, but she doesn't agree with you about the emancipation of women."

"I know that. From now on I'll let her do the talking. You know, I renounced love, children, the intimacy of those I loved most. Everything that I am, and everything I could do, I put into a new conception of art. I warmed myself in the sunshine, only to discover how changes in the sunlight affected the light of colors—new, unknown colors. I gazed in astonishment at landscapes which were constantly being transformed, and at people in whom the sunlight revealed character and wisdom, virtues and vices. I trembled with anxiety before the miracle of living forms that were never the same. I like *your* sense of wonder, Milena. When I came back from Munich and I saw you then, a little girl with braids, I remember how I trembled at the look of wonder in your eyes."

On the verge of tears, Milena knelt down and laid her head on Nadežda's knee. Nadežda caressed her, let her hand rest on Milena's head. "Then the war came—my third. I was in Venice. Surely I don't have to go to the front again, I thought, and live in a hospital tent? Do I have to go through it all again—the blood and sweat, the wounds, the groans? When I read in the newspaper that Princip had assassinated Ferdinand, and that Austria-Hungary had sent our government an ultimatum, I wept aloud. People were walking past me, like leaves floating in the wind. I couldn't look at Tintoretto and Bellini any more. Those great works in San Rocco seemed to disappear, and the walls looked bare and white like the white walls of our peasants' homes, shattered by shellfire. I gazed at Bellini's *Earthly Paradise* and saw our huts and sheepfolds going up in flames. Afterward, when I came out and was walking along the Grand Canal, the old stones of the palaces were soaked in sunshine, and the pillars, the façades, the sculptures all seemed to be draining away into that dirty water. I walked around the Piazza San Marco and felt ashamed to hear my heels tapping on the clean, level stones of the square. I felt a wild desire to be walking in mud up to my knees with our peasants and oxen. Apis sent word for me to stay in Venice and work for the Serbian cause, but I couldn't. If he'd told me to set fire to Vienna, I'd have agreed. So I came back to Serbia. You saw me in Niš."

"Yes, in that heavy rainstorm. In the park on the bank of the Nišava, where we took shelter under a lime tree, and you assured me that the war would be over by autumn."

"So I did. We all believed it, because Russia had joined the war, and Russia is a Great Power."

"We were wet through, and you said to me: 'Milena, tomorrow you must go to a hospital. Tell your friends that Nadežda wants you all to work as nurses!' " She didn't raise her head from Nadežda's warm lap; she wanted to stay there a long time.

"I didn't know there'd be so much misery and suffering. Once on the battlefield I tore up my blouse to bandage the soldiers' wounds. I carried those poor boys from the battlefield on my back, and the blood from their wounds soaked through my clothes. My back was wet from blood and sweat all day long. At sunset I looked for a stream so I could soak myself in it. What was the good of art and creation? Light was for bayonets, and the sky a pathway for shells!"

Milena jerked her head up and looked at Nadežda's face: she had never seen her like this before. She turned toward the paintings on the wall: a hospital tent, wounded men on a stretcher, a burly officer with whiskers.

"You're the only one who has found something positive in our misfortunes."

"Those aren't paintings—they're my attempts to forget my own and other people's torments! Ah, my dear, how I'd like to rush back headlong into a life where I wouldn't hear men groaning and typhus patients raging, where people wouldn't have to suffer punishment for being Serbs and human beings."

"I can't look at wounds any more either," Milena said. "Or amputations. I can't look at the eyes of dead men any more. I simply can't!" She seized Nadežda's hand convulsively. "I can't! And now my mother has become a nurse, too!"

Nadežda stroked Milena's hand, then lifted her up and sat her on the bed. She herself sat at the table and drank some brandy. Milena trembled, wondering if she dared now ask the question on her mind. Nadežda said in a hoarse, broken voice: "War is always against women! We're never the victors in any war—we lose them all. We're left without children, without brothers, without husbands or lovers. Men have a hard time and die—more of them die than we do; but the peace belongs to them—the peace and the glory. They have their medals, we have our mourning, and as long as wars are fought in this world, women will have the same fate." She picked the best quince from the basket and gave it to Milena.

"Tell me something," Milena asked softly. "After all you've been through, would you still urge your students to volunteer as nurses?" She asked just to say something to postpone the real question for a few moments.

"Of course I would, Milena. In this dirty, bloody world we must be clean and good. What would this world be like without women's hands, without our compassion, our gift for making things beautiful, our ability to comfort?"

Milena took another bite of the quince in order to calm herself and collect her thoughts. "Nadežda, I've done something dreadful." With a sob, she told her about Vladimir. She told her that she believed he wouldn't have fled from the hospital, thrown grenades at the Austrians, and been killed, if she hadn't come up to him that night and said, "It's snowing, Vladimir."

"You feel guilty, don't you, my dear?"

"Yes, I'm deeply troubled."

"I can understand that." Nadežda placed her hands on her shoulders. "A woman who truly is in love blames herself for anything that goes wrong with the man she loves. Only women have such guilt feelings; men don't. At best some of them sometimes feel a prick of conscience and compassion for us. The wisest respect us. But we suffer whatever they suffer. When we love these crude, selfish males, we love them as if we'd given them birth, we embrace them as if they were our children. That's how it is. If you loved him like that, you're lucky."

Milena looked at her with amazement, then gratitude.

"I liked your young man, Milena. He was a real man. He died because he was proud. A hero! You should weep for such a man." She again walked up and down the room, then put her hand on Milena's head and stroked it. "Do you ever read poetry? You should, you know, or you'll die of sorrow. And now, my dear, I'll sketch you." She sat at the table and took her sketch pad and pencil.

"Did you know Gavrilo Stanković, Nadežda?"

"Of course. We were friends."

"He committed suicide two days ago."

"Major Gavrilo Stanković committed suicide? That's impossible!"

Speaking haltingly, Milena told her how it had happened.

"Ah, Gavrilo! That handsome head of yours was always full of nonsense. What a lover he was! What happiness for a woman to be embraced by him! Something must have hurt him, wounded him to the quick, for him to decide to take that way out. I can't understand people any more."

She fell silent and seemed to be weeping; Milena wanted to touch her. Then Nadežda gave a start, wiped her face, and took up her pencil. "Now you sit there relaxed and look at the rug. At the rate things are going, this may be my last painting."

Now they've attacked my lips, too; they bite them, they suck them. They're lured by the congealed foam on my moustache, and the mucus from my throat which oozes from the corners of my mouth. The skin of our lips is thin and tender, full of fine capillaries and nerves. These bloodthirsty creatures are soon disappointed; there's little blood in my lips, so they move off toward my throat; but I divert them by coughing. Sometimes I think they've already penetrated to the skin of my head; I can feel their legs sinking into my burning hot skin. I must protect my eyes. My vision. They're only waiting for me to relax my vigilance to rush in. They crawl over my eyelids and up my eyelashes, bending them with their weight.

The skin on my back has stuck to the brick floor and is disintegrat-

ing. It's probably making the bricks rot, too. I can feel the pain in the loose bricks. Which will rot away first, I wonder, the bricks or my pelvic bones?

I no longer hate Death and rarely fear it. Sometimes the point and purpose of Death rouses my interest.

Perhaps our Death, the circumstances of our illness and the manner of our dying, will secure for our descendants a measure of wisdom. What we're doing constitutes a permanent element in our history. Although people set little value on this particular claim to fame, there may be a time when it will bring some comfort. Our Death may even bring our country the curiosity and attention of a world that doesn't respect us.

Perhaps our Death will provide the reason and nourishment for some form of art.

Perhaps, at some time and for someone, it will provide an argument against stupidity, evil, or injustice.

Or perhaps our Death will simply be a further proof of our errors, and our failure to understand the world we live in.

So long as it has some reason, some point, it does not matter what it is.

I try hard to see in the burning and exhausted eyes of the Sick some sign of hope that we're suffering and dying for something. Anything. When I find it, I must confess that I feel better.

Some higher power has removed the former director. A few days ago the new director startled us with his shining white, beautifully ironed medical coat, and his retinue of doctors in similar bright white coats and caps. Then he threw us into dreadful confusion: "Good morning!" he said to us all. "It's my intention to get rid of the lice, and I'm asking you to help me."

He looked at us with eyes full of anxiety, then one by one he listened to our hearts with his stethoscope. There was a sudden silence: it was the first time anyone had done this since we entered the hospital. A historic event.

Dr. Mihajlo Radić, our new ruler, deserves mention in this Report. He's determined to change the existing order. He's anxious and worried, never smiles, keeps silent, and spreads silence around him. Still, he commands respect; he insists on cleanliness and what he calls working for life. If he hopes to save us that way, we're lost forever.

The mob hates nothing more than truth and cleanliness; they have an unlimited capacity to endure lies and dirt. They're fanatical only in their errors, and always on the side of what already exists. They're against anybody who calls on them to make efforts which bring no immediate satisfaction or advantage. My delirious comrades would find it easier to face a bayonet charge than take a bath. They find violence from officers easier to bear than the director's rules of hygiene. The cleanliness which could save us needs precisely the effort we're least fitted to make. From the beginning of the world, cleanliness has been achieved only by force; and violence in the name of salvation is the worst thing in our destiny.

To be dirty means to be free and tranquil. To be dirty means to be superior in relation to oneself and those who are clean. Freedom is the favor for which I would beg and pray, now and always.

My joy over the change of rulers was short-lived. Doctor Radić, like all reformers, believes that people are to blame for their own fate. In this respect all benefactors are both naïve and ignoble: people are to blame for their own fate only to a small extent. A man isn't to blame when a clumsy movement causes him to sprain his ankle, so how can he be blamed for the time and place of his birth? We aren't sick because of any pleasure, vice, sin, or ideas. We are victims. Therein lies our wretchedness, and perhaps our pitiful greatness.

Before my brain catches fire again from fever, I must say one more thing:

If a man doesn't know about his own body, he'll know nothing about his existence, nature, and the universe. All other knowledge is of a lower order. Anyone who wants to create something, to find out the truth about human life and its meaning, must first of all conscientiously get to know his own body and its Pains. These truths might change the world and make it a more comfortable place to live in for both the Healthy and the Sick. Only a full knowledge of Pain can change the course of human destiny. On the basis of this truth and experience it might be possible to establish a more rational order of society with institutions, laws, and moral standards suitable for human beings.

Wars and social upheavals, ruin and destruction, all our ceaseless strivings for change—all these things stem from man's lack of knowledge about himself. When we look at things from the end of life and see our fussing and squirming, our shouting and rushing around the *earth, we know that man's greatest misfortune is his ignorance of what he can do.*

But who am I saying this to, when nobody believes a Sick Man?

Why do I dig my nails into the time yet to come? Why do I torment myself, to gain some lasting significance?

5

FROM *Serbian News:*

EXTRACT FROM A STATEMENT BY THE SERBIAN GOVERNMENT IN THE NATIONAL ASSEMBLY:

CONVINCED OF THE DETERMINATION OF THE ENTIRE SERBIAN NATION TO PERSIST IN THE SACRED STRUGGLE TO DEFEND THEIR HOMES AND FREEDOM, THE ROYAL GOVERNMENT CONSIDERS THAT ITS MOST IMPORTANT TASK AT THIS CRUCIAL TIME IS TO INSURE THE SUCCESSFUL CONCLUSION OF THE MILITARY OPERATION WHICH, FROM ITS INCEPTION, ALSO BECAME A STRUGGLE FOR THE LIBERATION AND UNIFICATION OF ALL OUR BROTHERS STILL UNDER FOREIGN RULE, WHETHER SERBS, CROATS, OR SLOVENES. THE BRILLIANT SUCCESS WHICH HAS JUST CROWNED THESE OPERATIONS WILL ATONE FOR THE BLOODY SACRIFICE OF THE PRESENT GENERATION OF SERBS. IN THIS STRUGGLE THE SERBIAN NATION HAS NO CHOICE, BECAUSE ONE DOES NOT CHOOSE BETWEEN LIFE AND DEATH.

ST. PETERSBURG

FROM SPALAJKOVIĆ, THE SERBIAN AMBASSADOR, TO SAZONOV:

THE EMBASSY OF THE KINGDOM OF SERBIA HAS THE HONOR TO INFORM THE MINISTRY OF FOREIGN AFFAIRS THAT ON MARCH 24 IT RECEIVED FROM MR. PAŠIĆ, PRESIDENT OF THE COUNCIL OF MINISTERS AND MINISTER FOR FOREIGN AFFAIRS, THE FOLLOWING TELEGRAM:

I HAVE LEARNED THAT THE DIPLOMATIC TALKS IN CONNECTION WITH ITALY AND HER PARTICIPATION IN THE FUTURE ORGANIZATION OF EURO-

PEAN AFFAIRS ARE NOW TAKING A MORE DEFINITE FORM. IT APPEARS THAT TALKS ARE IN PROGRESS ABOUT REWARDING ITALY FOR HER NEUTRALITY, OR FOR HER ENTRY INTO THE WAR AGAINST AUSTRIA AND GERMANY, BY TERRITORIAL COMPENSATION AT THE EXPENSE OF THE SERBS, CROATS, AND SLOVENES. IN THIS CONNECTION THE SERBIAN GOVERNMENT DIRECTS THE ATTENTION OF THE TRIPLE ENTENTE TO THE FOLLOWING FACTS:

THE TRIPLE ENTENTE BEGAN THIS WAR, AS HAS FREQUENTLY BEEN ASSERTED, TO LIBERATE PEOPLES UNDER THE GERMAN YOKE AND TO ESTABLISH A FIRM FOUNDATION FOR A LASTING PEACE AFTER THE WAR. IT IS THE DESIRE OF THE TRIPLE ENTENTE TO ESTABLISH IN EUROPE A STATE OF AFFAIRS ASSURING THE FREEDOM OF ALL NATIONS, AND ALSO THEIR FUTURE WORK FOR THEIR INTERNAL WELL-BEING AND THEIR MUTUAL CULTURAL PROGRESS. IN OUR OPINION THIS AIM WILL NOT BE REALIZED IF THE FUTURE ORDER IN EUROPE IS BASED ON THE ASSIGNMENT OF FOREIGN TERRITORY TO ONE OR ANOTHER NATION AS A REWARD FOR SERVICES RENDERED. IF ITALY RECEIVES TERRITORY INHABITED BY SERBS, CROATS, AND SLOVENES, THIS WILL GIVE RISE TO DISCONTENT AMONG THE SOUTH SLAVS THAT WILL LEAD TO OPEN CONFLICT BETWEEN ITALY AND THE SOUTH SLAVS IN THE NEAR FUTURE. SUCH A CLASH WOULD BE THE OCCASION OF FRESH COMPLICATIONS IN THE BALKANS AND EUROPE.

NIŠ

FRANJO SUPILO TO ANTE TRUMBIĆ [CROATIAN POLITICIANS]:
I HAVE BEEN VERY WELL RECEIVED HERE. I HAVE TALKED WITH PAŠIĆ THREE TIMES, EACH TIME FOR SEVERAL HOURS, ON ALL SUBJECTS. HE IS IN COMPLETE AGREEMENT WITH ALL OUR VIEWS. HE RECEIVED ME GRACIOUSLY, INVITED ME TO DINNER, AND WAS IN GOOD SPIRITS OVER EVERYTHING WE DISCUSSED. OF COURSE I TALKED WITH OTHER SERBIAN MINISTERS AND POLITICIANS, WHO WERE ALSO FAVORABLY DISPOSED. I WAS RECEIVED BY PRINCE ALEXANDER, WHO WAS HERE FOR A FEW DAYS. WE TALKED FOR AN HOUR AND A HALF, INTERSPERSING THE FORMAL QUESTIONS WITH THE MOST AGREEABLE EXCHANGE OF IDEAS. I WAS ABLE TO POINT OUT A NUMBER OF THINGS TO HIM. HE MADE AN EXCELLENT IMPRESSION ON ME WITH HIS CLEVERNESS AND FINE FEELINGS. HE ASKED ME TO COME SEE HIM AGAIN AS SOON AS I RETURN FROM RUSSIA.

THE ARMY IS WORKING MIRACLES, AND THE PEOPLE ARE TRUE MARTYRS IN THEIR HARD WORK, SUFFERING, AND SELF-SACRIFICE. THE WORST THING IS THE TERRIBLE DISEASES, ESPECIALLY TYPHUS; THEY HAVE CLAIMED MORE VICTIMS THAN THE WAR. WHO KNOWS WHAT WILL HAPPEN TO ME, THOUGH

I TAKE CARE OF MYSELF AS BEST I CAN. IT IS SOME KIND OF CONTAGIOUS TYPHUS. TO HELL WITH IT!

NIŠ

FRANJO SUPILO TO A. SAZONOV:

ALL POLITICAL ÉMIGRÉS FROM AUSTRIA-HUNGRY—CROATS, SERBS, AND SLOVENES—WHO HAVE BEEN LIVING IN ITALY, SERBIA, OR SWITZERLAND, HAVE GONE TO LONDON AND PARIS TO BEG FOR JUSTICE FOR THEIR HOMELAND AND THEIR WRETCHED PEOPLE ON THE ADRIATIC SEABOARD.

YOUR EXCELLENCY! OUR SLAV SHORES, INHABITED BY SLAV SAILORS—THE ONLY REAL SLAV SAILORS IN THE WORLD—ARE OF VITAL IMPORTANCE FOR OUR NATIONAL SURVIVAL AND DEVELOPMENT. WE WISH TO KEEP THESE SHORES AND THEIR PEOPLE WITHIN SERBIA, NOT ONLY FOR SERBIA AND FOR OURSELVES, BUT FOR THE WHOLE OF THE SLAV PEOPLE AND FIRST AND FOREMOST FOR RUSSIA, OUR MIGHTY SISTER AND PROTECTRESS. THE STRONGEST PROOF OF THE IMPORTANCE OF THIS COASTAL REGION IS THE BEHAVIOR OF ITALY, WHO IS EXERTING ALL HER POWERS OF CUNNING AND BLACKMAIL TO SEIZE IT FOR HERSELF, AND IN SO DOING SHOWS NO SHAME IN TRAMPLING UNDERFOOT ALL THOSE FUNDAMENTAL PRINCIPLES OF NATIONALITY TO WHICH SHE OWES HER UNIFICATION. IN THE NAME OF THOSE MILLIONS OF PEOPLE, I IMPLORE YOUR EXCELLENCY TO SEE TO IT THAT RUSSIA DOES NOT ALLOW THIS NATION TO BE SPLIT UP AND SACRIFICED. THAT WOULD BE ONE OF THE GREAT MISTAKES OF HISTORY, AND WOULD BRING TO OUR LONG-SUFFERING PEOPLE FURTHER DECADES OF CONFLICT AND BLOODSHED. I BEG YOUR EXCELLENCY THAT IN THE EVENT OF PRESSURE FROM THE WEST YOU WILL ANNOUNCE THAT RUSSIA, TOGETHER WITH SERBIA, CANNOT SACRIFICE LANDS IN WHICH PEOPLES WHO ARE SLAVS BY CULTURE AND HISTORICAL TRADITION CONSTITUTE COMPACT NATIONAL MAJORITIES.

TO THE AMBASSADORS OF THE KINGDOM OF SERBIA IN ST. PETERSBURG, PARIS, AND LONDON:

INFORM OUR ALLIES THAT SERBIA CONTINUES TO SUFFER TO THE UTMOST LIMITS. DISEASE IS RAMPANT. THERE IS POVERTY AND WANT EVERYWHERE. ONLY IMMEDIATE HELP CAN SAVE US.

KRAGUJEVAC

FROM *Wartime Diary:*

A BARBAROUS ATTACK ON CETINJE. ON A QUIET, CLEAR, MOONLIT NIGHT AT MIDNIGHT PRECISELY, AN AUSTRIAN AIRPLANE DROPPED FOUR BOMBS ON

THE CENTER OF THE TOWN. THEY FELL NEAR THE PALACE OF THE KING AND PRINCE ALEXANDER.

FROM *The Echo:*
A BULGARIAN ATTACK ON STRUMICA. WERE THEY GUERRILLAS OR THE REGULAR ARMY? ABOUT TWO HOURS AFTER MIDNIGHT, A LARGE NUMBER OF BULGARIAN REBELS IN ARMY UNIFORMS LAUNCHED A SUDDEN ATTACK AGAINST OUR POST NEAR VALANDOVO. THOSE OF OUR FRONTIER GUARDS WHO SURVIVED HELD THEM BACK, AND THEY RETREATED TOWARD THE RAILWAY STATION. THE BULGARIANS HAVE OCCUPIED ALL THE HEIGHTS ON THE LEFT BANK OF THE VARDAR. THE FIGHT CONTINUES. THERE ARE CASUALTIES ON BOTH SIDES. MANY BELIEVE THAT THEY WERE NOT GUERRILLAS BUT MEMBERS OF THE REGULAR BULGARIAN ARMY.

NIŠ

ANRI BARBI, WRITING IN *Politika:*
CLASH OF NATIONALITIES
THE UNITY OF THE AUSTRO-HUNGARIAN ARMY HAS NOT BEEN ABLE TO WITHSTAND DEFEAT. QUARRELS AND FIGHTS ARE A DAILY OCCURRENCE AMONG THE PRISONERS.

IT HAS BEEN NECESSARY TO KEEP THE CZECHS APART FROM THE OTHERS, TO SEPARATE THE CROATS FROM THE REST OF THE SLAVS, AND THE HUNGARIANS FROM THE AUSTRIANS, WHO DO NOT WANT CONTACT WITH ANYBODY. EACH NATIONAL GROUP SPIES ON THE OTHERS. THEY ARE CONSTANTLY THREATENING EACH OTHER, ESPECIALLY THE OFFICERS. SLAVOPHILE CONVERSATIONS OR ATTITUDES WILL BE DENOUNCED AFTER THE WAR. THERE IS A PROSPECT OF OVER FIFTY DUELS.

THE SOLDIERS, DECEIVED BY THEIR SUPERIORS, NOT ONLY DID NOT EXPECT ANY KINDNESS FROM THE SERBS BUT BELIEVED—FOR SO THEY HAD BEEN TOLD—THAT THEY WOULD BE MASSACRED IF CAPTURED.

BUT THE SERBS, INCAPABLE OF SINKING TO THE LEVEL OF THEIR INVADERS, ARE STRANGERS TO VIOLENCE. THEY FEEL THAT A DEFEATED ENEMY, ONCE DISARMED, IS A HELPLESS HUMAN BEING WHO DESERVES TO BE PITIED. THE SERB'S FURY CEASES WHEN THE FEVER OF BATTLE SUBSIDES, AND HE BEHAVES WITH GENEROSITY TOWARD THOSE HE HAS VANQUISHED, BECAUSE HE DETESTS CRUELTY.

BOTH THE CZECHS AND THE CROATS, AND ALL THE SLAVS FROM AUSTRIA— ALL THOSE WHO KNOW THEMSELVES TO BE BROTHERS—REGRET HAVING EMBARKED ON THIS FRATRICIDAL WAR.

After a single day's training as a nurse, capped by Doctor Radić's advice—quite useless to her—to "use all her nursing knowledge in a spirit of love toward the patients," Olga Katić began her first working day with Mrs. Stefanović, who told her more about what to say to the patients than how to care for them. Olga was sure she would be able to look at bleeding and suppurating wounds, and to clean excrement from the seriously ill, if only she could do it without words of comfort and encouragement, without deceiving them with hopes in which she didn't believe. Sick people, however, cannot let the healthy be silent in their presence; they resent their silence. She realized this and felt depressed. So she cleaned and washed them, but kept on the go simply to avoid conversation.

"Say something nice to them, Mrs. Katić," Mrs. Stefanović would urge her. "They appreciate a kind word more than compresses or powders."

"But I can't think of anything to say!" she protested, tears welling in her eyes.

"You must think of something—you must!"

The only person to whom she spoke any words of hope and comfort was Bogdan Dragović, whom she visited every hour; but Bogdan was delirious and heard neither Olga's whisperings nor his mother's. Watching, Olga envied his mother as she tenderly wiped the sweat from his forehead and chest with linen towels, changed his compresses, and held his hand. She wanted to embrace this thin, exhausted woman, who when the doctors demanded that she leave the hospital replied, "You won't get me away from him while there's breath in my body!" Yes, Olga envied her, and was unhappy because she wouldn't let her help care for Bogdan.

When her spell of duty was over, she felt afraid of meeting Milena. She dared not let Milena see her in her present state, nor could she tell her how she felt, so at dusk she went out onto the highway in the cold wind and rain, and watched the Scotswomen in their tropical helmets digging garbage pits and drainage canals around their row of tents. A crowd of loafers and small boys and a few women from the town were standing in the rain, commenting on the strange sight: "These Englishwomen, every one of them is a great lady and could buy up Valjevo, and here they are digging in the rain!"

Until darkness began to fall and the Scotswomen withdrew into their tents, Olga watched thoughtfully as they handled their picks and spades with as much sureness and devotion as if they had been digging pits all their lives. She had no strength to marvel at them, but she felt an excitement different from the excitement with which she had made her decision that morning. To do good for those who were suffering involved more than just the joy of giving and self-sacrifice; for her it meant the effort to change herself, and the acceptance of an alien mode of life. It meant the loss of one self, and the birth of a new one. Was she capable of this? What would her prewar life mean to her now? All her thoughts and apprehensions resolved into a single anxiety: what was Ivan doing now, what was he having for supper, and where would he sleep that night? If he was a prisoner of war, captivity would change him. They would all be changed. Would they be able to love each other as before? She would write to Vukašin about this in her next letter.

From the road she went straight into the hospital. The separation of the sick from the wounded was still proceeding under the supervision of Doctor Radić, whom she couldn't avoid meeting.

"Aren't you feeling well, Mrs. Katić?"

"I'm all right, Doctor."

"Come to my office for a cup of tea and a chat. You and Mrs. Petrović must help persuade some of the women in Valjevo to come work in the hospital."

"I'm going on duty tonight."

"Why? You've been working all day."

"I'd like you to transfer me to permanent night duty."

"That's not a good idea. You couldn't take it, Mrs. Katić."

"Yes, I can. Please, Doctor, I'd like my night duty to begin this evening."

He tried to dissuade her, but she turned and went over to Bogdan, and placed her cold fingers on his forehead next to his mother's hand. Kneeling there pressed close against his mother, Olga could feel her trembling and heard her whisper: "I see that my son is close to your heart, and I pray that the Mother of God may protect your own son. I pray for him and for all Bogdan's friends."

"I do, too," stammered Olga, her cheeks burning because she didn't have the faith of the other woman.

"Your soul shows plainly in your eyes. That's why I dare ask you a favor. Will you and your daughter help me take him home tonight?"

"Of course I'll help you! We'll take a stretcher and the two of us will carry him out."

"At midnight, when the doctors are asleep, we'll carry him onto the road. We'll have Radojko, the major's orderly, waiting there with a cart. Radojko has been discharged from the hospital, but he won't go back to the army until we get Bogdan out of here."

Milena appeared with some tea for Bogdan, interrupting Olga's moment of intimacy—the link of sisterhood which she could feel growing between her and this little woman with bony hands stained with green and red. She told Milena to go to bed.

"I won't go to sleep until you come, Mother."

"You go to sleep and have a good rest. Please, Milena."

"I want to talk with you, Mother."

"We'll have plenty of time to talk," she said firmly, and went to help Dušanka, who with the ex-clown Rista was responsible for half the hospital. Just before midnight she would persuade her to go to bed. Then she and Petrana would sneak Bogdan out of the hospital. She helped Dušanka with the patients, carrying out all their requests calmly and without effort. There was no need for her to say anything because Dušanka talked to each of them, making jokes and even flirting in an innocent way. But when Dušanka asked her to come see "a second lieutenant, the most handsome patient in the hospital," Olga felt embarrassed. Could there be such a thing as "the most handsome second lieutenant" in this place? She refused to go along, but Dušanka wasn't offended. She said lightly, with a smile: "You know, Mrs. Katić, if it weren't for these handsome young men, I'd fall asleep from exhaustion. Perhaps I wouldn't have become a volunteer nurse in the first place!"

Just before midnight Olga persuaded Dušanka to go get a few hours' sleep, then found a stretcher and waited for Radojko. Petrana called to her, holding a lighted candle: "That poor man in the bed is dead. He's the third one in that bed since the major. Just hold this candle while I dress Bogdan and get him ready."

Olga took the candle, but on catching sight of the dead man's staring eyes she dropped it. One of the patients swore. Petrana picked up the candle, held it for a few moments, then put it out, whispering, "Here's Radojko!"

"Have you dressed him?" he asked Petrana.

"Yes. We just have to wrap him in a blanket."

Radojko pushed her away, wrapped Bogdan in a blanket, and took him in his arms. Accompanied by Olga and Petrana, Radojko carried him into the corridor and placed him on a stretcher. "You hold on to him," he whispered to Olga, "so he doesn't fall off the stretcher. His mother and I will carry him."

"No. You and I will carry him, and his mother can hold on to him," said Olga, lifting one end of the stretcher. Radojko lifted the other end and they hurried out into the darkness and rain. Olga struggled behind Radojko, slipping in the mud, weeping as she remembered how she used to carry Ivan into the nursery when he fell asleep in her room. No burden had ever been sweeter to her. When they placed Bogdan in the oxcart, Radojko and Petrana started off quickly toward the town. Olga stayed behind in the darkness, until she could no longer hear the rattling of the cart. She wanted to embrace Milena at that moment, but it would be a pity to wake her, so she returned to the hospital and found Dušanka busying herself with the patients.

"I would have taken him away, too, if he were my son," said Dušanka.

Olga joined her in her tasks, without offering any explanation. Dawn found her in the room where Bogdan had been; in his place was the rigid body of the dead man from the bed. The wounded men got up and crawled toward the bed, surrounded it, and stared at it. Olga leaned against the doorpost, waiting for the doctor on duty. Since the suicide of Gavrilo Stanković, every man who had lain in his bed had died on his first night there.

Slowly and carefully, the patients removed the eiderdown from the bed and placed it over the dead man. With the same care they removed the pillow and the sheet, and examined the bloodstains on it. Then they pulled the mattress down onto the floor and felt it with their fingers. They tapped the headboard and checked the rods carefully, as if to see whether the bed were alive. A man without an arm took a knife out of his pocket, opened it with his teeth, and began to scrape off the pictures of the birds and roses on the headboard, the heads of the birds and the buds of the roses first.

"So that's how you feel about it, Miloje?" someone asked quietly.

"We've just begun!" said the one-armed man loudly, and went on scratching off the birds and flowers. Others grabbed their bayonets and also scraped at the flowers and birds, and peeled off the white paint. Then they broke the brass knobs and rods, at first cautiously, as if painting and fashioning the metal; then with furious anger they stripped off the decoration, smashed it, and broke up the bed. Some ran out and came back with picks and axes and fell upon the bed, banging, flattening, breaking every part of it. All this was done without comment; the only sound was the clattering of metal.

Olga leaned against the wall, not daring to move; she thought she must be dreaming. The wounded men came from the adjacent rooms and silently watched the demolition of the white bed.

"What are you idiots doing?" shouted Doctor Pantelić, pushing his way through the curious crowd. "Get back to your beds!"

The patients moved away from the distorted iron corpse and, smiling in triumph, returned to their beds.

"What happened, Mrs. Katić?" asked Doctor Pantelić in a frightened voice.

"I have no idea, Doctor," she replied, and went off to the nurses' room, where she quickly undressed and lay down next to Milena.

"Sleep, my pet," she whispered as she hugged her.

Everything around Mihajlo Radić was working against him.

People didn't seem concerned about being treated and cured, as if it were easier to endure without resistance, as if death were on that other side of life—the same side as their capacity to resist. People really had very little fear of death. They feared death which they could see or hear, or which they knew to be accompanied by great pain; but the majority did not fear that death which is quiet and invisible. Disease was combined with human stupidity and every kind of unpleasantness; helplessness, obstinacy, and vice were fused into one. So at the same time he had to fight both unscrupulous patients and selfish colleagues. He had to convince and supervise every single person. What he found worst of all was the way the orderlies stole medicines and levied charges on the sick and wounded for the help they gave them; as for the patients, the most painful failure was the discovery that in two of the wards the wounded had to protect themselves from rats by means of cats which they bought from the local boys.

Mihajlo slept in his clothes; he simply removed his boots and took off his white coat, so that it would not look crumpled during the day. He covered himself with a blanket, and often with his overcoat. He disliked doing things for himself, but felt ashamed to have a soldier or orderly do them for him. He found shaving and changing his shirt the hardest of his daily duties, but felt he had to, since as hospital director he had no right to make the staff and patients do things he was not prepared to do himself. Getting up at daybreak, first he visited the mortuary, to make sure that no living man had been thrown into the woodshed during the night. He had designated this the resting place for the dead, until their coffins arrived and the priest sang the funeral service in his presence, after which they were taken away to the cemetery. Next he visited the isolation ward, formerly the storerooms of the barracks, where the dying patients were placed, to be looked after with special care. Whatever the state of this world, a man mustn't breathe his last totally disgusted with his fellow men; and regardless of what kind of people they were, each one deserved a little compassion at least at the end. He came into the isolation ward as if entering a holy place, for everything there had the greatest significance for him: the dead, those who were still fighting death, and Olga Katić, who ministered to their needs humbly, like a priestess; she was gray from lack of sleep and hard work, but a light shone in her eyes. In her presence he felt a confusion which for a moment kept him from examining the patients; he stood in the middle of the ward and listened to her report like a culprit. Only when he had pulled himself together did he examine the most serious cases, accompanied by her in silence.

Her period of duty ended with his morning visit, and he would accompany her to the nurses' room, sometimes without either of them saying a word. Then with one doctor and a volunteer nurse he began his daily rounds, while three other medical teams did the same. He examined each patient without haste, asking about his pains, giving advice, and listening to his heartbeat. He was always afraid of making an error in diagnosis, although they all had typhus and wounds whose symptoms rarely admitted any doubt. For him, however, no illness was cut and dried, since he believed that a man never suffered from only one disease and one wound, but held to Hippocrates' idea that "the whole man is sick." Furthermore, he had to leave each patient with the belief that he himself had faith in the medicines he gave him and the words of comfort he spoke. He tried to make the patient feel better because of his presence, seeking to alleviate his pain by convincing him that he would recover, even before he took any medicine. Moreover, he knew that every man was sick in his own way, that everyone had his own pain and his own medicine, even when they were all suffering from the same disease; consequently, he had to speak different words of hope to each one. This was what he found hardest: language and knowledge have too few true and precise words of comfort. When he couldn't find real, convincing words, he would look the patient straight in the eye and say confidentially, "My friend, you must help me to cure you."

"How can I help, Doctor?"

"By wanting to get well and by following my advice."

"But I *do* want to get well."

"It's not enough just to say, 'I want to get well.' You must believe it and say to yourself, 'I must get well and go on living.' "

"Who can really believe that here, Doctor?"

Then Mihajlo would frown, get angry, and say in his deepest voice, "Remember this: the person who dies is the one who doesn't want to live."

If at this point a man turned his head in a gesture of negation and shut his eyes, he would put his hand on his chest and say quietly, "If you want to live, you must believe me."

When he was alone again after his rounds, he was troubled by these confident words which he himself didn't find convincing. After every successful effort, and the unsuccessful ones, too, he felt that to achieve his aim he would have to work beyond his capabilities and faith. He knew that he wasn't the man to perform heroic deeds: he lacked the unremitting self-confidence, the intoxication of self-deception; but his conscience—that tormentor—had laid on him the task of working without these qualities, in his own weakness.

Who knows what he might have done on the many occasions when his heart failed him, had it not been for the presence of Olga Katić, who hovered over him and saw the whole of him with her long, questioning glance? This beautiful, enigmatic woman stirred in him both admiration and despondency; he admired her readiness to sacrifice herself along with her daughter, but was unhappy to learn she was the wife of the politician Vukašin Katić. This was because he believed that many people can be lovable because of some quality, but not people who love power. Ever since high school, when he had known an uncle who was an ambitious politician, he had considered ambition the basest of all faults. How could such a wonderful woman love a man whose ambition was to rule over people and submit them to himself, even if he was doing this only for their own good? This was a question he often asked himself as he watched her working with the wounded. As he looked at her going about her duties and listened to what she said, he could find no answer to the riddle of her personality.

When Olga volunteered for permanent night duty in the isolation ward with the dying, he was delighted, but it made her more remote, since he had never loved strength in a woman and saw Olga as being far above his own very ordinary desires. The despondency passed, however, and he became filled with yearning for her. His duties in the hospital were permeated by the thought of her and became a struggle to win her respect and liking. Sometimes he felt ashamed of himself because of his moral urge to be always on the side of the minority, the people who know that a wise, respected man dies just the same as a fool and a rascal. Still, that minority doesn't act according to the logic of this inescapable fact, since they reflect at length about the pointlessness of human existence. So Mihajlo continued to act and speak as though Olga were always looking at him and listening to him; and he was afraid of being left without this moral urge within himself, although he knew from experience that no feeling so easily justifies and excuses faintheartedness as love.

He didn't have the courage to speak to her about his feelings, and didn't dare cross the boundary she defined quite clearly, forcing him always to keep their relationship official and to confine their conversation to concern for others. He was deeply troubled by her kind remoteness, and began to feel offended by her temperate and polite respect, irritated by her thoughtful silence when he talked about his own affairs. She had never asked him about his family or asked if he was married, yet every moment they spent together she seemed to show him the same compassion she had for the dying patients. When all was quiet he reflected at length on every meeting with her, recalling the expression on her face and in her eyes, the calmness of her gentle hands, her few and quiet words. He tried hard to transform the facts to his advantage, but realized that in love this was extremely difficult, perhaps impossible. Love, as he had long known, feeds on lies, sometimes with more success than on truth. The outcome of these preoccupations was always the same: he saw in a flash of illumination, albeit with sadness, that he had no right to reproach her about anything, and least of all to feel offended. Such conclusions brought him neither tranquillity nor hope. On the contrary, they left a sediment of unease, which offers lovers no pretext for any kind of vengeance for unrequited love; generous individuals are particularly prone to such feelings. So Mihajlo found it easiest to take refuge in sadness, which he used as a drug. That was for him the easiest way out, and the one truest to his own nature.

But what if she should fall ill? What would he do then? He asked himself these questions more and more often. As soon as this fear seized him, he would hurry to the isolation ward to make sure she was taking precautions against lice. Olga would receive his expressions of concern with the same schooled politeness and effortless kindness which she showed to all those around her. Today, however, she had been a bit put out by his detailed advice, answering him with a trace of reproach: "Doctor, you don't look after yourself in this way. You ought to, you know."

How significant this sentence was for him, this gentle but—he was sure of this—sincere reproach! This gave him the right to be with her more often and for longer periods, to watch her moving among the patients with dignity and quiet, carrying out their wishes with deft, gentle movements, patiently and silently.

If only she wouldn't get ill! He became increasingly anxious and restless, and had a passionate wish for a wild gambling party the following night. Not for enjoyment, but to punish himself with some sort of failure, to thwart that love of victory and delight in pleasure which still persisted in the "lower" part of his being. His duties couldn't be postponed, however: deaths among the patients were most numerous during the night.

Keep talking, men, I don't want to die in my sleep. Tell me how you were wounded. To hell with that—let's talk of the women we've had!

Why couldn't those spiteful bastards shut up at night? thought Miloje Dačić in his corner. What made those ill-tempered cripples compete with each other in lies? They broke up his first sleep, the only sleep in which he hadn't lost his arm and didn't have a scar that wouldn't heal, the sleep in which he was digging and reaping, wrestling with his friends on the threshing floor, and swimming like a fish. He stuck his finger in his left ear, having nothing to stick in his right, but he could hear them anyway: ". . . Bullets falling like hailstones! Our men, too. The C.O. right next to me—cut down by a machine gun. I wanted to run off, but the C.O. just looked at me and I felt sick with shame. How could I leave him? So I picked him up and carried him down behind our platoon. Bullets buzzing all around me. The C.O. was a dead weight. He was dying, but he kept looking at me with those eyes. If I had a heart of stone, I couldn't have left him. . . ."

I'll never again be able to carry a man, thought Miloje, when he gets his leg cut off by a plow, or when a log falls on him. I'll never be able to throw Zora in the manger. But what man is worth carrying anyway? Stupid!

". . . The Fritzies surrounded me with bare bayonets—I was scared shitless! So I flung myself down with the C.O., like I'd been hit in the head. I smeared my hands with blood from the C.O.'s wound, wiped my face with it, too. I stretched myself out, opened my mouth wide, and dug my nails into the ground. But you can't fool the Fritzies—they're worse sons of bitches than we are! They stuck me like a pumpkin."

You only carry children in your arms, thought Miloje—until they start to talk, that is. Will I be able to carry a child in one arm? Why not, until it goes to school? I'll have to manage a wife with my left arm; but you don't need arms for women.

". . . We'd occupied positions in the beech forest—a beautiful, thick forest on the heights. It was a fine, clear day, the kind that makes your ears tingle. Suddenly I wanted to climb to the top of a beech tree and look around. The leaves were beginning to fall, and I could imagine the tops of the trees, all rusty. The Austrian trenches were near, and you could hear them banging their mess tins and unloading boxes of ammunition. Something drew me up there, the beech tree was so young, with so few leaves, clean as a young girl. So I threw off my overcoat and my boots and started up that tree. 'Where are you off to, Sergeant?' asked the soldiers. I just kept on climbing, with my heart beating against the trunk. Then the C.O. ran up and really gave it to me: I'd give away our positions and everything we'd done would be fucked up. But something pulled me up toward the top of that tree, so I could see everything from up there, even if it was my last breath. 'You're a fool, Babović!' they were saying down below, and the C.O. was aiming his revolver at me. I wanted to laugh, I felt so good! I spit on my hands and pulled my way on up, from branch to branch, from one foothold to another. . . ."

I'll never again climb a cherry tree or a walnut tree, thought Miloje. Or a willow tree either, to watch the women bathing. I'll only be able to look down from a pole, or from on top of a loaded cart, or over the fence. Still, I'll have a good view and see whatever it is they all want to hide.

". . . And I got to the top, a branch no thicker than my arm, and there on the top of another beech tree next to mine—I could reach its branch—a squirrel! It was crouching on the branch with its tail up, looking at me. It just couldn't get over seeing me. My beech tree was swaying, and if it wasn't for a breath of wind I'd have fallen like a dead leaf. Something came over me, a warm feeling like there was no war on, like I was in church. I looked at the treetops, burning red, and the bark all shiny and smooth—you couldn't see the end of the woods. And so quiet and still. Why are we fighting this lousy war? I asked myself. Then a shot rang out, then another and another—the Fritzies were trying to hit me. I wasn't afraid, I swear, just surprised at them for shooting at the treetops, at the red buds and twigs. I hated them for shooting, and our men for shouting and screaming under me. I looked at the squirrel, and at the top of the beech trees again. Then something hit me in the chest and I fell down from branch to branch—still wasn't afraid—and when I blacked out I knew I was on the ground."

"You're sure you didn't dream this, Babović?"

"No, I didn't, I swear."

"Liar!" yelled Miloje, but they wouldn't keep quiet.

". . . The night before I was wounded, I dreamed I lost my cap. I was looking for it all night in the underbrush and couldn't find it. When I woke up and felt my head and found it was there, I knew something terrible was going to happen to me. . . ."

He was by himself, mowing Aćim's big meadow beside the Morava. As he swung his scythe, a quail fluttered out of an egg. He felt sorry for the egg; the quails were crying. Aćim waved his stick and said what have you been doing Miloje; you must mow that meadow yourself by noon. All the reapers are in the army now. The eggs spattered and the little birds ran out of them chirruping in front of his scythe. Behind him women turned over the newly cut grass and piled it into stacks. They were mowing the meadows all around Prerovo. The quince were turning yellow on the other side of the Morava and the clover was blue as far as he could see. When would he finish mowing? His arms were nearly wrenched off his shoulders; the women were threatening him with their forks; the clouds were black towers above the mountain; blisters were bursting on the palms of his hands; it was pouring. Miloje Dačić could feel in his shoulders that numb pain from reaping, he was sweating, the blisters were bursting on his right hand, he groaned. It was a sharp fierce pain; he knew it well, but he knew that his right arm had been cut off, so how could he feel pain from a burst blister on the ball of his thumb?

Water! Nurse, bring me water! Bring me some water, too! A drop of water would kill you now! All right, then, let me die. I'll give a blanket for a cup of water!

The worst thing about a man is speech, Miloje was convinced. You've no protection against the spoken word. You can't stop it by force, money, or wisdom. If there were no day, or at least no morning, it would be easier to put up with things until his scar healed and his spells of fever went away, and he could turn his back on Valjevo. He didn't really feel like going to Prerovo, not until his left hand had learned to obey him like his right, and it had got some strength or skill, so that no one in the village would be sorry for him. No, he wanted them all to be afraid of him, or to envy him because of something that no one else could do. But his scar wasn't healing; he felt the spot last night and it was slipping farther down toward his side, right down to his chest, stretching his skin and making it smart; and his head ached worse than yesterday, and everything was more blurred.

"Good morning, soldiers!"

Miloje shut his eyes and turned his head to the wall: Tola! He was bringing him some hot toddy, he knew, and would torment him with questions about how he had slept, and offer him bacon and garlic. As if losing my arm wasn't enough, I've got him hanging around my neck!

"Three soldiers dead without a candle, old man, but they've got souls. Light them each a candle, and you'll get it back in kind."

"Only three deaths last night?"

"Four that we know of. That blacksmith got a candle for himself."

"You don't think three's a lot, old man?"

"What do you mean, a lot, my boy? Until the new director came, there was seven deaths in this room every night. One morning there was nine. Just let me give Miloje his toddy, and I'll light the candles for the dead."

"How about some of that brandy, old man?"

"The new director says he'll kick me out of the hospital if he catches me bringing you brandy. I can let you have some garlic, and something to eat."

Miloje clenched his fist: why did God have to stick that father around his neck?

"Drink it up, Miloje, while it's hot. How did you sleep last night?"

"Why should I sleep?"

"A man grows while he's sleeping. Your wound'll heal while you sleep."

"I don't need anything to make me grow or heal my wound."

"Well, never mind how you feel about things, just drink up this toddy and have a bite to eat."

To turn his father off Miloje took the mug of toddy and drank it quickly, but refused to eat the bacon and garlic. Garlic was a medicine, Tola insisted; no one who ate garlic got typhus. He didn't care if he died, he wouldn't take a single bite of garlic. Not because he didn't like it, but to spite Tola, himself, and his illness. At least he could still say no!

Tola went off to light candles for the dead, then lit the stove. Miloje felt a little better when the new director walked in with his staff: "Good morning, soldiers! How did you sleep last night? Open the windows so we can get some air."

Now that fine gentleman, Doctor Radić, Miloje said to himself, would feel the dead to make sure they weren't just stiff, then play around for a couple of hours with the cripples and the typhus patients. Are you in pain, soldier? Feel better today? Just stick it out a bit longer, the folks at home are waiting for you. Ugh! Such fine words were poisonous, even when spoken by an educated man.

"Turn around, Dačić, so I can have a look at you. You're all right this morning—very good indeed. In a week or so I'll send you home, but I'll keep your father here to supply the hospital with wood until the plum trees bloom. Now why are you frowning?"

"Because I'm having such a good time. I feel so happy I could burst!"

Paun Aleksić, the former director, laughed out loud. Radić paused, then said: "You're much better than yesterday, much better. Give him two analgesic tablets."

Doctor Aleksić winked at Miloje as he went out behind Doctor Radić. That man knows what people are like, thought Miloje, and he knows how to make them shut up. He didn't make you wash your clothes, take baths, and get rid of lice like that smoothie Radić. Well, he wouldn't strip to the skin and take a bath in lye, or have his rags boiled in that pot. He didn't care if the lice turned into mad dogs and bit him all over.

"Got you . . . and you!" cried Sibin, lying on his stomach. Ever since Doctor Radić had announced that the louse spread infectious disease, he'd been killing lice and counting the victims.

"Shut up, Sibin, or I'll slug you!"

"Miloje, I killed six hundred and thirty-seven—seventy more than the day before. If we all killed a hundred lice a day, in a week those little bastards would be gone from the hospital."

"Fool! And the man who says you get diseases from a louse is a bigger fool! Nobody knows what's biting a man inside and eating away his soul! Nobody!"

Miloje's lips trembled as if he were about to cry, but he merely ground his teeth and turned his face to the wall.

Paun Aleksić had never had the faintest idea how a man could be affected by demotion from a position of power, even power in a wartime hospital. He struggled against these new feelings, he was angry with himself, even at times despised himself. The mountains loomed over Valjevo; the quiet, inaudible Kolubara roared in his ears all night long; the hospital had become a huge, terrifying building. The streets of Valjevo, which he avoided during the day, receded and became hemmed in by dingy buildings and fences which before, as director, he had never noticed. Everything now seemed large and menacing.

When he walked through the hospital grounds, his steps shortened; all the hospital windows appeared to be dotted with heads staring at him. He walked hesitantly, didn't know what to do with his hands, and looked at the ground, upbraiding himself: Keep your head up! Look everybody boldly in the eye and smile, Paun, as if you'd been made chief of the Medical Section of the High Command! These attempts, however, did little or nothing to restore even a remnant of his pathetic dignity. The voices of doctors and orderlies became threatening; everybody was screaming.

The day he was demoted he had to move into the "reception room" prepared for the Allied medical mission, now empty after the visit of the Scotswomen. His bed in this empty room was like a prison cot from which he was forced to listen, behind closed doors, to everything said and done by Mihajlo Radić: his intolerable nagging about conscience and goodness, pain and honor; his constant striking of matches, coughing, snoring in his sleep with an asthmatic rhythm; all his noises typical of a disturbed nervous system. His former deep, dreamless sleep, broken only by occasional jealousy on account of his wife, had been replaced by insomnia shot through with memories of daily insults and an insatiable longing for vengeance—against not only Radić but everybody.

He was no longer troubled by jealousy, which until now had been his greatest torment: he didn't care what his wife was doing, or with whom. His desire to spend every night with a woman was fading fast, and he began to think that, at thirty-five, he was already impotent. Before going to bed he would carry outside and scatter behind the doctors' privy the cigarette butts that in the morning would have betrayed his sleepless night to his orderly, Toma.

He got up early, as frightened as a common soldier at the blast of a bugle, dressed quickly, and listened for Toma. Brka, who formerly had made the fire in his stove, was now serving as Radić's orderly, so he could no longer soak his feet in hot water and alcohol; all his orderly did now was to pour out some lukewarm water for him to wash with after shaving. Toma's chatter was insufferable and he behaved without proper respect, but Paun put up with it because Toma was his only source of information about the hospital and the new director. Toma's reports galled him, but he couldn't help listening. He learned of the shameless exultation of doctors, nurses, and orderlies over his displacement. However much it annoyed and depressed him. Only in their hatred could he see himself as still having some significance. In their biting remarks he wanted to detect some hint of fear of his return. To generate that fear, he ordered Toma to convince those who most hated him that he had written letters to the High Command. Let them sweat! He had indeed written letters to important people: he would grab at anything to get out of Valjevo and save himself from a wretched death.

Even Srećko, the former hospital accountant—that embezzler of public funds and falsifier of tax accounts—avoided him. Now and then he would give him a leering smile, and once he even said, "Don't worry, Doctor, in Serbia it's those who lose their jobs that eventually get promoted. You'll see!"

Doctor Pantelić behaved like a cat on hot bricks and seized every opportunity to put him down. The Russian, Sergeev, behaved with offensive politeness and shunned him like a leper, while that pseudo-philosopher Simić, although inferior in rank, didn't even bother to greet him, and Doctor Nandor, a Hungarian prisoner of war, acted like a free man in his presence. The volunteer nurses giggled when he passed, and said things which made him flush with anger.

His medical duties were not a form of slavery; it was as though he had never in his life been a doctor. He couldn't understand why he had taken up such a bloody, dirty profession in the first place. Night duty was like punishment for a crime. The only patient for whom he felt concern, and worked on with all the skill at his command, was Miloje Dačić. Not because of his father, that cunning old fox who had the knack of making himself indispensable in time of misfortune, and thus important in his own eyes. No, he liked Miloje because he was so pigheaded—the most stubborn creature he had ever met—and exerted all his powers to save him because he believed such defiant and stubborn people to be the measure of the spiritual health of a nation.

How worn out he was by all those "reforms" of Mihajlo Radić, that ambitious "new broom"! The changes introduced in the hospital—strict hygienic measures, the disinfecting and delousing, improvements in the therapy, care, and feeding of the patients—had hit him like an undeserved punishment. It made no difference that his mind grasped the significance of Radić's measures; the frenetic persistence with which Radić implemented them aroused his spite, and he saw all Radić's mistakes and delighted in his failures. He even wished secretly that the epidemic might get worse and the number of deaths increase. It would be easier to live in a land without all this evil human progeny!

"This will kill me!" he whispered when alone, and his throat dried up from a sudden burning sensation of misery.

He stood in front of the mirror: he had grown older and thinner, his hair was going gray, his face wrinkled. Is this me, Paun Aleksić? Did my pitiful authority give me power and strength? Did that authority make me strong, confident, and happy? He nodded in agreement, and looked at his face with astonishment. Did he despise himself? No, his feeling was more one of pity.

Outside he could hear a frightful screaming and banging. If in their death agony the typhus patients killed the doctors who were trying to save them and set fire to the hospital, that would settle many accounts. A great conflagration: that was what this world deserved.

In the Warehouse of the Dead Olga Katić spent the whole night changing compresses, dispensing fever pills, holding the hands of the dying, and lighting candles. Now she could do it all without repulsion at the smell of festering wounds and the patients' excrement; at times she was afraid, but never tired. Sometimes, as the human hearts pounded with their last convulsive beats, she longed for a moment of solitude, so that she could think of nothing but Ivan, and of their parting in the railway station at Niš. In those moments she wanted to recapture the time that she had lived, and her awareness of its passing and permanence—its passing in Vukašin, its permanence in the children. That time had stopped when the train moved off, carrying Ivan away from her, a baby waving his rosy little hands from the open cattle car. All that time was compressed into the despairing whistle of the engine which she could hear whenever she was quiet, afraid to hear it stop, afraid to hear the clatter of the moving iron wheels fade away, a sound that would live forever in her heart.

When she went to bed in the mornings—not to rest, but to hug Milena and wait for a telegram from Vukašin—she would notice that time was passing and wanted to cry out, Let everything stay as it is—don't let Vukašin's telegram arrive! For in the wake of that telegram time might come crushing down, killing in her the hope that Ivan was alive, a hope which she felt in her flesh and bones. If he were not alive, then she would feel it, her belly would know it, her heart would beat differently, she would breathe differently, and never be able to sleep, never feel hungry or thirsty; she would never be able to utter a single word, or do all the things she did for the patients: her hands would not obey her, her legs would refuse to support her.

"Don't you feel well, Mrs. Katić?" Mihajlo Radić asked. She was outside in the darkness and rain, leaning against the wall of the Warehouse of the Dead.

"I'm all right, Doctor Radić."

"Is it your son that's troubling you?"

"Yes, and my whole life as well. Everything that I've been."

"If we're preoccupied with ourselves, the sickness will overcome us."

"But if we aren't preoccupied a bit with ourselves, how can we deal with the dying?"

The glowing end of Mihajlo Radić's cigarette was flickering in the darkness, just as it had in the train the first time she had met him.

"I find it hard to believe that you've become a nurse because you feel you've sinned in some way and need to atone."

"I do feel that I've sinned, Doctor. I feel it in the presence of the patients; and I'm afraid."

"Afraid of getting ill?"

"No, it's not a fear of sickness and death. My sorrow for my son is stronger than that fear. This fear is something different. I can't explain it."

"Those who can, don't feel very strongly."

"I don't know, Doctor. I don't understand anything any more."

"You understand something very important, Olga. You understand suffering," Radić said in a whisper that seemed so near she was startled. No one had ever said anything so meaningful and so beautiful to her. She waited for him to say more.

"You know, Olga, if people don't suffer, if they don't understand pain, they don't deserve respect or love. I couldn't love a happy, healthy woman for long."

"Is that what you really think?" she said, moving closer to see his eyes.

"Yes, that's what I think. That's why I'm not tranquil, let alone happy."

"Do you think that a weakness? Do you envy those who are strong?" She noticed a muscle twitching in his cheek as he moved his cigarette slowly to his lips.

"The only people I envy are those who are sure of their faith. Any faith."

"What can one have a strong faith in, except God," said Olga, speaking a little louder.

"Do you believe in God, Olga?"

There was sharpness in Radić's voice. She realized that for Radić, God was not the one and only God. "Oh, yes!" she exclaimed. Yet she didn't really believe all that much; she rarely went to church. Vukašin's ideas had deprived it of meaning for her, he had excised both God and faith from her life because of what he was.

"Every good deed leads to some kind of faith, but . . ."

She didn't listen to the end of his thought, but hurried past him—past the spark in the darkness—back to the hospital.

"Don't leave me, Nurse! Take me away. Tell the doctor to come!" called Marko, who was suffering from gangrene.

"She was with you a while back. She hasn't seen me since last night. Please come, Nurse!" That was Ljubomir, whose pneumonia had turned septic.

"Give me some milk or water, damn it—something wet!" shouted Peter, who couldn't speak without swearing. This didn't offend her. People who suffered so much had the right to do anything.

"Don't swear, you swine! Your own mother wouldn't do what she's doing for you!" said Svetislav. He was a student who knew Ivan, and every time she asked him how he felt, he'd say with a smile: "I'll be better soon. Thank you, Nurse."

"For the love of God, help me . . ." That was Miodrag, who'd been calling out for some time; his groans turned her stomach, but she must go to him right away. She was holding Dragutin's hand, though, and he implored her with tears in his eyes: "Swear to me in the name of your children that you'll see that I'm buried in a dry place by myself. Don't throw me on that pile!"

"I promise you, don't worry; but you're not going to die, Dragiša," she whispered, staring at his hand: was there anything in the world more sacred than this coarse, dry, dirty hand? She wouldn't flinch before the last convulsive spasm of his face, or that glassy stare as he struggled for breath.

Now she must go to Mileta, who had sepsis in his stomach and was crying pitifully for his mother. Gently she asked him if he wanted anything. He shook his head and continued to moan for his mother. He would live a bit longer; those who cried were still resisting death. She passed on to the next.

"What can I do for you, Peter?"

"Give me some water to wet my lips, goddamn it."

"I can't do that. You know the doctor has forbidden you to have water."

"What's my fucking life to you and the doctor?"

How could she answer him so that he would never swear at her again?

"Don't look at me like that—I'm still alive, fuck it!"

He won't die either, she concluded, and went over to Lazar, who was flailing his arms.

"The lieutenant has died, Nurse."

She left Lazar and went to Branko, who a few days ago had exposed his gangrenous feet to his mother, saying, "Just look what you've given birth to! Look at these rotting feet!" His mother had wept silently, covering her face with her hands. "Get out!" he had shouted. "I can't bear to see people crying—not even you, Mother, not even you!"

Olga leaned over him: his eyes were wide open, staring with an expression of disgust. She closed his eyes and crossed his arms on his chest. When she heard his mother's moans, pity caught at her throat. She reproached herself for pitying the living, a reproach that reached far back into her distant former life.

And so till daybreak: she listened to them, changed compresses, gave them milk, lighted candles. The patients' despair increased her own sense of hopelessness, but when they had hope, hope flared up in her that Ivan was alive. Good people stimulated her faith, while the coarse and spiteful crushed it; but she did her best to be the same to all of them. When she was able to sit down for a moment and rest her eyes on the green sprigs of privet on her table, she reflected about the conversation she'd had that night with Doctor Radić, and was astonished to discover that this man understood something she thought only she knew. She was surprised too by what lay underneath this, by his concern for her. What did he want? Good deeds lead to love, he had said. Her whole body trembled; she could feel the patients looking at her. The all-seeing eyes of those on the verge of death compelled her to judge herself as if she, too, were facing the Last Judgment: yes, she had lived easily, superficially—wretchedly, in fact. She had really had no idea what human beings were like, nor of what life was like in this country. Nobody was to blame for this, not even Vukašin. With full awareness she had delighted in the false values of wealth and gentility; nursing all sorts of illusions about her own pride, she had wanted to appear "happy" to those around her. Next to the jar of privet sprigs lay a needle and a spool of white thread. When she had come on duty the previous night, Veličko had called to her and whispered, holding the needle and thread: "This is all I have in the world. You've shown me more kindness, ma'am, than anybody in my family. Please take this needle and thread. I know it's nothing to you, but take it, won't you?"

"It means a great deal to me, Veličko. Thank you. I'll keep it all my life."

A few tears had appeared in Veličko's clouded, dying eyes. He continued to fight for life for some time; she saw him once more alive, and then was summoned to light a candle for him. A needle, and a spool of ordinary white thread! In all her wealth, her jewelry, her diamond rings and necklaces inherited from her mother and her grandmother, among all the beautiful things she owned, was there anything more precious than this needle and thread?

"Please come, Mrs. Katić!" She started at the sound of Radovan's voice and quickly went over to him. "Tell the orderlies to carry me outside!"

"Why would you want to go outside? It's raining."

"Maybe, but I don't want to die in here. I want to see mountains and fields while I'm dying, and trees and houses. That's what I've given my life for."

"Don't be afraid, Radovan. You're much better than yesterday."

"I'm not afraid, but I'm dying. I want to die on the bare earth."

He refused the lump of sugar she offered him and continued to beg to be taken outside. She listened, unable to understand him.

"What happened tonight?" asked Doctor Radić later, bending over her as if to put his hand on her shoulder. She trembled with pleasure: why didn't he lower his hand?

"What happened? Nothing special," she said, surprised at this question.

She could hardly wait for Doctor Radić to finish his examination of the patients, and for her replacement to come, so that she could go away and rid herself of some inner burden.

The strength had gone out of Tola Dačić's arms and legs, and even the words failed him that had always supported him in his misfortunes. He wasn't hungry or unhappy, he wasn't even particularly dirty. He sensed that if he and Miloje survived this epidemic, neither one would return to Prerovo the same as he had left it, nor would they find the village the same as before. The epidemic had come to the villages and their muddy lanes from the towns and the public roads, and was now doing its work there. He was worried about Aleksa and Blagoje, although there had been no word about them from headquarters, which should mean that they were alive.

Miloje's wound was healing slowly and giving him a lot of trouble; his strength was ebbing in low temperatures and frequent spasms of fever. He was fading away, his face had a waxen look, and he had shut himself up in his silence. He had no words for his mother or his brothers, or indeed for anything in Prerovo. When Tola met his glance, he knew that his son didn't see his father; a hatred was streaming through him. He didn't even groan; he only clenched his teeth sometimes. Soldiers were dying all around him; every time a candle appeared he bared his teeth, then turned toward the wall or stared at the ceiling. Sometimes Tola believed that Miloje had gone bad, become twisted into a knot of malice and rotten luck, and that neither typhus nor any other disease could touch him. He was upset by such thoughts: perhaps the sickness had already entered his soul; everything threads its way there first, including bullets.

For some reasons not clear to Tola, the demoted director had taken a personal interest in Miloje's wound—that same Paun Aleksić whom Tola had attacked because of his heartless treatment of the sick and the dead. He wouldn't have worried about Aleksić's change toward Miloje but for fear that this might offend the new director, since he and Aleksić hated everything about each other. He knew from years of experience that one had to be most careful about the gentry's feuds and ill will. Never mind that Mihajlo Radić was in all respects a good-hearted man, and that his authority in the hospital had brought changes for the better. Or that he, Tola Dačić, had helped him with all his heart, without any compulsion or profit to himself: with the three schoolboys that Doctor Radić had sent to help him, he was cutting down trees in the neighborhood and carrying wood to the hospital. He was so tired in the evening that he couldn't eat, and when he took Miloje his toddy, half the mug was spilled because his hands were shaking from fatigue. After he had lit the fire in three stoves, given Miloje supper, obeyed all those who asked him to do something, and told the wounded some funny stories about priests and their wives, he would climb up to the attic, to his resting place by the warm chimney; he would rub his neck and chest with crushed garlic soaked in vinegar, pour himself some brandy, and fall asleep without any fear of the sickness.

Each morning before the night shift went off duty, Tola got up, started the fires, lit candles for those who had died, and covered their faces with handkerchiefs. Then he crossed their arms on their chests, bared his head, crossed himself, and said, "May God forgive you, soldier!" After that he took the serious cases to the lavatory, and sold a bit of brandy and tobacco. Before Doctor Radić and his team came to do the morning rounds, he and the boys would go out into the fields by the Kolubara and above Valjevo to cut wood. At the beginning he used to cut the dry wood belonging to men of property; he'd select the larger orchards and fields, pull out the stakes from the big meadows, and pull down only fences of large holdings and places where no black flags hung from the eaves. During the past few days, however, he had cut down whatever was nearest the hospital and would burn best.

In addition to his anxiety about Miloje and his two other sons, during the past few days he had worried about the animals. In the fields along the Kolubara and by the road wandered emaciated cattle and an occasional nag, all of them collapsing from hunger and staring at the sky with huge, clouded eyes. Feeling sorry for them, he would pluck out an armful of dry stubble and gather up dead leaves and take them to a cow; the cow would chew noisily, looking at him in surprise, but in the morning he would find it dead. The carcasses lay rotting in ditches and along boundary paths, with dogs and crows swarming around them. Wherever he saw a flock of crows croaking ominously, he knew that a cow or a horse had died. Carrying an armful of wood into one of the wards in the evening, he would exclaim: "The cattle are dying, folks—dying of hunger! What will we plow with in the spring, and how will we sow the seed? Where will we find more animals for the soldiers' baggage trains?"

"What plowing and sowing! We will all be dead by then, old man!"

Such remarks made Tola angry, and he was offended that not even Doctor Radić wanted to hear about the animals; he just shrugged his shoulders and took a puff on his cigarette. So he decided to go to Vojvoda Mišić and complain that the cattle were dying like flies. He was sure that Mišić, even though now a vojvoda, must know that without animals Serbia would have neither life nor freedom.

The sentry in front of the First Army headquarters turned him away with the butt of his rifle: "Clear out! Don't you know there's an epidemic? The vojvoda isn't seeing anybody!"

"This isn't the first time I've been to see him, soldier. Just ask the officer on duty to tell the vojvoda that Tola Dačić is here."

"Clear out, I tell you!"

He couldn't persuade the soldier to even let him see the officer on duty. He returned to the hospital sad and humiliated, sat next to Miloje, and told him that Serbia was in such a sorry state that even Vojvoda Mišić wouldn't talk to anybody, he was so worried.

Miloje was silent for a few moments, then said, "Could you do just one thing for me?"

"Of course, my boy."

"Just one thing. The last thing I'll ever ask."

"Anything you want. With my knife, if need be. What is it, Miloje?"

"Don't tell a living soul in Prerovo, not even my mother, that they've cut off my arm."

"Why should I boast about that? What'll you do, my boy, when they send you home on sick leave in a few days? And when the war's over?"

"That's none of your business. All I want is for no one in Prerovo to know I have only one arm."

"Well, I can see to that."

"Swear it in the name of Aleksa."

Dačić got up and went off to the hospital attic, to his sleeping place by the warm chimney. Something evil was roaring through that chimney.

At the end of the day, crushed by fatigue, Mihajlo Radić went into his office and resolutely turned the key in the lock. He didn't want anyone to disturb his brief period of solitude. This was the first time since he had become director that he had taken advantage of this right. Today the most essential services had somehow been set up and had started to function. With the help of some Austrian prisoners a bath of sorts had been set up in a former stable, for which water was heated by a threshing engine. That morning the entire hospital staff had taken baths, including himself, then the hospital platoon and the prisoners who worked in the hospital, and finally the patients.

Vats for the dry disinfection of the hospital bedclothes and the clothing and linen of the patients had started to function.

About ten women recruited from Valjevo had started their duties in the hospital the previous day; they had been joined by a group of schoolboys and apprentices, so that now there were two nurses and one orderly on duty in each ward. There were seven doctors, though three of them, not counting Paun Aleksić, had been compelled to perform their duties only with great difficulty. The hospital was no longer a pigsty; basic hygiene had been introduced, lavatories set up, and a graveyard established nearby so that burial could proceed according to municipal regulations and the rites of the church. With the help of boys from Valjevo, Tola was keeping the hospital supplied with wood. There was less stealing, and the sick and wounded received cooked food regularly with milk or tea, despite the food shortage. Medicines and hospital equipment had begun to arrive by way of the Allied medical missions.

Meanwhile the Scotswomen's hospital, with its exemplary order, cleanliness, and care for the patients, had had its effect on all the native hospitals, including his. The doctors had recovered their morale; the Polish Doctor Hirschfeld, with his laboratory, culture, and knowledge, had had a stimulating effect on their self-confidence; people went to his daily lectures as if to a religious service, and came back radiant with renewed faith: Serbia was not alone in her misfortune, there were people ready to sacrifice themselves to save her and work for her survival. A major struggle against the epidemic had been set in motion: the medical authorities were in agreement that typhus was carried by the louse; the government was taking extraordinary measures, the newspapers had dropped items about the military victory and begun at last to talk about the epidemic and its threat to the entire nation. It was expected that there would be a general prohibition of travel by rail, and new hygienic regulations. Vojvoda Mišić had forbidden the soldiers to go on leave and limited the movement of military personnel. Preparations were under way for the general disinfection, whitewashing, and cleaning up of Valjevo. All this had brought about a noticeable decline of deaths in the hospitals, although the influx of patients was as great as ever, since the disease had spread to the villages.

These were the so-called objective facts which had, in his head, a certain importance and persuasiveness; but they existed more for others than for Mihajlo Radić, more for official reports and public attitudes than for his solitary moments and moods. In the last resort, he was at odds with reality as he always was, and found it impossible, here in the hospital during this epidemic, to achieve any peace and harmony within himself, and between himself and the world. He would die as a believer who had no faith, a weakling who pretended to be strong, a man without hope who instilled hope in others. How did he come to have such a clearly formulated opinion about himself? He shook his head and threw his unfinished cigarette into the stove.

Fully dressed and with his boots on, Mihajlo stretched out on his bed by the blazing stove. He folded his hands behind his head, to keep his restless fingers occupied. He relaxed and began to enjoy the dusk like a religious rite. This time belonged to him, for it was then that he could be most intimate with himself. He dozed, but didn't fall asleep. He let himself go completely, offering no resistance to memory, no defense against any thought. He flowed along with the tide of painful recollections, and tossed around in the swell of his own dark grief. Supposing he survived the epidemic, what then? Olga Katić would leave the hospital, and he would be a man of sorrows, without hope. He no longer dared to hope for any joy in his life. The appearance, the very existence, of Olga Katić had deprived him of any illusion that he might fall in love with another woman after Danica, and in that love find for at least a moment some counterpoise to the futility of his everyday life. However exciting, enigmatic, and beautiful she might be, nothing could have happened to him after Danica's death if he hadn't met a woman with virtues like Olga's. No, that wasn't true. Elizabeth and Milica—both had been in love with him, and everybody who knew them considered them exceptional girls. Yet they had aroused nothing in him but tender friendship.

Then Olga had entered his life that night on the train to Valjevo, only apparently by chance, as a fellow-traveler into the epidemic. In fact, she was fate itself, relentlessly mocking and punishing him for his failure to understand Danica's waiting and silence. Why had the suffering on Olga's face been the first and most striking thing he had noticed? Why had her pain, whose cause he hadn't then known, at once aroused feelings of love in him, and now a great longing to embrace her in this charnel house and graveyard, to make her submit here and now, to his ever-present desire? Once again, the night before last, as he was accompanying her to the sick friend of her son, he was suddenly struck speechless by his desire to take her in his arms. His yearning pierced him with a sharp, fierce pain which he didn't try to resist; rather he savored its sweetness, despite the fact that on that walk in the late evening, when they were almost touching, she had been talking about her son. He had no feelings of remorse or guilt about this woman, a mother suffering for her only son. Was it her suffering that had moved him so deeply, and given him the right to love her? Why was he bothered by this? Love and love only, both the wish and the act, can never be a sin.

What innocent vileness, and what a base excuse! Love was the mother of a sin for which there was no atonement and which he had drowned in debauchery. Since Danica's death, hadn't he made three or four trips a year to the brothels of Budapest and satisfied his desire by buying women's bodies, sating himself to the point of self-contempt and disgust? After these adventures it was a whole week before he felt free from defilement and able to embrace his innocent sister, kiss his mother's cheek, and look his younger brothers straight in the eye, while he made up some trivial experiences in Budapest.

What had he got from Olga, except suffering? What else but pain, since she gave no sign of noticing his love and sadness? Sometimes her failure to notice seemed like the indifference of which only the arrogant are capable, and sometimes like the cruelty of experienced women, who know that they are loved. Why did this torment him? Hadn't he clearly understood from his early youth that the pain of love was the pain one shouldn't fight against or seek to alleviate? That pain was the lower limit of human happiness, and the only means by which its existence could be known. Only a person who had never loved could be opposed to the suffering caused by love; and people who lacked the courage to grasp any great joy or well-deserved suffering. Why was he toying now with these facile and banal ideas which didn't even convince himself? He was digging inside himself, preparing a place for the sickness in his soul. Or was it already floating around in his plasma?

Suddenly he heard panic-stricken yelling and gunshots. He jumped up and ran outside, where orderlies and prisoners were fleeing from the bath and disinfection center, pursued by a mob of naked men wrapped in tent flaps, rags, and matting, all of them shouting and cursing.

"What's going on?" he asked an orderly who was running toward him.

"Their clothes have burned up in the boiler! There isn't a stitch left!"

"My God, what did you do? Why couldn't you idiots look at the thermometer?"

The naked bodies were rushing toward him. He had no reason to run away, and no right to, and he would not. His hands in the pockets of his medical coat, he looked calmly at the naked men approaching, some of them with unsheathed bayonets. "They've burned our clothes, you bastard! To kill the lice, you're killing us, too!"

Near him a bayonet glinted, accompanied by a curse; he moved back to the bottom step leading to his office. He had no store of clothing, no words of comfort to offer them. All he could do was identify with them, nothing more. He took off his medical coat and threw it to them. They grabbed it, two of them, scuffled over it; one got it and threw it over his shoulders. Radić removed his jacket and threw that to them. A naked man with a crutch grabbed it by the collar. Then he took off the white sweater his sister had sent him and threw it to them, but it fell in a puddle. He went into his office, got his overcoat and the blanket, and carried them out to hurl to them, too, but the naked crowd suddenly retreated, turned around, and ran into the hospital. Mihajlo stood on the steps with his teeth chattering; where the crowd of naked wounded had stood he saw now, in the gathering dusk, Olga Katić, staring at him, dumbfounded.

Olga saw his medical coat, jacket, and sweater in the mud: there was nothing this man wouldn't do for other people. Once more her eyes opened wide and her lips trembled: Vukašin wouldn't have behaved this way, or any other man she knew. Quite simply, she saw him now as a miracle worker, a beneficent madman, and perhaps for her a savior who had stirred hope in her in the Warehouse of the Dead. She could remember every wisp of straw on the floor as the orderlies carried in the dying on stretchers. He had talked about the purpose of the isolation ward, interrupting himself now and then to tell the orderlies not to set the patients down roughly. "It's our duty to save a man from his last pain," he went on, "from the feeling that he's lost and abandoned, condemned to die. We mustn't deprive a man of his last hope. As long as he exists before our eyes, hope for his life must exist in us. Mrs. Katić, make sure you use the Christian names of your patients, not their surnames." She had listened carefully. Her heart missed a beat as she recognized that something new was beginning in her life. She had given him a long look of agreement: "Yes, I'll remember." From that time on she had served him in all the things he strove to do, faithful to herself and to him, served him with an increasing devotion, presumably because there was no room in her for feelings of admiration for this man. When she did have such feelings, she resisted them, and not for any feminine reasons.

So things had gone until that night in the Warehouse of the Dead, when at midnight her whole being ached to see the sky, and he had found her in the darkness and the rain, leaning against the wall; he looked anxiously at her as no one had ever done before, and she had felt a sudden desire to tell him all about herself. She had given him some hint of this, left something of herself with him. After that, whenever she met him she wanted to reveal something of herself and hide it in him—things she wouldn't have dared tell even Vukašin, who wouldn't understand, rendering her defeat inevitable and unimportant. For she had long ago grasped the fact that only a woman's defeat was unimportant. She and Mihajlo Radić had never continued that midnight conversation, though he had tried to do so on a number of occasions. She had resisted any further delving into herself in front of him, because she knew where it would lead. She shuddered at this betrayal of Ivan—Ivan, not Vukašin—but now this man had done something which made it impossible for her to ignore him.

She wanted to come close to him, to touch his face and look into his eyes, and discover in them what was behind his self-sacrifice, behind the words "human love can prove itself stronger than the feeling of the pointlessness of our existence." Such words were difficult to prove. She had grown tired of listening to such grandiose pronouncements and lofty principles from Vukašin, and knew from experience how much smoke accompanied their fire. All the good that Mihajlo Radić did wouldn't have aroused her respect and admiration if he hadn't done it in his own special way. No doctor worked with his hands and fingers like Radić when examining his patients. He played on the human body as if it were a musical instrument; his fingers divined and saw under the human skin. He listened for a long time to each patient's heartbeat; every groan from a wounded man touched him. Of all the people she had met, he had the deepest understanding of pain. He understood it, pondered it, treated it. He was thin and sad; now he was helpless, ugly, and a bit ridiculous in his half-dressed state. She would have liked to wrap him up tenderly in her coat, like a brother. Suddenly she felt that the windows were open, that everyone's eyes were on her; she knew a woman dare not cross that frontier determined by human malice and lack of understanding. She wanted to say something to him with her eyes and her silence.

"Where's your revolver, Captain? A mutiny must be suppressed with a revolver!" cried Paun Aleksić.

Mihajlo Radić couldn't turn away from Olga's gaze to look at Aleksić. He waited for her to say something while his eyes asked: Have I made a mistake? Have I disgraced myself?

She came up to him, bent down, picked up his clothes from the mud, shook them, and handed them to him. "You'll catch cold," she said, and hurried away to the nurses' room, frightened by her own feelings.

"Don't worry about the soldiers' clothes, Director. We'll take care of them before the evening is out!" said Doctor Pantelić in front of the door.

Radić sat down by the stove to get warm. For the first time Olga had whispered something kind to him, done something for him outside the range of her duties, something personal. Was it compassion, or had she acted with understanding? The clothes she had picked up lay on his lap; she had shaken the snow and mud from them, and handed them to him as if he had been naked. He touched the jacket and sweater hallowed by her touch, and felt Olga's gentle presence in the vibrant, living lightness of his things. It was as though they were her dresses, her linen. He fingered his sweater; the roughness of the hem calmed down in him that sensual experience of her body. Again he wanted her, as he had wanted her the night before last, when she had grieved over her son. He wanted her and he hated that man, Vukašin Katić, who had a right to her and could do with her as he pleased.

His orderly brought in supper and got the fire going. Then Mihaljo wrapped himself in his overcoat and went out into the raw, still evening. The sky was deep and star-studded. When had he last seen so many stars in the sky? In the hospital everything was quiet, as if all the inmates had died, except for one who was calling out for his mother. He went into the hospital and told the doctors on duty to continue the bathing and disinfection the next day as scheduled; Pantelić reported that by the morning the soldiers whose clothing had been burned would be clothed again. He looked into every room to let people see him, then continued on his way. The nurses and orderlies on duty withdrew into the darkness, as if to hide. He went into the operating room, where Sergeev was cleaning away sepsis from a collarbone smashed by a bullet, helped by Milena Katić. She smiled, which rather surprised him, since during his morning rounds she had looked at him so imploringly that he asked if there was anything wrong. "Oh, no, Director," she had said, in a voice that made him blush. He had made up his mind that when he met her alone he would stop her, put his hand on her shoulder, and say something that would arouse her confidence in him.

"You saw what happened?" he said, rather softly and confidentially, almost touching her cheek, which excited him. He had never come so close to the eyes and lips of her mother.

"Yes. I liked the way you handled it."

He turned around and strode toward the window. It wasn't until after the orderlies had carried out the wounded man and Sergeev had told Milena that she was free until seven o'clock the next morning that he looked at Sergeev.

"Don't you envy me, Mihajlo Radić," Sergeev said in Russian, "for being perhaps the only surgeon in this war who can escape from sepsis and amputations into such wonderful eyes, into the face of such a beautiful girl? How's that for the fortunes of war? If beauty can't save the world, contrary to the dubious belief of Dostoevsky, the world can certainly last longer with it. Don't you agree?"

Mihajlo moved a bucket filled with pus-stained gauze, leaned against the wall, and stared at the blood-spattered operating table. "What am I doing wrong, Nikolay Maksimovich? Tell me, as a brother."

"You know, Doctor, Gogol thought illness should be viewed as a grandiose battle, and that we can fight it only as the anchorites fought with the devil."

"How should we interpret that here, Nikolay Maksimovich?"

"A man cannot vanquish illness and the devil alone."

"Are you telling me that I'm not acting wisely?"

"You believe too much in reason, the least of human attributes."

Mihajlo looked again at the bloodstained table and said: "Then we have no future. We shall perish in this epidemic and slaughter."

"Whoever lives for the future has given himself up to death. He has acknowledged its absolute power."

"How are we to resist it, Nikolay Maksimovich?"

Sergeev paced in the room, then stopped. "Two days ago, Mihajlo Radić, I listened to you talking about hope. For you, hope is in what's to come, and what's to come is good. That's a mistaken notion, a common error. Hope comes from the past, from what was good in it. That's the hope with which we can launch this grandiose struggle against illness that Gogol talked about—Gogol, the most unhappy thinker in all Russia, who fell ill and died from his thoughts. Well, let's go to my room for some cognac."

"Sorry, I'm having supper with Doctor Hirschfeld."

They went out into the hospital courtyard together, then Mihajlo hurried off toward the gate. Suddenly he remembered Philip Simić's invitation to drop by his laboratory, so he made his way to the pantry of the former officers' kitchen, which Simić had fenced off with packing cases and a hanging tent flap. On the kitchen table he had arranged a Primus for heating, above the table a shelf with some twenty jars containing preparations and chemicals. There, as he put it, he "thought about health and wandered in my spirit along the paths of the unknown." Mihajlo moved the tent flap aside and approached Simić, who was standing between two gas lamps, bending over a sheaf of white paper where with the tip of a feather he was nudging two lice on a piece of cotton soaked in a chemical.

"Doctor Hirschfeld's wrong. Sulfur vapor doesn't kill the louse, Director. Please tell him that tonight."

"What does?"

"Here are the results of my experiments: in liquid gas the louse dies in two minutes; in benzine, in thirty seconds; in carbolic acid, two minutes; in naphthalene, four or five minutes; in lysol and in a solution of spirits of camphor, one minute."

Mihajlo stood over Simić, who continued to push the two lice onto a small wad of damp cotton with the feather. How comically serious it was, he thought, as he waited to see what would happen to the lice when Simić pushed them against the cotton. Sensing their danger, the lice kicked about with their little legs and tried so hard to save themselves that they aroused his pity. "All right, I'll tell Hirschfeld. Now tell me what I've failed to do that you'd have done if you were the director."

"You've failed to do the most important thing. You don't use the big stick; there's no court-martial in the hospital. Those are the only effective measures against human stupidity. Humanity such as yours and so-called Christian compassion are just decadence. At least two hundred thousand filthy Serbs will pay for it with their lives." He offered Mihajlo his iron chair.

Mihajlo merely took hold of it and said with unusual brusqueness: "Doctor Simić, I don't exclude the possibility that people can be driven into paradise with a 'big stick.' Or even into freedom. Of course it's possible to acquire knowledge as a result of force, and to lead people to justice. All that can be done. But we'll never save people from pain or suffering by using force and the 'big stick.' That's out of the question."

"Every illness must be treated by conquering sentimentality and self-pity; that's Nietzsche's teaching. The ability to be equal to an enemy is a condition of health. Forgive me for mentioning Zarathustra's great saying once again: To be ill is a kind of resentment."

Mihajlo frowned; to him mathematical laws and chemical formulae represented an abuse of memory, and the citation of other people's ideas was the same as stealing.

"Did you see that mutiny, Doctor Simić?"

"Yes, I did. I was delighted to see all those naked warriors shouting and jostling—especially with bayonets. That, Captain, was their first manifestation of strength, their first real step toward health."

"You're determined to mock me. Is this what the rational part of your mind really thinks?"

"No such idea entered my head! I respect resistance and rudeness. Rudeness is one of the finest virtues. Keeping silent makes for bad character, it even upsets the stomach. All silent people have something wrong with their digestive systems."

"You're quoting other people again and making jokes that are out of place."

"For years I haven't met a man who speaks his own mind—intelligently, at any rate."

Mihajlo looked at him with pity: such a finely sculptured head, such regular features, yet full of someone else's ideas that were not in harmony with life.

"How many more days do you need for the incubation of your infection?"

"Four or five."

"You feel no fear of the disease?"

"The only fear I acknowledge and respect is the fear of truth."

"Only that?"

"Yes, I fear that great abyss."

"Aren't you afraid of an abyss from which you might not return?"

"In the face of that event, I have feelings far more important than fear."

His fear blazed with pain and a kind of proud, challenging will and determination. With admiration and pity, Mihajlo hurried out into the darkness. When he entered the Grand Hotel, it was crowded with officers talking at the top of their voices. He walked up to the table where Doctor Hirschfeld was waiting for him, held out his hand, and said in French with unnecessary brusqueness, "That sulfur of yours is no use at all!" At once he regretted having spoken, for a French officer, a stranger to him, was also at the table.

Flushed with embarrassment, Doctor Hirschfeld said: "Allow me to introduce Doctor Georges Embert. He has just arrived, and I've asked him to have supper with us. Doctor Embert is a member of the French Epidemiological Mission headed by Colonel Robert. Eighteen doctors have arrived from France. The lice are going to be conquered, Doctor Radić."

Mihajlo wanted to embrace the bearded and moustachioed Frenchman wearing a lieutenant's uniform, but the Frenchman dampened his ardor by his stern face and military salute, which put the emphasis on formality.

"It's not for me to thank you and express my admiration, Doctor Embert. All the same, your arrival is a great event for Serbia. Eighteen French doctors, plus people from Russia, England, and Switzerland—Serbia is not alone in her present misfortune."

"We Frenchmen are performing our duty as Allies. When we arrived in Niš, we realized that was little enough."

"I think Doctor Hirschfeld has convinced you already how little is needed to give us hope. For centuries we've been alone."

"Are you sure that sulfur vapor doesn't kill the louse, Doctor Radić?"

"My doctors have come to this conclusion as a result of their experiments; but please, let's talk about sickness and medicine after supper. Waiter, bring our supper at once, and some good red wine."

"During the ten days I've been in Serbia," said Doctor Hirschfeld hesitantly, "and of course that's too short a time to make any serious conclusions, I'd say that you Serbs have no God. That's a spiritual assumption of enormous significance."

"But we are Orthodox!"

"I know. So are the Russians, but they have their God, their Russian God. The Germans are Protestants, but they have their pure-blooded German God. *'Gott mit uns!'* exclaimed Kaiser Wilhelm. The French are Catholics and also have their God, and it doesn't really matter that they've combined in Him two irreconcilables: Gothicism and Descartes. Likewise we Poles and the Jews. I greatly fear a nation that has its own God, Doctor."

Mihajlo Radić tried to smile, and as he poured the wine he decided to give the conversation a lighter tone: "You can set your mind at rest on that score. The Serbs have no God of their own. Not because we don't want one, but because we don't believe that any God could be on our side. That's been our experience for centuries."

"What are the last words you Serbs utter, your dying words?" asked Doctor Embert, with pity in his voice and his eyes.

"I've watched hundreds of soldiers die on the battlefield and in the hospital, and nearly all of them address their last words to their mothers."

Doctor Hirschfeld pondered these words and let his gaze wander over the restaurant, filled with smoke from bad tobacco, and the smell of officers' boots, meat, and onions. It wasn't until Mihajlo Radić offered him supper for the second time that he spoke again: "You Serbs have a remarkable will to live. You carry the idea of eternity in your national character. The strength of that idea in you people is most impressive. That in itself is a deeply religious feeling. I was particularly aware of it during my long talk with Vojvoda Mišić."

Preoccupied with his own troubles and incapable of conducting a conversation where he had to choose his words with care, Mihajlo tried to change the subject to the problem of blood groups in relation to the causes of cancer—a subject Doctor Hirschfeld often discussed. But now Hirschfeld refused to take it up; instead he suddenly raised his voice so that all the officers at the neighboring tables could hear him: "Do you know what I'm afraid of when I think of the future of you Serbs? I am afraid that the suffering you're now experiencing may destroy your capacity for wonder. I know of no greater human misfortune than to be without this power."

He fell silent. Mihajlo also remained silent, but then he said in the manner of someone making a confession:

"Believe me, gentlemen, it matters a great deal to us that you foreigners should get to know us. Only then will you not regret your efforts and sacrifices."

"No need to fear our disappointment. We're here to do our duty," said Doctor Embert firmly.

"You must know that we're an extremely unhappy nation."

"How come you have such remarkable generosity and kindness toward your enemies? I intend to write a book on how you Serbs treat your prisoners of war."

Mihajlo Radić leaned over the table. "Perhaps you haven't noticed yet how easily we disappoint the very people we love. Please bear that in mind!"

"Doctor Radić," said Hirschfeld, "today Europe is responsible for the greatest crimes, she's on a level with the cavemen. No need for you to feel ashamed of your poverty and lack of sophistication. You Serbs kill only because you must, and therein lies your moral superiority over Europe today. Europe has forced you to kill! You're killing for freedom. That's your historical good fortune. Yes, you kill, but I'm amazed that a warlike nation such as yours does this with so little hatred."

Mihajlo was silent for a moment, then said with obvious sincerity: "I have no great belief in our nation, Doctor Hirschfeld, nor in humanity, nor in any great ideals. Now and then I believe in an individual man, one who's tormented by pain." Then, regretting this misplaced sincerity, he drank two glasses of wine, one after the other.

"I understand you," Hirschfeld added, "and I like an honorable modicum of love for everything. Still, today as individuals we're forced to think and concern ourselves not only with those nearest to us, not only with our own nation, but with the whole world—with humanity! We must do this because the very foundation of our most important values is crumbling away as a result of this war."

"Doctor Hirschfeld, I firmly believe that the world will continue to exist as long as there exists in it a single man who's prepared to die for another man, from whatever motives. The world exists on such sacrifice."

"It follows logically from such a belief that a single man, sacrificing himself from bad motives, could also destroy the world. Do you follow me?"

"Yes, I do. That's why our reasons for hope in high ideals are uncertain."

"That's not true, Doctor Radić; but do tell me what proofs you have that sulfur vapor isn't an efficient means of disinfection."

Mihajlo was glad when this conversation and the meal were over. He related briefly everything he knew about the action of sulfur vapor, and promised to bring some proofs the next day. Then he excused himself and hurried to the hospital to see Olga.

He went into the isolation ward timidly and stopped by the door. In the center of the room, as always, stood a table covered with an embroidered white tablecloth, and on it a glazed yellow jar with some green sprigs of privet, illuminated by a lamp placed near the edge of the table so as to give the dying patients on the floor the best possible view of the greenery. The chair behind the table, on which Olga usually sat, had been overturned. He saw Olga in the semidarkness kneeling beside a patient. Taking care not to tread on anyone, he tiptoed across the room and stood over her. As he waited for her to turn around, he gazed intently at her slim, bent back, her sloping shoulders flowing into her long neck, under the roots of her hair. For the first time he seemed to see her naked: from the dark nest of her hair he saw the tender undulation of her backbone, from the base of which spread the whiteness of her gently outlined thighs. She turned toward him, still holding the patient's hand.

The expression in her eyes—a mixture of reproach, entreaty, and helplessness—made him tremble; he bent down and took the patient's other hand to feel his pulse, but it was lost in his veins and hardly detectable. The patient opened his eyes with a half-pained, half-scornful smile which flickered over his whole face and finally came to rest at the edge of his lips. He closed his eyes again and whispered, "It's simple . . . so simple."

Mihajlo felt that time had stood still within him—time in which hope existed as long as he was troubled by the insignificant and transitory state of himself and other people. It's not in that transience that the poverty of life lies, he thought, as he gazed at the dead face with its open eyes, and at the lips with which the dead man had perhaps solved the riddle of his own pointlessness, but only for himself, thus depriving it of significance. The poverty of life comes from fear of its transience and its inescapable end, from the powerlessness of human reason to master that senseless fear, and that pitiful, crazy dependence on this world, and on the coldness clenched in its fist. But what would life be without that fear and that dependence on its sudden termination, the final monstrosity? He looked at the patient's hands; he knew from experience that the hand is that part of the body which resembles its living owner longest. It was a beautiful, elegant, impractical hand. What had it done with the greatest joy? He put it down on the dead man's chest. The hand slid toward the man's side, then stopped; it had finished all its tasks. What was their significance, and how long had they lasted? Were they something really important, or something no one knew about? What had that hand failed to do that it could have done and wanted to do? In that question lies the root of the deepest sorrow for those who have died.

The patient next to the dead man began to wail, "Don't let me die, Doctor!"

Mihajlo put his hand on the man's burning, sweaty forehead. "What can I do for you, my friend?"

"Doctor Vojtekh gave him an injection of morphine half an hour ago," Olga said, then went away.

The patient began to cry. Mihajlo stayed with him in silence for a few moments, then went over to Olga, who was standing by the overturned chair.

She was staring thoughtfully at the sprigs of privet. What did that world *simple* mean—death or life? Until Ivan had volunteered as a soldier and Milena as a nurse, Olga had lived a life in which death existed only for others, far away from herself and her family, so far away that she felt no fear of it. Was her life without feeling for death an authentic life?

With effort, Mihajlo put the chair upright so that she could sit down. Unconsciously, Olga gave a start and moved away from the chair and that act of courtesy. She raised her eyes from the sprigs of privet: did "so simple" mean life or death? Did this man, who had devoted himself to the sick, perhaps know something about it?

Mihajlo met her inquiring glance and saw on her face the same expression of suffering he had seen in the train: the enigmatic, beautiful suffering to which he had surrendered and with which he had fallen deeply in love. He wanted to lay his hand on her shoulder, and his hand ached from that desire, realizing its impropriety. He went out slowly, head bent, into the night.

Only after the first sitting for Nadežda's portrait of *A Serbian Nurse*, as she had begun to call her picture, did Milena think that the girl in the picture resembled herself. Subsequently the portrait began to take on the form and expression of Nadežda's dead sister Andja. At the last sitting Nadežda exclaimed delightedly, as she showed her the painting: "Look! Your mother will be thrilled!"

Milena was dumbfounded: it was completely Andja—the face and bust, and especially the eyes and the mouth! The nurse's cap and apron, with their dirty white color, simply heightened the recollection of her recent death.

Nadežda's face clouded. "Don't you like it?"

Milena had never heard her use that tone of voice before; she stared at the picture of the dead girl, embarrassed because she had upset Nadežda, who was waving her glass of brandy about, so that in her anger she spilled it before she had even taken a sip, and woke up the nurse asleep in the other bed.

"Dobrila, please look at Milena and this painting, and tell us what's there that isn't Milena."

Dobrila winked at Milena and smiled consolingly. Without even looking at the picture, she said: "Why don't you like it? We can't see ourselves any more; and who knows, perhaps we never did." Then she snuggled under the blanket and went back to sleep.

Turning the painting to the wall, Nadežda said: "Something's wrong with you, my girl. There's darkness in your heart—and no wonder!—so you can't recognize yourself. You'll be surprised to see how much you'll like the painting tomorrow. Come at noon. Then you'll see!"

But she hadn't gone—neither yesterday nor the day before. She was afraid both of the painting of the dead Andja and of Nadežda's disappointment. She was becoming quite obsessed by the likeness in the picture; Andja's threatening eyes seemed to look at her from the walls of the operating room, and from the gauze and the surgical instruments; and the moment she closed her eyes, two dark jets below the dirty white color bored into her from the painting—Andja's eyes! She was afraid to tell her mother about her feelings, knowing how easily Olga surrendered to superstitious fear.

Anyway, neither she nor her mother had time for confessions and anxieties. They shared the same bed, but the night-duty schedule was such that they hadn't slept in it together even once. Occasionally at the time of the change-over her mother would lie down next to her and hug her, and they would both tremble from the same fear; it was always hard for her to tear herself away. Whenever she managed to leave the operating room for a moment before her shift was finished, she would run up to the nurses' room to catch her mother in bed. When there was nothing to do in the operating room or the bandaging room (which rarely happened), she would run off to her mother in the Warehouse of the Dead, to talk about Vukašin's last letter and keep silent about Ivan, whom they usually referred to, indirectly: "Strange that there's still no news from Geneva!" Then they would discuss Bogdan, who had now gone home, and whom they both visited every day, though not together, Olga going in the evening with Doctor Radić. And now there was Nadežda's strange picture: the only person she could discuss it with was Dušanka, but she was in no state to listen to anybody, being so desperately in love with Doctor Simić that she could talk about no one else.

Three days after her last meeting with Nadežda, a soldier with his arm in a sling caught her at lunch. "Miss Petrović has given orders that you're to come see her at once!"

Milena left her lunch and went to her mother in the Warehouse of the Dead, told her about the portrait, and asked if she should go see Nadežda.

"Why on earth not? You know very well that all her paintings are crazy and look more like her than like what she's painting," said her mother calmly, and ran off to pick up a candle that had fallen from a dead man's mess kit and set the straw on fire.

Milena didn't wait for Olga to put out this latest of the frequent deathbed fires, but went out and made her way slowly and anxiously to Nadežda's room.

She found Nadežda putting cold compresses soaked in brandy on the chest of Dobrila, who lay with her eyes closed.

"How long has she been like this?" asked Milena, standing by the door. She wanted to run out, as if seeing a typhus patient for the first time, as if she hadn't just left a room where some thirty soldiers had died.

"It struck her at dawn yesterday. Sit down. Do you wear only one pair of stockings?"

"Yes, woolen ones. I'm not cold."

"That's no good. Tell your mother you should both wear two pairs of stockings. Like I do," she said, lifting her skirt to show Milena her legs. "Cotton ones, right up to your thighs, over your underwear. You must sprinkle plenty of naphthalene on them and your knickers. Then pull your woolen stockings over them, after soaking them in kerosene every morning; and fasten your suspenders tight, so that none of those disgusting lice can get in and kill you!"

With a feeling of awkwardness, Milena removed her eyes from Nadežda's enormous legs and thighs, their layers of underwear bound with rubber and black woolen stockings. The portrait was on the table but turned to the wall, which made it easier for her. Surely she wouldn't paint now, in front of Dobrila? She would tell her that was most inappropriate in such circumstances. Nadežda washed her hands with brandy, wiped them on a clean towel, then took a soldier's mess kit full of prunes and offered some to Milena.

"In addition to bacon and garlic, the best thing to eat now is prunes. Take a handful. I'll have some brandy. That's a good preventive medicine, too. Sometimes I even drink kerosene. You can see the state Dobrila's in. No hope for her. It'll be my turn next. I'll leave nothing behind me—a few little sketches, some exercises in still life. Still life, indeed! Flowers in vases. Gilt frames, drawing rooms, mirrors—disgusting! What I want to draw is living nature in all its variety. I want to paint all Šumadija, the Morava, the whole of Belgrade and the Sava and the Danube. I want to paint a regiment, a division, the First Army. I want to have half the nation in my painting. I want to stretch my canvas from Lapovo to Resnik." She poured more brandy and sat at the table. "I want so badly to finish at least this painting! I'll send it immediately to my big-eyed nephew Rastko. He'll be a painter someday. If anything happens to me, who'll pay for his education—who? Why haven't you come to see me for three days, you naughty girl?"

Milena opened her mouth to say she was afraid of the portrait, but recoiled from the idea and said tentatively: "I just can't get away from the operating room. There are lots more cases of gangrene and sepsis. Unbelievable. Sergeev is cutting off as many arms and legs as Napoleon's surgeon Leuriet."

"As many as who?"

"Napoleon's surgeon Leuriet. At least that's what Sergeev says."

They stopped talking and listened to Dobrila's groans. Nadežda was staring at a sketch of a powerful bearded officer. As long as she doesn't bring up the painting, thought Milena, as long as she doesn't turn it around and say, "Now, my dear, just think of what the countryside around Valjevo will look like when the plum trees are in blossom!"

"Our women are dying, the country is dying, Milena," said Nadežda softly. "The women *are* the country. They're like the fields and meadows, the orchards and vineyards of the land itself. They give birth, as the fields and orchards give the countryside its beauty—its red and green colors. As for the men, they're the roads, the rivers, and the forests. They're the State and the army, force and power, buildings and laws. I'm often amazed how men get interested in painting and color. I can understand their interest in philosophy and literature and everything that uses words; but painting, that seed of light, that need to be on a level with nature . . . ! Well, let's get down to work. Don't sit sideways; look at the rug. And don't listen to Dobrila; think about Vladimir or Ivan."

"How can you paint now? What for?"

"What for? I've never needed to paint more than right now, when so many are dying in this pesthouse where we don't know who's alive and who isn't! Where everything is murky and muddy and dirty! That's the color of life right now."

"A painting is such a small part of life, Nadežda."

Nadežda jumped up and stared at Milena in amazement. "Small? For me, *life* is small for the painting I want to paint! I'll die without having done anything at all! What have I been doing all these years?" She sat down and dropped her hands on her knees. She was silent for a moment, then continued in a tone both reflective and menacing: "The whole world should be hurled into everlasting darkness if there are no eyes to see light as it should be seen! Freedom is worthwhile only to the extent that human eyes can grasp light and human hands can express it."

Milena looked at her; she didn't mind her talking, so long as she didn't paint.

"I was younger than you when I decided to become a painter. I had some inkling that it would bring a curse on me, but the light and the prospect of fame lured me on. I'm speaking to you from the heart, as if you were my sister Andja. You know, I see her in you. Don't hide your eyes now! Sit up straight and look at me! There's nothing in human experience as exciting as the kind and gentle look of beautiful eyes. Men's eyes, too, Milena. My, how beautiful you are! Eat some more prunes—they're good for you."

"Do you love fame very much?"

Nadežda's eyes flashed, and she blushed from a joyful shame. "You are Vukašin's daughter, you have the right to ask anything you want! Of course I love fame. I love fame as an artist more than the love and embraces of a man, more than all the good things of this world. To be famous because of beauty and truth of heart and vision in a land where only heroes are glorified—nothing in life equals it. What more can a woman do in Serbia? Milena, I have a terrible, uncontrollable desire to feel the green leaf of the laurel with my fingers, to squeeze it, rub it between my palms, then clap my hands like a gypsy singer and laugh at the world and myself—at myself most of all!"

Flushed and trembling, she got up and walked about the room, then returned to her chair and looked at her drawings and at the paintings on the wall. Suddenly she gave such a groan that Milena held her breath. "But to be an artist in a poor, unenlightened country! A country where all that people need is bread and shoes, and occasionally brandy. To be absolutely unnecessary to the people you live for, Milena—to be ridiculous, crazy, pitiful—is there anything harder and more unfortunate? On top of that, to decide on one further act of folly: to want to create a new art! A new art in a land where there's no classic art or living art of any kind, except embroidery and kilims made by peasants. Oh, my dear, how splendidly and dreadfully crazy that is!"

Her hands were shaking. Milena wanted to comfort her, but didn't know how.

Dobrila threw her blanket off and cried out: "Shame on you! Shame!"

Nadežda covered Dobrila, returned to her chair, picked up the unfinished painting, and stared at it. "There's no need to finish any painting. All you have to do is begin. Leonardo and Vermeer, perhaps, have finished a painting, produced something total. Some of our frescoes in Studenica are like that, too, and one icon in the patriarchal church in Peć. I can go on with the painting without you. Tell your mother she must come see me this evening without fail. I feel like a bit of feminine conversation about Belgrade, and I don't have anybody I can talk with about Rastko."

Milena quickly put on her coat, hurried out, and set off for Bogdan's house. If only she never need see that painting again, that painting beside which Dobrila, a schoolteacher from Požarevac, was lying now in delirium, and beside which she would die.

Bogdan was waiting for her, shaved and smiling; she couldn't recognize him. That smile on his worn, emaciated face so astounded her, that only when he suddenly became serious and sad was she able to walk over to his bed. "Any news from Geneva?" he asked.

She shook her head, sat next to him, and took his hand as though it were Ivan's.

Bogdan's mother brought in a bowl of soup. "He's getting better. Since this morning he's been much better!" she said.

That night four patients died while Olga was on duty in the isolation ward; she stroked the fingers of all four while they were dying. All these deaths cut deep into her hope. She could hardly wait for Mrs. Stefanović to relieve her. The big acacia tree, overlaid with hoarfrost, glistened in the fog; as she walked past it she remembered with a pang of sadness how before the war trees covered with hoarfrost aroused in her a mood of solemnity, a kind of devout attention to silence.

On the pillow of the bed she shared with Milena she found a letter from Vukašin; she read it quickly with excitement, surprised by its contents, but soon sleep overwhelmed her. She woke up after noon and while still in bed read it several times:

Dear Olga,

I didn't reply at once to your letter, which I received a few days ago, not because I don't agree with your decision, but because more and more I'm at odds with myself.

To follow our children in a fate which they have chosen against our will is not the fulfillment of our duty according to moral or civil law; such things are done in obedience to the law of love. One doesn't pass judgment on love; I now realize this, too late. I must tell you I'm unhappy to the depths of my being, to the last drop of my peasant blood. I understand you, and I'm deeply touched by your strength, and by your staying with Milena in that hellhole in Valjevo. Last autumn I too barely restrained myself from asking General Mišić to place me in Ivan's platoon, so that I could go to war with him and look after him at least until we experienced some reverses —to light a fire while he was sleeping in the open, to dry his socks, to find him a piece of bacon. However, as you know (and there's a great deal that you don't know), I'm a man who has always strenuously resisted my feelings and my loves with ideas and principles. This has often struck you as crude ambition and love of fame. Well, now, I must write you something on this subject, sitting in this cold room to which we came as refugees, and which I've turned into a pigsty with my untidiness. Here and in my head (though more and more infrequently) Montaigne has established some sort of order by his invitation to enter the peace of modest surroundings, and to accept with dignity everything which is inevitable.

From the time when Ivan went away to the front—the time when I parted from him and came back to you—I've wanted to open my heart to you, but you haven't let me do this. Even after my return from Maljen, and when I came back from Valjevo without Milena, in your generosity and kindness toward me, and your strength to suffer without flinching, I didn't feel I had the right to speak with the sincerity I owe you. I've always sensed in your suffering a feeling of reproach toward me; sometimes I think that in your silence there's an element of scorn. I know this feeling doesn't arise simply from our disagreement that night when we learned the High Command was sending the students to the front—that night in Niš which marked a turning point in our lives. For a long, long time there has been a fundamental and growing misunderstanding between us. From the time when Ivan went to high school, and especially after he went to study in Paris, you've made me feel, both by your words and by your silence, that I owe our son a debt of love. And you were right. This is what I must write about tonight. For years I've felt the same pain as Montaigne's Maréchal de Monlic, whose words I continually hear in my head. I, too, together with this despairing father, believe that no pain can be so inconsolable, no suffering so well deserved, as the pain of unfulfilled love toward one's child, as the suffering caused by a debt of love to one's son. My son who's now missing.

How can I convince you, his mother, that I'm not the only father left with a debt of love to his son? How can I make you see that I'm not the only man who has punished himself by not showing his son as much love as he felt and wanted to show?

I have long understood that the good fortune of success should not be

attributed to the uncertainty of love. This much I understand, but no more.
That's because I am the son of my father, Aćim Katić, and have strenuously
desired that the chain of a certain kind of fate be broken in me. This,
perhaps, has been my destiny. Bear with me a little, Olga, and read these
words with the belief that our life together deserves. I must somehow
explain why it is that I now owe a debt of love to my son.

It was the misfortune of my father, Aćim, that he loved in me only his
son, nothing else—the one who continued his name and would inherit
his house and property, his reputation and fame, what he owed and what
was owed to him, what he had done and what he had failed to do; a son
who would be able to do what he had not been able to do. My father's idea
of human happiness was to be a powerful man, to have power over other
people. You will see that in his son my father loved himself, as most fathers
love their sons. What a blind sort of love, and how inevitable the suffering
it brings!

When I left Prerovo and grew up, when I had studied in Paris and seen
Europe, I was no longer simply the son of Aćim, no longer his other self.
I had become a man with different characteristics and a different purpose in
life. I was a stranger to my father, even his opposite. When I came back
from the world, I didn't come back to him—his son did not return to him.
He felt cheated and betrayed. Then my father, Aćim, came into conflict
with this other man in his son, and he—that is, I—came into conflict with
the stranger in his father. A rift between us was inevitable. Our ideas, our
worlds were stronger than the tie of blood. Those men inside the father and
the son were stronger than father and son. We became opponents, irrecon-
cilable in our opinions and aims. We were not prepared, and indeed were
unable, to accept each other as time and circumstances had molded us. So
my father and I clashed over the very foundation of life, its purpose. He
saw happiness in power over people, but I decided that my aim in life was
to serve general ideals and virtues. I couldn't be for my father the sort of son
he wanted, and my father didn't want to be the father of a son who didn't
take after his father. After my return from Paris I was disappointed with
my father and felt betrayed, just as much as my father was disappointed
with me and felt himself betrayed.

The drama of my father and myself, Olga dear, is the drama of masculine
fate in human life—a life lived, sincerely and consistently, in a state of love.
As long as the world exists, father and son will deal each other the heaviest
blows. While people exist, they will suffer most deeply because of love; and
love and suffering have the same soul, though their faces are different. My
father was not such a weakling that he could be a hypocrite, and I am not
such a hypocrite that I could appear a weakling. Both he and I wanted a

great deal from life, and a great deal from each other—too much to be able to act otherwise than we did. We did indeed love each other, in our very blood, and have not ceased to suffer because of our love up to the present day. We're not to blame because we cause each other so much pain, and of course I caused him more than he caused me. Still, we aren't guilty of that; but because of it we're unhappy.

In making this confession to you (from whom, out of vanity, I concealed everything to do with my life in Prerovo), I'm not asking for forgiveness. I only want to make it clearer to you, Olga, what sort of unhappiness I wanted to save my son from. I wanted—I was afraid to give the impression that I loved him simply because he was my son, and because you gave birth to him. I was afraid to show him as much love as I felt. I was waiting for him to grow up, to acquire qualities of his own, to form his character and choose his aim in life quite freely. I was waiting for him to come back from the world, which takes our sons away from us. I could hardly wait for him to become a man—a man and my son, my son-man. Unfortunately for me, it was only when we parted in Kragujevac, the last night before his departure for the front, that I saw the man that was coming into being in Ivan, the man he would be. That last night, about which I've spoken very little, I saw in our son a man who deserved all the suffering and disquiet of love. Please believe me now, I did succeed in conveying to him something of my knowledge and my feelings. He understood this marvelously and kissed me when we parted. I embraced him; and it was he I embraced, not myself! Then he hurried off into the barracks, racing with his own shadow.

Yet I'm not sure whether he loved me, and loves me, as much as I love my father. If only I could believe that he loves me the way I love Aćim!

There is one thing I'm sure of: there's no faith I wouldn't profess, no God to whom I wouldn't pray, no sacrifice I wouldn't make to have just a little hope—a shadow of a hope—that I'll be able to fulfill my debt of love to our son, my son.

You're lucky that you owe him no debt of love! For that I thank you.

Look after Milena and yourself, Olga. If there's anything you need, get in touch with Mišić. As soon as the Assembly adjourns, I'll come see you.

> *From the bottom of my heart I embrace you both,*
> *Vukašin*

Olga decided not to show Milena the letter. She had her lunch, then walked slowly through the field by the Kolubara.

"My man . . ." she said aloud in the wintry silence. This is the first time I've addressed you like that, and you're both farther away and nearer than you've ever been. In times like these we shouldn't utter one word without good reason. Silence is kind and honorable, Vukašin. But I can't be silent about your letter.

A Serbian woman, if she loves and respects her husband, refers to him as "my man." You know I've never liked the "folksy" fashion of imitating the people, so I've never referred to you as "my man." Still, at this moment I don't know how a woman could show greater respect and love for her husband, the father of her children, the man with whom she shares bed and board, life's troubles and its joys, than if she feels he's "her man." Your letter has given me the confidence and courage to feel that I can call you "my man"!

What are we to each other now? I'm afraid of this question, because I feel that nothing destroys love like the whole truth about it. I've loved you deeply, so I've been able to think of you as the man I loved. That's what you've become for me, although in reality you weren't like that; my opinion of you didn't coincide with that of the people around us. I realize now—thank God that it's only now—that someone who loves knows only one side of a person, the side turned toward him. Probably people who dislike him know the other side, and those who are indifferent know just a little, if anything. Isn't this the way you've long thought about me?

Do you know why today you are "my man"? Because never before have you shown me so much love and trust as in this letter about our Ivan. Perhaps I've been too superficial. Or have you changed? Surely we didn't need such disasters all around us for you to say what you said in your letter. Why couldn't you have said all that before? You loved him enough to be able to do what you could do. I admire you, yet I pity you more. I'm glad you are as you are, glad from the bottom of my heart, my man! How dare I feel any joy, how can I utter the word today? Now let me weep a little.

I'd be sorry if you reproached me for thinking of you as "my man" after receiving your letter, because in fact you aren't only mine, or indeed mine at all. Part of you doesn't belong to anybody, and part of you belongs to everybody. Then there's that long silence between us, which keeps getting longer, and the fact that every morning you're hidden from me by a kerchief over my eyes while you get out of bed and leave our room. And your exaggerated care, and your overemphatic words when we're with friends; your feelings of superiority toward all domestic details; your sternness when I tried in vain to remind you of our former "irresponsibility." Not to mention your unwavering devotion to your principles, which often make everything around us and outside us seem like dirt. No, Vukašin, that's not true. Here in this bare field by the Kolubara, I didn't intend to recall our prewar life, still less to reproach you. I know that you're a better man, and one with deeper feelings, than all the husbands of my friends and acquaintances. I have no reason to feel dissatisfied with my partner. It's disgraceful even to think of such a thing today. The suffering here reminds me of the need for humility and makes me feel sinful on account of the good fortune I had before the war, without any merit on my part. The thing that has most astounded me in the hospital, Vukašin, is how much people suffer through no fault of their own, and how little a person needs to be happy.

Why can't I tell you the most important thing? Ivan, our son, is alive! I feel it, I see him, something tells me he's alive. You must feel this, too, and protect yourself from fear by this feeling, because we *must* have faith, we simply must. I want to tell you how well I understand your feelings of pain and guilt. Is there at last a misfortune in which I can comfort you? All my life I've wanted to do this, but you never needed it. You've always been so strong, so very strong, my poor darling! I'm not just babbling: it's the strong people, the very strongest, who are the most unhappy. And I? I've existed, as the moon exists, illuminated by the light of the sun. I shone with your light, while I was in it. I wanted to be in it always, though I knew that moonlight sheds no warmth. The most important thing for me was that I should be seen, and that others should be seen through me and because of me. Now I don't care any more, Vukašin. Before the war I wasn't as vain as you thought I was. However, as I noticed long ago among our friends, husbands are the last to notice any change in the hearts of their wives, those with whom they mix blood and bone, as you said during our quarrel in Niš, our first quarrel. Sometimes all you have eyes for is our wrinkles and the circles under our eyes. My God, what nonsense!

I've met a man here, a doctor, who has an almost incredible feeling and understanding for human suffering, and I—no, not a word about Mihajlo Radić! I'll talk about him after the war.

She stopped under a tree covered with hoarfrost. At the top of the tree she caught sight of a huge crow which cawed when it saw her, then flew away, shaking the branch and again scattering hoarfrost over her. Caught in a moment of betrayal, covered with leprous patches of frozen crystals, she remained still for a few moments, wishing that a blizzard would bury her. She walked away with long, heavy steps.

You say to me, Vukašin, "You're lucky that you owe our son no debt of love." That love can be a debt is just another of your masculine principles. Love, my dear, has nothing in it that can be measured and calculated, nothing that can be paid off and equalized according to role or circumstance. But why should I turn a knife in his wound with these thoughts? I'll write him a few comforting lines, mostly about Milena, and that will calm him. Until now he's never really been unhappy; he's known only how to be anxious and to reflect, to think about the future of Serbia and the Balkans. Poor Vukašin—my man!

Dusk began to settle on the fields and blot out the glistening hoarfrost on the trees. She listened a little longer to the silence, but she didn't hear it now as she had years before, when she had stood alone in the woods of the Deer Park while Ivan and Milena were sledding. She turned and hurried back to prepare something for Milena's supper, something she liked.

By the light of a candle stuck in a bottle which Tola was holding, Miloje raved all night in a fever, and stuck out his swollen tongue at his father. Tola changed compresses soaked in brandy or vinegar, promising him all the while that he'd take him away to Prerovo before the dogwood blossomed in front of their house, the biggest dogwood in Prerovo; as soon as the dogwood was in flower, he said, every kind of sickness fled from the villages; by the time summer came, his wound would heal and there wouldn't even be a scar; he wouldn't make him do any work, he would go every day to fish in the Morava with a basket net. Then he reminded him of the scent of the willows and the river at dusk, and how the young girls would come up to bathe in the rapids, lifting their petticoats ever so high, staring at the riverbanks and the cornfields. At times Miloje would turn away in a gesture of negation and wander off in delirium.

Paun Aleksić came to see him twice before dawn and pushed some powders into his mouth. Before the general round at daybreak,

Milena Katić brought Doctor Radić to him; he gave him an injection and said to Tola: "He's in a bad way. This will soothe him and he'll have a good sleep."

"So you think he won't pull through?"

"You must have faith, Tola."

"You haven't got much to offer me, Doctor."

"While he still breathes, it must mean a lot to his father."

"That's right, Doctor. Well, thank you." But Tola no longer believed the doctors.

As soon as it was light he set off to the town to buy sugar to make toddy and to look for the medicine that he had heard guaranteed a cure. He had eleven dinars left; he'd spend one dinar on the sugar and the remaining ten for medicine. In front of two shops there were lines of about a hundred people; he chose the shortest line and stood there. But he had a hard time getting into the shop: there was a constant succession of tearful women, many of them in mourning, whose children were ill with scarlet fever or typhus, so he gave up his place to one of them and went back to the end. Then when he was just ten paces from the shop, he gave up his place to two wounded soldiers and again went back to the end. When he somehow managed to creep forward to the threshold of the shop, splashing his wet feet in the mud, an Austrian prisoner came up to him, confusing him with his good, clear Serbian: "Please let me buy some sugar for my sick comrades, old man."

"Why did you put on that Austrian uniform, my boy? You spoiled your looks with that cap of Franz Josef's."

"I'm a poor Serb from Jelačić's Seventy-ninth Regiment."

"Who's Jelačić?"

"A Croatian baron. May the earth spew up his bones!"

"If you were my son and under that man's command, I don't know what I'd do. You're in a bad way, so I'll give you my place; but throw away those Austrian rags! Come see me in the Second Reserve Hospital, and I'll give you some Serbian britches and a sheepskin jacket. A cap, too—you can take your pick. Our soldiers are dying all the time." As he went back to the end of the line, a woman in mourning said to him rudely, "You may be an old man, but you're a fool!"

"Maybe I am, ma'am; but better a fool than a heartless creature seeking vengeance."

"That man stuck a bayonet in your son's guts, even if he can speak

Serbian! Do you think people are giving sugar to our boys in Austria and Hungary?"

Tola didn't answer. A fog was sweeping up in all directions, concealing everything. This was the third time he'd gone back to the end of the line: if there was a God, He would return good for good. If there wasn't, then Tola Dačić from Prerovo was a fool.

A sound of military music came out of the fog; the people in line for sugar fell silent and turned around. The music was being played by Austrian prisoners, behind whom came a horse-drawn gun carriage bearing two coffins; accompanying it were three officers and three soldiers with guns. They were tense and stern, and looked at nobody. Tola removed his hat. The music made his throat feel dry; tears came to his eyes.

"Our children are dying like flies, and you're playing music!" shrieked a woman in mourning. The others joined in: Shame on you! Everyone's sick, and they're playing music! Let them go play under Mišić's window! Music for the officers, but the soldiers are thrown into a lime pit without so much as a funeral. What's happening to Serbia?

Embarrassed by the cries of the women, the musicians began to play softly and some even stopped, but one of the officers drew his saber and brandished it. "Go on playing!"

The prisoner-musicians continued to play the funeral march, and disappeared into the fog in the direction of the cemetery.

"If only those Czech musicians would play at my funeral!" cried a wounded man behind Tola.

Tola pulled his fur hat over his eyes and abandoned himself to his thoughts. The morning was well advanced before he reached the counter of the shop. "A kilogram of sugar, please!"

The shopkeeper threw him a bag already prepared.

Tola took it and held it in his hand. "That's not a kilogram, mister. That's only half a kilo."

"If that's not enough for you, go across the road!"

"Please measure it, mister. I'll pay you double if it's three-quarters."

"I've told you, go across the road; and leave me alone, there are people waiting."

"There isn't any across the road. This isn't right! My son's on his deathbed."

"If you need it, give me two dinars and take it!"

"Why two dinars, when it's only worth five groschen?"

The shopkeeper seized the bag from him and handed it to a girl who was waiting.

"What do you want with two dinars, swindler? If you have no fear of God, aren't you at least afraid of the lice? They've taken over!"

"Get out of my shop and beg in the street!"

"Two of my sons have given their lives for this country, and you can't even give a full bag of sugar, you bastard!"

Those in line shouted at him to get out of the way and take his grievances elsewhere: they had sick people waiting to drink something sweet and hot. Tola didn't know what to do: if he gave two dinars for the sugar, he wouldn't have ten left for the surefire medicine, but if he didn't buy the sugar, how could he make toddy for Miloje? He didn't resist as people pushed him out of the shop. In the street he remembered Vojvoda Živojin Mišić and hurried through the fog toward the First Army headquarters. He'd tell Mišić what the freedom he had fought for meant now for the people and the poor, and ask him this question: Živojin Mišić, tell me for the sake of my four sons, have we fought all these battles just for the shopkeepers?

"No one allowed in! Off with you, old man!" said a sentry from the steps of the headquarters.

"I'll be on my way shortly, soldier. I just want to ask Vojvoda Mišić a simple question: Who's boss in Valjevo? Him or the shop-keepers?"

"You'd better ask that in your still—but when all your pals with you are drunk."

"Now listen, soldier, I'm Vojvoda Mišić's first cousin, so don't fool around. Take me to the officer on duty; he'll know what to do."

"Come back when the epidemic's over!"

"The epidemic isn't just the concern of the vojvoda! It concerns me, too, and all Serbia!"

"Get lost!"

"All right, my boy, all right. I'll be on my way; but give me your solemn promise that you'll tell the officer on duty to tell the vojvoda that the lice and shopkeepers are running Valjevo!"

The fog engulfed the marketplace; it was hard to see more than ten paces ahead. A pile of coffins, some unpainted, some painted blue, loomed up in the fog. He went up to have a look.

"Pinewood, ash, and oak here! Painted and unpainted! Take your pick, folks, to suit your pocket and the gravedigger!" cried the coffin seller.

Tola squinted at a blue coffin with a lid and thrust his hands in his pockets.

"I'll meet you halfway with the price," said the salesman. "I can see you're not a rich man."

"They're not long enough for me," said Tola seriously.

"What do you mean, not long enough? We know the measurements."

"Not *my* measurements, you don't!"

Another coffin seller called to him: "Mine are oak, old-timer. They can lie in a puddle ten years, not even the edges will rot. Too much? Well, I've got some made of willow."

"I'm looking for one of walnut."

"Would that be for a colonel, old-timer?"

"For a general, my boy."

Tola continued on his way. Some children's coffins emerged from the fog, and gray rows of women and boys selling white shrouds and black cloth laid out on small tables, incense and candles, bunches of privet and sweet basil, bottles of wine, and little dishes with boiled wheat decorated with a cross made of sugar.

"For soldiers and poor wretches whose mothers can't prepare a funeral feast!"

"Naphthalene! Naphthalene!"

"Camphor here, just a few bags left!"

"Hair ointment from France! Smells like love's young dream and kills lice! Just the thing for ladies and gentlemen, officers and civil servants. Come smell it, Lieutenant!"

Tola walked on slowly, looking at the goods. He passed some peasant women with baskets of dried beans, potatoes, and plums who were surrounded by walking wounded more interested in the women than their wares.

"Guaranteed against typhus!" someone cried. "Step this way, folks! Good for scarlet fever and all children's diseases! Just rub the chest of a patient with typhus spots in the evening, and by morning his skin'll be as clean as a newborn babe's! I'm a pharmacist—here's my diploma."

Tola made his way through the noisy, jostling crowd toward the man with the diploma.

"Shall I read your fortune in the embers, soldier? I'll tell you what's happening now at home for a groschen."

"Can you tell me what my wife was doing last night?"

"Indeed I can, soldier! I write letters to lovers and sweethearts! Usual price, three groschen. If you want verse, it's more. This way, soldiers! The women and girls are in tears waiting for your letters!"

Two Austrian officers were buying a suckling pig and a turkey. Their orderly picked up the piglet in his arms; it gave a squeal and they hurried away. Tola stood listening to the piglet squealing in the fog. Arm in arm, a couple of drunken soldiers came staggering up in front of him. "Why so gloomy, old man? Have a swig and cheer up! Come on, old-timer, have some brandy! When a man's drunk there's nothing to fear."

Tola got out of their way, but a man seized his coat sleeve, saying, "Give me five eggs, and I'll tell you what causes typhus!"

Tola pushed him gently away. A soldier said hoarsely: "Aspirin, that's the thing! Only aspirin'll bring your temperature down and save your brain from rotting away. How much have you got, old-timer?"

Hurrying on, Tola came to some tables with rows of bottles and bags.

"Take this for typhus—it's like peeling it off with your hand! A medicine from Russia!"

"Something for scarlet fever, cholera, and dysentery or the bloody flux! A dinar a bag!"

"Step this way, folks, step right up! A new medicine, just discovered! Come see for yourselves, folks!"

Tola went up to a group of people around a table with bottles and a dish of red liquid. The salesman lifted his hand up high, holding something between his thumb and forefinger.

"Take a good look—I'm holding two lice! One's an Albanian girl, the other's a Turkish lady. Now keep your eyes peeled! When I throw them into this liquid in the dish, count with me." He threw the lice into the dish and called out: "One . . . two . . . three . . . four . . . They're dead! Look! The little bloodsuckers are dead!"

"No, they aren't—one's wiggling! You're a liar!"

"Wiggling? It's you that's wiggling! If it's wiggling I'll give you ten dinars!"

"Well, it *is* wiggling!"

The salesman took the louse out of the dish, put it on a piece of white paper, and asked, "Now is it still wiggling, mister?"

"You squeezed it with your fingers!"

"Here's your ten dinars. Now go squeeze one with *your* fingertips!"

Tola walked toward another salesman who was scarcely audible: "The only thing that can save us, folks, is Science. God and Science! The medicine I'm offering you was discovered by an Englishman, Professor Blake. It was made in London—look, here's the name of the firm. This isn't some old woman's rubbish, this is real chemistry, folks. Let's face it, typhus is fatal!"

"How much is that medicine, mister?" asked Tola.

"Fifteen dinars. That's enough for a cure."

"Too much, mister! Far too much."

"Who would you be buying this medicine for?"

"My son. He's a soldier. Lost an arm by the Drina."

"Are you saying that fifteen dinars is too much to save your son's life?"

"I'd give all Valjevo for my son's life, but what's the good of that, when Valjevo isn't mine to give? I'm not a shopkeeper. All I have in the world is eleven dinars."

"Sorry. Go borrow some money. This cost me fourteen dinars in Salonika, and it's only right I should at least charge for my traveling expenses."

Tola disappeared into the fog and walked toward another salesman in a fur jacket and leather gloves, who assured him that he had some medicine used in the French army, the only one in the world whose soldiers weren't dying of typhus.

"How much for a bottle?" asked Tola.

"Twelve dinars for a small one, twenty for a bigger one."

"Could I have one for eleven dinars, mister?"

"Look here, old man, I'm not the Red Cross!"

Tola continued on his way through the market, but could find no medicine for eleven dinars. In another shop he bought two bags of sugar, with the same false weight and the same price as in the other shop. Returning to the hospital, he found Miloje in front of the stove; he was taking his nicest buttons out of a bag—the ones he had won in a game—and throwing them into the fire.

"There you are, neighbor! Take them!"

Tola came up and tried to take him back to bed, but Miloje jerked himself away, took out his knife—the nicest knife in the division—and began to hit the wall with it until finally it broke.

"Now you can have it, neighbor!" he said, and started to go outside.

Tola put his arms around him and carried him back to his bed; this time he made no resistance. Miloje began to gasp, then lost consciousness. Tola took hold of his hand and stayed there all night, holding it.

In a tender letter full of disquieting detail, his wife had announced his promotion and transfer to civilian duties; but after his removal as director and all that had happened in the hospital, Paun Aleksić was not so credulous as to believe his wife, in whose loyalty he had little confidence. Naturally he didn't tell even the pharmacist Milan Belić, his closest friend, about his promotion and change of job. Then four days later Belić burst into the operating room with a newspaper in his hand.

"Just listen to this! 'Doctor Paun Aleksić, captain in the medical service, first class, has been promoted to the rank of major in the medical service and awarded the order of the White Eagle, third class, for outstanding service to his country.' Do you hear that, my friend? Look! Read it for yourself." He thrust the paper into his hands.

Aleksić dropped his tweezers on the operating table, but didn't raise his eyes from the septic neck wound he was operating on. When he heard Belić's words, his whole body grew rigid.

Belić clapped him on the shoulder. "Congratulations! But you've shut up like a clam! Hurry up, I'll be waiting for you in your room."

He seemed to have suddenly become deaf. He picked up the tweezers in total silence in which he saw only the movements of his own hands. He finished dressing the wound, then went at once to his room, where Belić was waiting with two glasses of cognac. Belić immediately handed him the copy of *Politika,* so that he could read Prince Alexander's decree. Either because of alphabetical order, or perhaps by order of merit, his name was first in the list of those promoted and decorated. When he had read it a few times he felt overcome with joy—joy that spilled over into the sweet fury of vengeance accomplished. He drank his cognac in one gulp, but still didn't say anything. Belić clapped him on the shoulder again, and spoke exultantly of his former depression and lack of confidence in the government. Aleksić remembered Srećko's words of encouragement: "Don't worry, Doctor, in Serbia it's those who lose their jobs that finally get promoted—you'll see!" He didn't hear what Belić was saying; he was picturing the face of Mihajlo Radić and the rest of them when they saw *Politika*. This triumph really did atone for his defeat and humiliation; vengeance heals all wounds.

"Life is strange!" he exclaimed.

"Life is like the drum in a lottery, my friend. Someone turns it, and we're all shaken up. One in a hundred gets half his stakes, and one in a million gets the big prize. That's what you've got. Now go blow it on whores and gypsies—good luck isn't something to be careful about."

"No, Milan. Nothing is a matter of chance."

That evening he didn't go to the party given by Mrs. Predolac to celebrate his promotion and the medal. He decided that a quiet triumph would have the most devastating effect on his opponents, would make them suffer most and at the same time feel ashamed. To make them feel ashamed would be the sweetest part of his victory.

He wouldn't allow even his orderly to rejoice in his victory, and forbade him to address him as "major" until the epaulets were stitched on his uniform. He gave much thought to his conduct during the next few days, pending his departure from Valjevo. He wanted to surprise and confuse his colleagues.

When he left his room, there was an expression of great anxiety on his face. He talked inaudibly and moved slowly and heavily, as though ill. He was obliging to everybody and volunteered for extra duties. He enjoyed the congratulations offered with unconcealed spite, with the hypocrisy typical of the vanquished. But his triumph wasn't complete: alone among the hospital staff, Mihajlo Radić and Olga and Milena Katić didn't congratulate him. Although Radić tried hard to behave as if nothing had happened, he was obviously impatient in Aleksić's company—clear proof of his pain, but for Aleksić not nearly enough.

As for Doctor Pantelić and Kaća and Ruška, Pantelić's former mistresses, there was no limit to the cunning and duplicity born of dependence, especially in women. Nevertheless, what surprised and infuriated him most was the attitude of Doctor Sergeev: when they met, or when they were forced to be in one another's company, he averted his head and didn't speak. To others unable to conceal their dissatisfaction he reacted with a thoughtful, melancholy smile. He wasn't sure whether this always had the desired effect, but he didn't care, in spite of his new discovery that the defeated notice every little detail about the victor, quite independent of their intelligence. In addition to the joy of gratified vanity, albeit cunningly concealed, his satisfaction was heightened by the revelation that only the recovery of lost power makes that power real, that only the restoration of lost authority confers authority for any length of time. What a greenhorn he'd been!

Because of the inefficient administrative machinery, he still hadn't been sent the official notice of his transfer to civilian duties, so he had plenty of time to draw other significant conclusions: rulers and doctors—those who lord it over people and who treat them in sickness—get to know them best; both submissive individuals and healthy ones are rare. The ruler who believes implicitly in human submissiveness will be knifed or poisoned by his valet, while the doctor who believes in health is a fool who'll never make a living. "People are evil and mean," he said to Belić when they met by chance one morning. He always thought the worst of people in the morning, when he woke up; afterward, he grew tired or got used to them, turned a blind eye to many things, and forgave them.

Finally the official letter arrived: he had been appointed district medical inspector at Požarevac. The new orderly, Brka, had come into the operating room and told him to see the director at once. Naturally he didn't obey immediately: he continued bandaging the wounded, enjoying the fact that he was keeping Radić waiting—he could imagine him striking matches, lighting cigarettes, and pacing up and down in the office. Why was it that all the so-called moral and conscientious people were gloomy and anxious and miserable? If they lived and worked so conscientiously, why were they so despairing? What was gnawing at them?

It wasn't until he had bandaged all the wounded that he went to see Radić; he had every intention of looking gloomy and absent-minded, but was smiling slightly when he entered.

"You wanted to see me, Director?"

"Yes, on an official matter." Radić got up from the table, walked over to the window, and stayed there with his back to Aleksić.

The room whirled around Aleksić: could it be that he had been deceived, that the newspaper announcement was an administrative error? "What is it that you wanted me for?" he asked.

Radić walked slowly back to the table and said in a thick voice, "You mean, what do I want personally?"

"Yes."

"I want to see whether you'll blush to the roots of your hair when you read this letter."

Aleksić snatched the letter from him and read it twice, three times. Yes, he was indeed appointed district inspector at Požarevac! He concentrated all his strength to look at Radić as he deserved, and to think up the right words to say.

"Such malevolence and vulgarity don't become your philanthropic nature, Captain!"

"Never mind that! Just tell me, don't you feel any shame at all? People are dying all around us. Answer me truthfully."

"Why should I be ashamed, Director?"

"Because of what people will think, Inspector!"

"Such feelings belong to moralists like yourself. I don't feel ashamed in front of people. Least of all in my own eyes." He now felt relaxed and confident.

"Then why such sacrifices for this riffraff?" stammered Radić, pale and stunned.

"Only fools sacrifice themselves for filth. As a doctor you should be able to make a different diagnosis of the world and the people in it."

"For instance?"

"It would be logical for you to love people dearly, since you've resolved to sacrifice yourself for them."

"What motives can you have in this present war and epidemic?"

"To survive, and to be recompensed for my trouble. To succeed."

"To succeed?"

"Why not?"

Radić's lips trembled. He must teach him a lesson. He added quietly: "I pity you profoundly. Your ideas are all wrong; and I must say I find your ambition distasteful."

Radić dropped into his chair.

That was just how Paun Aleksić wanted to see him, now that all their scores were settled. All that remained now was to turn his back, smile slightly, and leave him sitting there, dumbfounded, at his desk. Which was exactly what he did.

His departure from the hospital, he decided, should be as follows:

while the municipal carriage waited in front of the steps, he, wearing his new civilian clothes, would send his orderly, Toma, to summon to his room all the doctors, medical students, volunteer nurses, and of course Mihajlo Radić. He would greet them with a sad expression, pour each a glass of cognac, and say humbly: Ladies and gentlemen, in taking leave of you with such mixed memories, I want to be true to myself, so you'll remember me that way. War is war, and that's nothing new. There've been harder and easier wars than this one, people have suffered and lost much more and much less than we today. Much blood is flowing, and a lot of excrement, too. Yet one thing is absolutely certain: life is the miracle of the universe—its one true miracle! —and this miracle—life—is always above suffering, disease, and death, and of course above all our ideas, our lofty thoughts and feelings. Real people—sensible people—see life this way, and that's how they live it. They enjoy it whenever they can, and as long as they can. Others believe that life and everything in the world exist because of them and their ideas, so they destroy life like a broken-down old nag, or a tool belonging to someone else, or government-issue clothes and footwear. I hope that those of you who've lived with me during this epidemic know where I stand. After I've gone, please think a little about what I've said: for big fools, life is one long tale of suffering to the grave; for little fools, it lasts but an instant, then vanishes; but the smart ones adapt themselves, whatever the circumstances, and enjoy it.

However, things didn't turn out quite as he had planned. First of all, the death of Miloje Dačić—that unforgettable pighead of whom he'd truly been fond—was a real blow to him. Occurring just before Aleksić's departure, Miloje's death seemed a bad omen, like a priest or a black cat crossing his path. Furthermore, Radić, Sergeev, and Olga didn't respond to his invitation, so they didn't hear his farewell speech. In fact, he delivered it with some confusion and even muffed a few lines, which was quite enough for Dr. Paun Aleksić to climb into the carriage without a smile and feeling somewhat hurt, and in this state to be driven slowly to Valjevo railway station.

"Give him an injection, please, Doctor! Let him breathe a few moments more!" Olga whispered to Mihajlo as she stood above Svetislav, the young man who reminded her of Ivan.

"Don't you see he's already stiff? Nothing more can be done for him."

She seized his hand and brought her face close to his. "Please do something, for my sake!"

Mihajlo trembled from her first touch, the first feel of her breath on his face, the first sensation of intimacy and the nearness of her eyes, full of tears and entreaty. With the clumsiness of a beginner he gave the boy an injection of camphor, and to conceal his confusion, knelt down beside Svetislav to listen to his heart with his stethoscope. Because of the loud thumping in his own breast, he could scarcely hear the beating, which came from deep down and grew more rapid; on the threshold of the abyss it gave a convulsive spasm, a tiny squirming movement in its own darkness, then, smothered with blood, was suddenly still. Mihajlo pressed his stethoscope still harder to the dark blue spots on Svetislav's chest, and that very moment felt a louse bite him viciously between his shoulder blades. He gave a start, removed his stethoscope from the dead man's chest and, without any attempt to conceal his horror, stared helplessly at Olga's tear-filled eyes.

"Is it over?" she said despairingly. With Svetislav dead, something of Ivan was dead, too.

Mihajlo could feel the louse crawling down his spine; yet that morning he had put on a clean shirt and undershorts, and had shaken out his jacket and breeches and looked them over carefully. He shook his shoulders, expecting another bite. He looked at the tears flowing down Olga's face and saw on it the ravages of time; he hadn't noticed this before.

"He was only seventeen," Olga said desperately. Two nights ago she had promised him that if he "couldn't get about," she'd go to his mother in Jagodina and give her his few things and an unfinished letter.

Mihajlo bent down once more and pressed his stethoscope to the typhus spots: he couldn't hear any heartbeats. For a long time he stood still above this silence, while the louse crawled and scratched its way down his spine. He grew rigid under its slow progress, helpless, stunned by forebodings. He had never felt such fear before.

"Should I light a candle for him?" asked Olga with a sob.

"Yes, light a candle," he said, straightening himself. He wanted to say, It's bitten me! But she couldn't see him for her tears.

As though something had hurt him deeply, he left the Warehouse of the Dead without looking at her, and went out into the thin, icy rain. The entire space around him seemed compressed into the hospital precinct; the sky was falling onto the hospital roof, dripping quietly. There was nowhere he could turn with the louse on his back; what could he do with this final burden? He stopped under the eaves and lit a cigarette. Some convalescents and walking wounded came out of the hospital, accompanied by orderlies, on their way to wash their linen, have baths, and get a haircut; they walked slowly, as if to their own execution, indifferent to the rain. Mihajlo thought of his enormous louse. It was silent now, sated with his blood; or perhaps it had succumbed to the disease in its belly and had fallen dead this very moment. Why was he so terrified of this louse, by no means the first? He found one in his clothes nearly every day, and never knew but that one had already bitten him; but this one had bitten him at the very moment when the young man's heart had stopped beating. Could death have leaped onto him from that dead heart? Olga had been unaware of it. If she'd been looking at him, she'd have seen what had happened—but she hadn't, she was quite indifferent, she'd never feel afraid on his behalf. Never! Well, let it happen. Hadn't he accepted this fate back in Kragujevac, at the headquarters of the High Command, when he said he wanted to go where the greatest number of people were dying? To be a victim, a willing victim, was the most honorable form of lunacy today. It always had been.

Everything he did now was done in silence, while thinking about Olga. The pain caused by her indifference and the fear of illness intermingled in his mind, and he didn't try to separate them.

Certainly since he had come to the hospital he had never felt so hopeless as today, although it was his most successful day as an administrator: a considerable quantity of hospital equipment, blankets, linen, medicines, and food had arrived from Niš. At lunch Doctor Sergeev, provoked perhaps by his gloomy silence, had said to him in Russian: "Mihajlo Radić, you're working as if you wanted to wear yourself out and die here. To die at one's post means to die because of ambition, and this isn't always a virtue."

"Maybe, but if the alternative is to be like Paun Aleksić, I still think I've made the best choice."

He had quickly finished his lunch and gone to see Philip Simić, who was in bed in his laboratory. He had fallen ill a few days before and his temperature had shot up immediately; but when Radić had examined him and taken his temperature, in one of his spasms he had exclaimed tearfully and exultantly that here was proof of the incubation period of typhus: "This is the thirteenth day! *Typhus exanthe-maticus!* Carried by *pediculus vestimenti*—our dear little louse!"

Beside Simić's bed he found the nurse Dušanka, pressing a wet compress on his forehead; she was hopelessly in love with Simić. He wanted to smile at her and caress her round, rosy cheek, but she burst into tears. "His temperature is one hundred and four, and his pulse is terrible! You'll see."

He took Simić's hand from hers and felt his pulse. "It's nothing special; typical of this phase of the illness." As he took his stethoscope to listen to Simić's heart, he recalled his aggressive talkativeness the evening before he fell ill.

"I make a distinction," he had said, "between a louse and a man capable of sacrificing himself for the life of the spirit, or any kind of abstract idea. As long as there are people who can die for truth, justice, and beauty, or for untruth, injustice, and ugliness, or for any god living or dead, for belief in God or lack of it, then, Director, human civilization will continue to exist!"

"But surely, Simić, there must be some man, some individual who's worthy of our sacrifice," he had replied.

"Tell me who's worthy of your life or mine! Name one man for whom you'd sacrifice yourself! Naturally someone where there'd be no biological urge. Not your son, for instance."

"I told you his heart's in a bad way," whispered Dušanka.

Mihajlo removed his stethoscope from Simić's sweating chest. "His heart is excellent, don't worry. Just change the compresses frequently and in the evening give him two powders and some tea. I'll have another look at him later."

He went out into the rain, feeling anxious about Simić and sorry for Dušanka. He felt sorry for himself, too, which filled him with disgust; so in order not to think about himself and the louse on his back, he went to have a look at the patients—to listen to human hearts and their troubles, and to comfort and encourage the patients, without looking at their faces. It was dark when he finally left the hospital, exhausted by his futile efforts. He didn't feel like smoking; all those false words of comfort he had babbled to the patients had taken away his sense of taste. He felt an irresistible desire to play darts, to gamble, to lose.

He ran into Doctor Vojtekh and asked him to visit the isolation ward that evening in his place. At least she'll wonder why for the first time I'm not there to see the dying patients and sit at her table looking at the jar of privet sprigs. "Idiot!" he said to himself, and hurried into town.

The rain had stopped, and there was a cutting, icy wind, carrying with it the smell of carbolic and lime; the whole of Valjevo was being disinfected and whitewashed. The streets were empty; only an occasional passer-by hurried through the wind into the evening solitude of the disease-ridden town. The sound of distant wailing intensified the infrequent barking of the dogs and the rattle of some military baggage trains. He had heard from Paun Aleksić of a *salon* run by Mrs. Predolac, and stopped a woman with an armful of wood to ask her where this house was. But in fact he said: "Can you tell me if there's a café here where they play cards? Some inn where people gamble?"

"See that house with the big, lighted windows, sir? That's it."

"Do you know of a place where soldiers and poor people gamble?"

"Take the first turn to the right. You'll see a shoemaker's shop converted into an inn. The man's away at the front, but his wife looks after herself. They gamble and swig brandy there all night. Austrian officers, too."

The woman continued on her way, cursing someone, while he hurried into the lane on the right. The noise from a hovel, its windows covered with paper through which light filtered, made him quicken his footsteps. With a bold gesture he opened the creaking door and stood with one foot on the threshold, struck by the stench of tanned leather, brandy, and bad tobacco. The noise was cut short as the soldiers and civilians turned toward him, reluctantly and with embarrassment. The soldiers stood up, buttoned their jackets, straightened their belts, and saluted him.

"Sit down and go on with what you were doing!"

He shut the door behind him. Under a lamp suspended from the ceiling stood three tables crowded with card players; against the wall was a shoemaker's bench full of demijohns, narrow-necked pots, and brandy glasses; behind the bench, under a gas jet just above her head, sat a stout woman in a black headscarf who was looking at him sullenly. To put her at ease he ordered a glass of strong brandy and stood watching the gamblers, seeking out those who looked repulsive and criminally inclined, the sort of people who would commit any crime for money and endure any kind of disgrace. He selected a couple who seemed most like the partners he wanted: a wounded man with a bandage around his head, and a young civilian, probably one of those who had been pronounced unfit for military service on account of *vitium cordisa*. They were playing *einz*. He sat down at their table and waited for the two of them to cheat.

"You'll find the sort of players you want at Mrs. Predolac's. We're small fry," said the man with the bandaged head.

Mihajlo rose from the table, paid four times the price for his glass of brandy, and went out into the darkness. Tonight he couldn't even lose money! Where could he go? He'd stop in to see Bogdan Dragović; his temperature had dropped, so perhaps he could talk about something irrelevant but not completely banal. He buttoned up his overcoat and set off in the direction of the Dragović house.

The night air smelled even more strongly of fresh lime and carbolic. The mud and puddles were beginning to freeze in the cold wind. A light was on in the rectory, and this reminded him of the priest, Božidar: he could have a talk with him tonight on something more significant than the louse. Perhaps they could talk about God. No, better not; the priest's God was not one whom one would dare to doubt.

He knocked at the priest's house. The sexton answered, holding a wet towel in his hands.

"Is he ill?" cried Mihajlo.

"Not him, Doctor, but some of the children, the orphans. Father Božidar is in the church with the others and his grandchildren."

Mihajlo stood in front of the door of the kitchen, where the sick children lay on two specially assembled beds. That night he had wanted to gamble, and in Valjevo children were dying! That woman with the armful of wood whom he had questioned almost certainly had someone sick at home, perhaps a child, and he had been frightened of a louse, disappointed in a woman who loved her husband, and overcome by a feeling of hopelessness! How ridiculous! He brushed the sexton aside, examined the children, took their temperatures, gave them some of the medicines he always carried in his pocket, and told the sexton how to care for them until morning, when he would come see them again. Then he set out for the church with his overcoat thrown over his shoulders. He opened the door slowly and stood in the half-darkened narthex; a glowing light from the bema played over the iconostas, the chandelier, and the frescoes.

"Is that you, Ješa?" asked the priest in a loud, reverberating voice.

"No, Father, it's Doctor Radić."

Božidar opened the doors of the bema; behind him on the floor was a large brazier full of glowing embers. "What's troubling you tonight, Doctor?"

Mihajlo didn't reply. He couldn't lie. Walking on tiptoe, he moved hesitantly and stopped in front of the priest, who had a tall cap on his head and was wearing his cassock with a rough blanket flung over it. From the bema he could hear the breathing of the sleeping children.

"Come in and get warm, Doctor, and we can talk a bit. The night is long now, even for those who are healthy."

Mihajlo remembered the bema at Lazarica into which he had peeped as a child, suspecting that his grandfather was eating the consecrated wafers, the body of Christ, and drinking the communion wine, Christ's blood; he would watch his grandfather gaily putting on and removing his priestly robes with rather too much concern for his appearance, which had struck him as a profanation of that holy place, and he had felt doubts about this sanctity which even his grandfather didn't respect. It was his grandfather's fault he wasn't pious, and now he felt like kneeling down and making his confession.

"Doctor, the most holy place in the world is the place which guards life. God hasn't shut man off from anything on earth that works for life. He has implanted in his heart and mind some fine dividing lines between good and evil which man wants to eradicate. Because, being a sinner, he doesn't know the limits of what he can do."

Mihajlo went into the bema and crouched down beside the big brazier; the priest sat down on a three-legged stool, picked up a psalter, opened it out, and waved it to fan the embers into flame. Light and shadows chased each other around the bema above the sleeping children, the cross, and the crucifix on the table.

"God and pain. We have no words in our language shorter and more closely related, and no words of greater significance and mystery; and this is not chance. Have you ever thought about this, Father?"

"Well, that's how it is. There's all sorts of things going on inside a man's head."

"I've never asked you about your family. Where are they, Father?" he asked, for the sake of something to say as he looked at the little boys and girls lying around the brazier on rag rugs, covered with rough blankets, garments, and church banners, their breathing echoing about the bema.

"My home is broken up, Doctor. They say that war disperses a conquered country, but it never disperses the government and those who serve it. It breaks up homes, whatever's around the fireside of everyday life. My eldest son, Svetislav, was a teacher; he was killed while commanding a platoon. He left a wife and two children, thank God—that pretty little girl there and the lad beside her with the scratches on his nose; they had a fight today while playing, the little devils. My daughter-in-law was killed trying to escape from Valjevo last autumn; she fell under a baggage train. When Mišić liberated Valjevo, one of my parishioners brought the children to me. I have a daughter who married some good-for-nothing just before the Austrians entered Valjevo—one of these shirkers, he was, who took her off somewhere. My wife has gone to look for her. My younger son, Milorad, is in the Student Brigade; I haven't heard whether he's still alive. Milorad's a real socialist; as if it weren't enough to attack the government, the King, and Pašić, he's got to go after Jesus Christ, too—as if Christ were a police clerk, instead of the first man to suffer for the poor! May God preserve him, so life's troubles will knock a bit of sense into his head. Well, that's how it is. Here I am alone with two grandchildren, if I can keep them safe with God's help. Two of the children fell ill yesterday, so at night I bring the others here for safety."

"I've seen the sick children and given them some medicine. Don't worry, children recover from typhus much more easily."

One of the children broke wind in its sleep. The priest smiled as he waved the psalter over the brazier.

"Well, maybe. Just you go on singing," he said to the restless child. "We've never heard a nicer voice behind the choir of this church. I'll send that one to study theology, Doctor. His father and mother were both killed by the Austrians."

"According to you, Father, God and the Christian faith are always on the side of life. In everything from the funeral services you sing, to these children here in the bema. Yet according to the Christian faith—"

Božidar interrupted him: "Indeed you're right, Doctor! The Orthodox faith, our Serbian faith, is a faith for survival. Everything which serves and assists human survival comes from God. For us life isn't just dust and worms. We Serbs have no eyes for the dust, only for the hills. We don't fear the worms, but we do fear a heartless man. That's how it is: we don't exist in order to die, we suffer in order to exist. That's what our forefathers believed, and they survived; but your generation believes in politics—that devil's trade! You'll ruin Serbia with your politics, it'll cease to exist, my boy!"

"Are you afraid we'll lose the war, Father?"

"What I'm afraid of, my boy, is that we'll win the war as planned by Pašić and our politicians, by professors and their students. Have you read in the newspapers about us uniting with the Croats and Slovenes? I mean that declaration of the Assembly about the creation of a large state consisting of Serbs, Croats, and Slovenes? Three separate faiths, estranged by fire and sword, and divided by blood—but now they're to be combined in a single state! What louse or reptile shot this poison—this death-dealing sickness—into Serbian heads? I often ask myself this when I'm alone, Doctor, I ask it aloud. What kind of union can we have with the Catholics? After all the crimes committed by those brothers of ours in Austrian uniform, can anyone in his right mind believe in unity and peace with them? Why are you silent? You educated people are heading straight for the precipice, but why push this unhappy nation over it, too?"

"I'm not a politician, Father. I hate politics, maybe even more than you do. The one thing I approve of in the policies of both government and Opposition is the unification of all those unhappy people. I think it's better for us to be together, because then at least the Austrians and Russians won't be able to set one group against another. If we're going to be bruised and smothered, at least we'll be doing it to ourselves."

"You mean that we and the Catholics should share good and evil like brothers? That we should do this with those people who've been hanging Serbian priests all over Bosnia, and once over the Drina did the same thing to all our Orthodox clergy?"

"The soldiers haven't done all these things of their own free will. It isn't their idea. I don't think such victories over the Orthodox mean much to them."

"Ah, Doctor, you may have studied in Europe, but you can't see things just over your own garden fence. You can't see that many centuries have divided us, and that popes and bishops have fixed boundaries in the hearts and minds of these brothers of ours. Hatred for us has been implanted in their Catholic minds."

"For heaven's sake, Father, don't talk about these medieval divisions! We really *are* brothers. We've all suffered under foreign rule, we speak the same language, we eat the same bread, and we're menaced by the same evil."

"The only people like us are those Serbs on the other side of the Drina and the Sava. Our frontier should stretch just as far as they do, no farther; and if—God forbid—we move a step beyond this, we'll quarrel fiercely with our Catholic brothers the moment we find ourselves in the same sheepfold. Remember this, Radić: nations can be united only through peace and in time of peace. Today we're fighting under the flags of two emperors and two faiths. The best thing would be for us to end the war with the frontiers which the faiths in our hearts have fixed between us."

"It's popes and emperors—people alien to us—who have fixed these boundaries, Father, which will prove dangerous for us if we accept them. If we . . ." Mihajlo left his sentence unfinished, feeling that any attempt to oppose Father Božidar that night in the bema was pointless, especially on a political issue. He got up and put on his overcoat.

The priest straightened up and placed his enormous hands on Radić's shoulders. "God grant that you may outlive me, which by the laws of nature you should."

"No, you'll sing my funeral office, Father. I beg you, in the name of your grandchildren, that before you pronounce the final 'amen' you'll strip me of my rank and calling."

"Don't talk nonsense, Radić!"

"I'm not talking nonsense, Father. I'm already infected. I have perhaps two weeks left."

"I told you not to talk nonsense, Mihajlo. After the war, please remember this conversation in the bema, above these innocent, sleeping children."

"Let's not worry about our nation and the future, Father. That lies outside our power."

"I know what a man can do, and what he can't; but remember this: we Serbs have done our best to put an end to our existence."

"Still we'll go on, Father. We have strength inside us."

"No, we won't, Doctor. We prefer the tiniest shred of freedom to the possibility of survival; we've bitten off more than we can chew. That, my boy, is the vice of politics. We're infected with that vice, my boy, so we're a deeply flawed people, that's how it is. I wish to God that the priest Božidar Jevtović was sick in his mind and raving like the typhus patients in Valjevo tonight."

Mihajlo moved out from under the pressure of the priest's hands and with a quiet farewell left the church. Of all the ills the future might bring, the only one he took really seriously was growing old. "Come back early tomorrow morning and have a look at my children!" he heard the priest say behind him. The night was bitingly cold and he hurried along the street to the place where earlier he had met the woman with the wood. She had an unusually soft and pleasant voice, he reflected; tall, too. That vileness again! Then he dropped into the first house with lighted windows, where he found a sick girl. He examined her, gave her some aspirin, and explained how she should be treated. With a gesture of disgust he refused the money which the girl's grandfather offered him. Before he returned to the hospital he also called at some other houses with lighted windows, examined the sick, and gave them some medicine, bringing tears and embarrassment to the unhappy women there. An act of kindness which people were not expecting always brought the greatest joy. He was always moved by people's gratitude and found it sufficient reward for all his efforts. It filled him with an exalted vanity; he had often felt that the alleviation of human pain implied some kind of divine power, as the ancient Greeks had believed. Now, however, he experienced nothing of such feelings, nothing at all. He had ascended one rung in the ladder of goodness.

He walked slowly back to the hospital along the frozen highway. Had that louse now perished from *Typhus exanthematicus,* or was it still dozing in the hem of his shirt, sated with blood? How vast was the sky above him, how numerous the stars! From his louse to a star, and from that star to another louse somewhere beyond it, stretched endless movement and light. . . . If that created infinity, there was no final death. You idiot!

At daybreak Najdan Tošić, traveling by car, reached the outskirts of Valjevo and told his chauffeur to turn a little way off the main road; if he fell asleep, he was to be wakened at eight o'clock sharp.

He gave the man his pocket watch, wrapped himself in two new plaid rugs, and stretched out on the back seat.

"Shall we stop at an inn and have some hot brandy?" asked the chauffeur timidly.

"I don't intend to set foot in this lice-ridden town. If you're hungry and thirsty, you have a bag there beside you." He pulled his hat down over his face and closed his eyes.

He had been traveling since dusk the previous day, planning to arrive in the morning and find those poor silly creatures, Olga and Milena, and embrace them. Should he tell them the news at once, or prepare them? They'd ask first about Vukašin and he'd have to tell them the truth. The hardest thing would be to pack them into the car before noon and take them off to Niš. Milena was pigheaded like her father; it was clear whose daughter she was when she asked for her first doll. What crazy notion had Olga got into her head? She was a person of good sense, like the Tošići; all the older people in Belgrade had marveled at her intelligence. Now, from sheer caprice, she was working as a nurse in Valjevo, causing people in Belgrade and Niš to cross themselves in astonishment. Working with her daughter in this hotbed of infection!

Yet where could the poor woman go from the house of Vukašin Katić, that idiot politician who in this unhappy, poverty-stricken land, where there wasn't a house not in mourning, was demanding that patriotic provisioners should be court-martialed and hanged! The people were hungry, naked, barefoot, disease-ridden, and dying, yet that demagogue, just to be different, had shouted in the Assembly: "If we aren't prepared to wage war to the death against speculators and profiteers sucking the lifeblood of the nation, then, gentlemen, I call upon you to capitulate honorably to the Austrians and not to destroy our people. In a land without honor there can be no freedom!" That peasant radical from Prerovo was playing the part of a Serbian Robespierre. That upstart so delighted by the title "the Moral Sword of Serbia" bestowed on him by stupid journalists! It was pitiful, both tragic and comic—but dangerous for all in these desperate times.

Why bother about Vukašin Katić now? He was trying to save his cousin and that wretched girl whose beauty had brought her no common sense. Even with beauty and wealth, she'd never find happiness! When he read the telegram to Olga and gazed into those candid green eyes . . . For him she would never grow old, with that forehead of a Renaissance madonna, that wonderful skin, that noble pallor of her face over which there sometimes spread an enigmatic smile. If only she weren't his cousin, or there were one other woman like her in this lice-ridden Balkan peninsula!

The chauffeur was chewing his food, which got on Najdan's nerves and kept him awake. He waited for the man to finish, but these simple folk ate slowly, they savored and enjoyed their food as though their fathers and grandfathers had been viziers and sultans. It didn't matter, he couldn't sleep anyway. He thought about what he ought to say when summoned before an Assembly commission investigating army supply frauds—a commission presided over by his cousin-in-law, Vuka-šin Katić! Monstrous!

"Eight o'clock, Mr. Tošić."

"Ask where the Second Reserve Hospital is and drive straight there."

He removed the rugs, smoothed his tie and his suit, put on his hat, sat up in his seat, and pulled on his black kid gloves. He hadn't the slightest interest in Valjevo as he stared into the foggy morning swarming with soldiers, women, and prisoners, but he couldn't help noticing that all the houses had recently been whitewashed, and that there were white patches of spilled whitewash on the pavements on either side of the road. Gates, fences, pigsties, privies—all had been whitewashed. His nostrils picked up the smell of fresh whitewash, carbolic, and something else he couldn't recognize. He told the chauffeur to drive faster. Though the town was small, the incidence of death was great. There always had been a terrible disproportion between life and death in this wretched Serbia; human misery here had always been greater than the power to understand and overcome it. Someone ought to explain this to those foreign ladies in tropical helmets who were hurrying between their white tents like deer, in perfect order. How many centuries would we need to learn sense and bring order and symmetry into this land of ours? Those hospital tents looked like white tombs, the headquarters and harem of some vizier who had strayed far from home.

They stopped in front of the hospital gates, where a group of women were quarreling with a soldier. "No visitors!" he shouted. "I'm telling you in plain, simple Serbian: no visitors as long as the epidemic lasts!"

"Shut off the engine and wait here," he told the chauffeur. Cramped and numb from a night in the car, he walked slowly through a group of soldiers, who divided and fell silent as he approached, and stood stock still by way of a salute. He could hear murmurs of protest swelling behind him as he cautiously neared the long, low building, having resolved first of all to announce his arrival to the director of the hospital and to wait for Olga and Milena in his office. Presumably there wouldn't be any lice there. He felt extremely uncomfortable under the glances of the soldiers, who watched where he was going. He asked for the director's office and an orderly took him there. "You'll have to wait until noon to see the director," the man said.

"Why?"

"He'll be examining patients until then."

"Tell him someone from Niš would like a few minutes with him."

The orderly went out and Najdan stayed in the office, looking it over and trying to decide what the man who lived there was like. Typical masculine morning disorder, a mediocre suitcase under the bed, cheap cigarettes. Maybe he had lice, too. An ascetic or just primitive? Maybe the two were the same. He stood beside the window, then recoiled: someone was being carried out on a stretcher—a dead man, perhaps. Again he looked around the room as he paced, suffocated by the smell of cheap tobacco and soaked leather. Ever since the outbreak of the war, that smell of soaked, rotting leather had permeated all public places.

The orderly returned and said that the director asked his visitor to wait until he finished his rounds. Najdan Tošić found this most inconvenient; even at the High Command he had never waited more than five minutes.

"Could you ask Olga Katić to come? She's a volunteer nurse here."

"Of course I can! Are you her husband?"

"No, her cousin. Please hurry! Just a minute, do you smoke?"

"When I have anything to smoke, sir."

He gave the man a pack of cigarettes, one of those he always carried for such occasions. As he waited he felt impatient and agitated. Soon Olga appeared in the doorway, all the color drained from her face, unable to speak a word, questioning him with her eyes. He was amazed at her tired, worn face; in one month she had aged ten years! The pain of it brought tears to his eyes.

"Has the telegram come?" stammered Olga.

"Yes. He's a prisoner of war, Olga. Everything is all right." He stepped forward to embrace her.

Olga stood rigid. Najdan was startled by the sight of her face and lowered the arm he had raised to embrace her. Suddenly she turned and ran down a slope to the hospital—to Milena, to embrace her tightly.

Feeling sadder still, Najdan withdrew into the office. He had no idea where Olga was going. Presumably she had read Vukašin's speech to the Assembly and agreed with it, as she always did—the woman for whose happiness he, Najdan, would have placed his head under the ax at that moment! Why was he making such efforts, striving so hard to outwit corrupt people who cheated even themselves, to preserve from thieves those who stole from themselves? Why did he feel ashamed of his supply activities, his one besmirched glory in this era of brigands? Why was he accumulating wealth for her and her children, when they had no need of it, when they despised these things! What about his visit here, taking his life in his hands, so that he could show them the telegram from Geneva, share his joy with them, and rescue them from this graveyard? He leaned against the wall and stared in front of him.

"Uncle Najdan!"

He started on hearing Milena's cry. Before he could have a good look at her she had flung her arms around his neck and was kissing his cheek. It took him a few minutes to collect his thoughts and give her and Olga the telegram, which they both read aloud. He looked at Milena: she had grown thinner and acquired a sharpness of expression in which exhaustion and hardness were intermingled. He had feared to find such traces of the war on her face, overshadowing her beauty.

"Why hasn't Father come with you, Uncle?"

"Your father? Haven't you read today's papers?"

"Who reads newspapers in a hospital these days? What's happened, Uncle?"

Olga sat down and read the French text of the telegram over and over again: "I am happy to inform you Stop Your relative Ivan Katić a corporal in the Serbian army is a prisoner of war Stop His health is excellent Stop He is temporarily in a camp near Linz Stop You will shortly be informed of his address through the Red Cross Stop I have sent him two thousand crowns Stop Dear Mr. Tošić please continue to count on my friendship Leopold von Berger."

Najdan waited for Olga to look at him before he answered Milena, who had come up to him and put her hands on his shoulders. "What's happened between you and Father, Uncle? Does he know about the telegram?"

"Aunt Selena told him last night."

"Why didn't you show it to him?"

"I'll be talking with your father in my capacity as a destroyer of our people. I'll answer to him as president of an Assembly commission investigating army supply frauds." He waited for Olga to look up from the telegram before he went on.

Milena moved away. "My God, what's going to become of us?" she said in a whisper.

Olga gave no sign that she had heard what he said. This wounded him deeply, and contrary to his usual custom he cried out angrily: "Yes, your father will send me to the gallows! That's what I've deserved and waited for—for my cousin-in-law to put a noose around my neck! Do you hear that, Olga?"

Olga went on reading the telegram. Milena felt sorry for her uncle, but she was sure that her father was fighting for honor and freedom, and didn't know what to say. She burst into tears, aggrieved that not even at this moment could all members of her family be happy.

"Does it have to be like this, Uncle?" she stammered, her eyes full of tears. She tried to embrace him but he moved away, offended by Olga's silence.

"Ask your father why it must be like this. Now get ready so I can drive you to Niš. The car is at the gate."

Olga raised her head and looked at him absently. Superciliously, too, he thought. She made no effort even now to conceal that hint of gentle scorn by which she indicated disagreement. He knew so well that twitching at the edge of her lips, remembered from their games as children those sparks in her long, dreamy glance. He was driven to despair by the fact that even at this moment she couldn't forget Vukašin, and wouldn't indicate by a single look or word, or by a touch of her hand, that he was her cousin, and assure him of their friendship. This is a terrible war, he thought to himself.

"We'll lunch together in the Grand Hotel, Najdan, and talk things over," Olga said at last.

"No, Olga, we'll have lunch in the car on our way. Aunt Selena has prepared all the things you like."

"There's just one place where I'd like to go with you, Najdan, but that's impossible."

"I'm not going back to Niš without you! I won't leave you both here to die!"

"Najdan, dear, don't let us part today with hurt feelings. I can't leave here."

Milena turned around: she had never seen her uncle so unhappy. She came up to embrace him, but he shouted: "It's because of you that I put up with this humiliation! Because of you and Ivan!"

"It's not my fault, Uncle. I love both you and Father."

"It's *my* fault," said Olga. "I don't want any of the wrongs from my prewar life to continue."

Doctor Radić came in. "Forgive me, someone sent for me. I suppose it was you, sir?"

"Yes, I asked to see you," said Najdan Tošić, introducing himself without shaking hands. "I've come for my cousin and my niece. I consider that they've both paid their debt to their country."

Olga jumped up from her chair, crying, "My son's alive, Mihajlo!" She wanted to embrace him, but only touched his hand. "Read this!" She handed him the telegram, then collapsed on the bed with a stifled cry.

Mihajlo stared at the telegram, unable at that moment to understand a single word of French.

Milena looked at the floor, wondering what on earth was happening.

Najdan stood over Olga for a long time, full of despair, then said to Mihajlo Radić: "Well, you see how things are. Forgive me for interrupting your work. Please tell a couple of orderlies to come with me to the gates and get a case of soap and another one of eggs—my gift to your hospital. Milena, I'll be waiting for you at the gates at eleven o'clock." He bowed slightly to Radić and went out.

"Uncle Najdan is the most unhappy of all of us now," Milena said to her mother.

Olga got up from the bed, wiped her face, and hurried after Najdan to explain why neither she nor Milena could leave the hospital.

* * *

At dusk Milena ran to Nadežda's room and cried out from the door: "Ivan's alive! He's a prisoner!" In the half light of the darkening room she saw Nadežda sitting at the table with her peasant kilim wrapped around her and a towel over her forehead, splashing color over her dead sister's portrait with a brush, working by the light of the stove.

"I told you he was somewhere in old Franz's empire. He won't need his glasses there. Oh, my God, if only my eyes don't give out!" She opened the stove doors and examined her picture by the firelight.

Andja's portrait was destroyed, painted over with something that looked like a bat, a large louse, or a small dragon. There was something tense and menacing about it.

"What's this?" stammered Milena, relieved that the painting was destroyed, yet fearful of what was painted over it, which told her more clearly than the towel on Nadežda's forehead that she was ill. We'll all die, she thought, Mother and I, everybody. She leaned against the wall. Dobrila was breathing hoarsely in her bed. Nadežda bent her head toward the picture and picked up the kilim, which had slipped from her knees.

"Where's your nurse? Why hasn't your lamp been lit?" asked Milena.

"Because true colors are best seen in the darkness. Like truth. I told you girls that back in high school. It's since dusk that I really got going. I've been painting like a madwoman—as once before, after a meeting with Gavrilo Stanković. There she is! Look, Milena—the lady who's ruling over Serbia! Her shape is always changing—it changes just like the light; but I'm not satisfied with the color—can't find the right one. Perhaps white—a deep, dull white. A treacherous color. Something to make them shudder when they look at it."

Milena came up and took Nadežda's face in her hands. "You're burning hot—lie down! I'll make you some tea. I'll bring Radić—the best doctor in Valjevo."

"A violent chill seized me last night. I know when the nasty creature bit me! It bit me in just the spot where some stupid man once did. Not by chance, either—certainly not, my dear. You know, Milena, love and death are the closest of all emotions. I've always longed to fuse them together, but I could never find the color. I must finish painting this portrait tonight; tomorrow, in a different light, who knows how it'll be? Tell me now whether you like it! I dare you now to say you don't like it!" She turned the painting toward Milena; it was in the shadow now, dark and ominous: a louse, a dragon, a bat . . .

"Yes, I do like it! You must do some more tomorrow; but lie down now and let me cover you up. You're shaking with fever, Nadežda."

"I won't lie down until I find that primeval white. A stark contrast to that pure green, squeezed out of that ripe summer when they declared war on Serbia."

Milena ran out, found a doctor, and told him about Nadežda.

"Yes, I know. I saw her half an hour ago and gave her some powders to bring her temperature down. She should be feeling better by now."

"But she won't lie down. She's painting, Doctor."

"Don't worry. You know yourself that typhus patients often behave strangely, even comically. Then they get tired. I'll come as soon as I've given some injections."

Milena ran back to Nadežda. She was kneeling on the floor plastering color over the painting, at the edges of which the white ends of a nurse's apron and veil were still visible.

"Just remember what your old teacher is telling you, Milena. The future will be a painting—an infinite, unseen painting in bright, crazy colors. The whole world will be one painting. Don't have any doubts, my child! People will live in colors, in a triumph of colors. The freedom of beauty, equality in beauty, the justice of beauty . . . People will be as happy as their eyes can make them. You don't believe me? How can you not?"

"I do believe you—I believe everything you say!"

"Colors are brave and wise, evil and stupid. Colors are vices and virtues. Just tell your father that! Colors are freedom! And tell my nephew Rastko!"

"Do lie down! Your teeth are chattering. The doctor will be here any minute." She clasped Nadežda under her arms and tried to lift her, but staggered under her enormous weight.

"Ah, my dear, our vision is powerless. The most important color, the one that contains all colors, hasn't yet been revealed to us. The one that'll make it possible to paint death. I've only caught a glimpse of it—you can see it in the embers of an open stove, as I did a short while ago. Then the ash covered it; but perhaps I'll see it again."

Nadežda dropped her brush. Shivering from cold, she raised herself up a bit. "Cover me up, Milena," she whispered. "I'm cold again, all violet from cold."

Milena covered her with the kilim and stood over her with tears in her eyes. She was afraid to light the lamp. Soon the doctor would come, and the two of them would lift Nadežda from the floor and put her on the bed. Milena covered her with all the blankets she could find in the room.

"Can we do anything else?" Milena asked the doctor when he came.

"Not now. She's taken some medicine for tonight. It's a bad beginning."

"Please send a nurse to stay near her tonight. I'm on duty in the operating room with Doctor Sergeev. I must go immediately."

"Don't worry. I'll stay here with Nadežda."

Milena went out. Remembering that she hadn't told Bogdan about Ivan, she hurried to his house. When she entered his warm, lighted room, she took a deep breath of the fragrance of old wax, which made her think of candles. Speaking softly, she said: "Nadežda's ill, Bogdan. My God, who'll be left in this country?"

"Thieves, perhaps, and those who preserve some shred of hope."

"Ivan's alive! He's a prisoner of war in Austria!"

"Ivan!" Bogdan raised himself up. "Now I have reason to fight!"

Milena came up to his bed and curled up in his arms.

In a somber mood she returned to the hospital, glad that no one could see her. She felt a sudden exhaustion and fear of falling ill, and it pained her that she no longer felt any joy over the long-awaited news about Ivan. She found her mother preparing to go on night duty in the Warehouse of the Dead, and told her that Nadežda was sick.

Olga dropped her veil and sat down on the bed. "If Nadežda has fallen ill . . ." she whispered, but didn't finish her sentence, or the thought in her mind. It clouded the day's joy. She looked at Milena. "Are you all right? Why are your eyes so dull?"

"I'm all right, Mother. I've been crying because of Nadežda."

Olga felt her arms, forehead, and neck. "You're not all right! Dušanka, give me a thermometer!"

All three were silent while Milena held the thermometer under her arm. Milena took out the thermometer, carried it to the lamp, and said calmly, "Ninety-eight point four."

Olga took the thermometer to check the reading. "You must go to bed at once, even if you haven't a temperature. Dušanka can make you some tea. I'll ask Mrs. Stefanović to stay on duty a bit longer while I go see Nadežda. I'll take Doctor Radić, too."

As soon as Olga had gone out, Dušanka began to talk. "Milena, I couldn't keep quiet any longer. I swallowed my pride and told Philip I adored him. I told him I was ready to die for him, if that was what he wanted. Milena, he burst out laughing! 'Nurse,' he said, 'do you really think that you can catch me with your sickly sentimentality? Please spare me, won't you? We have to work together.' He said it to my face!" Dušanka began to sob.

Milena hugged her, powerless to offer any comfort.

At noon the next day Milena found Nadežda unconscious, her hands splotched with paint; there were patches of color on the pillow and the kilim, too. The painting was on the table: a large, multicolored patch of thick primary colors, spread on with fingers and scratched by nails.

"The minute she regains consciousness, she asks for this daub and her paints," said the nurse who was looking after Nadežda and Dobrila. "She spreads on the paint with her fingers, then gets angry—'It isn't you, it isn't you!' she says. She often mentions someone called Andja. But the doctors say her heart is very strong."

Milena stood a few moments beside Nadežda's bed, staring at her flushed, sweating face and parted lips; she could hear her grinding her teeth. When her eyes fell on the painting, she felt dizzy; the garish splotch of color seemed to be spreading over the table and onto the floor.

She returned to her room to sleep. She dreamed about Vladimir, his head bound up with red-stained bandages, lying on the sandbar of a river which was and yet was not the Sava; she was awakened by his cry just before he jumped in. Then she was engulfed by sleep once more and continued to dream about Vladimir: he was always wounded; only the place where she met him changed. At daybreak her mother came and lay down beside her. "You *have* got a temperature—you're ill!" Olga cried.

"No, I'm not, Mother, I've just caught a cold. Don't cry, Ivan is alive. I'll take some aspirin, and I'll be all right by noon, you'll see. Dara, give me two aspirin. Don't get up, Mother, I want you to lie beside me. Just hug me and don't worry."

Milena took the two aspirin tablets and fell asleep in her mother's arms. When she woke up Olga was no longer there. Feeling that she had no temperature, Milena got up joyfully, but she felt weak. Her legs wouldn't support her, and she was nauseous. She sat down on the bed, shivering. Her friends crowded around.

"Don't you feel well?" said Dušanka with a sob.

"It's nothing. I got chilled when I went to see Nadežda."

With great effort she got dressed and went out. On the stairs she stopped; she thought she was going to be sick and her head felt dreadfully heavy. I'm going to die, she thought, without any sense of sadness. She simply must see Nadežda once more; perhaps she would never see her and Bogdan again—Bogdan who last night had embraced her in a different way, not like a sister; he had been trembling, and for a long time didn't want to separate his cheek from hers. It was the first time she remembered it being like that, and the memory disturbed her.

Doctor Radić swung into view, smiling; he had a cigarette in his mouth and his stethoscope around his neck. He had become distasteful to her after what had happened in his office the previous day, in front of her Uncle Najdan. "I was on my way to have a look at you."

"Why?"

"Your mother says you have a temperature."

"That's just how it seems to my mother. I feel fine, Doctor. I'm hurrying off to see Nadežda, then I'll come on duty."

"Still, I'd like to listen to your heart, just to be on the safe side."

"No, please don't! But thank you, Doctor," she said, her face clouding. She turned around and set off toward the road, summoning all her strength to walk firmly and quickly. The cold wind cleared her head a bit; it was as if walking and her wish to see Nadežda had restored her strength.

She found Nadežda propped up on her pillows, staring thoughtfully at a piece of paper torn from a sketch pad.

"You're feeling better!" she cried joyfully, and sat down on the edge of the bed. She wanted to take Nadežda's hand, but recoiled: it was covered with paint.

"Look, Milena, I've managed to paint it after all. That's it. I saw it last night, quite suddenly. It was so simple, and I've tried so hard! If I hadn't fallen ill, I'd never have seen, never understood."

Dobrila extricated herself from the bed and began to totter about.

Arms outspread, she managed to reach the wall. Then she lifted her skirt and, rolling against the wall, began to urinate.

"Nurse, where are you?" cried Milena, unable to move from Nadežda's bed. As she called for the nurse, Nadežda gripped the iron bar of the head of the bed.

"Look at it, Milena. Please look at it, my dear," cried Nadežda.

Milena caught sight of a black dot on a white surface in Nadežda's hands. The dot began to move, creeping faster and faster over the white paper, hurrying toward the edge; then it bounced away from the edge, came back, hurried off in the opposite direction, bounced away again from the edge, fell down, and at the very end of the paper jumped up in the air, fell down, and began to move in circles over the white paper: a black insect, a butterfly, a little wisp of light in the darkness, a firefly, a firefly sinking down into darkness. . . .

When the doctor restored her to consciousness and offered to make up a bed for her beside Nadežda, she summoned all her strength and got up. "Will someone please take me to my mother?"

A nurse helped her on with her coat, took her by the arm, and led her outside. Clearly, she was ill. She didn't feel frightened or sorry. In the street she felt an overwhelming desire to see Bogdan, so she set off in the direction of his house, telling the nurse that she had a brother in Valjevo and wanted to go to him.

She stepped into Bogdan's room exhausted, her teeth chattering and her mind clouded. She smiled at him, then was lost in the grip of darkness.

If the fever doesn't overwhelm me, I won't allow myself to sleep tonight. It'll be quieter in the hospital, and all night long I'll be able to listen to my heart.

It came into being in darkness and has remained there; it was created from chaos, in order that it might determine the freedom of one form of movement. From the frontier of timelessness, the heart has given pace and direction to time.

When did its first movement come into being? By whose will or compulsion? Right from the start, with the highest sense of purpose; nothing about it can ever be a matter of chance. It must have been from that central flow of movement which sets in motion everything in the universe, and in which all laws are contained. The easiest thing is to believe that this movement comes to an end in us, and is re-

placed by a state of tranquillity. The heart is a seedling of eternity;
I'm sure that is so!

By its force it has determined a man's shape, given him strength,
greatness, or poverty, and most of all uncertainty—that tormented
creature in the damp darkness of his breast. That truth underlying
human joy and pain, that source of honor in our body, its voice, and
the conscious measure of our span of time.

The heart!

That tireless organ, never seeking its own advantage; the servant
of every fool and criminal; that life-bearer without a single fault,
which has never left any task on earth unfinished because of weari-
ness, and which has destroyed everything it has set out to destroy.
For human folly does far less harm to any human activity than the
heart.

I am unhappy that I can't see it, can't take it in my hands, can't
kiss it or breathe my last breath upon it, and marvel at its immeasur-
able, unerring, selfless power. What would I not give to hear the last
beat, the final sound, of my heart! I don't want to die until I have
expressed my gratitude to my heart.

My neighbors tell me that all night long I was grinding my teeth,
as if biting somebody. I dreamed last night—about spring, while an
exhausted, drowsy wind descended on the roof of the Hospital. This
dream dispersed my sadness, but increased the horror of my end.

For I shall not know the spring which will arise from this Sickness,
to give me one significant truth about human beings.

I am sorry that I will not see what the hyacinth looks like, or the
color of the first new dandelion in Serbia; but what will the flowering
apple and cherry trees mean to the living? If the healthy don't suspect
that eggs lie concealed in the blossom, and that from the pistils of
the flowers little white lice will crawl out, stay a while in the pollen
of the flower's pistil, then move into the branch and the bark and
wait there until someone comes to pick the fruit, so they can fall on
his neck; if the sowers walking behind the plow don't believe that
there are eggs in the very subsoil of our meadows; if those who come
to pick lilac don't shake the flowers well and soak them in carbolic
solution before carrying them into the house—then it will be clear to
any fool that not even this Sickness has implanted a protective fear of
flowers in us humans. Even foolish people will grasp that not even
this Death has ignited the smallest spark of rational foresight in the

dullness of human self-confidence. In that case our Death will be quite pointless. Heedless of the warning, the Healthy will renew and multiply their fatal delusions.

But why in these last moments am I worrying about the future? If I'm not mistaken, I did say once that the future was the time that belonged to Death.

The Healthy think that those on the point of death envy them. An inalterable delusion! I am no longer afraid of the things they fear; nothing can crush me any more, or surprise me or make me laugh. For this reason I sincerely pity the Healthy. They don't know that the only space in the world absolutely necessary to a man is room enough to lie down in; the only time necessary to him, the time while he is in love; the only possessions, enough to keep him from hunger and thirst; the only knowledge, that of his own body; the only right, that of daring not to love someone whom he doesn't love. Over and above this, some small measure of freedom to please himself and amuse himself. Now I'm biting my tongue not to blurt out the most important thing of all.

Judging by the looks of my neighbors and the nurses, I won't last long. In the eyes of those lying in the corridor, I see hope: they'll inherit my mattress and my blanket. Whatever one leaves behind, whatever one deprives people of—even if one leaves nothing and doesn't deprive people of anything—Death brings some advantage to the living.

I'm now quite sure that Sick People know most about human beings. Only a Sick Man has this unerring knowledge of people. Neither a slave nor a poor man has this power; they're prevented by hatred. No writer, philosopher, or scholar has this power, because ideas hide the faces of human beings from them. Only a Sick Man, I'm convinced, sees people as they really are.

If I could, would I now obliterate the world? I confess that I would!

No joy or happiness gives us the power we need for the last hour, for this final power.

All our activity, all our life, everything is now in question. We haven't created or achieved anything lasting. But why do we live if at the end we have no belief in ourselves? Why keep trying if no gift or virtue, no reputation or significance endures to the last hour? No such things exist, believe me!

All day I've tried hard to repudiate this assertion, but without success.

If only I could somehow not dirty myself before I yield up my spirit! But perhaps for this very reason Death is a marvelous and righteous act, giving filth to the earth, the world, and people, but the soul to heaven, living breath to the heights. That convulsive, final, and surely painful separation of the human into filth and stench, visible and invisible—that is the Death of man. What a fabulous discovery! Was it really worth so much suffering, so much walking over this earth? Especially since I still don't know how painful that last step will be.

I'm lying. Life is worth living only so that a man can shit once more.

The process of dying brings knowledge without the slightest significance.

Perhaps people will be saved when they have attained the conditions and power to choose their Death; when they find some means of making the process of dying pleasant, clean, and perfect.

If I'm now convinced that in this last hour there's no such thing as a happy or an unhappy life, I'm sure there's such a thing as a happy Death. In the last resort, this is the one thing worth troubling oneself about; but only a dying man knows this.

This is the most significant knowledge, and the most useless!

Do swans really sing as they die?

6

CHARLES GAREN, A DOCTOR IN THE FRENCH MISSION TO SERBIA IN 1915,
WRITING IN THE *Franco-Macedonian Almanac:*
THIS IS AN UNDERNOURISHED NATION, REDUCED BY WAR TO WOMEN
AND CHILDREN. IN THIS GRIEF-STRICKEN COUNTRY I'M CONVINCED THAT
I'M EXPERIENCING THE LIFE OF OUR PEASANTS IN THE MIDDLE AGES. IT
IS A PRIMITIVE WAY OF LIFE, BUT COMPACT. EACH FAMILY MAKES ITS
OWN BREAD; SPINS WOOL, HEMP, OR FLAX; WEAVES LINEN AND SERGE;
AND PRODUCES FOR ITSELF ALL THE AGRICULTURAL TOOLS IT NEEDS, AND
ALL THE FOOD FOR ITS MEMBERS AND ITS ANIMALS. IN THIS HOLY AND
TORMENTED NATION THE PEASANT IS OFTEN CRUSHED BUT KEEPS ALIVE,
SELLS LITTLE, EARNS ONLY AS MUCH MONEY AS HE NEEDS TO PAY HIS
TAXES. THESE TAXES ARE SPENT ON THE ADMINISTRATION, AND ON WEAPONS
AND MILITARY EQUIPMENT TO WAGE WAR FOR FREEDOM.

MORE THAN THEIR SIMPLE AND PRIMITIVE WAY OF LIFE, MORE THAN
THE PICTURESQUE GARMENTS OF THE MEN AND THE BRILLIANT CLOTHES
OF THE WOMEN, THE GREAT DISTINCTION OF THE SERBS LIES IN THE
WONDERFUL AND DEVOTED SPIRIT OF THE PEOPLE.

THIS NATION WHICH PAYS HONOR TO OAK TREES, AND WHOSE RURAL
FESTIVALS REMIND ONE OF THE ANCIENT CELTS; THIS NATION WHICH
LIVES OFF ITS OWN SOUL, WHICH SUPPLIES IT WITH FOOD AND CLOTHING;
THIS NATION WHICH HONORS ITS TREES AND ITS DEAD, STILL MAINTAINS
THE CULT OF ITS OWN PAST. THE HISTORY OF SERBIA LIVES IN THE HEARTS
OF ITS PEOPLE, IN THEIR SAD AND MELANCHOLY SONGS, BUT ALSO IN

THEIR SONGS OF HEROES. SOMETIMES AT NIGHT WHEN I HEAR THE SOLDIERS SINGING AS THEY RETURN TO THEIR HOMES FROM THE FRONT, I FEEL THAT I KNOW THE PAIN OF THIS LONG-OPPRESSED RACE AND THEIR UNDYING HOPE OF FREEDOM.

AH, MY PEASANTS! YOU HAVE ADOPTED ME AS ONE OF YOUR OWN, AND YOUR TENDERNESS AND RUDENESS ARE WELL KNOWN TO ME. FROM ME YOU HAVE LEARNED OF THE STRENGTH OF MY COUNTRY, FRANCE, AND I HAVE DELIGHTED IN YOUR CURIOUS, ATTENTIVE FACES, WHEN I TOLD YOU ABOUT MY PEOPLE AND MY TOWN OF BORDEAUX AS YOU SAT GATHERED AROUND ME.

I SHALL TALK ABOUT YOU TO THE PEOPLE OF MY OWN BLOOD, AND DEMAND OF THEM THAT THEY LOVE YOU.

NIŠ

FROM *Politika:*
THE SHOPKEEPER'S SCANDAL. GREED AND CUPIDITY. CONTRACTORS SHOULD BE LYNCHED!
NEW CURRENCY HAS BEEN WITHDRAWN FROM CIRCULATION BECAUSE IT'S UNBEARABLY UGLY: THE SOLDIER LOOKS LIKE A CORPSE AND THE PEASANT WOMAN LIKE A BARMAID!
THE RUSSIANS ARE NOW IN THE CARPATHIANS. BATTLES SUCH AS THE WORLD HAS NEVER SEEN.
OVER 700 ALBANIANS ATTACK OUR FRONTIER AT ĆAF.
TWO HUNDRED BULGARIAN GUERRILLAS INVADE OUR TERRITORY.
THE RUSSIANS ARE MASTERS OF THE CARPATHIANS.
ARRIVAL OF M. REISS FROM SWITZERLAND TO INVESTIGATE AUSTRIAN ATROCITIES IN SERBIA.
PRELIMINARY TALKS OF THE ALLIES WITH ITALY.
OUR SEACOAST: WE DO NOT WANT THE OUTLET TO THE SEA OFFERED US BY THE ALLIES AND THE ITALIANS; WE WANT, AND ARE FIGHTING FOR, THE LIBERATION OF OUR ENTIRE COASTLINE!
FATE OF CROATIA STILL UNCERTAIN.

FROM *Politika:*

JUGOSLAV MEETING IN NIŠ
THE MEETING WAS OPENED BY DUŠAN BRANKOVIĆ, A NATIONAL LEADER FROM DALMATIA. "UNIFICATION, AND A COMMON DESTINY FROM NOW ON. SERBIA IS NOT ASKING FOR US; WE ARE ASKING FOR SERBIA!"

FROM *The Tribune:*

FRANJO SUPILO'S SPEECH AT THE JUGOSLAV MEETING IN NIŠ:

I HAVE BEEN ASKED BY A COMMITTEE OF CROATS, SERBS, AND SLOVENES FROM THE ADRIATIC COAST TO INFORM YOU OF THE SITUATION THERE, AND STAND BEFORE YOU WITH MIXED FEELINGS OF PAIN AND HOPE. I HAVE COME HERE TO ADDRESS YOU AS A CROAT AND WILL SET FORTH OUR COMMON WORRIES. FIRST OF ALL, THE THING WHICH HAS MADE IT POSSIBLE FOR US TO THINK OF UNITY IS THE BEAUTIFUL LANGUAGE IN WHICH I AM SPEAKING TO YOU, WHICH WE CALL CROATIAN AND YOU CALL SERBIAN [LOUD APPLAUSE].

IT HAS TAKEN A LONG TIME FOR US—I MEAN THE EDUCATED CLASSES OF OUR PEOPLE—TO REALIZE THAT WE SLOVENES, CROATS, AND SERBS ARE BROTHERS AND UNDERSTAND ONE ANOTHER, JUST AS OUR PEASANTS UN-DERSTAND THE FIRST WORD THEY HEAR WHEN THEY MEET ONE ANOTHER. THIS FACT IS THE VERY BASIS OF OUR UNITY AS A PEOPLE, AND FROM THIS UNITY THERE HAS GERMINATED THE IDEA OF POLITICAL REBIRTH AND POLITICAL UNIFICATION. THIS IS WHY I IDENTIFY MYSELF WITH YOU, AND WHY WE FEEL THAT WE ARE NOT GUESTS HERE, BUT IN OUR OWN HOMELAND [LOUD APPLAUSE].

ALL WE ASK IS THAT WE AND SERBIA SHOULD COMPOSE A SINGLE NATION-STATE. DISASTER THREATENS US IF THE ITALIANS TAKE POSSESSION OF OUR COAST, OR IF OUR NATION IS SPLIT UP INTO SEPARATE GROUPS. IT IS A GREAT DUTY WHICH SERBIA HAS TAKEN ON HERSELF, BY FORCE OF CIR-CUMSTANCES. SERBIA MUST TAKE THE RESPONSIBILITY FOR THIS ONEROUS TASK. IF SHE DOES NOT, THEN THERE CAN BE NO FINAL SOLUTION TO OUR PROBLEM. I MUST EXPRESS TO YOUR KING AND YOUR SOLDIERS, WITH TEARS IN MY EYES, MY GRATITUDE FOR ALL THAT SERBIA HAS SUFFERED, BOTH FOR YOU AND FOR US.

DRAGUTIN GUSTINČIĆ SAID IN SLOVENIAN: "THERE WILL BE NO PEACE UNTIL ALL THE SLOVENES ARE INCLUDED IN A SINGLE STATE TOGETHER WITH GREATER SERBIA."

Vukašin Katić was hurrying to a meeting of the National Assembly, frequently tipping his hat to people, but ignoring those who greeted him from the cafés and shops of Niš. The pavements were thronged with upper-class people from Belgrade, and with Serbian and Austrian officers, so he walked down in the street among the convalescent typhus patients, wounded men on crutches, and tattered soldiers with their feet wrapped in rags, so emaciated that their caps seemed two sizes too big. He slowed down and looked hard at them for confirmation of what he intended to say in the Assembly. The street smelled of white-wash, carbolic, and putrefaction, but for him Niš was contaminated also by the rapacity of army contractors, the cupidity of petty merchants in the marketplace, and the selfishness of draft dodgers and the dregs of all Serbia concentrated in its wartime capital. Seeing few others in Niš, he was continually filled with rage and protested both in words and by silence. The hatred he had felt as a student toward commerce and petty tradesmen—a feeling inherited from his father, a peasant rebel, and learned from the socialist teacher Svetozar Marković—rose once more within him. Although he had regarded himself as a politician without prejudice or illusion, recently he had come to see that he had many prejudices, and that their range was growing wider; he also saw, with some bitterness, that anyone who hadn't lived through a war and survived it didn't know his nation, or what people were really like. His anxiety about Ivan, although alleviated by the news he was a prisoner, inflamed his indignation at a world which saw in war and the epidemic an occasion to acquire wealth and flout the law.

It was in such a mood that he had spent the whole night preparing his speech for the Assembly; he was determined to demand the resignation of Pašić, because of the government's unwillingness and incapacity to stop the graft of army contractors, the rapid rise in prices, and the corruption concealed in the poverty of war and the spread of disease. Now as never before, he felt he had the right to say everything to everybody: Ivan, Milena, and Olga stood behind his words. Today he would speak in such a way that this would be visible—in such a way that everyone listening would understand that behind his moral and political condemnation lay not the partisan passion of an Opposition politician, but a higher concern for the fate of Serbia, and a conviction nourished by his own sacrifice and his determination to confirm every word he spoke by action.

In front of the palace of King Miloš Obrenović in Niš, where the sessions of the Serbian National Assembly had been held since the beginning of the war, there had been such a large gathering of people only once before—the previous autumn, when the unification of all the Serbs, Croats, and Slovenes had been proclaimed as the war aim of Serbia. As Vukašin walked past the people, the murmur of voices died down, then swelled again: the newspapers had announced that in his speech he was going to attack Pašić and the government, using evidence not known to the public. He felt glances directed at him to be more hostile than sympathetic, and slowed down so they could have a good look at him. When confronted with explosive questions from reporters, he stopped for a moment as if to reflect, but not even by a flicker of an eyelash did he indicate his readiness to satisfy their curiosity, which cost little and was easily sold.

"Mr. Katić!" cried a voice behind him. A messenger handed him a telegram: "Milena ill. Come at once. Olga." Everything went dim. He walked toward the exit of the building as if rolling down a steep slope; someone blocked his way and brought him back. He surrendered to the dark pressure of people whose faces he hardly recognized; only when there was complete silence, with Pašić's beard swinging to and fro in mute welcome, did he realize that he was in his seat in the Assembly, with a burning sensation in his throat and his eyes hurting from the tears he fought to restrain. He felt desperate because he had agreed to do something unconnected with his personal affairs, something which suddenly seemed quite pointless. When Andra Nikolić, the president of the Assembly, called on him to speak, he remained seated, astounded and overwhelmed by the applause of the Opposition. He wanted to cry out, "I'm not on your side any more!" so as to break the silence in which the president announced once more that the debate would be opened by Vukašin Katić, leader of the Independent Radical Party.

"What are you waiting for, Katić? You haven't forgotten your speech, have you?" said a jeering voice near him.

He got up and walked to the rostrum, baffled by the applause. He didn't know what to say. He hadn't forgotten what he had decided to say the previous night, but now he had different ideas about everything he had intended to say. He remained silent, looking at the floor, listening to the sarcastic comments of the government supporters: "We're waiting to hear our moral mentor!" He remembered how his father had stood, likewise bowed and silent, at the general assembly of the Radical Party when he, his son, egged on by Pašić, had violently attacked the views of his father and his peasant-rebel supporters in the name of the young Radicals and intellectuals. He could hear the sound of his father's stick on the rostrum.

He raised his head and began: "Gentlemen, I'm not going to speak now in the name of my party and the Opposition. You will soon understand why, at this moment, I speak only for myself." The silence, and the rigid faces of the deputies, reporters, and spectators, cut through him like a knife. He was silent for a few moments and then, grasping the reading desk with both hands, he continued in a firm but muted voice: "Our vital anxiety is not how we shall achieve victory in this war. That victory will be decided by the Great Powers, as all our victories and defeats have always been decided by Europe and by Russia. The question for Serbia today is this: how shall those of us who survive justify the great sacrifices we have made, and will continue to make? I firmly believe, gentlemen, that freedom alone is not enough to atone for this time of death. Not even the union of Serbia with the South Slavs can atone for so many graves in Serbia—"

"Defeatism! That's what this is—defeatism!" cried the government supporters.

Without feeling at all offended, he looked them straight in the eyes, waited for the noise to die down, then continued to speak about the price to be paid for the national objectives—the subject on which he and his friends had kept silent since the November meeting of the High Command and the government in Valjevo. In the sudden silence of the Assembly—in which he could no longer see anyone who shared his opinions—he could hear the tapping of Pašić's stick.

"Human dishonesty and greed," his voice boomed, "has so flawed and disfigured our country that it is difficult to defend it on the frontiers in the trenches! The first line of defense of our country is here, in the Assembly. It is in our present capital that we must dig trenches!"

"That's right!" he heard two voices say. They were socialists: their agreement meant nothing to him, nor did he pay any attention to the comments of his friends, who declared that the defeatist tone of his speech would do the party a great deal of harm. Nor was he affected by the attacks of the government deputies, who vied with each other in denouncing his defeatism. He seemed to see no reason to defend himself, which confused everybody. A swelling murmur arose among the deputies, reporters, and spectators: silence was a new tactic on the part of Vukašin Katić, who was famous for his speed in settling accounts with those who opposed him. All he wanted now was to get away from this place, where no one had any idea what was in his heart and mind.

When the session was adjourned, Pašić stopped him at the door and said in a confidential voice: "Come see me in my office this evening, Vukašin. I need you badly."

He nodded vaguely, unable to resist that great white beard which reminded him of his father. He was surrounded by reporters, but turned away and hurried to his office. Pašić had summoned him, yet he must leave for Valjevo today. But how, when travel by train was forbidden because of the epidemic? Should he go in a private car? Najdan's? He would sooner die than go in Najdan's car. Should he ask Pašić for a permit to travel by train? Special influence—disgraceful! How, then, could he go to Valjevo? In his office he stared at a photograph of Milena in her school uniform, carrying a bag over her shoulder. Then he recalled her in her nurse's veil and apron, sitting on the edge of his bed, saying sternly and reproachfully, "Do you remember what you said once to Ivan and me, Father?" He had told them that even parental love must be the reward of virtue. Yes, that's what he had told his children, and he believed it. He had embraced her and told her to go back to the hospital, to her duty. She hadn't shut the door when she left.

A sob convulsed him.

He didn't return to the afternoon session of the Assembly. He lay down on the bed, smoking and waiting for darkness to fall, so that he could go to Pašić's office. He still didn't know how he would get to Valjevo. This visit to Pašić was more painful than the one the previous autumn, when Pašić had sent for him to persuade him to enter a coalition government. Why did Pašić need him this evening, when his attack on the government had been supported by only two deputies, and socialists at that? A warm south wind was blowing, bringing the smell of disease and infection. He would walk to Valjevo!

"Just a moment, Vukašin!" said Najdan Tošić, blocking Vukašin's way. "I only want to say a few words to you. I've heard what happened in the Assembly today."

"We two have nothing to talk about."

"Oh, yes, we have!" said Najdan, walking alongside Vukašin. "According to your moral principles, it's the patriotic duty of us businessmen to lose money, while blood is being shed for the nation; but in what war was trading ever a patriotic activity? People will give their blood for their country, but their money, never! If we give all our money to help the war, what'll we have left for the peace? What's the use of freedom to people who are poor and hungry? After the war, Vukašin, we'll have to give the people work and money, so they can build houses and raise families—so they can *live*. The State will survive, but it can't live with empty coffers!"

"Is that why you're filling your coffers?"

"I'm not filling them with that particular end in view, but my full coffers will help us all in peacetime. A man must make use of every opportunity!"

"Even for plunder?"

"To acquire wealth and property, Vukašin! Since the beginning of the world, wealth has been worth more than freedom. You can do almost anything with wealth, but only certain things with freedom. People either get rich in time of war or they fail. Surely you don't need a dirty contractor like me, with blood on his hands, to point out the lessons of history."

A group of gravediggers returning from the cemetery walked toward them; Najdan paused until they had passed. Vukašin hoped that the sight of them would silence him, but Najdan continued in a somewhat quieter voice: "Every task has its appointed time; this is the time for traders and contractors. What sort of a businessman would I be if I didn't take advantage of it? Money is there to be got. Never pity those whose money is taken—they always manage."

"Will poverty-stricken widows with sick, hungry children manage? And war orphans and invalids?" Vukašin moved on in an effort to shake Najdan off.

"Of course they will! They'll take money from someone else, or steal it. Those who have more will take pity on them. Orphans don't die of hunger because they have no money; they die of hunger only when no one has money, when there are no rich people. That's how it is. Enough of those idiotic socialistic ideas which you are trying to peddle as patriotic slogans! The world is not a monastery. It's a marketplace, a brothel, a casino!"

"What world? Whose?"

"The whole world! Everyone is in the marketplace; those who can't help it are in the brothel, and those who have something are in the casino."

"Then what is my country?"

"My country and yours, and everybody else's, is a full pocket and a full treasury. Those of us who make money decide the outcome of our national aims and the extent of our victory. We do it, and not you people who scribble fine phrases for the newspapers and strut about the Assembly, fighting for ministers' armchairs!"

Vukašin stopped suddenly; he felt like seizing Najdan by the throat, but merely said in a hoarse voice: "That's enough! Milena is ill!" He hurried on, leaving Najdan speechless in the darkness.

In the Prime Minister's headquarters, officials were arranging mattresses on the floor and heating up supper on stoves. A policeman conducted him to Pašić's office and told him that two sick officials had just been moved into the cellar, because there was no room for them in the hospital. So the louse had crawled into the offices of the government—it would infect even the ministers! In this unhappy land, in these disease-ridden times, whom was he opposing? Whose government was he protesting?

"Come in, Vukašin," said Pašić, standing in the doorway. Vukašin walked into the room and sat down in a large leather armchair.

Pašić sat on the edge of a sofa. "I hear your son has been taken prisoner. The worst is over now, unless his health deteriorates. And your wife is working as a nurse, I hear? A remarkable woman!" He was silent for a few moments, then went on: "First of all, my friend, I want to tell you this: to predict evil for the nation is a greater mistake than to predict happiness. Neither those who predict good nor those who predict evil really know the people."

"You're telling me you didn't like my speech?"

"You must say what you believe to be true, but remember this: an honest word reaches only an honest man. As for the nation as a whole, you must either believe in it or say nothing. Those who don't believe in the people have no reason to be in politics. Politics is a job for optimists."

"The time has come, Prime Minister, when those who believe in old maxims will make the biggest mistakes."

"If I could come up with new maxims, I'd abandon the old ones at once. Let me tell you why I asked you to come here: the Allies are pointing yet another knife at our throat. Right from the start they've been putting pressure on us to give Macedonia to the Bulgarians, and now they're trying to make us give up Dalmatia and the islands to Italy. They're carving up Croatia. As for Istria, the less said the better; they regard that as Austrian territory."

"So I've heard. Last night I saw Franjo Supilo. He's in despair."

Vukašin lit a cigarette. Pašić hadn't summoned him to tell him about new Allied pressure on Serbia.

Pašić ran his fingers slowly through his beard and stared at the floor for some time. "Our great Allies reproach us for being impatient to unite with the Croats and Slovenes. We're asking a lot, they say. If you get Bosnia and Hercegovina and the coastline as far as Split, that's enough; that's what the English and the Russians are suggesting."

"The English don't conceal the fact that they're our enemies, and nothing will change that. After the assassination at Sarajevo, they said that Serbia should be sunk to the bottom of the sea."

"I know. Still, we must ask from the English only what it's to their advantage to give. What suits them must suit us. The same applies to all the Great Powers."

"It's perfectly clear that in this war too the Great Powers will make agreements only at the expense of the small nations. That's the law of the world. Let's not cherish any illusions, Prime Minister." He was anxious to end this conversation as soon as possible.

"It doesn't help to complain. They can't hear us. We must ingratiate ourselves with people in St. Petersburg, Paris, and London and voice our complaints on their doorsteps. Others have left for St. Petersburg and London. You must set out for Paris immediately."

"Paris? That's impossible!"

Pašić continued as if he hadn't heard him: "Tell the French that the Serbs and Croats are a single people with two faiths. Tell them that although we Serbs lived for five hundred years under the Turks, since the time of Napoleon we've learned all that Europe knows about the rights of nationalities and freedom. We must get it into the heads of sensible people in England and France that on our side we merely want the rights which are the basis of their own national aims."

Vukašin interrupted: "Prime Minister, I must go to Valjevo. My daughter has typhus."

Pašić was silent for a moment. "Poor child! You must go by the night train to see her. I'll give you a permit for the official coach. But come back as soon as possible, so you can leave for France. You must do this, my friend."

"I can't, Prime Minister, not until my daughter is better. I can't leave."

"Tasks affecting the fate of a nation have to be done only once in a lifetime. What isn't done now can't be made up for later."

"If something should happen to her, what would I do, Prime Minister? And my son's in a prison camp."

Pašić looked at him relentlessly, and said quietly as he got up: "You must go. I'll make out a travel permit, and you can leave for Valjevo at midnight."

Vukašin felt he no longer had the right to resist. What would be left of him and his family after the war if his conscience kept forcing him to make sacrifices?

Olga hadn't sent the telegram to Vukašin the day Milena fell ill; the whole night passed before she pulled herself together and wrote, "Come at once."

When Bogdan's mother told her that Milena had fallen ill, Olga and Doctor Radić hurried to Bogdan's room, where they found Milena hanging on to Bogdan's arm and moaning. "Don't let them take me to the hospital! Save me, Bogdan! Swear that you won't let me leave this room!"

Bogdan comforted her and gave her his solemn promise. Petrana assured Olga that Bogdan had another room, and Doctor Radić agreed that this was the best place for her to be nursed. Long moments elapsed before Olga summoned the strength to undress Milena and lay her down on Bogdan's bed. Milena's fear of being taken to the hospital, and the bewildered way in which she clung to Bogdan, suddenly awoke in Olga a feeling of guilt, which flared up into anxiety for Milena's life and for her own relationship with Mihajlo.

During the first night of Milena's illness, which the two of them spent at her bedside, Olga was amazed to discover that she saw in Mihajlo Radić not only a doctor who might save her child, but a person in some way more necessary to her at this time than Vukašin. My God, can this be true? she said to herself, and moved away. He was seated next to Milena, listening to her breathing and her pulse, speaking only when it was necessary to change her compresses or bring her some tea. In his absorption in Milena, Olga saw much more than a doctor's professional anxiety, and felt deeply grateful to him. When he got up to go to the hospital at daybreak, she almost cried out, Don't leave me now! After he had gone she put out the lamp, sat in his chair, and put her head down close to Milena's; a deep shudder overwhelmed her, and she shook as though with fever.

"You're shivering, Mrs. Katić—you're ill! Holy Mother of God!" whispered Petrana, standing over Olga with some tea and honey on a tray.

Olga straightened up. "No, I'm not ill. How's Bogdan?"

"No temperature again last night—may the Mother of God be merciful!"

Milena was still asleep, breathing heavily. Olga hurried to the post office to send a telegram to Vukašin. On her way back to Milena her whole being was filled with hope that Vukašin's arrival would change everything and save her from the great uncertainty engulfing every aspect of her life.

Just before noon Doctor Radić arrived, stern and silent in a way she had never seen him before. He came up to Milena, examined her, felt her stomach, and listened to her heart; he did these things for so long and with such intensity that Olga exclaimed, "Say something, Doctor!"

He merely nodded. On his way out, in front of the gate, he said, "Olga, please believe that Milena will come out of this all right."

He spoke with such conviction that Olga didn't dare ask for explanations or proof. She returned quickly to the house and stared at Milena's face, waiting for her to open her eyes, so that she could see in them confirmation of Doctor Radić's assertion: did they have that look which she had seen so often in the eyes of the dying? In the Warehouse of the Dead she had discovered that those on the point of death died first in their eyes; death first of all broke up something in the light of the pupil, clouding it. As she looked at this dimness in the patients' pupils—this slantwise glance from the very end of life, when a shadow filled all the wrinkles in the face and darkened the forehead, and a wave of trembling spread over the body, and the movements of the hands became aimless and confused—she realized that she had always believed in the soul, and in the pain of its separation from the body. Milena opened her eyes: her expression was burning and feverish, but there was nothing at all of that other look in her eyes. Olga smiled at her and kissed her forehead.

This faith sustained her all day, but during the night it darkened: Milena's temperature went up, and the delirium of typhus possessed her. Mihajlo Radić restored her hope; he spent the second night with her at Milena's bedside, as silent and anxious as the first. When they parted he said, convincingly, "I'm sure Milena will get well."

On the fourth night Milena's condition worsened, and Mihajlo Radić didn't go to the hospital at daybreak; remaining at Milena's side, he gave her an injection of an English antipyretic. Olga noticed that he took these powders himself; she was frightened by the expression on his face, especially his exhausted eyes.

"Do you have a fever?"

"No, I'm just tired."

She wanted to continue the conversation but his face clouded and remained so until the door slowly opened and Vukašin appeared. Mihajlo Radić got up and moved away from Milena's bed.

Vukašin walked up to Milena like a penitent. Olga stiffened at the expression on his face and retreated to another corner of the room. He took both his daughter's hands and pressed them to his lips and face, whispering as he bent over her: "Look at me, my darling! Look at me."

Milena opened her eyes and muttered: "Don't let them take me to the hospital, Father! They'll kill me."

"I won't let them take you! Don't be afraid!"

She jerked her hands out of his, plunged them into her hair, and began to tear out handfuls of hair, gnashing her teeth as she did so.

"My poor child!" cried Vukašin, terror-stricken, as he grabbed hold of her hands.

With a shudder Olga recalled her first encounter with her sick daughter and looked at Vukašin's bent shoulders; they were shaking. She grew rigid in the silence. More strongly than ever before, she was tormented by guilt: by staying in the hospital, she had endangered Milena's life. She had done this under an impulse which, that night in Vojvoda Mišić's house, had been stronger than her fear for Milena's life and more important than anything she had ever felt. The feeling that Mihajlo Radić had awakened in her, altering the whole course of her life, had surpassed her fear that Milena might fall ill. My God, is this really true? she thought. There was no room left for any fear for herself, none at all! Yet why hadn't this punishment been exacted from her? How was it that she had never thought that all three of them could find themselves together, silent as they were now, not looking at each other, listening to each other's sighs? What would happen when their glances met? The silence seemed endless. She must say something at once. When she and Vukašin were alone, she would tell him everything; it was too important to be passed over in silence. She had never told a lie, and now least of all had she any right to do so. Did she want to save some kind of honor and dignity? Was there anything in herself worth saving?

Vukašin and Mihajlo Radić were talking; she could only see the movement of their lips. Mihajlo's glance was sometimes perplexed, sometimes threatening—unfamiliar to her. Vukašin was looking at him with concentration, but gently; it was rare, very rare, for him to look at anyone like that. Mihajlo said something quickly and lit a cigarette, breaking the match as he had done that night on the train; Vukašin was listening attentively, his arms folded. She could hear the dark, hoarse tone of his voice, typical of when he was deeply moved or excited: "I'm grateful to you from the bottom of my heart, Doctor, for everything you've done for my wife and daughter."

Olga's face burned with shame; she could have hugged Vukašin for these words spoken with the sincerity of a man of pure feelings. She walked up to the window and leaned against it. Why didn't Mihajlo Radić leave?

"I'll be here this evening, Mr. Katić, by seven at the latest."

This isn't the last time the three of us will meet, it occurred to her. She would hear the two of them talking every day—Vukašin with respect for the doctor treating his daughter, but Mihajlo perhaps with a feeling of scorn for the politician, the man striving for power. Today she must cut through the tangle inside her, pluck it out forever. But what unworthy element should she repudiate, what must she stifle and what must she do against herself—and how? Mihajlo Radić left. Vukašin's hand fell heavily on her shoulder. "We haven't even greeted each other, Olga."

She took his hand and pressed it to her cheek, her eyes full of tears.

He embraced her gently and kissed her forehead. "Forgive me," he whispered. "Forgive me for leaving you alone for several days with Milena ill. For leaving the two of you alone. I thought I was doing some good these last few days, helping the cause for which our children have sacrificed themselves."

"That's what I wanted to do, too, Vukašin."

Milena groaned, and he went up to her. "I'm here, Milena, and I won't go away without you. Can you hear me, my darling? You'll soon be well again, I'm sure of it."

Olga brought chairs for Vukašin and herself, and they sat down beside Milena, gazing at her exhausted and sweating face. It was time to change her compresses, but Olga couldn't do it; she had to say something to Vukašin first. Yet all she had in mind seemed quite without significance before the fate over which they sat, bowed in silence.

"I have confidence in that doctor. I don't know why, but I have," Vukašin said finally.

If I speak a single sentence about Mihajlo Radić, she thought, I'll have to tell him everything. She took the burning compress from Milena's forehead and went out to soak it in vinegar.

They spent the day looking after Milena, fearing the coming night, and waiting for Mihajlo Radić; but he didn't come when he had promised, and still hadn't arrived at nine o'clock. Milena was delirious. Vukašin became restless, and Olga decided to go to the hospital to look for Radić. She put on her coat and was just going out when Doctor Sergeev appeared in the doorway.

"Mihajlo Radić has come down with it," he said in Russian. "He's lying in his office, with a temperature of a hundred and five. That's what happens in this world, I'm afraid. Death takes the special few, but lets the mob survive." He went up to Milena's bed, took out his stethoscope, and began to examine her.

On his fifth evening in Valjevo, Vukašin Katić decided to call at the First Army headquarters. He gave his name to the officer on duty and waited in a half-darkened corridor saturated with carbolic and naphthalene, remembering that November night when he had walked along the same corridor from the courtroom, feeling like a criminal, after the secret meeting of the generals and the politicians. That night, in order not to become a traitor to the national cause, he had betrayed some of his own convictions: he hadn't opposed sending the students to the front. Not because he was afraid of Prince Alexander, Pašić, the generals, and his political opponents. He had yielded before Živojin Mišić, his friend, in the face of his gloomy conviction and the menacing movement of his thumb over the war map of Serbia.

Vojvoda Mišić came to meet him and embraced him. "I've been

worried about you, and waiting to see you ever since you arrived. Louisa tells me that Milena has spots now, which means the disease will disappear in a few days. No need to worry about Ivan. A lot of their people are here with us, so they have to look after ours and feed them properly." He led Vukašin into his office and brought a chair up to his table for him.

Vukašin listened in silence. He was embarrassed by the intimacy of this strong man, but at the same time grateful for it.

"Nadežda Petrović is in critical condition," said Mišić.

"I went to see her today. She didn't recognize me."

"Tomorrow I'll go see her. I'd like to please her, but I don't know how. Should I give her a medal for bravery? You know her better than I do."

"If she's conscious, it would please her more to get a sprig of flowering dogwood. Forgive me, Živojin, for delaying until now my congratulations on your promotion and the victory on Suvobor. Don't frown and don't try to deny the victory. It was dearly bought, Živojin, but you're worthy of it."

"Vukašin," said Mišić, rolling a cigarette slowly, "I'm not the victor. It's the soldiers. The men who gave their lives—hungry, barefoot, without overcoats, walking in mud and snow up to their waists. I just arranged the troops, and on some occasions I botched it. That could have cost us plenty if Potiorek had been a smarter commander, if he hadn't been fighting against us with contempt and hate in his heart. No great task should be undertaken with hate. Even when we're defending our country, we mustn't do it with hate in our hearts."

"How are your childen? Are they well?"

"Yes, they're all right, but the lice are destroying my army. Of four divisions, one is wiped out. And the silence, Vukašin! Not a single bullet fired. I don't look at the map any more. Every morning my officers bring me reports from the hospitals: how many sick and dead. Instead of trenches, we're digging graves. The baggage trains are carrying corpses instead of ammunition and shells. The buglers are playing funeral marches, not sounding the charge." He fell silent, his lips and hands trembling.

They smoked in silence. Then Mišić gave a start and hit his knee with his fist.

"I've forgotten! I'm put out by this, but I can't do a thing. A telegram arrived for you from Pašić." He handed it to Vukašin: "Come back to Niš as soon as possible. You must set out on the journey we discussed. Pašić."

Vukašin crumpled the telegram and raised his arm to throw it in the stove, but put it in his pocket instead.

"What'll I do, Živojin?"

"Where is Pašić sending you?"

"To France. To promote our union with the Croats and Slovenes."

"I hear our Allies are offering Dalmatia, Istria, and the islands to Italy as a reward for entering the war. Is that the last word?"

"That's what they've told our government, and they're putting pressure on us to give up Macedonia to Bulgaria."

"Nice friends and allies we've got!"

"Pašić believes it may be possible to persuade the Allies to be more lenient. That's why he wants me to go to Paris. Olga will be heartbroken."

Mišić walked over and stood beside the window, staring into the darkness; then he came back and put his hands on Vukašin's shoulders. "Tell me, Vukašin, do you people in the Assembly and the government know—does the Opposition know—how many Croatian units there are in the Austro-Hungarian army? Almost half of Potiorek's army was made up of our brothers!"

"That, Živojin, is the strategy and politics of Vienna. They want to force us to slaughter each other and so kill in us any desire for unification."

"Why are they fighting so eagerly? Why don't they surrender?"

"How can they not fight when there are Austrian officers behind them who'll kill anyone who disobeys orders? You know that better than I do."

"Yes, I know it. And the atrocities committed against us by our brothers in Austrian uniform. Do people in Niš know this?"

"Yes, they do. But they have to keep quiet about it because there are plenty of Serbs from Bosnia and Croatia in the Austrian army."

"There are, but fewer; and they surrender as soon as they can. Do people in Niš know that the first troops to enter Belgrade were Croats, and that the Croatian tricolor flew over the palace beside the Austrian and Hungarian flags?"

"They know that, too, Živojin. These are the old dirty tricks of Vienna."

"Don't these facts tell you politicians anything?"

"Of course they do! They tell us none of us must ever again fight for a foreigner, never be against each other—a reason for our unification."

"What makes you politicians so sure that the Croats want to be united with us?"

"Of course they do. All elements with any national awareness want union with the Serbs—a united state. I've been with Croats in Niš on several occasions lately; I feel much closer to Franjo Supilo as a politician than I do to Pašić. And then the Croatian volunteers . . ."

"A few students, five writers, and a hundred Dalmatians!"

"Throughout history the majority has never been on the side of progress. The most important events have been set in motion by a handful of bold, farsighted people!"

"There are few Croats of this type, very few!"

"In the present conditions, Živojin, all this must be forgiven. The Croats are an unfortunate people, more so than we are. For centuries they've been fighting for others, and now they're being forced to give their lives in a war against their own freedom and their brothers."

"When people look at each other over gunsights and bayonets, there is no brotherhood! Not even all the Serbs are my brothers. I'm surprised, Vukašin, that you believe that people who haven't lived together, who don't know each other, can desire the same thing."

Vukašin straightened up, astonished by Mišić's words. It was true that Mišić was a conservative in politics and a peasant at heart, but it didn't bode well that he should think as he did. Vukašin wasn't in the mood for such a conversation, but he felt he must go on.

"The Italians who were united under Cavour didn't know each other, nor did the Germans united by Bismarck. Even their languages were less similar. But we speak the *same* language, Živojin!"

"Do we, indeed? Only individuals and nations on an equal footing speak the same language. A free people and a subject people do not speak the same language, even when they understand each other. The Croats, to their own misfortune, are a subject people."

"All of us in the Balkans are slaves, even when we believe that we're free. We must unite so that we *can* speak the same language."

"What will this unification with the Croats and Slovenes achieve? In what way will we all be better off?"

Vukašin shrank from a clash with this man who had never been closer to him, and whose human support was essential to him at this time. He said in a quiet, melancholy voice: "If we're to survive in the face of the German and Russian Empires, and the ambitions of Italy in the Adriatic—if we're to remain free—I don't see any alternative to union with all the South Slavs and the creation of a single state. We'd be the most powerful nation in the Balkans—something quite new between Vienna and Istanbul."

"But the victors and vanquished cannot unite. Unification would only increase hatred in everybody. If by some misfortune it should come about, then we'll have lost the war!"

"If it doesn't happen, we'll lose all future wars. Only by uniting into a single powerful and democratic state can we South Slavs become part of Europe, on an equal footing with the other countries, and share in its civilization. There can be no more splendid purpose for our generation, Živojin. That's our mission. If we don't succeed, we'll remain a hotbed of quarrels and intrigue, and the Great Powers will continue to bargain with our blood."

"Fine ideals, but no substance. How can we forget the past? Dare we close our eyes to reality?"

"There's no reason for us to close our eyes to reality, but if we don't look forward to tomorrow, we'll remain blind. I'm troubled by your point of view. It can only lead to the old unhappy state of affairs."

Mišić came and sat down behind his desk. "Listen, Vukašin. It's my job to work for the defense of our people on the battlefield. But I feel uneasy. I fear the embrace of a brother who wields a bayonet. I am afraid of being under the same roof with someone who hasn't shared my suffering."

"This war must see the end of our internal conflicts in the Balkans, Živojin. If we wish to survive. And our fratricidal wars cannot be prevented except by unification and liberation. There is no other way."

For some time they smoked in silence. Vukašin felt better now that they were no longer arguing; but Vojvoda Mišić took off his cap and said, raising his voice: "Just let me tell you one thing more, Vukašin. The unification of peoples divided for centuries is of no use unless they've made equal sacrifices of flesh and blood in order to obtain it. Yes, flesh and blood! We aren't all fighting equally hard for this union; on one side nothing is being spilled but ink. That's no way to unite people who've been separated for centuries—it's impossible!" He banged his fist on the table and stood up.

"There's a great deal of truth in what you say," Vukašin said cautiously, "but we must have a correct understanding of the times we live in, Živojin. We live in an age when only large states can survive and make progress. Only great states have any future, especially in the Balkans. If we Serbs and our Croatian and Slovenian brothers can't look beyond the trenches of today—if we remember only our wrongs and our wounds—then we've lost the war for our grandchildren. I'm firmly convinced of this, Živojin."

Mišić's orderly, Dragutin, brought in coffee. Mišić waited for him to leave, then sat down and continued: "*I* am firmly convinced that for a great state everything must be on a grand scale. What have we got? Politicians! A politicians' affair, that's what our unification will be. Don't be angry."

"Our unification is a matter of historical sense, and national sense, too, in which even you believe, Vojvoda."

"A nation, Vukašin, must always have greater strength than is needed for the aims it sets itself. Only such a nation can be happy."

Vukašin sipped his coffee in silence and didn't listen any more to what Mišić was saying. He remembered Milena's face, disfigured by livid spots and blisters filled with inky blood, and her bloodshot eyes, her hoarse breathing, the convulsive way in which she seized his hands. A south wind shook the windows. Vukašin got up. "Good night, Živojin. I'll drop in tomorrow about noon."

Mišić invited him to his house for supper, but Vukašin firmly refused. Dejected, he went out and hurried back to Milena.

Olga was waiting for him in front of Bogdan's house. "Milena isn't asleep. Bogdan is telling her what it was like when he and Ivan were fighting on Suvobor; but I just can't listen."

"Calm yourself, Olga. She'll certainly get better, but we still have our worries about Ivan, and about getting together under the same roof again. Pašić has sent a telegram asking me to come to Niš immediately and then leave for France. I'm on the rack again, torn between my children and my country."

He embraced her gently; she bent beneath the pressure of his hand, unable to respond to his desire for intimacy, restraining her sobs.

"Don't upset yourself any more," he said. "I won't do anything ever again that you and Milena don't agree to. I've come to understand something of this world and our fate in it."

Olga wanted to remove herself from his arm, so that she could see his face on the first occasion that he had spoken such words. Has he changed, she thought, or has he seen the change in me? Does he suspect something?

"I've come to understand something too, Vukašin. I won't oppose you any more. You must go on with the things you have to do."

"I can't leave here until Milena is on the road to recovery."

"She'll be a lot better in a few days, unless something unexpected happens, pray God it won't. You must go to France—that's what Ivan would say. It's Nadežda I'm crying for. She died this evening; I saw her. The nurses were covering her with lilacs."

"Nadežda! That marvelous woman!"

"Not so loud. We must conceal Nadežda's death from Milena."

Vukašin moved away from his wife, to observe a moment of silence for Nadežda alone. Olga walked past him, to keep silent her fear for Mihajlo Radić, whom she had visited briefly that evening and found in a condition in which only Doctor Sergeev saw any hope.

Vojvoda Mišić put on his overcoat to go have his supper, then paused. Vukašin hadn't shaken his convictions in any respect. In talking with his friend, he had opposed his ideas on the national aims— opposed a man who was a violent opponent of Pašić in all matters except union with the Croats and Slovenes. For both of them this was the great national aim. All politicians proclaim high-sounding aims, dangerous aims, and for these dubious and dangerous aims *he* must wage war, give orders that cause regiments and divisions to be slaughtered, bear the title of vojvoda, and rejoice in fame. His military oath was choking his conscience. . . . .

The telephone broke through his silent musing; he lifted the receiver. Hearing the asthmatic coughing of Vojvoda Putnik, he waited for him to speak first.

"Good evening, Mišić. I'm not calling you for a report about the hospitals. The situation on that front is improving, thank God. I don't want to hear a word this evening about illness and infection."

"I was intending to call you in the morning, sir, to inform you that there isn't a single grain of animal fodder in the First Army stores. The animals are dying, and my baggage train is reduced by half."

"I know all that! Have the soldiers let the animals loose in the fields to find food? The grass is coming up and the trees are in bud. The animals can feed on that until hay and oats arrive from Russia."

"I gave orders yesterday, but we've run out of salt. If the animals aren't given salt to lick with this green stuff, which is quite inadequate as fodder, and water to drink with it, they'll be ill."

"I've asked the Minister of War to obtain salt as quickly as possible."

"In a few days' time we won't even be able to give the soldiers half rations."

"I've asked Pašić to call an urgent meeting of the government; the chief quartermaster will report on the food-supply situation."

"As regards the hospitals and food for the patients, I have to resort to requisitioning. Private trading will be punished by court-martial."

"Mišić, I haven't called to hear your complaints. I don't allow either you or the other army commanders to do what I can't do myself. If it makes things easier for you, you have your wives and God."

"We need our wives only until we become army commanders, and God when we lose the war."

"On the contrary, Mišić, God is essential if we're to become army commanders; if we lose the war, all we need is our wives."

"It all depends on our war aims, sir."

"The Russians have requested us to launch an attack across the Drina and the Sava as soon as possible, so as to carry the war into Austro-Hungarian territory. They've asked us to take the Montenegrin army under our command and move toward Ljubljana and Budapest."

"I can't hear you, sir."

"I can understand you perfectly well, Mišić. Please do not lose sight of this fact."

"I won't. We could move toward Ljubljana and Budapest with two French airplanes, until a bullet shot us down like stray greese."

"I can't hear you, Mišić. The line is bad again."

"How are we to cross the Drina and the Sava with a sick, hungry, barefoot army?"

"Someone has cut in on our conversation. Hello, Putnik speaking. This is the High Command.".

"I can hear you perfectly well, sir."

"Grand Duke Nikolay Nikolayevich says the Russians will invade Hungary and smash the Austro-Hungarian army, if the English, French, and Serbian armies go immediately on the offensive on all fronts and force the Austrians to withdraw troops from the Russian front. Did you hear me, Mišić?"

"May I ask a question, sir?"

"Within twenty-four hours you must send a report to the High Command concerning First Army requirements for crossing the Drina toward Zagreb and Ljubljana."

"I can give you that report immediately."

"There's no hurry, Mišić. Is it raining out there?"

"There's a south wind, and by the look of the window I would say that it's raining slightly."

"Let's hope so. It's time there was rain."

"If only it would snow!"

"Military commanders can believe in miracles—after the battle. Don't you agree, Mišić?"

"I hear that our Allies are going to give Dalmatia to Italy if she enters the war; and the Adriatic islands."

"There's a terrible wind here in Kragujevac, enough to blow the windows out. Good night, Mišić."

"Get me Colonel Milić," said Mišić to the officer on duty. "Mišić speaking. Good evening, Milić! By noon tomorrow I want a detailed report on the state of your division and everything required for an advance across the Drina."

"I suppose the Austrians haven't moved against Serbia again, sir?"

"No, they haven't. This gives us our chance to move into Austro-Hungarian territory. The Russians are coming down from the Carpathians. The English and French armies are also preparing an offensive. Hello, Milić! Can't you hear me, Colonel?"

"I can give you the report right now, sir. Forty percent of the men in my division are sick, not counting those who've died. The condition of the animals is even worse. I have no baggage train."

"You have until noon tomorrow, so think carefully about your report. Good night, Colonel. Get me the commander of the Drina Division. Hello, Smiljanić! Spring is on the way; can you hear the wind blowing from the mountains? There'll be leaves on the trees in the woods by Sunday."

"The wind brings sickness, sir. There's been a sudden increase of deaths in the hospitals today."

"The sun will warm us and burn away our sickness. We soldiers and peasants must get down to work. We must prepare the plow and the seed."

"This year we won't have anything to plow with or sow."

"As long as our nation exists, we'll find some means of plowing and sowing; but each to his own task. Your task, Colonel, is to prepare your division for an advance across the Drina as soon as possible. Be conscientious and resolute. Good-by, Smiljanić. Get me the commander of the Danube Division. Good evening, Kajafa. You haven't gone to bed yet?"

"I've been talking with the chief of staff, sir. He tells me that the Allies are pressuring our government again to give up Macedonia and Dalmatia."

"Kajafa, you know what I think of soldiers who meddle in politics."

"Sir, allow me to convey to you my poor opinion of politicians who aren't soldiers. As for soldiers who don't think—who's cut us off? Hello, Vojvoda! I simply wanted to tell you that soldiers who don't think die like fools and kill from fear or for plunder."

"It's our good fortune, Kajafa, that we have something to think about: how to get the troops in a fit state to advance across the Drina and the Sava as soon as possible. Hello, Kajafa! Why don't you say something?"

"I'm thinking, sir."

"The situation with our Allies is such that we must be ready for an offensive at any moment. The Russians will come down from the Carpathians and the English and the French are about to launch a big offensive. If the Serbian army isn't ready to attack at the same time, Serbia will lose its dearly bought good name with the Allies. What are you thinking about for so long, Colonel?"

"Our good name with the Allies. The great admiration expressed by the Allies for Serbian victories. About how Serbia is about to become the sacrificial lamb. Have I overstepped the bounds of my competence, sir?"

"If we don't undertake the offensive required of us, that'll be the end of our union with the Croats and Slovenes, Kajafa, and good-by to Dalmatia."

"If we cross the Sava and the Drina in our present state, it'll be good-by to Serbia, too!"

"You've overstepped the bounds of your competence, Kajafa! By noon tomorrow, please send me a report on your division's requirements for crossing the Drina."

He slammed down the receiver and walked wearily to the window. The wind shook the pane and spattered it with rain. He opened it and said to himself: "May the heavens empty and drown this and all other headquarters! And the hospitals and cemeteries. And submerge all roads that lead into the unknown!"

Adam Katić and Aleksa Dačić were traveling home on leave, among the first allowed to do so when the epidemic was almost over. Meeting in a train crowded with soldiers, they embraced like brothers. When they began to talk of their war experiences, Aleksa said that the corporal in his platoon had been Ivan, Vukašin's son, and that he had been reported missing in their last battle because he had lost his glasses the day before. But he concealed the fact that in his pocket he was carrying Ivan's notebook, which he had found in a knapsack thrown in the underbrush; it was full of comments on the fighting in which he, Aleksa, had taken part, yet his own experiences were not what Ivan had recorded. He told Adam that he had been promoted to corporal and awarded a medal, and vowed that he would finish the war either a sergeant with the Karageorge Star or dead. Adam remained unmoved by the news about the cousin whom he didn't know, and recounted to Aleksa in great detail how he had lost his horse, Dragan, which Aleksa had loved and had sometimes ridden; but now the news of this loss didn't affect him at all. These two were contemporaries in age, rivals in the pursuit of war widows, a young master and a young hired man, the one a cavalryman, the other a foot soldier in the First Army. As soon as they caught sight of the Morava they fell silent: for a long time neither had heard anything about their families at home. It was a bright, sunny day with a wide blue sky overhead. The poplars and willow trees were green, the unplowed fields yellow, the hedges already in flower.

When they got off the train at Palanka, Adam didn't want to walk to Prerovo, but set off in search of a carriage—in vain, since all the carriage drivers had either been drafted or had died of typhus. He decided to wait until dusk and then set out, so that no one would see him coming on foot. He didn't say this to Aleksa in so many words, but suggested they lunch together in the Hotel Europa and then find someone to drive them to Prerovo.

Aleksa didn't accept this invitation. He was in a hurry to get to Prerovo and to pass through the village at twilight, when all the people would be in their courtyards or the street, where they could see his corporal's star and his medal. Walking briskly, he set off toward the village, overtaking several soldiers on the way. He reached the outskirts just as dusk was beginning to fall, and removed his tattered overcoat so that his corporal's rank and medal would show. Calling to the first woman he saw in a sheepfold, he asked about his folks at home. She told him right off that his brother Miloje had died of his wound, and that his sister-in-law and nephew were ill. Aleksa's face clouded, and he slowed down but didn't weep; he would do that later when alone in the dark. He loitered about Prerovo, staring into every courtyard, learning from the mourning flags on the eaves who had died or been killed; there were many. The road was empty, as were the courtyards. No dogs barked and there was nobody for him to greet. As soon as he caught sight of a child he called him by name and greeted him, and stopped in front of every woman, just so that he might be seen. No one cried out in joyful surprise at seeing him, which pained him: after all, he wasn't coming home from the fair! What was the point of risking your life if after the war there was only silence? He swallowed a few scalding tears for his two slain brothers, then at the side of the road caught sight of a smile, the first he had seen; it was a woman sitting on a pile of hay, a woman in mourning. He felt rather embarrassed and wanted to greet her and then hurry on, but she stopped him, leaning on her pitchfork.

"Aleksa, how thin you are! I heard that you'd been killed, too."

"The war's still on, Jelka. When did your brother die?"

"In the autumn—a shell got him." She sank down on the hay beside her pitchfork.

He opened his mouth to say that her brother's death was an easy one, then realized that she now had a dowry of fifteen hectares of land in the Morava valley and a courtyard full of buildings. He looked at each building as if seeing it for the first time, as though he hadn't known them well enough as a hired man. Then, without saying good-by, he hurried on down the lane.

He decided not to go straight home but to drop by the district office and the inn, so that Aćim Katić would see him, and the school-master, Kosta Dumović, and some other old men who were usually sitting in front of the inn. He would tell Aćim about his grandson Ivan; he wondered whether he should give him Ivan's notebook or take it to Vukašin Katić. Vukašin was a powerful man in politics and had been a minister; Aleksa might need his help to get some sort of government job, and perhaps Vukašin would give him a reward.

The only person he found in front of the district office was the drunken drummer Radoje, who wept when he saw him and said that his son had been killed, Miloje's inseparable companion in tiddly-winks and fishing. But just now Aleksa didn't want to see his tears and listen to his weeping; you had to go to the war, and whoever came back—well, so much the better for him. By chance no bullet had got Aleksa yet, so he was coming home on leave, but one would get him sooner or later. In front of the inn he didn't find a living soul! Where could they be, those old men who had sat around Aćim Katić in front of the inn at twilight on warm evenings ever since he could remem-ber? Surely they hadn't all died of typhus. He looked in the doorway of the inn: there were sick people lying on straw pallets on the floor, some of them children. A black-bearded doctor in a white coat was feeding a small boy who was being held with great difficulty by Natalia.

"Where's the inn now?" he asked those who looked at him in astonishment from their mattresses.

Natalia smiled at him joyfully and ran up to embrace him. He dropped the overcoat he'd been holding under his arm and looked at her sadly in embarrassment, wondering how to tell her that Bogdan Dragović had said she was his girlfriend. She looked at him joyfully and clapped him on the shoulder in congratulations for his promo-tion and medal; the doctor came up to them, smiling. Natalia said he was a Frenchman named Charles Garen who was treating typhus patients in Prerovo and the surrounding area while living with Aćim Katić. Aleksa nodded, avoiding her eyes: he would tell her about Bog-dan tomorrow, when they were alone. Natalia said that his sister-in-law's illness was passing; as for his nephew, Radoša, his spots were already drying up. Aleksa saluted the Frenchman and strode off to-ward his own house, then took pity on Natalia and turned back; he called her over and told her that his corporal, Bogdan Dragović, had been wounded and taken prisoner.

"You mean he was wounded, *then* taken prisoner?"

"Yes, he was seriously wounded, then taken prisoner together with his commanding officer, Major Gavrilo Stanković."

"You don't know any more?"

"No, I don't, Natalia."

She burst out sobbing and struck her head against the trunk of an old acacia tree. Aleksa turned around and hurried to his house; he didn't stop any more, not even in front of the old men sitting in silence on their porches. He no longer wanted to meet or see anybody.

"So you're alive, Aleksa! Welcome home, my boy!" cried Aćim Katić from his porch, banging his stick against the railings.

"Adam is still in Palanka, but he'll be here by evening," said Aleksa, and continued on his way to his own poverty-stricken courtyard, with two black flags hanging from the house. He opened the gate slowly, caught sight of Tola standing in the doorway, and stepped across the threshold, waving his arms but unable to speak. His nephews came out of the house, squeezing between their grandfather's legs. His mother Andja pushed Tola out of the way to embrace him; Tola shook hands with him only after Aleksa had silently offered his hand to his sister-in-law. Once Aleksa had sat down under the big blossoming dogwood tree and begun to distribute little knives and Catholic religious pictures on gold chains to the children from his spoils of war, Tola slipped off into the plum orchard to cry where no one would see him, and to kill the last two chickens for Aleksa's supper.

Meanwhile, after lunching in the Hotel Europa and learning from friends of his father that everyone in his house was well, Adam waited until dusk and then set out for Prerovo. He walked slowly, allowing himself to be overtaken by other soldiers in a greater hurry to get home. He kept stopping to listen to the Morava and to breathe in the scent of the leafy willow trees; he picked some young poplar leaves, rubbed them between his palms, and smelled them: they brought back memories of how he had galloped along the Morava as a boy and a young man, over meadows, piles of hemp, and watermelons. Everything that had been part of his prewar life was gone forever. He didn't know why, but he knew that this was so; it was in the scent of the poplars, the poppies, and the rotting tree trunks. The same sadness was in the Morava as it fought its way over the rapids; it rustled through the leafy treetops of the poplars with a sound similar to that in the ash trees at night, when Natalia had gone away to Belgrade to study and he hadn't seen her until Christmas. It was better for him not to have seen her during that vacation or that summer; now he no longer wanted to ride his horse through the meadows of Prerovo and along the Morava secretly at night. Somewhere in the darkness a woman began to wail for her son. Who would do that for me if I'd been killed, he wondered. If his mother were alive he'd now be hurrying home, not dragging his steps, sniffing at the leaves, and listening to the river; but he didn't remember his mother; he had only seen her with George in two photographs. It was a long time, very long, since he had been conscious of his mother; the thought slowed him down. The night stars had appeared and the new moon was descending onto the mountain.

In front of the first house in Prerovo he stopped to listen for the dogs; surely the typhus hadn't killed them, too. There were no lights anywhere. He'd go straight to Vinka. It was from her farm that he'd gone off to the war at dawn, from her ample breasts, leaving her in her nightgown, half naked and weeping on a heap of maize. Yes, he'd go to her first, and onto the maize again. He set out for Vinka's house along an empty lane; it was dead quiet, as though the frost had Prerovo and the Morava fettered in its icy grip. He felt afraid, he didn't know of whom or what. He had never felt such fear in this lane, not even when he'd gone to women with angry husbands and expected to hear their double-barreled shotguns firing into the hayloft from an ambush. He hadn't trembled like this before his squadron charged. He grasped at the fence and stood for a long time to calm himself: it was quiet in Vinka's courtyard. Perhaps her father-in-law and mother-in-law had died, or perhaps her little son, Boja, was ill. He walked toward the gate, but that wasn't the way he used to come to her, so he jumped over the fence, snapping the binding rope. The sound reverberated through Prerovo and the rope tripped him up. He took off his torn shoes and, carrying them in his hands, set off toward her window on tiptoe. A dog yelped at his heels; he nearly stumbled; the dog recognized him and sniffed at him. With a trembling hand he touched its head in the darkness, then tapped on the window three times, scratched the windowframe, gave another two taps, scratched again. With all his strength he squeezed against the wall. The silence engulfed him like a wave. He knocked again, more loudly and impatiently.

"Is that you, Adam?" Hearing the voice of Vinka's mother-in-law from the doorway, he tried to run away as he had done before the war, but his legs gave way and he said in tones of surrender, "Yes, Mileva, it's me."

"You won't see Vinka any more. Nor me or her son. My old man, Stanoje, is gone. He and Vinka died within three days of each other, and the priest buried them together."

Adam kicked the dog away and walked straight to the gate, his feet scarcely touching the ground; he continued through plum orchards, past haystacks and sheepfolds, over fences, just as he had when he had last returned from Vinka, carrying a stolen watermelon to his father for them to eat together, after which he had saddled Dragan and gone off to the war. Now he was carrying his torn peasant shoes. As he passed through Tola's plum orchard he stopped: was that someone playing a flute? Was it Tola playing because Aleksa had come back? He didn't know. He wouldn't use the jumping-place, but mounted the fence, broke the binding rope, and jumped into his own courtyard.

"Surely you're not coming back from the war at night over the fence, my boy?" said George's voice in the darkness, in front of the cooper's shop.

Adam came up to his father and embraced him. "Well, what can I do? I've lost Dragan and I've been transferred to the telephone service."

"You're in the telephone service? So Vukašin wasn't lying? Zorka, Milunka, light all the lamps in the house!"

From the porch Aćim gave a cough and banged the rails with his stick.

"Here I am, Grandfather. I left as a trooper and I'm coming back as a foot soldier. To hell with the war!"

"For me you've come back a vojvoda, my boy! Come on in, don't dilly-dally. This gentleman is a Frenchman, a doctor. He doesn't understand anything we say, but he's saving our lives."

Adam greeted the Frenchman with reserve; the latter looked at him with delight and repeated a few Serbian words. His stepmother, Zorka, and his grandmother Milunka ran up to him; he submitted to their embraces and babbling. George asked him to come have supper in the new house. Adam refused to sit at the dining table in his dirty, bare-footed, ragged state; he would do this after he had taken a bath and changed into civilian clothes. They had supper in silence: Adam because of his grief and weariness, George because of his happiness as a father, and Aćim from a wish to discuss alone with his grandson the matter most important to him. After supper Aćim invited Adam to his room; the moon was up, so he didn't light the lamp. He asked him about the fighting and his deeds of heroism. Adam didn't feel like talking about the war; he wanted to hear from his grandfather who had been killed or died of typhus, and what life was like in Prerovo with so many people away at war.

But Aćim was persistent: he wanted to find out what had been Adam's most heroic deed, so Adam reflected a moment, then said reluctantly: "I'd been ordered to take some mail to Mladenovac. I was standing on the platform of Valjevo station with a crowd of soldiers, cripples, typhus patients, all sorts of riffraff. There was a soldier with typhus lying on a rug with his tongue sticking out; it looked as though he wouldn't last long. Standing over him was an old man who'd lost an arm, and he asked us soldiers to carry his son into the train. But who wants typhus? We turned our heads away and didn't say anything, just waited for the train. Then the old man begged us, each of us in turn, and offered to pay something. 'How much will you pay, old man?' asked an infantryman. 'Do you think it's worth a pair of oxen?' 'That's a lot, soldier, too much.' 'So it is, but I've got children,' said the soldier. 'Well, here's a ducat for you, my boy,' said the old man, but he wasn't very pleased about it. 'That won't even buy a cow!' said the soldier, which is true. Then we could hear the whistle of the train as it came into the station, and there was some awful pushing and shoving. 'Here's a ducat and ten dinars,' said the one-armed man, and he began to weep. Then the soldier, a real bastard, said: 'Give me a bit more for a pig. Then if I get sick and die, I'll leave my children a sow. At least they'll have something to grease their gizzards with next winter!' The old man swore in the name of his sick son that he didn't have another cent. By now the soldier's buddies were telling him: 'A ducat and ten dinars—that's worth having, you fool! Your life isn't your own, anyway. The Fritzies'll finish you off without a cent of compensation. This way you may catch typhus, but you might get over it, and whatever happens there'll be some money for your wife and children.' 'Then why don't you earn it?' said the soldier. The train came in, there was a lot of jostling, doors got broken, the old man was whimpering, but the soldier held out for two ducats. I don't know what came over me, Grandfather. I felt furious at the soldier and at the old man with his goddamn ducat. So I took the man with typhus in my arms, and his rug, too, and carried him into the train. The old man pushed something into my pocket, but I shouted to him to keep his lousy money for the man who would take his son off the train. After that I took off my overcoat and jacket and shook the lice out the window, and for about two weeks I was hardly alive."

Aćim made no comment, and Adam went off to bed.

He got up only when he saw the sun shining above the bare ash trees, and the first day of his leave brought him no pleasure. Nor did the subsequent days, in a house overburdened with anxiety on his account, and in deserted Prerovo, where typhus was still claiming victims. The women he had known before the war had either died or were ill, or were in mourning and incapable of nocturnal adventures. The few who did roll up their skirts when they met him couldn't rouse his desire even at dawn. He was again troubled about Natalia—as he had been that summer when they had galloped beside the Morava, and she had fallen and broken her arm just as he had leaned over toward her breasts. But Natalia had time only for those who were ill; she spent her time visiting typhus patients, and if he met her she looked straight through him, all passion extinct. He knew why and it didn't please him. He went from village to village with his father and grandfather in the dogcart, looking for a horse that would be a worthy successor to Dragan. They went around the entire neighborhood, but there was no horse of the type he wanted anywhere; the war had taken the best ones, leaving only nags and foals.

Nor did Aleksa Dačić know what to do with himself during his respite from fighting. He didn't want to work for hire during his first leave, and not just because he'd decided that he wouldn't work again as a hired man ever; he was turning over in his mind the idea of marrying Jelka before he returned to the army. Her brother had been killed, her father had died in the war with the Turks, so she had only her mother and fifteen hectares of land, plus a courtyard full of buildings, so that not even his grandchildren would need any more. Jelka was not particularly good-looking, but she was tall and had strength enough to plow, and to bear children who would survive wars and epidemics. He pondered how he, her hired man before the war, should propose to her, his former employer, and was afraid she'd cut him to the quick with her condescending smile.

He spent all his time now catching fish in the Morava; afterward he fried them in a deserted watermill and made great efforts to read Ivan's notebook. His brain was confused by these strange, incomprehensible words about something which was part of his experience and yet quite different from it, so that he could no longer be sure what had really happened on Suvobor. Sometimes Ivan's clever verbal tricks and paradoxes made him angry, and sometimes he felt disappointed in this young man who'd read so many books, yet didn't feel hunger and cold the way the rest of the platoon did; but most of the time he was simply confused by these words that he could hardly read through to the end, and saddened by the fate of this unhappy man whom God had branded in his head, the very place where it was most important for a man to be sound and whole. For some reason he couldn't bring himself to part with this notebook; if someday he could, then he'd take it personally to Ivan's father, that fine gentleman Vukašin. As he was returning from the Morava, he walked slowly past Jelka's house to greet her and ask her a question, no matter what; only now and again was she in the mood for conversation. When he passed and saw her silent and downcast, he searched his memory for all the widows in Prerovo and the girls with dowries, and compared their properties and state of health.

Every evening Adam and Aleksa sat by themselves in the flowering apple orchard, telling each other how they had spent the day; as they smoked they listened to the spring croaking of the frogs, which came up from the Morava in waves of sound, so that it was impossible to hear anything in the village. They both thought, and occasionally said, that life was better for the frogs than for them. When they went off to bed, they didn't forget to remind each other how many nights they still had before they must return to the army.

Milena woke up late in the morning and through the open window caught sight of a blossoming tree in the sunshine; she smiled at Bogdan and his mother, who were beside the bed. Could that really be a fruit tree in bloom? Bogdan understood her bewilderment and told her it was a quince tree.

Olga confirmed joyfully that Milena's illness was now rapidly subsiding; she put the thermometer under her arm and saw that for the third day running she had no temperature. She begged her to drink some milk with her medicine. Milena did so, but with great difficulty, out of pity for her mother.

"You've shaved off your moustache!" she whispered joyfully to Bogdan.

"I've decided to change myself."

Olga looked hard at him: we all want to do that, but how? she asked herself.

In broken phrases, trying to smile, Milena told how Ivan's letter had described Bogdan as having the largest moustache in the platoon. Bogdan interrupted her gently by telling her about their quince tree, which produced the biggest fruits in this part of Valjevo.

Milena asked her mother whether there was a letter from her father; he had promised to send her letters written on the ship from every port. Olga was beginning to feel anxious; French ships were being sunk by German submarines. Hearing the roar of a car, she listened to it drawing closer and didn't reply to Milena.

Bogdan walked slowly to the window and said to someone, "Yes, they're here." He remained beside the window even when Najdan Tošić opened the door brusquely and embraced Milena, then Olga, with tears in his eyes.

"Bogdan, this is my uncle," said Milena.

Bogdan turned around and shook hands with Najdan, depressed by the arrival of this elegant gentleman with a car, who quite inappropriately thanked him for the hospitality shown to his cousin and his niece. Then Najdan turned to Olga. "Has Milena a temperature?"

"Not for two days."

"Splendid! Now, my dears, please get ready to travel at once. I've bought a wonderful little house in Niška Banja for you to recuperate in. Aunt Selena has taken some of your things there, and also some of our furniture from Belgrade. Olga, don't look so astonished! Aunt Selena will have supper ready for you. I'm *not* going back to Niš without you!"

"But, Najdan, do you think it is a good idea right now?"

"I don't want to hear any 'buts.' Vukašin reached Salonika a week ago. We have some English doctors in Niš, and I've made all the arrangements for Milena's treatment. I've been told by the best medical authorities that there isn't the slightest reason why Milena shouldn't travel if she has no temperature—and she hasn't!"

"Let me get a little better, Uncle," whispered Milena, looking at Bogdan, who, unable to bear her glance, had turned away.

Olga's pleas to postpone the trip at least until the following morning, and Milena's tears because she felt she couldn't leave without seeing Nadežda Petrović, were firmly rejected by Najdan, with a certain vengeful love and a passionate desire to save Olga and Milena, and to do what Vukašin had been unable to do.

Olga agreed that they should leave at once only because Milena had demanded to see Nadežda, whose death had been concealed from her; she didn't wish Milena to know about it until she was stronger.

Betrayed in one of his hopes and feeling miserable, Bogdan went out of the room; his mother, Petrana, helped Olga and Milena to get ready. Najdan, deeply moved but also impatient, carried their things to the car. Olga dressed Milena, who was still weak; she longed to cry out, I'm leaving Mihajlo Radić at the most critical stage of his illness! Milena couldn't stand on her feet, and everything was black around her, but she wouldn't let her mother and uncle carry her to the car; she wanted Bogdan to take her. They called him; with his last ounce of strength and dull pains in his chest, Bogdan took hold of her under the arm and somehow managed to get her to the car.

"Promise me that you'll come to Niš as soon as you get a letter from me," she whispered.

He nodded his head, then turned away so that she couldn't see his eyes. Olga hugged Petrana, then Bogdan, whispering that now he was her son, too. She sat down close beside Milena in the car.

Najdan ordered the chauffeur to drive carefully but fast; he was happy and wanted to show this happiness to Olga. He waited for her to speak, but she couldn't. Only when they passed the hospital did she speak, asking the chauffeur to stop. She got out and stood at the gates, remembering her arrival: the dogs, the corpses, and Mihajlo Radić between them, standing in the fog.

"Mother, let's see Dušanka and Sergeev. I don't want to go without seeing them," she heard Milena say. Then Olga saw Mrs. Stefanović and managed to catch up with her. She told her that her cousin had come to take Milena to Niška Banja and that she had to go with her; she asked Mrs. Stefanović's forgiveness for leaving the hospital before her. Mrs. Stefanović assured her gently that she would do the same in her place, and went off to call the doctors and nurses to come say good-by to them.

Olga hurried into Mihajlo Radić's office, where she found Dušanka tending him.

"His temperature's higher than yesterday, and his breathing is harder," said Dušanka quietly. Grief had dampened her spirits and made her look quite plain.

Olga told her that Milena was in the courtyard with her uncle and wanted to say good-by. Olga sat down in the chair and stared at Radić's gaunt face; his eyes were closed. For the first time she took his hand, and was afraid that he would feel hers. She bent over him, thinking to herself: I'm going away, Mihajlo. I'm leaving you and leaving some part of myself, too. My very bones are unhappy. Dare I say this now? You don't know I'm going; your pain blinds you. If you don't recover, good, sad man that you are, I won't be able to regret that you could not know I'll repent. I had no choice. I believe that you would understand all my reasons, just as you've understood my suffering. Will you really never regret that I couldn't do the greatest thing of all?

She took his hand between both of hers.

I didn't meet you for the first time on the train. I knew you all along, you were in my mind. Last night I remembered a line from Pushkin: "My entire life has been a pledge that somewhere in the world I would meet you." Well, that's what you are for me; but how can I assure you of this, in a way that wouldn't be unbecoming to the three of us, and that would be wholly true? As true and real as my suffering for my son. Now only that truth can save me, but I don't want to be saved, I'm not interested in that any more. I don't even want to be saved by you. There's a great darkness inside me, it's good that you can't see me now!

I've come to you because you're the only person with whom I haven't felt fear for myself; there are no closed doors in you. In Vukašin's life there hasn't been much room for me; he's been absorbed in his own affairs. This isn't his fault. He has loved me as much as he could love, and that was not so little, really. But you are somehow weak, though in a good sense, and downcast and sad, and so you're closer to me, much closer. You could hear my silence. I don't love you because you're better, but because you're closer, more like myself, and because you're different, my dearest. You have no idea how difficult it's been for me to remain faithful to my husband, nor how great a yearning has swayed me, how I've sunk under the weight of my love for you.

It wasn't easy for me to accept you. When we were alone there were moments when I despised you, and sometimes I was frightened by the look in your eyes while we were standing among those bodies, but I was perhaps—and I must use this word—happy. Yes, I was happy, and at the same time in despair. You realize that you turned everything upside down in me—or perhaps only here in the hospital was I really born, perhaps from the soul of one of those patients while holding his hand. No, it was from *your* soul, while I was listening to you. I suppose this is something that rarely happens in our lives. Something of you was born in me. During these forty days I've become a different person, and it was you who created me. Something which I hadn't been, yet had some idea that I might be and was afraid to be. I was yearning in vain for a self that no one around me either knew or wanted—not even he whom I've had neither reason nor right to deceive in his belief that he knew everything about me, the man who thought I was entirely his. As indeed I was.

Gently she wiped his sweating forehead with her scarf.

Dare I tell you the worst thing against myself? I'm going away and will never see you again. Never. You, my good, kind, tender friend, have completely destroyed my former life, a life of wealth and beauty, but empty. Did you know that? Perhaps that would have pleased you. You told me you were a gambler. But this life is all I have, and I don't want to abandon it, in spite of everything. I don't blame you, not at all; I'm grateful to you. Whenever I'm alone and shut my eyes, I'll see you—always sad for some reason, poisoning that sadness with tobacco, and unable to keep your hands still. In every moment of quiet I'll be listening to your breathing. I'll embrace you, and do everything I haven't dared to and never will be able to do. One evening when we went to see Bogdan I touched your hand and I wanted so badly to kiss you; I don't know why I didn't. Why couldn't you sense what I wanted? Why? Well, I've told you now. I don't know what else to say, I'm a person of silence. From now on my silences will be even longer. And now let me weep a little, my poor sick friend.

She brought her hand to his face.

I must go. What will I take of you? Who am I now, and what will

I be like when I leave your closed eyes? I was proud, that's what those who loved me said, but those who envied me said I was conceited, and all who hated me considered me selfish and wicked. Now I'm just an ordinary woman. It's you I have to thank for that. If you recover, please never try to find me; but you'll live in me until my dying day. Under the hoarfrost in some wood, in dark silence or on a starry night —then most of all. Can you sense my desire? Yes, Mihajlo, it's happened, my dear sick friend, so near to me . . .

Olga got up, bent over his face, and almost touched it. She placed Mihajlo's hands on his breast, then slowly walked out and stood on the steps. Patients were sitting there warming themselves in the mild spring sunshine, listening to one of their companions play the flute; the old acacia tree was about to burst into leaf. The car horn honked; it was surrounded by nurses who had come to say good-by to her and Milena. She left the hospital grounds much more slowly than when she arrived.

In the evening Aleksa Dačić told Adam Katić how at twilight he had asked Jelka to marry him, how she had taken her time before nodding assent, and then burst into tears because she was mourning her brother. Adam embraced him and cried out: "We'll have a big wedding! I'll bring musicians from all over the district!"

"Do you think it's right, Adam, to have a big wedding now? Half of Prerovo is dead or dying."

"What's wrong with a big wedding? We're not deserters, we're from Mišić's army. Who knows if we'll survive till autumn? I want to have a wedding! I want to dance and live it up! If only I'd bought a horse!"

Aleksa fell in easily with Adam's wish, and that same evening he told his mother and father what he intended to do. His mother was amazed that Jelka Bajić had agreed to marry him, though there was no handsomer fellow or better worker in all of Prerovo, but she was violently opposed to a big wedding: it was less than forty days since Miloje's death; where could his soul go if there were a celebration in the house? Tola found it difficult to believe that so much land and property would come to his son, and said he should do as his heart and the law of humanity directed him, according to which law births and marriages had never been forbidden. So Aleksa decided that the wedding should be in three days' time, on Sunday, in the bride's house. The two of them sat under the dogwood tree discussing the wedding and reminding each other of what had to be done, until the moon disappeared behind the clouds.

At dawn each of them began his appointed task in preparation for the wedding. At first there was general astonishment in Prerovo over something which could be expected only from the Dačići at such a time, and all those who were still alive and healthy began to protest about having the noise of a wedding and its music interfering with their funerals and weeping. Adam went up and down the Morava looking for gypsy musicians, and came back gloomy and angry: the best ones and all the young ones were away at the war, the old and crippled had succumbed to the infection. Showing the same persistence, however, with which he had sought a successor to Dragan, Adam rushed in the two-wheeled cart from village to village, invited all the soldiers on leave to come sing, and sought out convalescing musicians. On the eve of the wedding he brought into Jelka's courtyard a cart full of hungry gypsies and bass players. He gave them fried liver and a jug of brandy, and ordered them to play as if Serbia had defeated two empires. He was worried about Mikan, the first fiddler, who'd been complaining and grumbling all the way to Prerovo.

When the gypsies began to play, the women from the neighborhood started to wail loudly so as to drown out the thrumming of the bass fiddles and the squeal of the violins. The women who were helping Jelka and her mother went off to hide in the hayloft and weep, and all the women in mourning in Prerovo withdrew into their houses, sat at the bedsides of the sick, or clasped the clothing of the dead to their bosoms. A few children hung over the fences and stared at the musicians.

Even Aleksa, who with Tola and George was putting the suckling pig and the lamb on a grill, was startled by the sound of the music; it was as though he had met an Austrian machine gun on patrol. His arms dropped limply from sorrow for his brother and for the neighbors who had died, and he wanted to tell the gypsies to shut up. But George said kindly: "Aleksa, you have only one wedding in a lifetime. It should be the kind of wedding we had here before the war."

Tola was of the same opinion, and made a great effort to be merry and to stifle his sorrow for his dead sons. But the wedding guests didn't come; only a few small boys gathered around the musicians. Adam sat at the empty table, drinking wine, telling the gypsies what songs to sing, and plying Mikan with strong brandy to burn up his illness, so that the wedding wouldn't lose its best musician.

Aleksa put his hand on Adam's shoulder and said despondently, "There won't be any guests at my wedding."

"Tonight the two of us will get all the soldiers on leave from the Morava division to come sing."

They divided the villages between them, mounted their horses, and rode furiously through the greenish moonlight, past croaking frogs and the song of nightingales, to summon people to come sing at the wedding. They called their comrades-in-arms, who were already half asleep, and begged them to come the next day to the wedding. Just before midnight they came back and found total silence in Jelka's courtyard, with Tola and George sitting by large heaps of embers, sleepily turning the pieces of meat; they walked past the fires and silently went home to bed.

Aleksa spent a wakeful night, in a state of hope that was stronger than weariness or the desire for sleep. He remembered his hardships as a hired man, and how Jelka's father had whipped him with a branch because he had been playing and the pigs had gotten into the hemp field. He vowed that he'd never humiliate the hired men and servants; and if he didn't pay any more than George Katić, he'd certainly give them better food and drink than any other man in Prerovo. If only this damn war would end and he came through it safe and sound; his medal and his corporal's rank were enough for his authority in peacetime, enough to let him look people straight in the eye. Then he'd set out to double his property; after the war there'd be plenty of empty houses and land going for a song. He'd spread out in all four directions. He'd be Aleksa Dačić, a man of property, you couldn't see to the end of his land. Yes, Aleksa Dačić would be somebody.

He was wakened by the sound of music and trembled at the thought of his victory, which was being proclaimed all over Prerovo and the valley by the fiddles. He shaved, put on his new suit, and hurried to Jelka's house—from this day on, his own. Adam was waiting for him, shooting off his gun and cursing Mikan, the first fiddle, who had started to run a fever and been removed to the hayloft; Ruva, the second fiddler, was also complaining. Aleksa was upset; it was important that the bass players shouldn't fall ill, because they could be heard on the other side of the Morava. He was worried too lest there be too few singers, and he be ashamed of his wedding. Meanwhile Tola, already tipsy, was staring at him, and two women were preparing a dining board ten tables long. Aleksa went to visit Jelka in her room—*their* room after today—and found her sitting despondent and silent over her wedding dress. He felt sorry that she didn't seem pleased to see him, and said to her in a serious voice: "When I come back from the war, that'll be our wedding, Jelka. And I'll come back, don't you worry."

The sun rose high above the Morava but the courtyard was still empty; some ten soldiers arrived, Aleksa's war comrades, and a few boys, mostly orphans and hungry. Adam wouldn't let the gypsies rest and kept firing his gun, which brought curses from the women in the neighboring houses. It was time to set out for the religious ceremony, and still the singers hadn't come. Aleksa's face darkened; gloomy and angry at all of Prerovo, he set out for the church down the empty lane, his bride between himself and Adam, accompanied by the ten soldiers and the children running alongside the gypsies, who could hardly drag their instruments along, and played louder only when Adam shouted at them and brandished some money. Natalia and the Frenchman peeped out at them from Aćim's inn, now a hospital; Aleksa called to Natalia to bring the Frenchman to the wedding without fail, but she went back into the inn as if offended, or so it seemed to Aleksa. He was hurt.

When they reached the church, the priest's wife told them that the priest was at the cemetery performing funeral services, so they would have to wait. Jelka got even sadder, but Adam and the soldiers started dancing and kept on until the priest arrived to perform the ceremony, which he did hurriedly, as if the church were on fire.

The rest of the ceremonies were performed in the same hurried manner, and only the most essential at that; but Aleksa was no longer offended, for he had got what he wanted. Tomorrow he would start plowing and sowing, and would keep on until he had to return to the army. The wedding breakfast began; all the singers crowded around two tables; the other tables had no people, but were laden with jugs of brandy, bread, and roast meat. The soldiers soon got drunk and started to sing and shoot off their guns. Adam didn't give the gypsies a moment's respite; when Ruva, the second fiddler, rolled his eyes feverishly, Adam gave him a ten-dinar piece and begged him to keep going at least until sunset. Tola, now drunk, moved in and out among the singers, clapped the soldiers on the back, and offered the children food. At twilight they began to dance; only the soldiers and the boys joined in. The soldiers wanted to dance with the bride, so Aleksa ordered her to do as they wished; she joined in, and the soldiers took turns dancing with her and holding her hand in theirs. At sunset the fiddler Ruva tottered toward the dancers, dropped his fiddle, and sprawled on the ground. When Adam gave him ten dinars he got up and went on playing, pleading all the while that he had just got over typhus and was about to collapse.

The soldiers went on dancing a little longer, then said good-by to Aleksa and his bride, and hurried off home. This made Adam angry; he poured out all his money in front of the musicians and, hoping that Natalia would come, ordered them to go on playing until their strings snapped. Aleksa sat with Tola and George Katić at the head of the long, empty table and talked about the sowing. Adam called to Aleksa and the bride, and the three of them danced in the moonlight. The bride was too tired to go on, so only Adam and Aleksa were left, watched by their fathers in tipsy admiration. When he had lost all hope of Natalia's arrival, Aleksa paid the musicians, and Adam piled the gypsies and their instruments into the cart and drove them to their village. The croaking of the frogs, celebrating their own weddings, re-echoed through the silence under the high moon. The Prerovo dogs scrambled under the wedding tables to fight over the bones.

Aleksa and Jelka went to their room and sat on the bed without touching each other. They sat in silence for a while, then their eyes met and, for the first time, their desires: he serious and joyful, she filled with fear and apprehension. "We have nine more nights, Jelka, but we must cram years into them. God knows when this war will end." Then he began to take off his shoes and undress.

She extinguished the lamp. Her fingers fumbled with buttons and hooks, and the moonlight pushed her into the shadow against the wall; she just barely managed to get into her nightdress. He waited patiently on the bed, naked and slantwise like a plowshare. Then he grasped her firmly around the waist, laid her carefully on the bed, and embraced her slowly and powerfully: he was filled with such longing for his wife that he felt he must make every movement on her and in her as if he would live only for as long as he embraced her, and as if the day would never dawn again.

When the roosters announced the dawn, she was happy, while for him it arrived too soon. When the light of early morning replaced the moonlight, casting dark shadows on her face and breasts, Aleksa gave her a kiss on both cheeks and whispered to her to go back to sleep, while he prepared the plow and the oxen. He dressed quickly, washed himself from an earthenware jug, then strode out to look at his courtyard, which stretched out in the early morning light: he would fill it with children and animals. He went out into the stable and for the first time harnessed his own oxen. When he had loaded a cart with the plow, hay for the oxen, a barrel of water, and saddlebags with bread and meat for the two of them, he went into the room and woke up his wife. She dressed quickly and a little shyly; they climbed onto the cart and set off for plowing, eating bread and cheese on the way.

The sun rose, but the lanes of Prerovo were still empty. There was a sound of wailing for the dead, and some women were cooling towels for sick people in front of their houses. Aleksa hurried the oxen on and reckoned in his mind how many days he would need to plow and sow the best meadows. He would have to overstay his leave by three days, for which he would be jailed ten days. Never mind: he would be plowing his own meadows and sowing seed for himself. As soon as they left the village, the yellow expanse of an unplowed field stretched before them all the way to the Morava. It pained Aleksa to see those flowering yellow weeds. He got down from the cart, turned it into a ditch, harnessed the oxen to the plow, put the bags with seed on his shoulders, and told his wife to bind the hay and carry it behind them, together with the barrel of water. He went through the underbrush with the plow and oxen, whipped the right-hand horse, and began to plow the empty field a row at a time, and kept on in the direction of his own meadow on the bank of the Morava. Behind him his wife walked along the dark, glistening furrow, carrying food for themselves and the animals.

The plum trees are now in bloom around Valjevo

Vojvoda Mišić, his cap pulled down on his forehead, was at his desk speaking on the telephone. "Yes, I can hear you, Vojvoda. According to all reports, the epidemic is declining rapidly. The hospitals are empty; but the First Army is still in a bad way."

"The Russian High Command," said Putnik, "has informed us that the Allies are to launch a general offensive in May. Our army must be ready for an advance into Austria-Hungary."

"The difficulties are insurmountable, sir."

"I know that. I feel the same way you do about our difficulties, but they must be overcome, Mišić."

"I'm afraid that's impossible at the present moment."

"If this is impossible, then our survival and our freedom are impossible, and our national aims, too. The commander in chief and the government consider that if we aren't prepared now to offer the Allies the help they ask, they won't satisfy our national aspirations at the peace conference."

"Sir, I believe the only sacrifices that aren't in vain are those which we make for our survival—our own survival."

"I understand you; but I'm ordering you to prepare for movement and action."

"I've made three urgent requests for footwear for the soldiers. How can they go across the Drina barefoot?"

"I'll send some boots if we have any."

"The soldiers are carrying ammunition in their pockets. I must have cartridge belts and satchels."

"As soon as we get them, I'll send them to you."

"Half my draft animals have died of hunger. Those still alive are so weakened by starvation that they fall as soon as you yoke them. Can you hear me, Vojvoda? Please send the necessary animals for my baggage trains! And fodder for the animals! And food for the men! And boots and overcoats! I need belts, cartridge belts, bayonets! Do you understand me, Vojvoda? Hello—High Command! Who's cut us off? Mišić speaking; please connect me with the High Command at once!"

The apple trees are now in bloom around Valjevo

Vojvoda Putnik, speaking from Kragujevac: "How are your preparations going, Mišić?"

"It's raining here, Vojvoda. Pouring."

"It's pouring here, too. The Russian High Command requests that our main operations be in a northwesterly direction, to be near the right wing of the Italian army."

"If my army is to cross the Drina, it must have pontoon bridges and boats. Because of the heavy rain, the Drina is still rising. It's a fast and treacherous river, as you know."

"Lord Kitchener, the British Minister of War, has sent the following telegram: Italy is mobilized and ready to attack Austria. The English High Command expects an offensive from the Serbian army. Hello, Mišić! Lord Kitchener expects Serbia to launch a strong attack at the same time as the Italians. Why are you silent, Mišić?"

"This direction of attack favors our allies."

"And our union with the Croats and Slovenes. Can you hear me, Mišić?"

"I understand, Vojvoda. I'll move the army in that direction. But the rivers are rising and it's still raining. I haven't a single pontoon bridge. Please ask Lord Kitchener and Grand Duke Nikolay Nikolayevich most urgently to send us pontoon bridges and boats, and hay and oats for our animals! Can you hear me, Vojvoda? Please ask for tents, boots, and overcoats from France!"

All the fruit trees are in bloom around Valjevo

Vojvoda Putnik, from Kragujevac: "Is it still raining, Mišić?"

"Yes, sir. The roads are flooded."

"Perhaps there'll be a miracle to save us."

"I still don't put my trust in heaven."

"The commander in chief has informed the Allies of his agreement that the Serbian army should unite with the Italian and Russian armies. Why are you silent, Mišić?"

"I must ask you again to send at least forty kilometers of telephone wire, and at least ten telephone and telegraph installations. Otherwise we won't be able to communicate."

Mišić went on holding the receiver, listening to the panting and wheezing in the distance. Wherever they went now, it must be into that distance. How would they survive? Wisdom and courage, the will and strength to endure more than their opponents—these things no longer sufficed. Only a miracle could save them, but not an ordinary human miracle, like the one on Suvobor. How could they survive when opposed by those whom they considered their friends? How could they be saved from their Allies?

He told his adjutant to get the car ready and sent his orderly,

Dragutin, to tell Louisa he'd be away for two days inspecting positions. Then he got in with his adjutant and Dragutin and drove off toward the Drina.

The rain was still pouring down; the roads were empty. Dead cows and horses lay rotting in the ditches. Broken munitions carts, and here and there a gun carriage, were soaking in the rain. He and Dragutin both stared at the unplowed fields and heeded their prophecy of hunger. As they went through the villages, both of them counted to themselves the houses without mourning flags; they also counted the chimneys that were smoking and the unwhitewashed houses, empty as a result of the enemy occupation or sickness. If they caught sight of a village cemetery which had sprung up by the side of the road, they turned their heads away. As soon as Dragutin began to lament the unplowed meadows, Mišić silenced him by saying that never before had there been such plum blossoms; if there was a good plum crop, Serbia wouldn't go hungry. To whomever they met—old man, woman, or child—Mišić gave a salute. The car could hardly move along the road, which was almost washed away; frequently it got stuck in the mud and had to be extricated with the help of women and sometimes cattle, too.

When the road began to descend toward the Drina, Mišić told the driver to stop, then stepped out into a green clearing near a copse of leafing beech trees rising above some unburied corpses left from the battles. He started westward toward the Drina, which had flooded its valley as far as the eye could see, all the way to the Sava. No foot soldiers could now get across it—not even the First Army; and the rain was still falling. Mišić took off his hat and crossed himself as he stared at the flooded valley and the sky: O Lord, he prayed, send the floods over Podrinje and Posavina and save what's left of our army, and save Serbia's life from her friends. Only You, O Lord, have the power to work this miracle.

His orderly, Dragutin, stood a few paces behind him; he took off his cap and crossed himself after the vojvoda, praying to God that the rain might stop and the Drina not flood the fields: it was time now for plowing and sowing.

Swirling mists are rising up: the space around me is dissolving. Objects exist for me in this mist; but all the time it is growing darker and darker. I can no longer distinguish people's faces.

In the state of nausea that grips me inside my former uniform, it seems miraculous that there ever existed something which I could eat and drink. I'm now finally reduced to my bones, and to some part of me that can still think a little or remember. Though only from time to time, in broken fragments. I'm struggling hard to remember everything important in my life. Was there anything important, or have I forgotten it? I'd like to feel some pity for my mother and father, my sisters and brothers, my wife, my friends, and some good people whom I met on the way to war and the Hospital. I can't squeeze out a drop of pity for these rigid gray shapes, or this distorted, disordered, freezing civilian.

I'm alone, but I'm not complete. I'm losing bits of myself, my extremities are disappearing. I no longer possess most of my feet; they're thrust out into the chill of the universe, into some day and night of former times. I'm now without movement and height. My hands are of the greatest significance, especially my fingers—their number, similarity, and movements. They are the final power of my will. How much longer will I have them? I press them to my lips with the touch of a mother and a lover, and kiss them with what warmth still remains in my blood.

I am now that part of me that is striving and struggling to think; that convolution twisted up inside my skull. But the world is all coldness and distance: faraway voices, a jumble of words, aimless movements, vileness without limit.

I'm thrusting my fingers into the past, into the end of the world, the universe. Never mind if they are cold and frozen in those distant places; let them move about a little in the infinite. They are living their last moment. Let life claim them, my fingers. For Death I have my breathing. In my mind I embrace that last wisp of warmth and movement.

Ah, but I have my heart. A fabulous gift, though its progress is slowing down. That's what I am. Wherein lies that power, now and in earlier times?

I would say that I'm living my last experience: the departure of my heart. I think about it and listen to it, and see its pitful stumbling into the infinite, through timelessness.

I suppose I've been thinking about one more patch of darkness with just a little flame, circling the remains of my inner vision. I've been listening to the footsteps of my heart, I've been embracing my breathing, kissing my fingers—the one remnant of myself in the world. I've tried hard to envisage God, but without success. I've struggled to hear Him in the silence and the wind, to see Him as light and darkness. I can't accept Him as the origin of all things. There are moments when I think the end has come. I'm not afraid.

In some of my lucid moments, I've had a burning desire to see my own face, to see what I have been, most of all, to other people. What have I been to them? I don't really care. When I manage to see myself completely, then everything is so simple: just to live, no matter how or where or by what means; and contrary to all reason, since death will free me from my torments. Everything I have thought, all my burning desires, everything I have said can be summed up in one word: life! I know that I've endured the greatest difficulties, the most acute suffering. I know what an unhappy man I am because I haven't been able to believe that this end is not the end.

I'm still struggling hard to feel my heart, and its desperate effort to jump over some barrier. There it is, obstinately skipping around: tap, tap. It's time I said to this vain beating of my heart, Thank you.

Before I use my last strength to scatter excrement from myself, and so confirm the fact of my foulness, I wish to forgive my cruel and wretched country for my death. I forgive the world in which I have lived all the evils I have endured, and I love all my sufferings.

Once more the dawn and dusk have come and gone, although I have scarcely noticed their passing. I like this abolition of the crude differences between day and night, that confrontation between light and darkness which dims the clarity of light and contributes to human unhappiness. This reconciliation between light and darkness, the one flowing into the other, is for me the final grace of a world in which I will soon cease to exist. It's a bridge into the unknown.

But in this damp darkness of my existence, my heart still creeps on, scarcely audible. Its beat is now muted, nourished by my last impulse of love. It is repaying with its strength the gratitude which I have always accorded it. It is so weary that I cannot overcome a feeling of compassion for it. It is, somehow, very considerate in its manner of stealing away from me; it intends to do so while I'm asleep. But I have seen through its intention, and this last trick finds me awake! We're having a little game with each other, cheating and deceiving each other, seeing who will win the battle of wits.

I still have one more game to play with myself. Shall I be able to bring myself not to sign this Report? If I don't sign it, I'll nullify the reason for composing it, but at the same time I'll gain a victory. My last victory: a victory over the tragicomic suffering of human transience. Why should we resist transience? It's the foundation of everything we have been and done. Transience is the creator of all our joys and pleasures, and also hope and other superior feelings. For some reason I want to master self-love—the first and last defense against Death. That poor, wretched resistance to the powers of transience. By this means I must affirm the sense and point of my existence, and its nullity and that of all humankind. That is the outcome of transience, but it is also the essence of human greatness and its most lasting form.

And so, for anyone who may chance to listen,
I remain,
An Unknown Sick Man